MW01241987

W. G. TUTTLE

WAR FOR THE SPHERES

A Novel

THIS IS A W. G. TUTTLE BOOK PRODUCTION

BLURRED INK, LLC

Riveting fiction.

Novels
Those Who Long
Try To Sleep
October Midnight
War For The Spheres

Short Stories
Adamah - A Book of the Serpent
Scranton October 1894
SURvIVe
Cut-Up
Where Did THEY Come From?
Standard Issue Spirits
Vacation's End
A Fatal Thing

Book cover illustration by **Vincent Di Fate**, an American artist specializing in science fiction and fantasy illustration. He has produced art for numerous companies, publications, and organizations, such as NASA, IBM, and Scientific American Magazine. In addition, he has consulted for several entertainment companies, such as Walt Disney Productions and 20th Century-Fox. He was inducted into the Illustrators' Hall of Fame in 2019 and the Science Fiction Hall of Fame in 2011. He has also received numerous honors and awards, including a Hugo Award in 1979 for Best Professional Artist.

For more information, please visit **vincentdifate.com**

For my wife Shawn

CHAPTER ONE

Millions of people sardined in a dense area like Manhattan can suck the life out of a man. Hayden Bakley felt so. He wasn't claustrophobic or anthropophobic, for he didn't fear people. There wasn't much on Earth or in space, he feared. An astronaut, he would rather be up there with artificial bodies, satellites and other orbiters, instead of the organic bodies roaming about the city. Even when cramped inside some space vessel, personal space seemed open, comfortable. Perhaps the vastness of space outside the ship walls fooled the senses into thinking so.

Not in downtown Manhattan, where on the other side of the walls, floor, and ceiling of his hotel room were people. Worse yet, in a car, a rental no less, Hayden sat stopped at a red light. Unlike a room, there weren't any curtains in the vehicle to draw. Driving meant paying attention and when regarding people, two senses, hearing and seeing, were necessary and too many.

It had snowed most of the day, but the city had little to show for it. Vehicle, human, and all sorts of ancillary traffic absorbed, trampled, and melted the ice crystals, leaving nothing but dirty tracks, marks, and prints in ugly slush.

Mobs of people crossed the street in both directions,

somehow dodging each other with no interruption of flow. The light turned green, yet, latecomers stepped off the sidewalks to cross the street as if their organic material were made of steel instead of the vehicles operated by impatient drivers. Beeping ensued and Hayden asked himself, *What the hell am I doing here?*

As the last stragglers crossed, a man among them, wearing a trench coat, tried his luck as drivers pulled forward before the light turned red again. Despite the weather, windows went down with damning words yelled out of them.

Trotting, the man spread his unbuttoned trench coat like a cape, wielded an ax from his side, and swung it at a man in front of him carrying a black briefcase.

A couple of cars back, Hayden sat up and watched as the axman struck the blade numerous times just above the man's elbow until the arm slid out of the sleeve and landed on the briefcase on the slushy street. It was then Hayden noticed the cuffs secured around the briefcase handle and the man's wrist.

Blood sprayed out of the sleeve and onto the slush like cherry syrup over a snow cone until the amputated man tucked his nub into the crevice of his other elbow and hunched over as he squeezed. His brown overcoat darkened as if dyed black and he dropped to his knees, then onto his side on the wet street.

The light turned red, and the hacker leaned the bloodied ax against his shoulder as if a lumberjack, reached down, picked up the briefcase, and ran off. The cleaved forearm banged against the side of the briefcase like a drum as he ran, leaving a sprinkled blood trail.

Drivers ahead of Hayden maneuvered their vehicles around the man lying in the slush. Hayden considered stopping, but in a fog, followed them around, seeing the man's body begin to relax as he peeked out his window. He sped down the street behind the other cars that got through. He'd seen some amazing things, but nothing like what he had just witnessed.

Over the speed limit and the caboose of a four-car train, Hayden checked his rearview mirror. People had gathered in the street around the dismembered man, blocking traffic. The car in front of him slowed in haste to turn, catching Hayden off-guard. He swerved to miss it, veered to avoid crashing into vehicles parked along the curb, then slammed on the brakes to prevent rear-ending the cars stopped at a red light in front of him. His tires slid in the slush and he thought for sure a collision was inevitable. The light turned green and the car in front of him pulled forward. Otherwise, he would have hit it.

He looked out his rearview mirror and no other traffic came his way. A loud explosion sounded behind him and a ball of flame grew from the street about where the robbed man laid. Numerous colors pulsated within the orange and yellow flame as it expanded and engulfed the onlookers. A dull clang and jarring of his car drew his attention out his front windshield as the axman slid over his hood, carrying the suitcase with the arm still attached.

An orange beam passed the windshield, then another. One appeared to hit a parked car and another a brick building, but upon contact, nothing happened as if they were merely lights. A short, slender person, wearing an unusual orange outfit with a hooded cloak, ran the sidewalk toward him and fired again in pursuit of the man with the briefcase. The weapon had range because the pursuer fired from a block away. The orange beam sped through the gray, snowy air, illuminating things as it passed.

Pedestrians fled the scene and drivers remained in their cars, beeping for traffic to move no matter the color of the light.

In a flash, an orange dash of light zoomed past Hayden's windshield and penetrated the center of the axman's back. The force curved his body forward, stomach-first, and his arms and legs flailed back as if parachuting out of a plane without a parachute. The man exploded as if he were filled with TNT and it sounded exactly like the earlier explosion that had occurred a block behind him, only louder.

Pushed by the explosion, panicked people raced their screams away from the intersection.

Hayden had seen lasers at NASA, but nothing like the orange blaster. Nor had he seen a human body combust. As the blaze of the explosion raced toward his combustible car, he braced himself, thoroughly expecting to be reduced to fragments of flesh and bone in a matter of seconds. Of all things to think at that moment, *At least it's a rental*, crossed his mind. The flame licked his windshield as it engulfed the vehicle. The inside of the car and everything in it changed colors as the colors within the flame changed.

The passenger side window shattered into tiny pieces. Instinctively, Hayden's arms raised to protect himself, but he already felt particles of glass penetrate his face. A hard object smacked into his elbow and forearm then banged onto the center console. A gust of warm air blew into the car through the window, blowing his hair about and unwrapping the scarf halfway off his neck.

The inferno retreated away from the vehicle and the wind died down. Hayden couldn't believe he and the car weren't broiled. Able to see out his driver's side window, he saw the orange-cloaked shooter standing on the corner near his car. A dark shadow veiled the face under the orange hood, but it appeared to Hayden the pursuant was only concerned about the blown-up man and not him or anyone else.

Many, tiny stings pinched his face all at once when he looked in the mirror. Particles of glass were embedded in his skin, reminding him of rock salt and the cuts of red specks made him look like he had the measles. Windblown hair resembled bedhead. Reflective glass fragments stuck to his leather gloves and covered him as if salted like a pretzel.

Hayden's eyes left the mirror and returned to the orange figure standing on the corner. With a resolute interest, the cloaked figure watched the flame recede to the man's last location until it disappeared. Nothing remained of the axman and the slayer's petite shoulders relaxed as if relieved.

Stepping off the sidewalk and onto the slushy macadam, the killer crossed the street; the black abyss under the hood moving side-to-side as if looking for something or ensuring nothing remained.

Just for a second, Hayden's eyes retreated inside the car. They stayed there. Sharing the center console and passenger seat next to him was a black briefcase, sitting upright with the arm still handcuffed to the handle and, now, the axman's hand still squeezing the handle in a death grip. Cleanly severed above the elbow, most of the arm down to the hand had survived the explosion. All along, he had thought the passenger window had shattered from the blast.

When Hayden had looked up at the blown-out window, the opening of the orange hood faced him, too dark to make out a face, but the eyes behind the shadow were on him.

A glance to the rearview mirror and traffic had stopped behind him. When his eyes returned to the orange figure, the exterminator was already in mid-stride, walking briskly toward him.

Not wanting any part of it, Hayden lifted the suitcase off the seat, ready to toss it out the window and drive off—if the car worked. A light cast on the inside of the windshield and he swore he heard a voice speaking. Startled, he let go of the handle and the briefcase fell flat on the passenger seat. On top of the briefcase, the dangling forearm spun on the cuffs and implanted in the flesh under the skin was a small screen. Its transmission came through the skin clearly, as if there weren't any skin over it, except for where some blood had dried, making parts of the screen appear darker.

A bald-headed man with broad shoulders implored Hayden, "Drive! Now! Don't give up the case!"

Hayden stared at the tiny television, seeing and hearing the man distinctly. Orange flashed in the corner of his eye and, when he looked up, the cloaked body stood at the busted passenger window.

The same strange fog came over Hayden.

Traffic had backed up behind Hayden's car, beeping for him to move.

Orange arms emerged out from under the cloak, reaching inside the car for the briefcase. Although close, Hayden still couldn't see a face under the hood.

The bald man yelled out of the screen in the forearm, "Drive, fool! Don't think! Drive!"

Before the grabber could get a firm grip on the case, Hayden snatched the briefcase, tossed it in the back seat, and took his foot off the brake to hit the gas. The orange form moved from the passenger window and the car sat still until it started. The backside window shattered into pieces and Hayden turned and saw the bottom of an orange boot back out from where the window had been. Orange-gloved hands reached through the window for the case in the back seat, when the car moved forward.

Someone in the car behind Hayden yelled, "'Bout time, buddy!"

Pressing the pedal to the floor, Hayden gradually picked up speed through the intersection. *A sloth could beat this piece of shit*, he thought. Whoever thought of stop-start technology didn't account for situations like this.

Hayden peered over his shoulder and saw the orange shroud still clinging to the back door. Failure wasn't an option for the one holding on, whose orange-gloved hands darkened red from glass still in the doorframe cutting into them.

Hayden had seen some brave souls leave Earth into the unknown, but this person had no fear. Bloodstained cut hands and having to be in pain, this soul didn't acknowledge it with a moan or wince.

Desperate, the veiled individual chicken-winged an arm over the door and reached for the orange laser, holstered in the orange belt around a slim waist.

Seeing, in the side-view mirror, the determined person in a hanging knee raise on the side of the car going for the laser, Hayden skidded into a left turn at the next intersection. The rental car creaked and leaned as if a boat turning sharply in the water. The case slid across the backseat toward the broken window.

The turn proved too much and the orange bandit, holding on with one crimson-stained arm, flew off the car door, and rolled into the intersection, while retaining the laser.

Looking in his rearview mirror, Hayden saw the orange body sit up and the black abyss inside the hood face him. Even without eyes, the formless stare pierced him. He adjusted the mirror to make sure the briefcase had remained in the car and it had.

"You still there?" Hayden asked.

Not hearing anything, he asked again. "Bald man! You there?"

Rechecking the rearview, he didn't see the orange outfit in the intersection or anywhere.

His eyes remained there too long and he ended up skidding to a stop to avoid the car in front of him.

When traffic moved again, he forced the rental across the lane as drivers beeped and cursed. Wanting out of that mess, he took the next right.

It wasn't a street, but an alley. The brakes on the rental screeched as Hayden slammed on them to avoid smashing into a car heading his direction. The other car jerked to a stop and bobbed a few times on its frame. Animated faces on the driver and passenger were a mere two hood lengths away and Hayden saw every detail and heard every cuss. For good measure, four erected middle fingers told him he was the one heading in the wrong direction.

Hayden grabbed the briefcase and got out. He wished thought of it earlier, but he bent down and retrieved the pistol case from under the driver's seat. His first time in Manhattan, it had to come along.

As he used the pistol case to push the door closed, those in the other car stared. The arms attached to the briefcase were enough for the driver to put the car in reverse and back up. Another car entered the alley behind them and the first car crept and beeped until both cars backed out of the alley and drove off down the street.

The wintry weather couldn't mask the garbage and piss odor in the alley. Constantly looking over his shoulder for the person in orange, Hayden jogged through the alley, carrying both cases. With the axman's hand gripped to the handle of the briefcase and its forearm erected straight as a radio antenna, it made it difficult to carry, not leaving much room for his own grip, while the hacked arm, dangling in handcuffs, annoyingly bounced off the side of the briefcase in a steady rhythm.

When he emerged out of the alley, none of the street names he saw sounded familiar. Not being from New York, he had no clue where he was, other than south, until he saw a sign, E 11 St, and figured he had a long walk to his hotel on Fifty-Seventh.

Eyes of people passing by gravitated toward the arms attached to the briefcase and they sped up and veered away to avoid any trouble. A woman screamed when she saw the appendages and Hayden tried pleading with her, "No, ma'am! Don't do that! It's not what you think!"

Addressing her made her move faster away from him. He had to do something about the arms.

Returning to the alley, he took off his overcoat and was just about to drape it over the arms and case when the screen embedded in the hacked-off forearm illuminated through the skin.

"You have the briefcase?" the bald-headed man asked.

Hayden positioned the forearm so he could see the screen. "Well, I don't know. I might have it. It still might be in the car. I can't remember."

"Okay, good."

"If you already know, why did you ask? What's going on? Who are you?" Hayden pushed.

"Someone trying to help you," the man said. He looked

away and pointed at something off-screen, then said, "You're on Eleventh."

"How do you know that? How do you know I have the case?" Hayden asked. "Drones? Tracking? Satellites?"

"Your hotel is on," the man looked off-screen again and said, "Fifty-Seventh."

"I'm flattered. You know everything about me and here I know nothing about you."

The man studied something beside him and then said, "Based on traffic, don't grab a taxi and don't go back to the car. Hoof it. It will be faster."

"Oh, that's good to know. Now, how about a weather report?"

"No, scratch that. Don't go back to the hotel."

"Why not? What about my things?"

"It'll become a funeral parlor," the man said, "and those things will be no good to you when you're dead. It's important you take the briefcase and both arms with you."

"Well, I'm having such a good time," Hayden said, "I was just wondering when I can see you again. And where?"

"As far away as you can."

"Will I make it?"

"To where you're going?"

"No, with you."

"I know where you're thinking," the bald man said, "and for now it's okay to go there."

"We've only been together a little while and already you can read my mind," Hayden said. "All right, I'm frisky enough to play along. Just have answers to all the questions I'm thinking."

"You better get going. I'll contact you if there's been a change of plans."

"No promises, I like that. I'll meet you there. Just one thing though. Wear a wig."

"Good idea. Buy a hat and don't take it off."

"A hat. How do I get a hold of…"

The screen darkened. No one would have ever guessed it

was under the skin. The arm looked normal, other than it wasn't complete and not attached to a body.

Hayden took out his pistol, loaded it, and wrapped his scarf around his hand holding it. When he draped his overcoat over the briefcase and arms, a dimmed light flickered inside the other forearm, the axman's. A faint, garbled voice sounded in and out of broken communication, but Hayden never heard it.

CHAPTER TWO

Getting out of Manhattan wasn't easy because Hayden had a lot to take care of without the benefit of going back to his room and grabbing his things. While making his rounds, he made sure he stopped at a store and bought a generic hat and an orange. Not liking New York, any hats with love or a heart on it was out of the question as was their sports teams. Not trusting the New York air, the thick rind on the orange made it the choice to buy.

Call it a quirk or an idiosyncrasy Hayden liked fruit. Not always though. As a kid, he couldn't stand it. Never ate it unless forced to.

Space changed all of that and much more. The economics of a small supply of fruit, usually gifted on supply runs, increased his and the other astronauts' demand for it. Even fruit they never liked or tasted before. When grounded, as Hayden was now, they still couldn't eat enough of it.

Because Hayden traveled alone, the airline didn't have any problems finding him a seat, but the itinerary was less than ideal. The flight would be the longest in his history of flying coast-to-coast. Three-and-a-half hours had passed with three more to go until he landed in Portland. A three-

and-a-half hour layover awaited him there. From there, another whopping three-and-a-half hour layover awaited him and his destination was only two-and-a-half hours away. He thought more than once, maybe three times, *Things do come in threes.*

His face still hurt and now his head hurt. The hat didn't help, so it came off. If things do come in threes, what's going to hurt next?

Thinking about what had happened taxed his brain the first half of the flight. Few conclusions came of it, except he would never go back to Manhattan. Not ever, for any reason. That part of the globe forbidden. Off-limits. May as well not exist.

The other, he needed more fruit. Fresh fruit. For now, the pouch of mixed dried fruit he carried onto the plane would have to do.

Adaptability made a sound, leveled-headed astronaut. Life had trained Hayden to adjust. It supplied lemons abundantly to his lemonade stand that was open year-round. Instead of lemons hitting him in the head, he became good at catching them on the fly and squeezing them into lemonade. Somewhere along the line, he was sure he profited somehow from this ability, but never enough to close the stand once in a while. Even if life continued to toss lemons his way, it would have been nice to find protection in his profit and let them pile-up and rot.

Making the best of his life wasting away trapped on the plane, Hayden decided to do what he had done sometimes in space—nothing. The passenger, in the seat beside him, looked bored out of her mind, searching for something to read on her laptop. As Hayden tilted his seat back to get comfortable into nothingness, a link entitled "Bizarre Explosion in Downtown Manhattan" on the computer screen adrenalized him and slothfulness may have to wait.

In his excitement, Hayden tilted his seat forward then back again because he could see the screen better.

"Hello," Hayden said.

The woman's head turned slowly to face him.

"Sorry to interrupt," Hayden said, smiling. "When you're finished reading, would you mind if I read that explosion article?"

"Which one?" the woman asked. "There are a number of them."

"I'm sorry. The Manhattan one." No way was he going to tell her he was there. "Terrible there are so many things like that in the world."

"It is."

Her eyes checked him over as if seeing him for the first time, although she had sat next to him the last three and a half hours.

"Here," she said, handing him the laptop. "I read what I wanted to and my eyes need a break."

Hayden accepted the computer. "Thank you. I'll just read this and give it back."

"When you're done, just set it on the tray. I'm going to close my eyes."

Hayden clicked on the link and read the article. Done, he scrolled back up to a video embedded in the body of the article and clicked the play button. The video started and its sound blurted out of the tiny computer speakers.

People peered over the backs of seats to see who couldn't operate their electronics.

Alarmed, the woman reached over and lowered the sound. "My fault. Conference call that I could barely hear. Use your earbuds."

"Sorry. Thanks again."

Using the earbuds this time, Hayden started the video over. Someone up a few floors in one of the buildings had recorded the explosion that had happened behind Hayden. The camera zoomed in on the man lying in his own bloodied slush on the street, struggling to stop the bleeding out of what remained of his cleaved-off arm. Visibly, the man's body appeared laxed, losing consciousness. When it went limp, the explosion erupted from where the man laid, and a ball of flame expanded like a new universe coming into existence, changing colors as it grew, concealing that entire section of streets and sidewalks. The flame appeared hot enough to consume anything in its path.

The blaze rolled toward the camera and the recorder yelled, "Get down!" as a blur of moving film played then stilled. Apparently, nothing happened because there wasn't any panic, just the man recording saying, "I think it's gone."

Blurring movement resumed and settled on a view of the street where the man had laid.

The fire cleared. Not dissipating, though, this shrank, receding outside-in. As more of the area became visible, nothing had been damaged nor had anyone been hurt. Even those standing around the man when the explosion occurred were still there. By their reactions, they appeared shaken and disheveled as if they had just came out of a tornado, but not injured.

When the fireball minimalized into nothing where the assaulted man had lain, the man was gone.

The video ended and Hayden checked the woman next to him, who sat still with her eyes closed.

He took the liberty of watching it again; confirming the detonation originated from inside the man and noticing, this time, all of the man's clothes and personal effects had disappeared.

It took watching the extraordinary video a third time before he realized the man's blood within the slush had also vanished.

If it weren't for the recording and eyewitnesses, no one would have believed the man ever existed or an explosion had taken place. Without any evidence, no structural damage, and no one hurt, except for the man with his arm cut-off, why should anyone believe. The only way Hayden could explain how the man was, then wasn't, was that the man had disintegrated in the same fashion the hacker had disappeared not far from his car after being lasered down by the orange pursuer. Immediately, he wondered why nothing else had been destroyed. As far as he knew, discriminative weapons of destruction don't exist.

Half a day had passed and Hayden's plane landed into Friday Harbor Airport on San Juan Island in Washington State. He didn't want to, but he put on the hat and carried his only carry-on off the plane. After retrieving his vehicle, he drove home.

Parked and the carry-on bag strapped over his shoulder, Hayden proceeded to the docks. Clouds appeared and dissipated at his mouth as he breathed and the cold air lightened his skin and reddened his lips. The dock bounced on the water as he walked and water slapped the logs.

The beauty of where he lived made him wonder why he ever went to New York in the first place. Nature had landscaped the secluded, bowl-shaped area as beautifully as any other on Earth. Deep green trees with snow adhering to them, as if sprinkled in powdered sugar, covered every slope and cascaded to undisturbed snow, blanketing rocky shorelines, banks, and a few plots of open land. Blue water filled the bottom of the bowl, creating a mystery as to what beauty might lie hidden underneath.

Most of the scenery escaped human tainting, which had been limited to the shoreline where Hayden lived, which, in itself, wasn't an eyesore, sprinkled with well-to-do homes, boats, and cars of residents. Even the vehicles of family and friends, visiting for the holidays, weren't bad to look at. No, the people living in this section of San Juan Island were blessed. Beauty was in the eye of the beholder, but for the rest of Hayden's life, only his eyes mattered and this part of the world suited just fine.

Perhaps the worst in Manhattan was walking the city, freezing his ass off after the excitement. People stared at him. There he was, cold and it was snowing, and instead of wearing his overcoat and scarf as a sane person would, his coat covered the briefcase and arms and the scarf the gun in his hand. His cut-up face looked like needle marks from injecting drugs straight into his head.

A close second was finding somewhere private to deal with the trouble he carried. Prying a dead man's hand off the briefcase handle and breaking the thumb of the other hand to slide it out of the cuff were two unpleasantries he wanted to forget but knew he never would.

For some reason, maybe the cold, or rigor mortis, both were a bitch to get off. The death grip held the handle like a vice and the damn thumb wouldn't break. After some crude finagling and significant effort, the thumb finally detached. Breaking a sweat in freezing temperatures while not wearing protective clothing could be a challenge, but he did it.

Perhaps the best part, or lucky stretch, was not crossing paths again with the person dressed entirely in orange.

It wasn't over, he knew. The eventful trip would linger on, for how long he didn't know, but the shorter, the better. The rental may be sitting in the alley or it might have been towed. Whose arms had he pried loose? Will the killer in orange forget about him or come after the suitcase? Who was the bald-headed man and how did he know things?

Hayden had gotten out of there alive and didn't want to live the rest of his life looking over his shoulder, wondering if the person in the orange cloak had the laser drawn to shoot him in the back and vaporize him. And for what? A briefcase. Life was good at spurring questions as it was hurling lemons and not so good at providing answers or instructions on how to make lemonade with them.

How stupid he was for letting the bald man talk him into fleeing with the briefcase. Why did he listen? Regret of that decision would haunt him and needlessly carry on this predicament until he no longer had the briefcase. It wasn't with him now, but it was coming. So were the forearms. Life would never be normal again until he got rid of them. All of them. But how?

He stepped off the dock and onto the deck of his small floating home docked for the winter, unlocked the door, and entered. It felt warm, but he swore he turned the heat down before leaving for the East Coast. The house was small, less than 500 square feet, single-story, and had only one hallway and four rooms: a living space, tiny kitchen, a combined bath and laundry area, and one bedroom with a walk-in closet, in that order.

Hearing something, Hayden stopped and listened. Not hearing it anymore, he decided his first-line of business would be to check the house. The living room and kitchen were clear. Proceeding down the hallway, about to check the bath and laundry, he saw a woman facing out the window-wall in the bedroom.

She turned around as he stepped into the room. "Back so soon?" she asked.

"Ora?" Hayden asked, surprised.

"Expecting someone else?" Ora asked.

He removed his hat. "How did you get in?"

"How quickly we forget."

Finding the memory, he said, "That's right. Mexico. I gave you a key."

"I'm impressed."

With his thumb and middle finger wrinkling the skin on his forehead, he asked, "What was the name of that hotel?"

"I'm no longer impressed," she said, then answered, "Palmilla."

"Of course you would remember."

"Not to be rude or anything, but," she flung the bangs out of her eyes, "what happened to your face?"

He spun the hat through the air like a Frisbee onto the bed. "God, I wish you respected me."

"Like you do me?"

Hayden pursed his lips then asked, "Any fruit in the house?"

"How should I know?"

"Well, did you pick up any groceries? Some fruit perhaps?"

"You act like we're married, Hayden. Not that it's any of your business, but I just got here myself."

Opening the bag, Hayden pulled out the pouch and said, "All I have is this dried stuff."

They stared at each other, but their stares weren't the same.

Her stare expressed she had made a mistake coming here.

His stare expressed his want for her. She looked beautiful, standing in front of a floor-to-ceiling glass window, which ran the entire length of two walls of the bedroom. A darkening wintry gray sky was behind her head and torso and dark blue water was behind her legs, which camouflaged her jeans. It took a couple of attempts, a true struggle, but his eyes pulled out of her allure and looked around the room. Everything seemed to be as he left it.

"Well?" Ora asked.

"Well ..." Hayden shrugged a shoulder and said, "Fine."

In frustration, her hands went into the air and came down, slapping the sides of her thighs.

"You don't believe me," she said.

"I do. It's fine."

She stormed toward him for the hall. "I shouldn't have come. It's obvious you don't want me here."

He grabbed her by the arm as she passed and whirled her around to face him. "I would never have gone to New York if I knew you would come."

"I wasn't sure if I was coming either."

"When did you know?"

"When I opened the door."

Hayden let out a childish, goofy chuckle, "Wow! You didn't think the key would work, did you?"

"No." She bounced on her toes. "But I was hoping."

"Hold that thought. I need a shower—bad."

"Yeah, you stink and need to brush your teeth."

"It's a little like being in space again, huh?"

"No. You're ripe. This is like that camping trip where you didn't shower or anything for a week."

A smile grew on his face, "You remember that?"

Looking up at him and caressing the air around his face, she asked, "What did you do? It looks like it hurts."

"Like bee stings with the stingers still in them."

"Well, go shower and I'll clean them up. I'm sure you have medical supplies stashed somewhere, just in case."

"In the bathroom. I'll bring it when I'm cleaned up."

Hayden went into the bathroom and undressed. Moisture hung in the air and the bath rug felt damp. He opened the shower door to run the water and noticed the tiles and things in there were wet. *'I just got in'* she had said.

The water in the shower ran for a bit as he retrieved the first-aid kit. Steam filled the shower and as he stepped inside, Ora's voice surprised him.

"We can't say we never lied to each other," she said, leaning against the bathroom doorframe.

"No. No, we can't."

"I'll go get some fruit if you want?"

"That'll be great. Take a left out of here and there's a store about a half-mile down the road. You can't miss it. You'll make it before they close if you hurry."

"Anything particular you want?"

"No. Just no oranges. I've had my fill of them today."

Night had set on the island and everything in Hayden's bedroom reflected in the window-wall as if a mirror; his gray bedcover reflected in the skylight above the bed in the ceiling of the bedroom. Hayden leaned back on pillows against the headboard of his bed, holding a brandy, while Ora worked on the cuts in his face. Three vines sat on the bed from three bunches of grapes Hayden had eaten.

"God, Hayden. It looks worse now," Ora said.

"Thanks for noticing," Hayden said.

"Want to tell me what happened in New York?"

"Not really. I've already spent too much brain power on it."

"Long voyage home, hey astronaut. Well, you're used to it."

"Long journeys sure. But not this."

"Not what? I want to know."

"Fine." He took a sip of his brandy, sat up, and told her what had happened. It flew off his tongue as if he were a seasoned storyteller.

"I still had the arms with me at the vendor, right. Well, my coat slides off and the guy looks at me and asks, 'Are they real? They look real,' and I said, 'No. They're fake.' He said, 'They sure look real, mister,' and I said, 'I know, right. The stuff they can make these days.' Just then, the screen in the forearm comes on and the guy hears it and asks, 'What did you say?' and I tossed a couple of bucks on the counter and said, 'Buy yourself a lottery ticket. Hope you win,' and left."

"Screens in arms. I don't believe it."

"Oh, believe it, sister."

"If you got caught with those things, your life would have been cast into litigation hell, not to mention your astronaut career would be over."

"It's already over."

Dabbing his head, she said, "You don't know that."

"Ora, I haven't been in space for two years. NASA won't be calling on Hayden Bakley for any upcoming missions."

"Well, I haven't been assigned for a year and I'm much younger than you are."

"Not that much."

"A decade is a long time, Hayden."

"Well, hell with them, then."

"I know you want to go back up. You wanted to stay up there even before they brought you down."

"Be honest, Ora. Did you miss me?"

A smile grew on her face. "Yeah. Things were just getting good. Sneaking around like we were teenagers." The expression on her face turned serious. "Well, maybe I was a teenager and you were some sicko trying to live out things you never got to experience while you were young."

Hayden gulped the rest of his brandy and stared at her.

"It's so easy for you, isn't it?"

"Tell me something. And be honest with me. Why did you go to Manhattan?"

Reaching like a blind man, he said, "Grapes. I need more grapes."

She grabbed his wrists and, when he was just about to break out of her grasp, her fingernails dug into his skin.

"Ow!" Hayden yelled, jerking his hand back.

"Then answer!"

"*Christmas.* That's all. Just to say I spent it in the Big Apple."

"That's all?"

"Yeah, that's all."

A stillness settled in the room as she thought, then she said, "I want to see them." Setting the washcloth on the nightstand, she got off the bed and walked toward the bag. "Are they in the bag?"

"I told you what's in the bag. You don't listen very well."

Just then, Hayden's cell phone rang.

Ora stopped and they looked at each other.

As the phone rang, Hayden said, "Maybe it's NASA."

More ringing and she asked, "Well, aren't you going to answer it?"

"I guess."

He picked up the cell phone off the nightstand and answered. "Hello."

A man's voice said, "This is the Office of the Inspector General of NASA. Are you familiar with NASA, sir?"

"Yeah, I know what NASA is," Hayden replied. "Apparently, you don't know who you called."

"Sure I do. Only insiders know that Nobody Answers when Somebody Asks NASA."

"*Stressed fruit fields*, is this Kip Stanton?"

"That's me. You should really see somebody about your fruit fixation."

"I did. Instead of meds, they said to consume fruit at least twice a day. *Jesus, Kip!* I thought this was a real call."

"It is a real call. We're talking aren't we?"

"Well, what the hell are you up to? Been up lately?"

"No. I've been grounded."

"Me, too. Two years. How long for you?"

"For good."

"Aw, man. I'm sorry. I haven't been told officially, but I'm probably in the same boat."

"Hayden, I have to ask you something."

Kip's an old friend, but Hayden's demeanor changed. "You said my name, Kip. That's not good."

"Actually, it is, Hayden. You have to believe me. I really am calling from NASA's Office of the Inspector General. Once I returned shortly after you, they told me I was grounded. Long story short, I'm a field agent of the Office of Investigations."

"This is an official call, then?" Hayden asked.

"I wanted to call. Many times. Just been busy."

"Becoming a field agent."

"Yeah."

To say the call irked the hell out of Hayden would be an understatement. They had flown a number of missions together and had become good friends. So had Kip and Ora. Of all the astronauts, it was Kip he worried most about when it came to Ora. They were closer in age and had flown missions together while Hayden was on the ground.

The call had a long-lost friend feel to it. Had Kip called, thinking the relationship was enough to sell something or, in this case, gather information? Still, Hayden knew he had to play his own game, wanting to return to space at least for one more mission, so he cooperated. Besides, he could have reached out to Kip, but hadn't.

"Fine. Ask away," Hayden said.

"Thanks for making this easier on me, Hayden," Kip said. "I'll try to do the same." Kip's tone became more business-like. "So, anything unusual happen while in New York?"

"New York, huh?"

"Yeah, Manhattan."

Hayden didn't like the Office of Investigations knowing his business. "I'm sure all kinds of unusual things happened there."

"So much for making this easier on me. You know I meant anything unusual happen to *you*?"

"Look, Kip. I need a friend to talk to, not an investigator."

"I thought we were friends. Besides, you know either official or unofficial, in the long haul they both count."

"I know. I was hoping you didn't."

"Come on Hayden, this is my work, now. Of course, I would know."

"You were always a good astronaut."

"And, so far, a good agent," Kip said.

"Seems you already know something unusual happened. Otherwise, you wouldn't have called."

"Yeah, I would have. You know I would have."

"Well, I should have called you, too."

"Wouldn't have done you any good. I was too busy…"

"I know," Hayden interrupted, "becoming an agent. What do you want to know?"

"Everything. From your perspective, of course."

"Can't we do it another time?"

"I know you had a long trip getting home, but I need it while it's fresh."

The fact Kip and the Office of Investigations tracked him from New York made him uneasy.

"Like I said," Hayden said, "You know so much, you probably know Ora's standing here in my bedroom."

Silence on the other end and Ora, knowing it was Kip on the other end from Hayden saying his name, cowered back as if she didn't want Kip to know.

Finally, Kip said, "Yeah. We knew she arrived before you got there."

Hayden pursed his lips and his eyes widened as he looked at Ora and repeated Kip's words for her benefit.

"Oh, you watched her arrive here before I got here," Hayden said, looking at Ora. "Interesting."

Ora's hands went to her hips, not caring for their knowledge.

"And other adjectives," Kip said. "Tell her I'll talk with her next."

"You assume she's staying?"

"Of course. You're both in your bedroom instead of the living room, so I assumed the couch was out."

"You got eyes on us, Kip?"

"Maybe," Kip said flatly in near admittance. "But I've also crashed on that pull-out couch, remember?"

"I do. If I don't talk, don't you need to get a warrant or something?"

"Or something. Why are you stalling? I said we're trying to help you."

"I'm not stalling," Hayden said, stalling. "In fact, ready to jot this down?"

"You know we're recording," Kip said.

"I figured. Here it is."

"Remember, from your perspective."

"It's the only perspective I got."

"When you're ready."

Hayden said a few words and laid the phone on the nightstand, which ended the call.

"Jesus, Hayden. What did you do that for?" Ora asked.

"Intuition. I didn't like it.

"You know he's going to call back."

The cell phone rang.

"See. Told you," Ora said.

"Let it ring," he said.

"Look to see at least whose calling."

"There won't be an I.D."

"Oh, men."

"That was too close to *omen*."

Ora stormed over to the nightstand and on her way said, "I didn't forget about those arms."

"Come on, Ora. Forget about it."

"How can I?"

She picked up the cell phone and there wasn't an I.D. on the screen. Kip's angry voice sounded out of the phone. *"Hayden! Hayden!"*

Hayden's shoulders shrugged as he looked up at Ora and said, "Picking it up answers it."

Panicked, Ora asked, "Well, what do I do?"

"Set it down and magically he shuts up."

The phone landed hard on the nightstand from her tossing it as if it were contagious.

"Easy," Hayden said.

"Well, now what?"

"First, we silence the phone, including yours. Second, I skip telling you what happened. I have a feeling Kip was only going to ask you how I appeared, acted, etcetera when you first saw me. The less you know, the better."

"Anything else, your highness?"

"Third, you have to leave. I'm in the middle of something."

Those words more than disappointed Ora, they hurt.

Until he said, "In the morning."

Later that night, Hayden's floating home bobbed gently on the water. Light from a dock lamp came in through the front window into the living room, while moonlight reflected off the water, casting a soft glow through the window-wall onto the bed, where Ora laid tucked under Hayden's arm and covers. Through the skylight above the bed, someone dressed and cloaked in all orange looked down on them.

CHAPTER **THREE**

Morning sunlight shined through the window-wall into Hayden's bedroom onto the bed, warming the comforter. Fleece sheets against Hayden and Ora's skin provided one of the world's most comfortable feelings. Besides fruit, Hayden believed in a comfortable mattress and took it seriously. No price was too great for such comfort. After sleeping many orientations in near-weightless gravity inside a sleeping bag in space, the one piece of furniture he could not live without on Earth was a firm mattress. Feeling gravity pull his body against a contouring mattress made it okay to be grounded for those hours he slept.

Hayden kissed Ora's forehead, threw the covers back, and got out of bed. Cold air touched his skin and goose pimples raised all over his body. Thinking the heat would kick on soon, he let it go, went to the bathroom, and took a leak. The toilet flushed but never filled with water. Thinking he would get to it later, he turned the handle on the faucet to wash his hands and no water came out. Waking comfortably and not alone had contained a promise of a good day. In a matter of minutes, the promise wasn't kept, and he expected his lousy luck would carry over into today.

On his way to the kitchen to make some coffee, this end

of the floating house felt much colder and the skin on his body tightened in self-defense. Maybe the heat went out. No heat and no water in the middle of winter.

Naked and pimpled, he walked into a ransacked living room. Furniture was out of place and a few pieces were toppled over. Every cabinet door was pulled opened as were the drawers with many of them removed and discarded on the floor. All that had been stowed away laid scattered, covering the rug and hardwood perimeter. Even the front door was left open. Instead of seeing a dock, he saw open water.

Shivering, he stood naked in the doorway and looked out. The house floated freely on the water away from the dock and land. Defeated, he closed the door and returned to the bedroom. Morning grogginess must have blinded him, only functional enough to get out of bed and trod the path to the toilet where he had trod many times before. A learned pattern and familiarity, achieved with practice, where eyesight was no longer needed in a state between being awake and asleep.

Awake and aware, now, by the cold, intrusion that had occurred while he and Ora slept, and their predicament, he saw what he had missed. Clothes hung over opened drawers and clothed the floor. The lone closet was open with hangered garments piled on top of one another there. Out the wall-window, in the distance, he saw the dock.

"Hey Ora, wake up," he said as he shook her shoulder, her now laying on her side.

Used to being awakened in space for shifts, she sat right up and as the covers fell off her torso down to her waist, she cried out, "Geez, it's cold!" and grabbed the blankets to cover herself.

"You'll warm up once you know what we're dealing with," Hayden said.

A crunching sound of unwanted friction came from outside. When Hayden looked out the wall-window to see what it was, the house pushed against a thickening piece of ice, floating on the water.

"That's not good," he said.

Not a practicing praying man, he still knew when to pray, especially on voyages into space and now was one of those times. It amounted to repeating, *Don't get lodged in that ice.*

"What's not good?" Ora asked.

"This morning," he answered. "I need to make some calls."

Hours passed and Hayden felt relieved to have the floating home secured to the dock once more. Some locals he knew had come to the rescue, but it cost him for their time and putting their assets at risk in such weather. The method for getting the home back to the dock had been crude: a motorized boat, some rope, and long poles to steer the house from hitting anything. Being the end house on the dock had cost him a little more to have the perpetual view of the water from his bedroom, but had also made re-docking easier. One neighbor had stuck around to help Hayden reattach the power and water cables, which Hayden had purposefully made sure the connectors on the house were above water level when he purchased the home.

After giving the man a few extra dollars, Hayden went inside, turned on the heat, and checked the water. Everything good, a knock sounded at the front door.

"I'll get it," Ora said.

A man stood outside the door. She opened it and asked, "May I help you?"

"I have a package for Hayden Bakley."

"Oh sure," she acknowledged, then yelled over her shoulder to Hayden. "Hayden! Package!" Turning back to the man, she said, "Come in out the cold."

The man stepped inside and she partially closed the door as Hayden approached. The man set the package on the floor then situated the handheld and wand to make it easy for Hayden to sign.

Hayden signed but never thanked the man for the

delivery. He showed the man out, locked the door, and carried the package into the living room.

"Draw the blinds," Hayden said to Ora.

As she drew them, there was another knock on the door. She headed for the door, but Hayden stopped her.

"Keep closing. I'll get it," Hayden said, on his way to the door. "The whole house."

He opened the door and a different man stood outside, holding a package. Hayden signed and took it, never thanking the deliveryman.

Taking the package into the living room and setting it beside the other one, Hayden had just sat down when another knock sounded at the front door. A third package came, so he signed, set it by the others in the living room, and sat down.

Ora returned from closing all the blinds in the house and saw the three packages.

"Gifts?" she asked. "You shouldn't have."

"I didn't," he said. "They're not gifts. Believe me. They're worse."

"Worse? Why?"

"I don't know where to return them."

"Well, what's in them?"

"Halloween is what," Hayden answered. "These things are two holidays too late."

"Why weren't they all delivered together?" Ora asked.

"Didn't seem right to trust all three to one carrier."

"Aren't you going to open them?"

"When I'm ready."

"Which will be?"

"After a couple of brandies over a slow fire."

"You must be freezing. It's flurrying out there."

Hayden built a fire in the fireplace while Ora poured some brandy in a glass. When he sat down in the chair in front of the fire, she handed the drink to him, sat on the arm of the chair, and twirled a finger in his hair.

"Rough day," she said. "Is it always like this?"

After a sip, he said, "Hell, no. It's why I live here."

The slight burn of the brandy and warmth from the hearth were precisely what he needed to warm up.

She stood and, while setting up a TV tray in front of him, she asked, "How did the house become loose?"

Enjoying the aroma of his brandy, he pulled the glass away from his nose and said, "Someone knew what they were doing and unhooked us."

His words got her thinking as she went into the kitchen. The sound of the oven door opening then closing came from there and she returned with a crock of French Onion soup and set it on a potholder on the tray in front of him.

"At night? Who would do such a thing?" she asked.

"A New Yorker, perhaps," he answered. "No one around here."

"Someone on the same flights as you?"

Her words now had him thinking of people he saw on his flights and layovers. Honestly, specifics were hard to conjure up. They had happened, of course, making his way from one coast to the other, but nothing out of the ordinary put him more on alert than what he already was. And after what he had witnessed, he had consumed more than his fair share of alcohol. Perhaps it was fair.

"I don't know," he said in a near whisper. "Maybe."

While Hayden lingered preoccupied in thought, Ora had gone back into the kitchen and returned, setting a spoon and a grilled cheese sandwich on the tray beside his soup.

"Well, eat and get warm," she said. "You want some more brandy?"

"In coffee, if you made some," he said.

On her way to the kitchen, she said, "All I got to do is hit start."

The coffee began to brew and she returned to the living room. When she passed Hayden's chair, he reached out, grabbed her arm, and pulled her close.

"Thanks," he said. "You didn't have to do all of this. Clean up in here and everything."

A shyness came over her and she said, "Well, after the day you had, you deserve it. I'll run to the store and pick you up some more fruit."

His eyes rolled off her toward the delivered boxes.

"We don't deserve any of this," he said.

Her head turned to follow his eyes to the boxes and returned to him.

"Deserve what?" Ora asked.

He didn't answer. His eyes fixed in a vacant stare on the packages.

"Hayden. Are we safe?"

The fire crackled and the coffeemaker gurgled. Occasionally, water splashed against the house.

Releasing her arm, he picked up the spoon and tasted the soup. Without looking up, he said, "No."

Ora drove to the store before it got dark. Warmed now, Hayden headed back to the bedroom to remove his sweater. A shadow in the shape of the Sun on the comforter caught his eye, but he didn't think much of it. Bird droppings, leaves, and other things have been on the skylight above the bed before.

Crudely, he folded the sweater, put it in the closet, and shut the door. The odd-shaped shadow nagged him, so he looked up at the skylight, hating he had done so. Such anxiety and analysis were okay on missions in space, but not in his home. It's been years since such feelings and thoughts had surfaced inside him in his dwelling. For the first time since buying the place, his sanctuary had been encroached.

Light filtered through a red splotch on the glass of the skylight. The dot itself reminded him of dark red cellophane paper. Only it couldn't be cellophane paper. Same-colored tentacles, but differing lengths and in numerous directions spread from its center like a streaking liquid that had dried and hardened. It appeared to be blood.

The temperature outside was cold, but not cold enough to freeze blood. It occurred to Hayden the vital fluid could always be animal, but more likely belonged to whoever ransacked and unhooked his home last night.

His eyes fell to the view of the snow-sprinkled green hills and whitening blue water outside the window-wall. The view didn't register the same to him as previous times. Its beauty had been tainted. If only he hadn't gone to Manhattan.

Early twilight set on Friday Harbor and Ora returned from the store, carrying a paper bag on her way to the house. A hooded silhouette stood on Hayden's roof. Startled, she stopped on the dock. Water bobbed the wood under her feet. A sudden wintery gust sprang from the water and pushed against her body and paper bag. Something banged and a yelp instinctively cried out of her as she cowered over the rippling bag. The hooded figure's head turned and looked down at her. Her body shivered as if her spine dangled from her brain, exposed to the elements, void of the insulation of her torso.

The gust ceased.

"Oh, good, you're back," the silhouette said.

"Hayden?" she questioned.

"Who else?" Hayden said. "Before you go in, can you set the ladder up again? The wind blew it over."

Ora set the bag on the deck by the door and leaned the ladder against the house. "What would you have done if I wasn't here?"

Hayden carefully slipped what he held into his coat pocket. "I don't know, Orange."

"Orange? Don't you mean Ora?"

"Right. Just a slip of the tongue. You've been great."

"If I've been so great at least remember my name."

His gloved fingers poked the side of his head. "Just an association."

"Well stop associating and come down."

Inside, Hayden added wood to the fire, while Ora put the groceries away. Waves, increasing in strength, gently rocked the house and flurries had turned into snowfall.

Fake flowers in a vase donned the center of the coffee table in the living room, surrounded by dirty plates, utensils, and a half-drank wine bottle from dinner. Hayden and Ora sat on the floor, leaning against the couch near the fire, each holding a glass of red wine.

"That hit the spot," Hayden said. "If I knew you could cook, maybe we would have stayed in more."

"I suppose if I agree, that would make me conceited," Ora said.

"Not at all. Better than eating out and there are some fine restaurants around here. You normally eat like that?"

"I cook for myself most nights."

Her phrasing didn't get by him.

"Yourself?" he inquired.

A smile formed on her face. "Why, sure. What did you expect?"

He shrugged a shoulder. "I don't know. I just thought …"

The smile on Ora's face extended farther. "You thought what?"

"Maybe somebody …"

'*Somebody*' was an insinuation of not just anybody, but someone in particular and it erased the smile from her face.

"Not somebody," she said. "You mean Kip, don't you?"

Looking down at his glass and pursing his lips told her it was so.

She sat up. "God, Hayden! You know how to ruin a nice time. I'm done explaining myself to you."

He shook his head and then said, "You didn't before and you don't have to now. It's not like we're married or anything."

Her body erected more. Not trusting herself, she set her wine glass on the table. "That's two for two."

He gulped a swallow of wine instead of a sip and said, "No. I've brought it up more times than that."

"*Clueless!* How did you make it through astronaut

training? How did you fly all those missions? I meant, I said about being married yesterday and you said it today. I've only been here two days."

"Two for two. Got it," Hayden said, finished the wine in his glass, and set it on the table. He picked up the fruit and cheese plate, ate a slice of cheese, then the last raspberry. "Any more fruit?"

Ora's lips smacked in disgust. "You should really see somebody about your fruit fetish. I must be a lunatic."

Eating another slice of cheese, he said, "*Mm-hmm!* See. That's what Kip said on the phone last night."

"That I was a lunatic?"

"Who's clueless now? No. That I should see somebody. Only he said *fruit fixation* instead of *fetish*."

"So?"

"So! It means you've been around him enough you're starting to think and talk alike."

Her hands went into the air. "Break time!" She got off the floor and started cleaning up.

He stood, grabbed some plates, and followed her into the kitchen.

"Oh, no!" he said. "No break! Not this time."

She set the dishes in the sink and turned around. "Fine. You want honesty. Kip, I, and others, we all think alike, Hayden. And what are we thinking? We're thinking what kind of man, in his forties no less, turns to fruit in times of crisis?"

His gesturing reaction came off like what was wrong with it. "What?"

"You don't find it even a little peculiar?"

Defensive, he said, "You know what? No. No, I don't. I just happen to go for what goes into the wine instead of the wine."

"And that's better?"

His head nodded. "I think so, yes."

Her glare targeted him.

Nervousness she was going to leave filled him.

"Well," she started, "I do too."

Relieved, he said, "Well, then what are we arguing for?"

She turned around and ran the water to wash the dishes. "We aren't arguing. Married couples argue."

"Ah, ha! You mentioned marriage each day. I only said it today."

"Get the rest of the dishes, before I make you wash them."

"Why would I wash them?"

"Because if I don't, you'll have to."

"I have a dishwasher right there."

She glanced to her left where he pointed and sure enough, there was a dishwasher under the counter.

"You forgot, didn't you?" he said.

Sitting on the couch in the living room, Hayden took a sip of wine and then reached for one of the boxes delivered earlier. Instead of grabbing box cutters, he opened the scissors from the kitchen and ran the blade along the tape on top of the box.

Beside him, Ora watched with interest, her hands cupping the outside of her glass.

The scissors knocked on the wooden coffee table when Hayden tossed them and he opened the flaps on the box. A smell released out of the box as if a small dead animal was inside, but it wasn't overpowering and dissipated quickly. Knowing now what was inside, he slid the box out of the way, brought another box closer, picked up the scissors, and opened it. A black briefcase emerged out of the box in his hand and his foot pushed the empty box away from him.

Cupping her hands around the glass, Ora sipped her wine, as if drinking from a bowl. She waited for Hayden to say something and took another sip. His demeanor toward the case had a similar reaction to receiving a gift he didn't want.

"Hayden. You okay?" she asked.

Turning and studying the suitcase, he simply answered,

"No," as if it were a bother to answer.

Another sip of wine, a bigger one this time, and she realized her consumption was much faster than usual. "What's in it?"

His narrow eyes examined every part of the briefcase. "I told you earlier. Halloween."

Setting her glass on the coffee table, she said, "Fine. Be a baby."

With his eyes fixed on the case, he said, "I'm not being a baby. Babies don't know what seamless means. Which this case happens to be. Can't open seamless, my dear."

"It must open. If it doesn't, then bash it open."

"Bash it open? The damned thing survived a laser blast that disintegrated a man and you want to bash it open."

"Well, what good is a briefcase that doesn't open?"

"If it's a briefcase."

"Why wouldn't it be? It sure looks like a briefcase."

"I don't know," he said. "You don't know. Maybe it was made to look like a briefcase. All I know is whatever it is and whatever is inside is worth a man getting his arm chopped off, then blown-up, and another man lasered in the back and then blown to smithereens."

"Lasered? Blown-up? What are you saying?" she asked.

"Grown-up stuff. Beyond typical adult behavior. Not baby tantrums."

"Well, what? You saw it?"

"Up close and personal. Both of them."

Ora sat erect. "Did you contact the authorities?"

"No."

"*No!* Two men had been murdered, Hayden."

"I know. I was there."

"I don't understand you," she said, shaking her head.

"Look! I thought about it, all right! If you want to leave, I won't blame you."

Her eyes lowered to her lap and then raised to him. "You think there's a connection between last night and this briefcase? Someone was looking for it?"

"I know so."

With determined eyes, she requested, "Tell me what you know. Then tell me if they're going to kill us."

"They're not going to kill us. They want what I got."

"Until they take it from you. Then they'll kill us."

Hayden went on to explain all that had happened in Manhattan, leaving out the gruesome details. When he finished, she didn't know what to say.

"If you want to leave, I understand," Hayden offered again.

"No," she answered. "You were there for me when space was making me crazy and you never reported it. Not exactly the best attribute for an astronaut is it?"

"Just like I'm not going to report this. Something tells me reporting it isn't going to absolve me or stop it."

Ashamed, she looked down. "You should have. Like you should now."

"I'll never go up again, Ora, if I do."

A finality pricked Hayden's insides from his toes to his scalp. This wasn't imagined. It was real. Real enough to hurt and make him wince and as final as losing a job, getting a divorce, and death. Even though he had taken care of her by not sharing with anyone her Astrophobia condition, her fear of space, and she owed him one, there was no way he was telling her or anyone about these fog-like funks he gets into where things become hazy and his body performs tasks without any connected thought. Of course, the brain commands the body, he knew, and that knowledge scared him the most. Not only because what he might do, but also because it made him unfit for space. It was his love for space, being an Astrophile, which had helped Ora's fear of it.

Looking up at him, she asked, "Why not? You didn't do anything wrong?"

Oh, how he wanted to ask her if she had done anything wrong? He had thought about it many times. When he wasn't with her on a mission in space, who had helped her with her phobia? Every time, Kip's face appeared in his mind as a lead suspect.

"Stealing is wrong," he said. "The case isn't mine, remember. But there's more. What I'm about to tell you and more importantly show you, I have a feeling I've done a bunch wrong. I'm part of whatever is happening."

"Well, reduce your stake. Turn everything over to the authorities and get out."

"Like Kip?"

"Yes, Kip. He knows you don't send an astronaut on a spacewalk without a tether. He'll make sure you're okay."

"Not this time. The tether would only be there so I can choke on it."

"After all you two been through, you don't trust him?"

"Not after that last call I don't." Hayden picked up Ora's wine glass and handed it to her. "Here, drink this down. You'll need it once you see how bad going to New York had changed my life."

Not having a clue how to open the briefcase and witnessing it survive one hell of a blast in Manhattan, he gave up on it, for now, set it on the floor, grabbed the flap of the other box he had opened, and pulled it in front of him.

"I would drink that down now before I show you what's inside," he said.

"I'm fine," she insisted. "Quit messing around and just show me if you're going to show me."

Out of the box came all sorts of souvenirs from Manhattan and he set some on the coffee table and some on the floor. His hand disappeared inside the box again and sounds of his skin, skidding and grabbing something plastic like a garbage bag, emitted out. Similar to a magician pulling a rabbit out of a hat, in his grasp came out something long, wrapped and taped in clear bubble wrap. Whatever was inside had a pale, washed-out color with one of the ends black or a deep red.

Eyeing Ora, Hayden saw she wanted to know the truth

and her body language seemed poised for him to proceed. He carefully peeled back the tape as someone who received a gift and liked the wrapping paper so much that he wanted to keep it. Next, the bubble wrap was unrolled as if a valuable vase was inside. Before unveiling the thing inside, he stopped and looked at her. Her eyes were too busy, examining the nearly exposed package on his lap to notice. Finally, she noticed him looking at her and her eyes met his. Apprehension contorted them in the mixed feelings apprehension brings. Without further ado, the last of the bubble wrap pulled back, exposing a man's forearm severed just above the elbow.

The red wine disappeared from her tilted glass as she drank and, somehow, she kept her eyes on the appendage. Her full lips puckered and, as she leaned forward to place the glass on the coffee table, the wine's acidic aroma gave way to another acidic odor, similar to a dead mouse. The sting of gangrene from the bloodied gauze pad made her bring the wine glass down on the table too hard and the stem separated from the bowl. Rather than trying to collect them, she let them fall on the table.

Hayden's middle finger and thumb pinched the wrist as if picking up a rat by the tail and dangled the arm over the bubble wrap on his lap.

"Need more wine?" he asked. "I'll take a brandy. The bottle, please."

"Why do you have an arm?" she asked.

"I have two."

"No jokes. You joke, I'm going to assume you've gone mad and I'll have to turn you in."

"No, I mean I have two of these. Here. I'll show you."

Carefully rolling some bubble wrap around the forearm and placing it back inside the box, he stood, grabbed the scissors, sat back down, and opened the third box. The scissors knocked on the coffee table and Ora shivered on the couch. With the flaps opened, to Hayden's surprise, this box was nearly odorless.

He set a souvenir of the Statue of Liberty on the table. More souvenirs came out of the box and then he tossed a t-shirt at her. She held it up and the screen-print on the front expressed love for New York City. Her hands collapsed on her thighs and she gasped when she saw Hayden holding another bubble-wrapped limb.

"See. Two," Hayden said.

Unwrapping this one equally cautious, he pinched his fingers around the wrist as he had done with the other and let the disembodied hand and forearm dangle in front of him; its raw end above the elbow was also covered with a bloodstained gauze pad.

Swiveling the arm with his fingers, he said, "They sure do look alike but trust me, they're different."

In front of her was the man she came to see, the guy who had helped her through some rough patches, helped her keep her job. The man she had worked with today to get the house back in order. The one she shared the most intimate and vulnerable moments in her life with. Yet, fear and mistrust came over her. There she sat, on a killer's couch, the killer mere feet away, showing her his souvenirs.

Hayden saw it all in her eyes and pleaded with her as he had with the woman who passed him and screamed just outside the alley in Manhattan, "Oh, no, Ora! It's not like that! I told you what happened. Don't you believe me?"

Her hands wrung the t-shirt. Her breathing became heavy and she began to hyperventilate.

"Ora. You have to breathe normally. Say something, Ora. Please."

Her chest rose and fell. Between breaths, she said, "Who … packs … body parts … and … sends … them … to … their … house … Hayden? … Who … does … that?"

"Ora. Listen to yourself. You're talking crazy."

Each breath elongated and in a struggle, she said, "I'm … crazy? … You … packaged … them … in … souvenirs."

"Just calm down."

As he crudely rewrapped the arm in the bubble wrap and

lowered it into the box, she lunged for the table and picked up the scissors into a stand.

Not caring about the arm now, Hayden dropped it in the box and began to stand.

Holding the scissors with both hands out toward him, she yelled, *"Stay down! Don't move!"*

His butt returned to the couch and his hands went up as if at gunpoint. "Ora. Think about what I explained earlier. I didn't do this. Now, I'm going to stand."

"No! Don't!"

As he raised himself off the couch, she swung the scissors across the front of his body and missed. His focus went to the scissors, then to her trembling face, disbelief on his own. He reached a hand toward her and she swung the scissors through the air with one hand.

"Fuck!" he yelled, his left hand retracted back against his body, its palm bleeding.

"Stay away from me, Hayden! I mean it! I'll cut your goddamn neck open!"

"Ora, stop! Get a hold of yourself. Get a hold of your fear!"

"My fear. Where's your fear? Afraid of getting caught. Afraid of what you did to those people. Why did you have to spend Christmas in New York, Hayden? Huh? Why New York?"

"Sh. The bald man's calling," he said.

"The phone didn't ring, Hayden!" she yelled. "It's all in your head, you sick fuck!"

"No, really. There's this little screen in one of the forearms and this bald guy talks through it and…"

Ora's scream went right into, *"Oh, my God! Shut the fuck up!"*

Hayden stepped back. "I'll show you I'm not crazy. I'm going to pick up the arm."

Out of the last box he opened, he lifted the forearm and there wasn't a lit screen, a bald man, or anything unusual, except for not being attached to a body.

"This is the blown-off arm. The guy's in the other one," he said.

More a whine than words, she said, "I came here for this? For you?"

Even under the circumstances, her words didn't get past him.

"I hear it, Ora. It's in the other box."

"What's in the box, Hayden? The tomahawk you used for stealing people's arms?"

Knowing time was running out on her doing something more violent to protect herself and his stinging hand losing a decent amount of blood, he sidestepped toward the other box, pulled it toward him, reached in, and pulled out the crudely amputated arm.

She stepped back and then stopped. A light emitted from the forearm and a man's voice sounded like it came through television speakers.

They stood there for what seemed like minutes, unsure what to do with the knowledge.

"You hear it, don't you?" Hayden said and expelled doubt out of his lungs and a calm relief remained, oxygenizing him to new life.

The man's voice rambled on in the background as Ora, upset, stared at Hayden, and began to cry. His relaxed face and reassuring eyes intensified her crying and emotions the longer she looked at him.

When she went to wipe her eyes and nose, the sight of his left hand stained red brought her out of her self-absorbed state.

"Hayden," she said. "You're bleeding."

"It's okay. I'll live. You didn't mean it," Hayden said and his eyes went to the scissors in her hand.

Her eyes followed his and the scissors eased out her fingers, hit the edge of the coffee table, and ricocheted off onto the floor. "I ... didn't ... mean ... to ..."

"It's alright."

"I'll wet a towel."

At first, Ora barely moved toward the hall, and then, as if adrenaline throttled her, she trotted into the bathroom.

Hayden kicked the souvenirs on the floor out of the way, sat on the couch, situated the severed arm on the table so he could see the screen, and pressed his cut left hand into a throw pillow.

The image of the bald-headed man came out of the inlaid screen and through the skin clear and defined as if the skin weren't there. Two-way communication was on the device as before because as soon as the hairless-headed man saw Hayden he yelled, "When I call you, you answer! Got it!" The man looked off-screen as if verifying something then looked squarely into the screen, "Hayden Bakley."

"Oh, you know my name, now?" Hayden said.

"I see you cleaned the blood off the arm. You're coming in much better."

"As are you. But I got to say I'm very disappointed you decided against a wig. Something wavy and frosted…"

"Shut up!"

"See, you're rude. Nothing irks me more than an improper introduction. You know who I am, now who the hell are you?"

"Someone trying to help you."

Ora returned, sat on the couch next to Hayden, tossed the bloodied pillow on the floor, and pressed the wet towel on Hayden's cut palm.

"So you've said," Hayden said.

"You have the briefcase?" the baldheaded man asked.

"Didn't we have this discussion before?"

"Bakley! Answer the question."

"Geez, so impersonal. Maybe … I don't know."

"You don't want to get on my bad side by lying. All of my ugliness is there."

"Which is your bad side? I can't tell. It's ugly everywhere."

Ora's eyes snapped on Hayden, but, all along, she recognized the sarcasm in what he said.

"If you know I have it, why do you keep asking?" Hayden asked.

"Trust, Bakley. You don't know how important you and," the bald-headed man looked off-screen again, "Frush are now for the moment."

"Call me Hayden and her Ora or the arm's going in the fire."

"Important. How?" Ora asked.

"You have the briefcase," the man on the screen answered.

"What he's saying, Ora, is the briefcase is important and whoever has it. Not us," Hayden said.

"Now we understand each other and you understand your place, perhaps you'll answer like your life depends on it because it does." Again, the unknown man looked off-screen, pointed, and said, "Your house moved locations. Oh, I see, it's a floating home. I take it you didn't move it."

"No," Hayden said. "Someone who knew what they were doing unhooked everything last night."

"Your rental papers in the glove compartment of the car," the bald man said. "They followed you."

"Tell us something we don't already know. What's in the briefcase?"

"A trump card which possessed and slapped on the table in victory by the holder will beat every hand at every card table in the world, leading to catastrophic outcomes. Not only will it be heard around the world, it will wave through space, unheard by human ears, but perhaps someone or something with superior hearing will hear it."

"Like world destruction? This part of a weapon?"

"In part, yes. It always comes to that. Domination is a better word, but, certainly, destruction plays into dominating. It already has in Manhattan. They want to rule the world, not destroy it."

"Who?" Hayden asked.

"An empire resides in that briefcase," the bald man said. "You ever hear of the British Empire? How about the

Mongolian Empire? Certainly, the Russian Empire?"

"Sure. But what do they have to do with…"

"When the British Empire peaked in the early 1900's, the Brits ruled nearly a quarter of the world's population and land. *A quarter.* The items contained in the briefcase could result in an empire that controls not only the Earth, but the space around it, and someday, maybe the solar system."

"The solar system," Ora repeated.

"No way," Hayden said. "You seem to forget about the Outer Space Treaty of '67 and other agreements since."

"No I haven't," the man on the screen said. "You fail to understand our daily lives reach the spheres. Satellites, Bakley. Communication. Reconnaissance. Navigation. Remote Sensing. Space Exploration. There's some on the ground, but everything's up there where you two have been. The war for the spheres began a long time ago and is one of the longest-running wars in human history. Yet, like the rest, it's generally ignored until someone thinks of it. Because of its ongoing nature, most stop seeing it as a war and as just the environment we live in. Don't be fooled. It is a war. Perhaps, the most important in human history. The spheres are the middle ground between Earth and the rest of the solar system into interstellar space. Whoever controls the airspace around our planet will certainly conquer Earth and, in time, the solar system. Not knowing what other life is out there if any, I'm guessing one-day interstellar space."

"So the briefcase can be opened?" Hayden asked.

"Of course," the man said.

"Well, how do I open it? I want to see this trump card."

A knock sounded at the front door.

CHAPTER **FOUR**

The screen, nested inside the forearm lying on the coffee table, blackened as Hayden and Ora's eyes snapped to the front door. A pale light, casting from the dock, outlined a black silhouette of a man's build facing the French-paned door.

Hayden's cut hand squeezed the wet towel as he stood, wishing he had kept the pistol he had ditched in the East River while in Manhattan. The damned city will haunt him the rest of his life.

There was no use in sneaking around. Whoever stood outside could see the entire living room. So, instead of picking up the fire poker, Hayden calmly walked into the kitchen, slid the butcher knife out of the knife block, and concealed it against the side of his leg as he returned to the living room. With only a few panes of glass between him and the knocker, another gun might come in handy in the future. Especially, in his current circumstance, which he doesn't quite fully understand.

Waiting for Hayden to open the door, the stranger outside shrugged his shoulders in irritation and knocked again.

The second knock had startled Ora as much as the first

and, sitting on the edge of the couch, she asked, "Who is it?"

Hayden flipped a switch by the door and the outside light turned on. Recognizing who it was, he said, "Someone hates me, Ora. They really do."

Disgust rendered his face unattractive as if plagued by a fast-acting disease.

Shaking his head, he turned to Ora and said dryly, "It's Kip."

"Kip! What's he doing here?" she asked.

There, but absent, it was as if Hayden's spirit had vacated his body.

"Hayden. Didn't you hear me?"

"Huh? Yeah."

"Well, aren't you going to let him in? It's cold out there."

"Let's get this day over with," he said and opened the door.

Kip entered the house, carrying a small black case.

"For a moment, there, I didn't think you were going to open the door," Kip said, remembering Hayden hanging up on him last night.

He set the case on the floor, removed his gloves, stuffed them into his coat pockets, and took off the coat.

"You have a place to hang this?" Kip asked.

Cold air blew into the house as if it itself needed warmed. Unphased by the cold, Hayden stood there holding the door—and the knife, his internal timbers keeping him comfortable.

"Wake up, Hayden, and close the door!" Ora said.

Dazed as if he had lost some of his mental capacities, Hayden slowly closed the door.

Kip straightened out his arm, holding his coat, and said, "Better get your mind right while you still have one."

Walking past Kip, Hayden grabbed the coat with his free hand and walked deeper into the living room.

An arrogant demeanor encased Kip in pride as he pulled the cuffs of his shirt out of his suit jacket. Self-importance melted off him and his eyes widened as he reached for Hayden from a distance.

"No! What are you doing?" Kip asked.

Without breaking stride toward the couch, Hayden let the wet towel in his palm fall to the floor, balled up Kip's overcoat as best he could with his cut hand, smearing blood on it, and underhanded it onto the fire before sitting on the couch next to Ora.

Kip knew, by the time he got over to it, it would be damaged and he didn't want a damaged coat, so he stood there, watching it smolder.

A silver gleam of the butcher knife, Hayden held over his head, drew Kip's attention from the lost coat and gloves. The knife plunged toward the severed arm on the coffee table.

Noticing the arm, Kip screamed, "No, not the arm!"

A sticking thud sounded when the tip of the knife sank into the wood of the table. As it wobbled, the blade reflected some orange and yellow of the fire.

A genuine sigh of relief expelled out of Kip. This wasn't exactly the entrance and impression he had wanted, but he was in the door. It went much easier than he anticipated, fully expecting to have to use force to enter.

Kip's nose raised in the air as the arrogance returned and he picked up the case and walked deeper into the room. His self-importance diminished when he saw Ora return to the room, sit beside Hayden on the couch, and hold a clean wet towel on Hayden's cut hand with a caring touch.

Her eyes noticed the butcher knife sticking in the table, but didn't say anything. Missing what had happened, she didn't even want to waste the effort to guess.

Insecurity behind Kip's wandering eyes made him slouch a little, because he had also noticed the flowers on the coffee table—Ora's touch, the fire—Hayden's touch, a lingering aroma of a just-eaten meal—Ora's touch again, in Hayden's place, so she came to see him, at least one night he knew, and two glasses of wine on the table. All of which were simple things in life and a sure sign of mutual comfortableness. But, make no mistake, the simple can be overwhelming—take death for example. All of this evidence harassed Kip's heart as if death itself squeezed it and, at the last minute, let go before reapplying pressure again, toying with his very existence.

The way Hayden's eyes looked thankfully into Ora's and her's longingly into his held the compression on Kip's heart a little longer than the previous times and there was no doubt, his two long-time friends had been together last night after Hayden had hung up on him.

Competitiveness had made Kip one hell of an astronaut and off to a good start at the Office of the Inspector General at NASA. Jealousy of other people's achievements had also driven him to his own accomplishments. Although he never felt strongly for Ora and believed he would end up with another woman, his jealousy for her, at this moment, brought out a competitiveness and he vowed to try harder.

In the past, Hayden had expressed to Kip that he, too, never felt smitten with her and that it was nice for however long it was going to last. Perhaps, he lied and, of course, things could always change. What Kip saw in Hayden's eyes told him they had.

Flames in the fireplace began to outnumber the smoke, which had reduced to occasional breaths, as Kip's overcoat and gloves began to burn.

In Hayden's absenteeism, Ora asked Kip, "Would you like a drink?"

A fake smile formed on Kip's face. "Sure. I know Hayden has brandy here somewhere. Without a coat, I'll need it when I head back out." He rubbed his hands to warm them and added, "Or gloves," then pointed to the souvenirs from New York City. "Do I get one of those for my trouble?"

As Ora began to stand, Hayden rose off the couch and said, "I got it," letting the wet towel drop to the couch and picking up a souvenir as he stood.

"Please sit," Hayden said and as his hand offered a chair, he handed Kip a miniature Statue of Liberty. "There's your souvenir for all your trouble."

Kip inserted Lady Liberty's head into his mouth, unbuttoned his jacket, and lowered himself into the chair while setting the case next to it. Removing the souvenir from his mouth and fondling the tiny statue, he said, "The good stuff, too. None of that cheap shit you offer people just to be nice."

"You don't know where that souvenir has been," Hayden said.

"I'm genuinely worried," Kip said. "I hope not up your ass."

"No. Now a miniature island of Manhattan, maybe."

"Or a rocket with NASA on the side," Kip said as he chuckled. "Damn you're slow. What are you doing, poisoning my drink? You should just hand over the bottle, you cheap bastard, since you burned my outdoor wear."

"Speaking of not cheap … who do you work for again?"

"The Inspector General."

"The Inspector General. I'm sure he pays you enough to replace them."

When Kip's eyes met Ora's, she pursed her lips and uncomfortably turned away. His nose went into the air then lowered as Hayden handed him his drink.

"I do okay," Kip said, setting the statue on the coffee table and taking the glass.

Hayden sat down with his own glass of brandy. "Oh, I'll bet. So, you want me to tell you, from my perspective, what you already know happened in Manhattan?" Hayden's eyes and slight tilt of head toward the severed arm on the table hinted sarcasm.

Kip's lips were wet from his sip of brandy. His eyes had followed Hayden's to the forearm then returned to Hayden. "You got it."

"And if I refuse?"

Kip's finger stroked the rim of his glass. "I'm not alone.

You will talk."

A silhouette of a man appeared in the bay window. The outline of the figure's head appeared smooth, so he was either bald or wearing something over his head.

"It's okay. He'll cooperate," Kip said and the man turned around and returned to the dock.

"He it?" Hayden asked.

"No," Kip answered. "Many."

"They must be demons. At your beck and call?"

Arrogantly, Kip's lips pursed to the side of his mouth, while he shrugged it wasn't a big deal.

"So, you must be Satan," Hayden said.

"Why couldn't you have said a good guy?" Kip questioned.

"Look. To get you out of here, I'm going to tell you what I know. I take you already knew about my ..." Hayden's finger encircled his face. "I had so much glass in my face I could have blown a small vase in my fireplace."

Kip nodded.

"If you already know what happened, why do you need to hear it from me?"

"Don't sell yourself short. You're an astronaut for God sakes. Guys and gals like us don't exactly grow on trees. Those who analyze videos and pictures can only speculate what they see because they weren't there. You were. We need your firsthand story."

The reasoning made sense to Hayden. Videos and pictures provided visual evidence, but other intangibles would, certainly, be missed, at best derived, but based solely on one sense—sight. The questions asked by Kip were sure to be of other sensory perception, what did he hear, what did he smell, did he taste anything, did he touch anything unusual, and when Hayden agreed, Kip's questions followed suit.

Hayden retold the story in greater detail than what he had shared with Ora. Kip asked his questions. At the end, Hayden saw the disappointment in Ora that he had left things out. This didn't go unnoticed by Kip.

"I guess I'm next," Ora said.

Kip finished his brandy and glared at her as a smooth, warm burn coated his throat.

Noticing Ora had a hard time maintaining eye contact with Kip, Hayden sat quietly and observed, having an inkling it was his long-time friend who had helped her with her Astrophobia on space missions when he wasn't there.

"No," Kip finally said. "I think we have everything we need." The bottom of his glass made a sound when he placed it on the coffee table and he stood, picking up the case beside the chair.

"Oh, no you don't!" Hayden said as he stood. "You owe me some answers!"

With a surprised look on his face, Kip said, "Oh, I'm not leaving. We're just getting started. Here."

He held out the small case for Hayden to take and pulled it back when Hayden reached for it.

"I know you have it. Even trade. Agreed?"

"With pleasure," Hayden said and he took the case and sat on the couch. Holding it now, he knew exactly what it was. "How did you …?"

Hayden's hands caressed his black plastic case that he had taken with him to Manhattan. There wasn't any evidence it had been tossed in the East River. In fact, it appeared in excellent condition. Yet, all the familiar scratches were still there but blended in better after being cleaned.

The case was his all right. There was no denying that. His fingers moved to the discs and spun the combination. He opened the gun case and the smell of new foam escaped like the smell of a new car; his pistol and clip packed perfectly in carved out molds. Everything was there in immaculate condition. Whoever had restored the case and cleaned the weapon and clip knew what they were doing.

Amazement on his face, Hayden said, "It's impossible."

Smug, Kip said, "Very little is impossible nowadays," as

he sat in the chair.

"No. You don't understand. I tossed everything separately into the East River. It all would have sunk and scattered."

"Everybody knows the East River has preservation properties. You should have seen all we found down there. Robotics. Furniture. An ice cream truck. Dead bodies. A couple fresh by the way. Are you sure everything's there?"

After eying the case and its contents carefully, Hayden looked up at Kip and answered, "Yeah."

"Check the clip."

Hayden's finger lifted the ten-round clip out of the foam and, when he saw the follower, his eyes widened in astonishment.

"Fuck!" Hayden blurted.

All ten rounds were missing.

"You might be," Kip said. "But I'm not doing the poking."

Disbelief made Hayden shake his head. "They're in the river. I dispersed everything separately in different places. You didn't find them is all. They're small."

"First of all, size doesn't matter. Secondly, we found one of them. Inside the head of Germany's President."

Hayden's zombie face livened and a twisted smirk stretched his lips. "I get it. This is some kind of gag to lighten the mood before you tell me I'm being forced to retire from space travel."

Kip folded his hands except for his straightened index fingers, which he placed over his lips like a Roman seal over a tomb to keep whatever inside in, shaking his head it wasn't a joke.

A laugh seeped out of Hayden and he said, "So what. I've never been to Germany. I don't even know who the President is over there."

"Was," Kip pointed out.

"Besides, you called me last night, remember? Here. At the house. Ora was here as a witness. And I have a flight track. New York to Washington. There's no way I could have gone to Germany. Not in two days."

Kip lowered his hands and rested his arms on the arms of the chair. "On a plane, no."

"That brandy went right to your brain," Hayden said to Kip and then to Ora, "No more brandy for him, Ora. He's cut off."

Kip leaned forward, placing his elbows on his thighs. "There's no record I called here last night, protecting me. Saying otherwise, you would be considered a liar. Ora's witness would be thrown out as an accessor. And there's no record of your flights. I'm sorry, Hayden."

"Oh, I'll bet you're sorry," Hayden said. "It's because Ora came here, isn't it? What? Did she slip out of your bed into mine?"

Fire filled the firebox of the fireplace, fueled by Kip's overcoat and gloves. Hayden's eyes bore holes through Kip, sitting in the chair, then larger holes through Ora, fueled by pain and jealousy that what he had suggested might be true.

"It's not like that, Hayden," Kip said. "Really. It's bigger than that. I'm here to help."

Human, like any other soul, Hayden's insides jerked as wild as a lie detector needle registering habitual lies as his imagination ran wild, entering the arena of the unrestrained, envisioning himself reaching out and gripping the knife stuck upright in the coffee table.

It's as far as he got. Control made him a good astronaut and it had put the kibosh on visualizing what he would do with the blade.

Or so he thought. When he came out of his brief fabrication, there he was, sitting forward on the couch with his hand wrapped around the handle of the butcher knife still stuck in the coffee table and the handgun case opened on the couch next to him. Unwarranted guilt tingled his body and slowly his eyes raised to Kip in the chair and then to Ora, who backed away to the opposite arm of the couch.

Hayden's hand remained on the knife's handle as if

superglued there and after an internal struggle, he let it go and softly said, "Sorry."

Neither Kip nor Ora said anything. They only stared.

"Go ahead, Kip," Hayden said. "The President of Germany was assassinated. Why?"

"We don't know," Kip said, adjusting in his seat. "We're working on it. And now, the main souvenir from Manhattan, please—the briefcase."

The screen lodged in the forearm lying on the coffee table illuminated and the baldhead and shoulders of a man filled the screen. He looked off screen, eyeing whatever he looked at, and said, "Mr. Stanton, you have company."

Hayden's eyes snapped to Kip. "'Mr. Stanton?' You know each other?"

Staring at Kip, Ora shook her head.

"Let me guess—the car?" Kip asked the bald-headed man.

"That's right. Bakley wrote his life story on the rental papers and left them in the car. A child playing hide-and-seek with a GPS and a plane ticket could have found him."

"Yeah, we'll have to work on that. Was the car destroyed?" Kip asked as he stood out of his seat, buttoned his jacket, tapped his forearm, and walked over to the bay window.

Light reflected off the window as if Kip held a flashlight. When Hayden and Ora saw it, they looked at one another, puzzled.

"Impounded," the bald man said to Kip. "FBI is cooperating with the German government."

"The assassination." Kip sighed. "So how many callers?"

"A bunch. At least twenty."

"Not Germans I take it."

Seeing his own reflection and that of Hayden's living room in the window, Kip reached into a pocket inside his jacket and put on what resembled sunglasses. Instantly, the reflection in the window cleared and nighttime outside appeared as day. A hooded-figure, dressed entirely in orange and cloaked walked backward on the dock toward Hayden's place as naturally as walking forward, aiming what Kip knew to be a laser.

Interference from the activity outside scrambled the screen inlaid in Kip's forearm and then the bald man's voice came in crystal clear again.

"No black, red, and gold," the bald-headed man reported. "Only orange."

"Tis the season for pumpkin pie."

One of Kip's men ran into view on the dock. An orange laser beam, already airborne, penetrated his chest before he got a shot off and in an instant, he disintegrated.

"They're damn close," Kip said. "What's the evac?"

Hearing orange, Hayden walked toward the window, already knowing who was close.

"Backdoor, on the move extraction," the man on the screen answered.

As Kip turned away from the window, Hayden saw a baldhead and shoulders on a tiny screen, projecting through Kip's left jacket sleeve as if his flesh, skin, shirt, and the jacket's material weren't there.

Staring at Hayden, Kip said to the bald man, "God, I hate that one," and then he smiled and said to Hayden, "Surprise."

With eyes bulged and the skin around them stretched tight as if plastic surgery had been performed, Hayden pointed and said, "You have one of those?"

Kip turned Hayden by the shoulders, "Yeah, yeah. We'll talk later. I'll take mine and you grab the other two and the suitcase and meet me on the back deck. No lights and don't forget Ora."

Hayden trotted back toward the couch. Not about to have Ora carry the severed forearms, he handed her the briefcase and said, "Back deck."

He grabbed the arms, ran down the hallway, and met her by the sliding glass door in his bedroom. His own arm wrapped around both forearms as if holding a grocery bag, he slid open the glass door and all they heard was the occasional slapping of water against the dock and floating homes; it was as if nothing was happening outside.

The Pacific Northwest winter drifted in and brushed against their bodies, causing goosebumps. Goose pimples raised on the forearms as if they were still alive and Hayden felt them prickle on his own arm as he held them. There was something spiritual yet morbid about it as if the dead knew something was wrong.

Which wasn't far from the truth. A conflict between those cloaked and hooded in all orange and those uncloaked and ski-masked in all black occurred among the trees, structures, and snow in its own unrhythmic beat of strategic maneuvering about like ninjas. Skirmishes of orange and blue laser beams cut through the night air, shedding light on everything they passed.

Both squads had arrived in stealth, transported into the area somehow without detection and alarm. It was as quiet as war gets. A Cold War of sorts, but more like cyber warfare, where real damage could be done. Instead of opened wounds, blood, and eventual decay in the grave, lasers expedited the process by immediate disintegration, in such case, a grave wasn't necessary.

Hayden and Ora stepped onto the deck and looked around; their breath condensed visibly at their mouths and noses. Startled by a clinking sound behind them, they turned around and it was Kip, holding Hayden's handgun case and the bottle of brandy.

"How long?" Kip asked.

"Fourteen and a half seconds," the bald man replied.

"That long, huh?" Kip acknowledged and then said to Hayden, "Wish I had my coat and gloves. It's freezing out here."

"You just got out here," Ora said.

Lights appeared through a light snowfall in the night sky over treetop tips on the hill. Night made it difficult to make out the exact shape of the craft, but it definitely wasn't a helicopter, resembling a plane more, but it's speed and smooth flight mimicked the comfortableness of a Peregrine Falcon glide without the wing flap. As the craft approached, the wings didn't appear long enough to carry the roundness of the fuselage. Ora thought it looked like a flying penguin.

"Alright," Kip said, "when I say jump, jump."

The skin tightened on Ora's pale face, which resembled a miniature moon in the darkness. The cold and Kip's words were the anesthetic and Doctors Surprise and Horror had performed the plastic surgery procedure.

"Jump?" Ora asked. "Where?"

"Toward the ship. Don't worry. They do this all the time and I've done it more times than I would like. Besides, we don't have a choice."

The squat aircraft dove toward the water and raced toward Hayden's home.

"Isn't it going to slow down?" Ora asked.

"Get ready," Kip said.

"We all jump at the same time?" Hayden asked.

No ripples in the water and no wind, the craft was about to pass and Kip yelled, "Jump!"

"I can't, Kip!" Ora said as she hesitated.

Kip wasn't there anymore because he had jumped.

However, Hayden was, who had also failed to jump.

They watched the aircraft speed away.

From somewhere unknown, an orange laser beam, larger than what the handheld lasers fire, raced across the snow plotted night sky like a falling star. Only it wasn't falling. It raced toward the peculiar craft and appeared to clip, of all things, one of the truncated wings because the lights at its end went out.

It was too dark to tell if the wing had disintegrated, but the lights on the body of the ship told them much of the plane had remained intact. The lights began to fall out of the sky in an arched-descent like fireworks ending their sparkle and the craft glided smoothly and quietly toward the ground until it disappeared behind the hill opposite it had arrived.

"Oh, Kip," Ora said.

Hayden's eyes lowered to the water and he tapped Ora's shoulder and pointed. In the distance, lights came toward them, level and smooth, just above the surface of the water. It was strange for them not to be bobbing up and down on the water like a boat.

Shattered glass sounded from inside the house, startling them fully back to the reality of their own situation and, for now, Kip was all but forgotten. Hayden closed the sliding glass door.

"Yeah, that will help," Ora said. "What do we do now?" She shivered.

"Look!" Hayden pointed at the snowing sky to lights from another airship coming over the hill.

"Oh, thank God!" Ora couldn't contain.

"Maybe it's not for us," Hayden warned. "Maybe that thing shot down Kip's plane?"

A flash of orange inside the house caught his attention and he snapped to Ora, "Lie down!"

They laid on their bellies as flat as they could on the deck. Hayden's eyes looked through the sliding glass door into the house, while Ora's watched the water. The deck was wet and cold underneath them from water splashing and freezing and the falling snow. Just lying closer to the water made it feel colder than when they were standing.

A figure in orange came down the hall toward the bedroom, slow, light on their feet, and deliberate like a careful burglar, sneaking where they shouldn't.

"One's inside," Hayden whispered and, seeing his breath, he covered his mouth, gesturing for Ora to do the same.

"The boat's coming," Ora said softly and, glancing over her shoulder, she reported, "So is the plane." Her hand successfully reduced the breath in the air to keep from being noticed.

"We'll have to assume it's for us. Come on."

As Hayden and Ora stood and grabbed their things, another form in orange looked down on them from

Hayden's roof. Erect and exposed, the wind hit their cold, wet bodies and they shivered. Besides chilled, both were scared.

The orange invader, inside the house, ran into the bedroom and toward the sliding glass doors.

Something must have happened to the assailant in orange on the roof because his head laid on its side and an arm dangled over the edge as if he had fallen asleep.

"Someone tucked him in," Hayden said.

As soon as he said it, another orange warrior appeared on the roof, this one standing.

Almost to the deck, the flying craft appeared to be the same kind of unusual ship Kip had jumped on. It glided over the water toward them and, in about the same timing as Kip's, Hayden yelled, "Jump!" and they both jumped.

The orange invader, inside the bedroom, opened the sliding glass door, but Hayden and Ora were gone.

Inside the short-winged aircraft, not only had they made it; a man in orange was aboard as well – the one from Hayden's roof.

Frightened, Ora instinctively swung the briefcase, hitting the man upside the head. After seeing what she had done, adrenaline raced through Hayden and he reacted similarly, swinging both of the forearms he carried. Simultaneously, they struck the sides of the orange-hooded head at its ears like clashing cymbals. Despite the blows, the orange intruder swung a fist with lightning-quick velocity in self-defense but missed. The extra reach the forearms had provided was greatly appreciated by Hayden.

A muscular man already on board, wearing an all-black, form-fitting outfit, detained the orange man in a chokehold and dragged him toward a door to take him to another part of the plane. Hayden stepped forward to help, but the man in black told him to step back.

In a struggle, orange hands reached back for the black arms around his throat. Unable to get a grip, the hooded man in orange slapped his own forearm and a lighted screen projected through the orange fabric there, which meant it had first gone through his skin.

Catching a glimpse of the screen as the men struggled, Ora didn't see a person on the screen, as she had seen the bald-headed man. Instead, she saw numbers. When she could see the screen amidst the two men moving, the numbers ticked backward and it dawned on her it might be a countdown.

Frantically waving a hand toward the men, she yelled, "His arm is counting down to something!"

When Hayden saw it, too, immediately, he thought of the other forearms, including Kip's and then asked the man in black, "What should I do?"

"How much time?" the hulking detainer asked through his cloth mask.

From her angle, Ora saw the time before Hayden and said, "Twenty seconds!"

Another man wearing all black entered the compartment and helped to move the unwanted visitor to an outer wall of the craft. Forcibly roughing him up a little, the two men shoved him into the sidewall of the flyer. An opening appeared there, where there hadn't been one, exposing the cold night sky over the harbor, as if the unwelcomed man's body were a huge orange eraser that had rubbed that part of the plane away.

Skillfully and lethally, both men in black kicked the orange intruder, one black boot to the chest and the other to the knee. Standing near the opening, they watched the man in orange be sucked out the plane as if gravitationally pulled by a black hole.

The doorway remained open and all in that compartment of the craft saw the orange man, outside the ship, pull his hood forward and then finger the screen implanted in his forearm. Behind him in the distance, a distinct line separated the black hills below and the metallic-blue night sky above. It surprised Hayden and Ora that they had reached such a height already.

Unexpectedly, the man in orange exploded in mid-air, sending a sonic boom throughout the bowled hills of Friday Harbor. As the ball of flame grew and raced toward the aircraft, it only had a chance to change color once before the opening in the plane closed and they saw no more. Oddly, the force of the blast hadn't affected the flight of the peculiar plane, which raced out of the area, avoiding where Kip's vessel had been shot down.

Hayden couldn't see his home but knew it was back there, somewhere, and wondered if he would ever be back. Either way, it was over. For many years, the floating home had been his sanctuary on Earth. Private with just enough interaction with a few, uninterested neighbors; most of which never knew he was an astronaut.

Friday Harbor was at the other end of the spectrum from Manhattan. He could breathe here and therefore live, not having to fight for air. Out here, there was plenty of it. Everyone was willing to share. Unlike the city, where everyone competed for it. A breath stolen here, another swiped there until eventually, life itself would dwindle to one last breath. Even then, no one was spared. In a world of self-preservation, there was no question that last breath would be sucked right out of the poor soul like snatching the last loaf of bread from a child in the bread aisle.

No, the dwelling back there was his only in name. Never again could it or would it be his sanctuary. Even if nothing was damaged and those in orange and black never returned and left him alone to live in peace, the floating home had been black-marked tonight—orange, too—by parties he never knew existed.

He had told Ora those boxes delivered to the house contained Halloween and people in black and orange costumes crashed Hayden's place, uninvited. For all Hayden knew, they continued to party below. Who knows? Maybe the man wearing a hat with a tan, *Manhattan*, had made an appearance and won best costume. *Manhattan*—the birthplace of haunts.

Like a rubber band, Hayden's mind stretched to the East Coast and when he let it go, it snapped back to the West Coast, jarring his head and ringing his ears.

His thoughts turned to Kip and he wondered if he had made it. It occurred to him he had forgotten to tell him about the blood he had collected from the skylight. It was still in his coat pocket at the house.

CHAPTER **FIVE**

The odd plane carried Hayden and Ora away from Friday Harbor, away from Kip. Seatbelts across their waists, Hayden held an arm around Ora, who sat tucked into him with her head on his chest, both looking out a window. They were alone in this particular cabin and it was quiet. The airplane didn't produce any sound as a typical aircraft would. When they didn't speak or move, each swore they had lost their hearing. They basked in the silence, but, for their own sanity, found themselves, on occasion, readjust in their seats or say a few words for sound, ensuring their ears still worked. Hayden's stomach growled and then Ora's. Their hearing was fine.

For a short while, the sparse lights below were the only way Hayden could distinguish between land and water. He had done it so many times before from space. In no time, the light dots out the window multiplied until there was a cluster of them. Hayden figured it must be Seattle.

After that, the farther they traveled, the speed at which they traveled, and the higher the plane ascended, there was no way of telling their exact location. Neither knew exactly how much time had passed and there was no one to ask. Scrambling to get out of Hayden's, they had left their cell phones there and the men in black, on board the unorthodox plane, had left a long time ago. After they had ejected the orange assailant out of the plane, they had confiscated Hayden and Ora's watches from their wrists, the briefcase, and the two forearms. They had locked the door behind them without any direction other than for them to remain seated with their seatbelts on.

Based on the estimated time the siege on Hayden's home had occurred, the best Hayden and Ora could figure maybe it was around midnight. If true, it sure didn't feel like it, in time or physically. Their adrenalized minds and bodies were too wired to sleep, yet, how they wanted to close their eyes and shut their brains down. Exhausted spirits trapped inside their excited bodies produced a confused, sick feeling in both of them. Operating in uncertainty made them uncomfortable, as it would most people, but with space missions as unpredictable as anything in life, they handled it better than most. After all, training and repetition went toward making them feel as comfortable as possible in unforeseeable circumstances. That education went a long way in increasing their tolerance.

Their relationship, too, had never been clearly defined, by any stretch of the imagination, and that had helped to cultivate a near-comfortableness with the unknown. Nothing certain about it, their fickle relations could only be blamed on their finicky needs and wants and this made it difficult for them to stay together long. In fact, outside of space missions, the several days into this unplanned rendezvous was a third of the way there to their all-time record of consecutive days spent together on Earth.

Outside of being alive, the only thing Hayden knew for sure was they were still in North America, because, in seeing lights on the ground, they hadn't flown over any large bodies of water. Another thing he knew, the plane would have to land, eventually. Unless, of course, the craft happened to be powered by some unending energy source that would never run out and the rest of the world didn't know of its existence. Still, what would they do—fly forever? There were at least the two men dressed in black on board. No, they would land, he just didn't know where.

Practically lying in his seat, wishing a long time ago that he could recline and move his eyes away from the window, which he didn't seem to have the willpower to do on his own, Hayden thought, perhaps, he might be falling asleep. His eyelids closed then opened and this continued for some time. His sight dimmed and, shade-by-shade, the window in view darkened over; any lights on the ground blacked out as if turned off. Maybe, his mind, body, and soul, not knowing what to do under the complex confusion of being wired and exhausted at the same time, were shutting down.

A still Ora in his arms, he could only assume her eyes were closed, possibly even asleep, so he let her be. His own being fought to stay awake and, through undecided eyelids, the windows tinted over until they were black and no longer transparent, while the few cabin lights on dimmed off. This type of extreme darkness he had only experienced in space. Even Ora's hair under his chin wasn't visible.

The airship never struggled during any of its maneuvers. Not once did it shake or vibrate. Even the wind outside brushed against it as lightly as if no wind at all. The capabilities of the vessel had Hayden believing it could be a spaceship of some kind and he wondered where they were heading and how high they could fly. They couldn't be too high or else they would have experienced weightlessness.

"Hey, Ora, wake up," Hayden said, squeezing her shoulder.

Not moving she said, "I'm awake. Just closed my eyes."

"Sorry. I didn't know where we were before, but now I *really* don't know where we are."

"What do you mean?"

"Look out the window."

She looked, he knew she had because he heard her sit up. It was too dark for him to see that she had reached out and felt for the window.

With her fingers still touching where the window used to be, Ora said, "I don't think it's the outside, I think it's the glass."

"How?"

"Tinted. Commercial jets are going to them instead of shades."

"I think I saw that somewhere, but this goes beyond tinting."

They both felt a slight bob of the plane. It was the first disruption the entire flight and they both wondered why.

Mere minutes had passed and the same section of the wall in the craft that had opened into a door opened now as if that part of the wall had controllably disintegrated away. A silhouette of a small-framed woman stood in the opening and said, "Come with me."

Either the unproportioned craft had landed and Hayden and Ora didn't know it, or they were docked to another ship out in space. The latter seemed doubtful because they felt the pull of Earth's gravity. Doubt, but not definitive, because there always could be a new technology out there that was not introduced to them at NASA.

The lights in the cabin turned on and the woman stepped inside. She wore a gray blouse, black skirt below the knee, gray nylons, and black high heels.

Hayden unbuckled his seatbelt and stood with not as much fury as he wanted, but it amounted to all the energy he had. "Any word on Kip?"

"Shut up!" she said, as two armed guards dressed in dark olive green utilities flanked her, pointing handguns, and the two men in form-fitting black outfits on board entered through the door they had left what must have been hours ago.

"Don't talk and follow me," the woman said as she turned around and, without looking back, added, "Shoot them if they do."

Ora unbuckled her seatbelt, stood, and, with Hayden, followed the woman out of the aircraft, while the armed guards brought up the rear. The men in black remained on board.

The floor of the ship transitioned seamlessly to a flat area outside, only noticeable from the lights inside the vessel. Beyond the light's reach, darkness awaited. As the woman walked briskly and knowingly into the pitch-black absence, lights came on where she stepped—one above, one on each side, and one within the floor—her heels clanking on what sounded like metal. As she proceeded down the hall, the lights, surrounding her on all sides, followed her and gave her a celestial aura. With darkness ahead of her, the length of the hall was impossible to know.

This wasn't a usual airport. This could be the boarding bridge to the terminal, but doubtful.

As Hayden and Ora followed, lights came on around them where they stepped and went out where they left. Looking ahead, the woman walked in light, and darkness followed her until it met their light and, peering behind, darkness trailed them until contrasting against the light surrounding the guards.

For a while, they walked this way, only the woman's high heels making any significant sound.

The dark gap between the woman and themselves widened and Hayden estimated they had walked at least a mile by guesstimating four trips around a track from his high school days when he ran middle-distance. Now and again, his eyes met Ora's; otherwise, they followed the woman's lead, keeping their eyes peeled. Since the woman ahead hadn't dropped off into oblivion, they assumed they wouldn't either.

A thin horizontal line of bright light appeared above the woman's head like a halo. It widened in front of her all the way to the floor as if heaven had opened its door for her to enter. When she walked into the light, her well-defined appearance unraveled into a smeared-edged black silhouette, which then separated into black blotches within the white light, resembling spilled ink on paper, until she disappeared entirely and only the light remained.

One of the guards commanded, "Pick it up!"

Hayden and Ora walked faster, yet, the other guard said, "Faster!"

Hayden and Ora's brisk walk intensified into a speed walk and then into a trot. The guards followed close behind and the lights around them kept pace.

Something dark began to rise slowly out of the floor and douse the light. One guard ordered, "Move!" while the other yelled, "Run!"

The guards caught up to Hayden and Ora and there was no longer a dark gap between them, the four of them running for the light before the door closed. Running full speed, Hayden grabbed Ora's arm and catapulted her in front of him. Now, the light around them cast three lengths of people. He pushed her forward and she, uncoordinatedly, skipped a step, avoiding the rising door and went through the opening into the light. Behind her, Hayden jumped over the rising door and ducked into the light.

The guards sprinted to make it. Arriving at the same time, one didn't slow down, diving headfirst over the door into the light as if into water, while the other tossed his laser through the opening in a brief hesitation to let the other guard through, launched himself, grabbed the top of the rising door, now nearly halfway up, with both hands like a gymnast mounting a Pommel horse, and, in mid-air, pulled himself through.

The second guard landed on the first and they both struggled against each other to get to their feet with their lasers. The door closed behind them and the bright light dimmed, while the woman observed, standing with her hands on her hips, and tapping a toe.

"You should have kept up," she said.

The military goons seemed out of place to Hayden, especially, when compared with the precise technology and skillsets of the men dressed in all black.

"Hired hands?" Hayden asked.

"I said not to speak!" the woman yelled at Hayden. "You spoke." Then, she said to a guard, "Glow a toe off."

The guards looked at each other to see who wanted to do it. One of them raised a laser and pointed it at Hayden's right foot.

"*Whoa!* Wait a minute!" Hayden said, holding his hands out in plea. "Glow a toe?"

Bothered, the woman said, "Make it all of them."

"Don't laser off anyone's toes," a man's voice ordered and immediately the guard lowered his weapon.

Since entering the light, Hayden and Ora hadn't had much time to look around. Doing so, now, they were in a small, dimly-lit room with battleship gray walls and some gadgets affixed to them.

"I apologize," the man said.

"And you are?" Ora asked.

"The elevator man. Take us up."

What appeared to be a control panel, the woman pushed up on a lever and pressed a button.

A perturbed look changed Hayden's face as he turned away and then he looked at the unknown man. "Elevator man? What the hell does that mean?"

"Perhaps some music might drive the point home," the man said.

Immediately, elevator music of the classical kind began to play. Hayden and Ora looked at each other.

Pleased with himself, the man said, "God, I love that."

"Where are you taking us?" Ora asked.

"There," the man said.

"There? Where?" Hayden wondered.

"Up."

Up may as well been open sesame, because the door of the room receded into the ceiling.

"Better let me go first," the man said and he walked through the door.

The man must be lying. The room seemed secured and stable under Hayden's feet. He hadn't felt anything—no movement whatsoever; nor did Ora. There was no way the room had moved.

"He walks faster than I do," the woman in the gray blouse said. "So you better catch up,"

As Hayden and Ora walked through the door, they overheard the woman giving the guards an earful, "You two should have burned down there!"

The woman's scolding waned as the door glided out of the ceiling and closed.

Stepping into a different room and the words *'down there'* had Hayden and Ora wondering if the room had actually moved. They had exited the same door on the same side they had entered the elevator room and it turning, while they were in it, seemed doubtful. Compelling evidence suggested the room had moved, which it must have, otherwise if the room remained put, they would have stepped into the same corridor. Unless it had turned in place.

Hayden and Ora stared, blankly, at the man standing at the end of a row of chairs, twelve in all, brown-leathered, spaced evenly about a foot apart, each having a rotating tan desk on the right arm, a cup holder embedded in the left, and all of them facing a clear-glassed window-wall with what resembled brown earth behind it.

The man gestured for them to sit, saying, "The last shall be first and the first last."

The man's voice echoed slightly. Three people and twelve chairs were the only things in the dimly-lit room. The walls were dark and the corners of the room were even darker. When Hayden and Ora had first entered, it wasn't noticeable, but with their eyes adjusted, the corners weren't at ninety-degrees. The off-kilter room was shaped as a parallelogram: a rectangle with its ends slightly slanted.

Hayden and Ora walked over together and sat down.

"May I get you anything?" the man asked. "Food? Drink? I would offer tobacco, but neither of you chew or smoke."

His knowledge of them didn't go unnoticed and Hayden

and Ora's eyes met once more.

"Hayden, a brandy perhaps?" the man offered. "How about some fruit?"

Unsure and untrusting, Hayden didn't answer; nor did Ora.

A hint of disappointment expressed through the man's face.

"Maybe next time," he said.

"I overheard your secretary laying into those guards," Hayden said. "She said something about they *'should have burned down there'*. What did she mean by *'burn'*?"

"The corridor you came through is really an exhaust shaft," the man said.

"Exhaust shaft?" Ora asked.

"Come now, you're both astronauts."

"Rocket exhaust?" Ora said.

"Precisely."

"Wouldn't a regular elevator be cheaper?" Hayden commented.

A surprised look donned the man's face. "You don't realize how far we traveled."

"That was a pretty short ride," Ora said.

"Speed accounts for that," the man said. A smile formed on his mouth as if sharing a dirty joke. "Come now. You don't believe a space agency's budget is all tied up in labor, do you? The bennies aren't bad, but the pay …"

"Space agency?" Hayden said. "NASA?"

"This arrangement is more comfortable, don't you think?" the man said instead of answering. "It's like we're old friends at a sporting event. The theatre," he accentuated with some flare, "and we're just talking. Casually getting in a word or two. Like *canyon!*"

Canyon, spoken louder than the rest as if voicing a verbal menu command, echoed inside the narrow room.

That's exactly what it was—a command. All twelve chairs rotated to face the glass wall. The man calmly sat in his seat, while his untrusting visitors' heads were on a swivel and their eyes on the lookout. Ora gripped the arm and rotating desk of the chair, holding on. Hayden looked down to the right, left, then right again, unsure. Behind the glass wall, the earth moved in sections. The left end moved left and the right moved right, while the center moved in unequally divided segments, some down, some up. Night's light peeked through the cracks where the separations occurred, like plate tectonics of the Earth's continents moving away from each other on a much smaller scale.

When the earth territories completely moved away from the window-wall, there wasn't a reflection of people or the room in the glass, as in Hayden's home at night. Somehow, the room seemed bigger, more open, but, of course, it wasn't, its dimensions hadn't changed. Still, the illusion worked as it always had in his own home.

From where they sat, a view of Earth's starry night sky filled the top-half of the window, while an un-starred black mass filled the lower half. Below that, the view down of an abyss appeared blacker, like deeper depths into the ocean, strangely interesting to look at despite its simplicity. All views appeared crisp, clean, and, without a glare in the glass, almost unreal.

Where the black mass touched the starry sky, some detail clarified as their eyes adjusted. Initially, the top of the mass appeared smooth and flat, but now it appeared jagged like an edge of a cliff. The area above the ragged edge lacked any noticeable topography, such as trees, and uneven impressions below sure reminded Hayden of a side of a cliff. The man did say, *'canyon,'* and it must be true. Or an illusion. As mysterious as the ride up in the rocket-elevator.

"Lights," the man spoke into the room.

Lights outside turned on and brightened as if controlled on a dimmer.

"Oh, my!" Startled, Ora pulled her feet up onto the chair and wrapped her arms around her knees, curled up.

Mere inches, from where her feet had been on the floor, was glass, the same as the window-wall, and through it, she could see a river at the bottom of the canyon.

Without question, Hayden and Ora believed they were inside the cliff of a canyon; the detail of the experience would be difficult to replicate.

The man-made lights outside achieved just the right brightness with Earth's natural lighting of the first hour of a new day. The breathtaking view of a river winding the canyon's bottom and the way time had etched its presence into the Earth as a potter using the wind of his own breath, water from his own spit, and the Earth's crust as his potter's wheel to form such a monument, tugged at the heartstrings a creator worked among its creation. For this monument and others like it, the work was ongoing and never complete. No rush, there was all the time in the world. At most, simple time divided into days and nights, before tracked hours, minutes, and seconds imposed its will on man.

The man whispered as if not to disturb the moment, "When the earth is together over the glass, where they connect, it appears as natural cracks to the million or so people that visit here every year. The outside of this room has been photographed and video recorded so many times, that when I see the pictures, I have a tough time figuring out which cracks separate and which ones don't. I know, of course. In time, I can identify them all. Only because I've looked out this window so many times. The hard part is reversing what I've seen in here and applying it to what I see out there."

"Is this the Grand Canyon?" Ora asked.

"Grand, indeed," the man spoke up. "But, no."

"What canyon is it? Where are we?" Hayden pushed.

The man's eyes rolled down in inner thought and in a near whisper said, "One day, perhaps, it may be called the throat of death."

Ora's arms squeezed her legs against her body, as she timidly rolled her eyeballs on and off the man.

"Cut the bullshit!" Hayden said, sliding forward to the

edge of his seat. "After what we've been through, we deserve answers. Now start talking."

"Where should we start?" the man asked.

In unison, all twelve chairs rotated away from the canyon to the right. When they had turned a little more than ninety degrees, because the right wall slanted a tad in the parallelogram room, they stopped.

"How about these?" the man continued.

A light snapped onto the dark wall. Hanging there, in the shape of a triangle, was the seamless briefcase at the top and, adjacently below, the two forearms with fresh white bandages on their nubs. In the center of the triangle hung Hayden's pistol case like a cherry centered on whipped topping of a sundae.

A rectangle section of the floor rose like a lift on what looked like two silver hydraulic poles.

Ora's slumped posture in the chair erected as she sat up.

Hayden stood out of his chair and yelled, "Goddamn it! Theatrics. All theatrics. Someone…"

The man rose out of his chair and yelled, "Sit down and shut the fuck up!" pointing at Hayden like a ruling judge, his eyes glistening and steady with intensity. The glare remained on Hayden for a moment and then the man unexpectedly swept away from him, led by his arm like a dancer, and moved swiftly toward the rising table.

Perfectly timed, the table's ascent stopped upon his arrival. Standing behind the table, he picked up something black out of a recessed cubby at its center and pointed it at Hayden. "Don't make me use this."

Instinctively, Hayden's hands went up and he kept them raised as he sat down.

The man's fingers loosened around the grip and the handgun dangled from a finger through the trigger guard. "Don't worry. It's not loaded."

"Crazy bastard," Ora said under her breath.

Hearing it, the man glared at her and then returned to Hayden. "I would let you see it, but you might hit me with it." A smile far from genuine formed on his face. "So, I'm just going to put it back where I found it."

After returning the gun to the cubby, the man gestured to the forearm hanging to the bottom-right of the briefcase on the wall—the one that had been hacked off in Manhattan.

"Ah, the cornerstone, where it all started," he said.

"Where what started, exactly?" Hayden asked.

A perplexed look contorted the man's face, as he looked past Hayden to Ora, shaking his head as if he had embarrassingly forgotten something and just remembered.

"I never answered your question, did I?" the man said. "Forgive me. You had asked me if I was from NASA. I am from that four-lettered-word space agency."

"Then why are you treating us this way?" Ora asked, nearly in tears, exhaustion getting the better of her.

"Because we have questions of our own. Such as, are *you* from NASA?"

Worked up now, Ora grunted her words. "What do you mean are we from NASA? You know we are!"

The man shook his head and said, "No. No, I'm afraid we don't."

"Stupid government fubar," Hayden said under his breath.

"And I have just the man who's going to find out," the man said. "If he can't, I'll get someone else who can."

Every light in the room went out, rendering it dark. Clothes shuffled on walking bodies. A dull bang sounded on the table. Silence for no more than ten seconds, then the lights snapped on the wall like a spotlight and the dim room lights rose like a sunrise.

"Boom!" a man yelled, standing behind the table and using both hands to point the gun in the direction of Hayden and Ora; his hands and pistol partially blocking his face. Chuckles grew into laughter and when the man lowered the handgun, it was Kip.

CHAPTER SIX

"**B**ut we saw you go down over the hill," Ora said.

All sorts of emotions waved through Hayden and Ora, nearly making them sick. Anger reared its ugly head above the rest.

Holding the gun up sideways for Hayden to see it, Kip said, "This is yours by the way." He spun it once around his finger then set it on the table next to the bottle of brandy he took from Hayden's house. A good amount of it was missing.

Not in the mood for jokes, Hayden stood out of the chair, scurried up to Kip, grabbed him by the lapels on his coat, and shook him.

"Glad you're alive and all, but what the fuck is going on?" Hayden blurted.

"I wouldn't shake me like that," warned Kip, his words a little slurred.

Ora stood and, walking over to them, said. "Oh, my God! Are you drunk?"

"Naaaa." Kip waved it off.

"You are!" she confirmed. "You're drunk."

"Well, what would you do if you survived a plane crash?" Kip asked.

"Look," Hayden said. "You're not going to survive *me* if you don't start talking."

Ora pulled on one of Hayden's arms. "Let him go. What's he going to say? He's drunk for shit's sake."

"Please let me go," Kip said to Hayden and then yelled into the air, "Get the man some fruit would you!" To Ora, he asked, "What would you like?"

"A big ass breakfast is what. French toast. Bacon. Eggs. Coffee. Definitely coffee. The works," she said.

Kip yelled into the air, "You got all that? Double it and don't forget to bring Hayden some fruit." His voice lowered. "They're tired and would like to get some sleep. Worrying about me and how I almost died." His eyes lowered and bounced between Hayden and Ora. "You were worried, right?"

"Torn to pieces," Ora flatly said.

"Worried sick," Hayden followed. "Now, are you going to talk or do you need to inform your boss you won't be coming in? Ever. Now, who was that guy?"

Kip's lips barely moved on his deadpan face when he answered, "My boss."

Hayden and Ora looked at each other.

"I tried explaining how I almost died," Kip continued, "but he wouldn't have any of it. He called me a wuss and here I am. That's how dedicated I am to my job. I just hope he remembers it on my next performance review."

A pleasant woman's voice sounded into the room. "Breakfast is ready."

Talking to the ceiling, Kip said, "Fine." A little louder, he said, "Unlock," and then in a more normal voice said, "Okay. Come on in."

Ora shot Kip an unpleasant look. "You mean we were locked in here?"

As a small round table ascended out of the floor on a single post, a man, pushing a food cart, entered. Two women followed. They were all dressed in chocolate-colored food service uniforms, the shirt collar, buttons, and cuffs cream-colored. The man removed towels, hand soap, and a washbasin from the bottom shelf of the cart and set it on the table with the gun and brandy. Before the round table fully ascended, one woman wiped off its top and then the other draped a white tablecloth over it.

The man met other servers at the door, who had brought two chairs and, efficiently, they placed them at opposite ends of the small table and left.

The three of them took turns washing their hands in the basin and, when Hayden and Ora sat down, utensils, napkins, and drinks were already on the table. The man server set a plate on the table in front of Ora and one of the women servers set a plate in front of Hayden. In unison, the servers removed the plate covers, revealing the food. As the other woman server reached to set a vase of flowers at the center of the table, Kip said, "They don't need that. Take it away."

Hesitantly, she did.

An afterthought, Kip added, "Thank you."

The male server poured hot coffee, including a cup for Kip, while a woman set an orange on the table next to Ora's plate and an apple by Hayden's.

"Your idea, I presume," Hayden said to Kip about the orange.

"Nope. Purely coincidental. I was in here with you, remember?"

Everything served, a woman asked Kip, "Anything else, Mr. Stanton?"

"No. That will be all."

The servers left the room and Ora started eating.

"Excuse me. I'll be just a moment," Kip said.

He went over to the long table and returned with the brandy bottle. "We can start ... hold on." Holding the bottle, he looked at the ceiling again and said, "Secure the room."

Neck bent, he waited, and, instead of a woman's pleasant voice speaking, a man's voice said into the room, "Room secure, Mr. Stanton."

The steel cap scraped against the glass threads of the brandy bottle as Kip opened it. "Okay, now we can start talking a bit until they come back to clean up."

Hayden noticed this had happened numerous times and asked, "Who's listening?"

The brandy splashed into the coffee in Kip's cup.

"You haven't touched your food," Kip said. "She's going to beat you."

"I'm going to eat slow and, while my mouth is busy, you're going to talk," Hayden said. "Agreed?"

"Fine." Kip took a sip for taste. "Whatever you say."

Hayden's knife cut easily through the French toast and he stabbed two small squares with his fork. "Well? I'm starting, so you start."

"Okay," Kip said, as he set his coffee cup on the rotating desk of the nearest brown leather chair and sat down. "Let me start by saying, I tried removing you from the equation by taking the briefcase off your hands at your place. That got interrupted, so you're eating breakfast inside a canyon. As you can see, I survived the plane crash with overwhelming fanfare." His hand gestured toward the things hanging on the wall, "As did your gun case, nearly all of its contents, and the brandy that I coveted as our ship fell out of the sky. All because of some countermeasures and nifty flying by our pilot. Otherwise, all of it, including me, would have been reduced to particles scattered by the wind around Friday Harbor and riding the waves to who knows where. I can give you the pilot's name if you would like to thank him personally."

In the middle of chewing, Hayden said, "I'm good. I suppose you don't want to share the particulars of how you survived?"

"That would be correct. I'm not in the mood to share particulars."

"We understand. It must have been an awful experience and you don't want to ruin our breakfast with the details."

"Your breakfast would be ruined anyway without my story. I may be the messenger bearing grim news, but you are the reaper himself. Death comes by your hand."

"What are you talking about?" Hayden asked as he chewed.

"You're eating, so I'll be a gentleman and come back to that," Kip said. "I will, I promise. So, I told you I work for the Inspector General, which is partially true. Now, the Inspector's office only gets allocated point-zero-two-percent of NASA's nineteen billion dollar budget. It would cover the basic day-to-day and a little extra, but there's no way we could do what we do on forty mill. A lot of allocations have other buckets, *Other Missions and Data Analysis* and shit like that. At most, we get about half. A few others we get more. For example, half a million in OMDA for *Earth Systematic Missions*? No way. Another two-hundred million in OMDA for *Mars Exploration*? Please. If I didn't work for the agency, I'm with the rest of America, shit, or get off the pot.

"Mars isn't a promise, it's a ploy. Brought up every so many years to allocate more money to NASA, which creates a baseline budget going forward. You never see NASA's budget dramatically cut. That's the beauty of it. The last time any major cuts occurred was in the early seventies after we landed on the moon and the race for space slowed to a grinding halt. Anyway, we get a good chunk of that stuff, so bam, by the time it's all added up, we're around a billion dollars a year. So, when you asked, *'Who's listening,'* well, the answer is OMDA."

"OMDA, huh," Hayden said. "That's who you work for?"

"Technically, yes. That's who pays the bills. But we don't have a name. Hell, I don't even have a title."

"So, you're not a Field Agent?"

"It's an accurate description, somewhat, but no."

"And that wasn't the Inspector General?"

"No. He's the elevator man. And my boss."

"So, what do you do, exactly?"

"All the stuff people think NASA should be doing, but isn't. Instead of reading about it in the papers, people read about what we do in science fiction stories."

"Would you like to elaborate?"

"I don't want to do this alone, so how about we call on our bald friend, shall we?"

Kip tapped his forearm and the bald man appeared on the screen, projecting through Kips' skin, dress shirt, and jacket. The pads of his fingers tapped gently the screen and Kip said, "Hover screen."

A hologram screen appeared in mid-air.

"Larger," Kip commanded and it expanded. "A little more," he added and the screen proportionately stretched. "That's good."

Ora's fork clanked on the empty plate and she wiped her mouth on her napkin. She picked up the orange, dug her fingernails into the rind, and pulled. Immediately, a citrusy smell hung in the air and strengthened as more of the fruit became exposed.

The conversation dragged too much for her. It reminded her of TV evangelists and the like who had spoken a lot of words but ended up not saying anything worthwhile to keep her attention. Kip was holding what he knew close to the vest. From what she knew of him, this seemed to be his way. Direct when he wanted something, equivocal when someone wanted something from him. Instead of flying directly to the moon, he'd take you all the way around the sun first and then to the moon. It wasn't a quality she admired. Maybe her exhaustion made it difficult to comprehend, but Kip had better take them to the loot fast or she would force him to take them there. Besides, it would give Hayden a chance to finish his breakfast.

"As you can see, I'm with Ora and Hayden," Kip said to the bald-headed man on the hovering screen.

"Ms. Frush," the man on the screen said. "Bakley."

"I'm going to tell them a little story," Kip said, "and you can fill in whatever I miss."

"Sure, Mr. Stanton," the man said.

"Okay…" Kip started.

"Hey, Kip," Ora interrupted, unable to keep her mouth shut, being so irritated by Kip. "Before you start. I just want you to know you're behaving a lot like NASA."

"How's that?"

"It's time to shit or get off the pot," she said, "and tell us what you know. If you're going to take us there, then take us."

"I will," Kip said. "At least as far as Baldy and I can take you. There are things we're unsure of. I'll take you that far and then I'll take you to some beds so you can get some sleep."

"See, that's the kind of shit I can't stand," Ora said. "We don't know what you know so how do we know you're telling us everything you know? Besides, you're drunk."

"You won't know. That's the power each one of us holds, Ora. They're called secrets. And I'm not drunk. Not anymore. I think I drank myself sober. Now may I begin? The fuel's running a little low and we may not make it to our destination."

"Ours isn't," Hayden said. "Remember, we could have died tonight, too. So get on with it. In plain English."

"It's my native language tongue, too," Kip said, as he struggled to stand out of the leather chair and moved over to the wall where the briefcase, two forearms, and Hayden's pistol case hung. "I even have a storyboard." Pointing to the bottom-right forearm, he said, "This arm here belonged to our guy, the one you saw take a laser in the back and disintegrate. His mission was to locate and retrieve this briefcase by any means necessary." His hand moved up to the briefcase. "He located the case, carried by the man in the brown overcoat." His hand moved to the bottom-left forearm. "Who had, casually, walked down the sidewalk to blend in. Our man followed and, in the crosswalk, maybe not the best choice, perhaps he was making some kind of statement, he successfully extracted the briefcase. Now, chopping the guy's arm off with an ax may have come across a little barbaric for innocent bystanders like you, Hayden, but any means necessary mean just that. I'm glad that guy got his arm whacked off because he was our enemy."

Kip's voice lowered. "But it cost our man his life. Now that he's dead, I can tell you his name, Del Kenton. So, you see, within the universe, this room," Kip waved his arms around, "and on our little blue planet, the wall," he waved his hand over the wall where the items hung and then pointed to each one as he mentioned them. "There's the all-important briefcase, priority one, so it's on top. There's us, represented by Del's forearm, may he rest in peace. Then, there's them, represented by their man's forearm. Which I hope there's enough of that guy to rot in hell." Kip pointed to Hayden's pistol case in the center of the triangle. "Unfortunately for you, you're in the middle of all of this now. The last and the least of everything up here. Any questions on the parties involved?"

"Yeah, I have a question," Ora said and she turned to Hayden and asked, "Are you going to eat your apple?"

"No. Go ahead," Hayden answered and rolled it across the table to her.

She caught it, rubbed it on her shirt, and took a bite. It was exactly what Hayden wanted to do to Manhattan.

"No questions," Kip said. "Moving on then."

"No, wait a second," Hayden said. "What about these lasers? I mean, I've seen lasers at work, but these things obliterate people. How did it get to this?"

"For a second there, I thought you were going to ask me how they work," Kip said. "Lasers have been around since 1960. The Soviets had a laser pistol back in eighty-four and they intended to use it in space, not down here. And now, progressive power has these things all over the place, in every military, on every vehicle, in all sizes, and even in our hands."

With apple still in her mouth, Ora said, "You know, Kip.

Your shit doesn't stink that bad. This is how you should be all the time."

As Kip stood under the spotlight, a hint of rose colored his cheeks and he lost the fight to hold off a smile. Ora swallowed the bite, smiled back, and bit into the apple, tearing off another hunk.

Sitting with his finger in the handle of his coffee cup, Hayden watched their interaction and wondered if that's how it started each time when they were on a mission in space while he was grounded. The cup handle felt like a trigger guard around his finger.

Embarrassed, Kip said, "Well, I just wish you weren't brought into this."

"Yeah, me, too," Hayden said louder than usual.

Kip cleared his throat and continued. "I meant the both of you."

Hayden finished his coffee and poured himself some more. Ora flashed an embarrassed glance at him then looked at Kip.

"Hayden, you happened to enter this thing at an opportune time for us and an inopportune time for you," Kip said and then spoke loudly into the air. "Can we have someone come in here, please, and tend to Hayden's cuts before we continue?" Facing the hologram screen, he said, "Sorry to bring you on, then let you go so quickly, Baldy. I'm going to shut you down and bring you up again in a bit. We'll get this rolling again soon enough."

As the large floating screen converged in on itself and disappeared, two of the brown leather chairs rotated on their own to face each other. An attractive woman entered the room. Her outfit was opposite the colors the food servers wore. Instead of chocolate with cream-colored accents, her main clothes: blouse, skirt to the knees, and sneakers were cream-colored, while her hat, buttons and trim on the blouse, belt, and nylons were chocolate-colored.

Carrying a black bag in one hand, she grabbed Hayden's hand with the other and said, "Come sit by me, Mr. Bakley."

"Please, call me Hayden," he said, as he stood and followed her over to the brown leather chairs facing each other and they both sat. Only a space of about a foot between the chairs, it was tight quarters, and she let Hayden situate himself first, then tucked her feet inside his.

"Here, rest your arm on the desk," the nurse said.

She tended to the cut on his hand first. "That's some gash. Who did this to you?"

Hayden's answer projected loud as if testifying on a stand in court for all to hear. "That woman over there."

His head nodded toward Ora and the nurse shot her a disapproving glare.

"Now, that wasn't very nice, was it?" the nurse said.

Hayden's voice projected again as he said, "No, it certainly was not."

"Oh, spare me," Ora said.

Hayden's hand cleaned and bandaged, the nurse went to work on the small cuts on his face.

"She didn't do this, too?" the nurse asked, looking at Ora with attitude, then dabbing a damp cloth gently on Hayden's face.

"No. I can't blame her," Hayden said and then, in a pout, added, "At least, I shouldn't."

"I can't watch this," Ora said. "You're pathetic."

"She always talk to you like that?" the nurse asked Hayden.

"No. Not always," he answered. "But, most of the time."

Ora stood. "I'm out of here."

Kip trotted over to Ora and insisted she sit down. "You can't leave, yet, Ora. Please sit down."

Reluctantly, she sat. Kip retrieved his coffee cup and brandy bottle, set them on the breakfast table, moved the chair Hayden had sat in to eat closer to Ora, and sat down. Ora grabbed the brandy bottle's neck like an experienced wino and drank a gulp.

"Ms. Frush. You know it's the A.M.?" Kip said.

Turned sideways in her chair, Ora watched Hayden bask

in the nurse's care. They conversed and smiled as if sitting outside a French café in Paris with the Eiffel Tower in view. The nurse's delicate touch and mannerisms were sensual and provocative. Of course, Hayden, the putz, fell for it. Why it is when a woman gives any kind of attention to a man, the man thinks she's interested. Although, this time, it appeared to Ora the nurse might be meddlesome and jealousy burned Ora's insides worse than heartburn.

Maybe it was the brandy. Already tired, she had a feeling swigging the alcohol might turn out to be a mistake.

The nurse finished, but she and Hayden continued to talk. And laugh. Her long, thin hand touching his. Now, both hands. Hayden swept his hair back with his fingers and her hand stayed there, on his knee. He did it on purpose, that sly devil.

The nurse laughed aloud at something Hayden had said. She found him funny and humor can sometimes be just as important as looks, which Hayden had, too. A lot going for him at the moment.

Hayden and the nurse stood together and, in the confined space between the chairs, their bodies were against one another.

"Sorry, I …" Hayden began.

"I don't mind," the nurse said.

"I'll just sit down and let you go first," Hayden said as he sat, blushing.

She pinched his chin in her fingers, gracefully collected her things, and walked toward the door. On her way out, she turned around, smiled, and waved at Hayden before leaving the room.

Ora looked at Kip first, then turned to see Hayden, and they were both still eyeing the door. Ora's eyes turned toward the ceiling as she shook her head.

Hayden tried turning the chair and couldn't, so he stood up and went back over to the makeshift breakfast table.

"All set, pal?" Kip asked Hayden. "Seriously, I had no clue she worked here. I'm going to be sick like every week from now on."

"You never took me to Paris," Ora said.

"What?" Hayden asked as he sat down.

"Tough act to follow," Kip said as he further loosened his already loose tie. "But as much as I enjoyed that, I guess we need to return to reality." As he walked to the wall where the briefcase, two forearms, and Hayden's pistol case hung, he said, "I told you once and I'm saying again, for all of us, we need to get our minds right while we still have them. I think everyone knows the parties involved. Us. Them. Are after this." After pointing to each arm, he pointed to the briefcase last. "And you two are now in the middle of it." He gestured to Hayden's pistol case in the middle of the triangle. "I already was, because it's my job. Speaking of minds, we should get Baldy back."

Kip brought the projected screen up again, the bald-headed man at its center.

"You didn't miss much," Kip said to the man on the screen. "I just reminded them of who the parties are and we're off again. So, now, if the complex nature of the parties wasn't enough, here's some more. Take it as a warning. It's all about extremes in this business. From being underground in this canyon to the spheres around the Earth, and one day, past that into interstellar space. However, as in real estate, everyone knows *location, location, location* is the key. And usually, it's the middle ground connecting those extremes that is the most valuable. And right now, that middle ground is the spheres around the Earth. The troposphere, stratosphere, mesosphere, thermosphere, and exosphere. Being astronauts, you already know their order and the properties of each, so, no need to go there."

The bald man on the screen chimed in. "And don't forget what I told you earlier, Bakley. Our lives down here reach up to those spheres via all the different types of satellites and even our own increased space exploration. You two know that already, but most people don't. To them, life is on the ground. I also spoke of the war for the spheres and how it's one of the longest-running wars in human history. Because of its ongoing nature, its predominately ignored, and those who do notice, it's not seen as a war, but simply the environment in which we live. The war for the spheres is the most important in human history. People may not see it now, but they will."

"Excellent, my man," Kip said as he snapped his fingers at the man on the screen. "Did you hear what he said? *The most important war in human history.*' And no one knows how complex this is going to get. There are the two main parties I talked about, but other ancillary groups are forming and most of them are building their own stuff, challenging NASA and other space agencies for jobs. Who knows what lifeforms will come from the cosmos and partake in this? Especially as our reach into space lengthens as our technology improves."

"Are we talking airspace, Kip?" Hayden interjected. "Because we all know there'd be enough for everyone, even these up-and-coming companies if we just cleaned up all the space junk up there."

Kip's fingers snapped at Hayden, "*Yes! Airspace!* The control and ultimate ownership of that airspace."

"See," Hayden said. "That's where I thought you were going with this and the skin-globe on the monitor went there as well. No one can control space or own it. The Outer Space Treaty of '67 and other agreements won't allow it."

"You're wrong," Kip countered. "Remember SDI back in nineteen eighty-three under Reagan?"

"Yeah, ugh, give me a minute. *SDI. SDI.* The Strategic Defense Initiative."

"Correct. Part of that proposal dealt with nuclear-powered lasers on satellites, which would have been a direct violation of the Outer Space Treaty. The same treaty the United States signed and ratified. And that was almost forty years ago. No one disputes the good that disintegrative lasers could accomplish. Just think what it would mean getting rid of all of that space junk, orbiting up there, and waste management down here. But that's not the goal. You could get rich off it and it would make a nice cover, but agencies and others out there see more than money. They also see power and they're busy planning how to get it as we speak. There's no way they're going to let a few words on some paper stop them. You saw the lengths they're willing to go. Firsthand, you witnessed it. It's what landed you here. There's a Law of War, but not everyone who served abided by it. I'm talking force. Fear of the future so groups with the means are out to control the future. It's a little less scary when it's in your own hands.

"When I say force—I mean force. War force. With technology and troops and ships and the whole nine. Whoever controls the spheres around our planet will conquer Earth. Guaranteed. And in time, they'll control the solar system and into interstellar space. Why? Because they'll be the gatekeepers, in or out. Orbital tracks will be rented out like parcels of land for satellites and things and they'll charge outrageous amounts to do so. If they were smart, they should charge so much that it would break a country financially and ultimately just break the country. That's what I would do. I wouldn't go selling any of it either. Either they pay, or go back to the Stone Age.

"Cost! It's the one true thing in the universe that dictates people's lives, holistically or individually. Whoever gets there now, in today's dollars, and gets a stronghold, will be difficult to dethrone later. But what keeps me up at night is whoever gets there first, or gets there and stays there, can weaponize anything up there. We're talking weapons of mass destruction orbiting around up there. All of a sudden, range isn't an issue. There are issues of reentry of all the usual space travel stuff, but if they're smart enough to gain control, they'll be smart enough to figure it out. Maybe heatshields at first, then who knows?" Kips' thumb and middle finger rubbed his temples. "I need a drink."

As Kip walked over to the breakfast table, Ora asked

him, "How far along is this? I mean is there anyone even close to having the capability to do such a thing?"

Pouring some brandy into his coffee cup, Kip answered, "It's early, but yes. They, not us, have devised a way of setting up a perimeter around the world real quick-like, foxholes, if you will, without having to dig them themselves. If they're successful, they'd be so entrenched up there, nothing else could get up there and overthrow them. Thankfully, that's not going to happen, because we have the briefcase." Raising his coffee cup, he toasted, "I'll drink to that."

Hayden leaned forward, placing his elbows on his knees. "You said we're important only because we have the suitcase. So, what's in it—deeds to space?"

Kip's finger wiped the rim of his coffee cup. "Maybe."

"Maybe? You mean don't know?"

"Not for sure. We've seen schematics of possible designs, but we've never seen what they settled on."

"But you know what they do?"

"The schematics were purposefully vague in case of interception, but enough was there for us to make heads and tails out of it."

"You sounded so convincing you knew, Kip," Ora said.

The finger Kip rubbed the rim of the cup with raised in the air. "I never said we knew. Not for certain."

"You never said you didn't," Hayden said.

"I did. A moment ago," Kip said.

"See. I told you he was drunk," Ora said to Hayden.

"I guess you're right," Hayden said. "What a waste of time."

"It wasn't a waste of time," Kip said. "Come on. Everything I said was true. Whatever is in that briefcase can do all I'm saying it could do. And maybe then some. That much we figured out."

No one knew where to go from there. The quiet in the room wasn't the wisdom of intelligent people holding their tongue but hiding their ignorance.

Finally, Ora said, "Is there anything else, Kip? We're tired."

Kip started to speak, but Hayden cut him off and asked, "I'm tired, too, but maybe you can answer this? Why do you have a screen in your arm?"

"Fair enough," Kip said. "I knew it was coming."

Kip poured some coffee in his brandy and plopped into one of the leather chairs. "I told you I was grounded for good, but I never said why. Two years ago, the last mission all three of us flew together, we returned to Earth. Two days later, I was called back in and given a physical. Deemed fit to go back up, I went on another mission. What that mission was, I didn't know at the time, but it involved some extra danger pay, so I took it. The mission was only supposed to be a couple of days, a week at the most, so no big deal.

"So, I'm in space, right, and I walk into this room and something grabbed me around the forearm. I panicked and tried to pull out of the grip, but my arm wasn't budging. I looked and it was one of those damn robotic arms. No one else was in the room. I start screaming my fool head off and, next thing I know, I feel the hand squeezing my arm like a boa constrictor. I screamed as loud as I could until the pain was so bad, I couldn't anymore. I literally choked up. Desperate, I pulled as hard as I could. I felt tearing in my elbow and shoulder, so I stopped trying to break free. By the time someone got to me, my forearm was as flat as a Vietnam tit."

Kip sipped his brandied coffee and continued. "Come to find out, *I* was the experiment. They wanted to see how fast they could replace a damaged forearm with one of these." Kip's forearm with the screen inside in it went into the air, then back down onto the chair desk. "When it was over, I found out the mission was classified for the surgeons and everybody else on board—*hush-hush* for me, so I didn't know what was coming. And, because of my exemplary service and body alteration, I had been accepted into what I'm doing now. I'm sorry I lied, Hayden. I'm not grounded for good. I was only grounded for a time. As I said, I didn't want to bring you into this."

Hayden pieced it together. "I see. When you said you were busy becoming a Field Agent…"

"I was on that mission," Kip said. "Up with my own arm, down with a robotic one. The very thing that destroyed my natural one. It didn't have a screen in it yet and, when I recovered, I went through their training. What else was I going to do? They rebuilt my arm for free. When I made the cut, they installed the screen. I've tried getting TV on it, but, so far, no luck."

"Have you been back up?" Hayden asked.

"No," Kip answered.

"Any chance you can go back up?"

"I think so."

"Oh, to be young again."

"Age doesn't have anything to do with it."

Ora turned so she sat sideways on her chair. "It looks so real. Can I see it?"

"Sure." Kip swallowed some of his drink and walked over to her. "The technology is called enh*um*anced. Think of *enhanced* and *human* intermingled together."

Her hands caressed his robotic hand. "It feels so real."

"It is, partially. Skin cells. Hair. Nails. All a composite of human DNA and synthetics, covering the robotics underneath."

Ora looked up at Kip. "Wait. So that means …"

"The other arms are designed the same way," Hayden finished.

"That's why they survived for so long after being detached," Kip said.

Hayden stood and walked over to the two forearms hanging on the wall and looked at them, shaking his head. "I thought they were real and I guess they are because I'm looking at them."

Looking down at Ora, Kip smiled, and slowly pulled his hand out of hers.

"There's something else," Kip said.

Embarrassment flooded Ora, not intending on caressing his hand for so long.

"Straight out of the playbook of the robotic claw that had squashed my arm like a grape," Kip continued, "these fabricated arms are strong. It's why we have them. Our man knew he had to chop the arm off because their man's grip would never relinquish the handle."

"I understand the usefulness and good of prosthetics, but when used like this, it's scary," Ora said.

"Speaking of scary, here, I'll show you." Kip set his cup down on the breakfast table and walked over to Hayden.

Ora stood and followed.

Kip removed both forearms off the wall and set them beside each other on the long table. As he removed the bandages near the elbows, death whispered from the raw flesh into their nostrils. His hand reached inside his jacket pocket and pulled out a pen. A click sound and he began to poke and prod the open flesh.

"Decomposition would be worse if this were all human tissue," Kip said. "Only the human elements are decaying. Their guy, lying in the street, was booby-trapped to self-destruct, so he blew up so nothing remained as evidence. Our guy, too. The blast disintegrated him, but, once death was imminent, he self-destructed. You said the blast was louder, right?" He asked Hayden but continued without an answer. "Well, it wasn't just because you were closer to it. It was a double-whammy."

The tip of Kip's pen dug out some of the human flesh and synthetic compound, exposing a section of robotics. Science fiction stories from their childhood came rushing back, bringing along with it all the wonder and fear in a child's imagination, where wonder could be quite wonderful and uninhibited fear could be quite scary. All of those stories about robots taking over the human race. Here it was, right in front of them: robotics, replacing the individual human, before they took over the world.

When Hayden bent down for a closer look, he noticed something peculiar about the fingernails on the hand of the other forearm. It might have been the angle or a reflection, but his interest took his eyes there. The nails themselves appeared normal and it wasn't a reflection he saw. Instead of the color of the flesh under the fingernails appearing uniform, these had some white at their centers, reminding him of grains of white rice, as if they had been jammed under the nails. The thumb didn't have any white and appeared normal.

Concentrating on the middle finger, Hayden squinted. The white underneath the nail appeared bleached from the rest of the flesh as if a small worm had curled up there, while the rest of the flesh had tanned from the sun.

Under the nails of the ring and pinky fingers, the pale areas appeared blotched the same way as the middle finger, but on the index finger, a line ran straight up and down.

Hayden stood erect to give his back a break and, in doing so, the blotches of white began to take form. His eyesight veered to the other hand and the flesh under its nails appeared a uniform pink, no white in them at all. His eyes returned to the hand in front of him and the bleached spots were still in the flesh under the nails in the same form he thought he saw them.

He turned away and closed his eyes to rest them. Impatience didn't allow him to rest long. Eager to prove or disprove what he thought he saw, he opened his eyes and looked at the fingernails. What he had seen before, he saw now, and he asked Kip, "What are these numbers under the fingernails?"

CHAPTER SEVEN

Moving to the other forearm and hand, Kip held the bloodied, gelled pen just above one of the fingernails and inspected it. He stood out of a slight hunched posture, looked at Hayden, and slouched again to inspect the rest of the fingernails.

"There's not a number on the thumb," Hayden pointed out.

Seemingly satisfied with what he saw, Kip stood and looked at Hayden. "I don't see any numbers."

Almost in a panic of unbelief, Hayden checked the fingernails. "What do you mean you don't see any numbers? They're right there! One-two-three-four!"

"Hayden, I don't see any numbers," Kip reiterated.

Frustration had Hayden shaking his head.

"Fine. You don't believe me," Kip said. His hand motioned from Ora to the hand. "Ora, would you so kindly come over here and tell us if you see any numbers?"

The two men spread apart so Ora had room. Hesitantly, she bent down in concentration. Checking and double-checking, taking longer than it should, she finally stood, bit her lip, and said, "I don't see any numbers."

"You two are pretending, right?" Hayden said. "To make

me think I'm seeing things."

"Come on! Really?" Kip said. "We don't have time for that."

Blood reddened Kip's face under the skin, telling Hayden that he wasn't messing around. An insincere smile of Ora's mouth tried hiding the underlying concern on the rest of her face, but it had failed, because Hayden saw it.

"You really don't see any numbers?" Hayden asked.

They shook their heads they didn't.

Combing his hands through his hair, Hayden mumbled as he turned away, "God, I must be crazy."

Kip's eyes met Ora's and then he walked over behind Hayden. "You're not crazy," Kip began.

Hayden turned around, grabbed Kip's lapels, and said, "I have blood."

A nervous laugh sputtered out of Kip, as his eyes looked down at Hayden's hands on him. "That's twice this morning. You must really like my jacket."

Frightened eyes on Ora's surprised face watched.

"Not *have*," Hayden said. "*Had*. It's not here."

Another spooked laugh slipped out of Kip. "Of course, you have blood, buddy. We all do."

Slowly, Hayden's hands relaxed. A gulp sounded in his throat and with flat hands, he ironed the lapels on Kip's jacket.

"There was blood on the skylight above my bedroom," Hayden said, softly. "I collected it. That's what I was doing when Ora came back with the groceries."

The mention of her made him turn his head hesitantly toward her, the expression on his face desperate for confirmation.

She nodded she remembered.

"Well, where is it?" Kip asked Hayden.

"In a coat pocket," Hayden answered. "Hanging in my closet."

"You have to get it. These guys don't leave traces like that behind very often."

Hayden walked over to Ora and put his hands on her shoulders. "I didn't tell you what I was doing on the roof, because I didn't want you to worry."

"I already was after everything else," she said.

"I know. I should have told you just in case anything happened to me and at least someone else knew about it."

"I'm sorry this is happening to you."

"I'm sorry this is happening to us."

They hugged.

"Okay, kids, break it up," Kip said. "We need a game plan for what we're going to do."

"We're listening," Hayden said.

"Well, first of all, in this business, the unusual becomes the norm," Kip said. "Not that you get used to it, but it's there. I think you see those numbers because they really are there and we can't see them. Eye specialist," he said into the air. "Even with this program, they're not doctors anymore, they're specialists. We're going to get you checked out."

"And then?" Ora asked.

"Not then—now," Kip said to Ora, then to Hayden, "You said the numbers were one to four?"

"Yeah," Hayden said. "Index to pinky."

"One to four, index to pinky. Got it," Kip said. "After your eye examination, another specialist will change your appearance. Cosmetically first, then if we need to make some alterations, that'll be done later."

He looked at Ora. "God, you're beautiful, but you, too, I'm afraid."

The same pleasant sounding woman's voice spoke into the room, "The eye specialist will see you now, Mr. Stanton."

"Okay, great," Kip replied.

A regretful look formed on Kip's face as he puffed up his cheeks and blew out the air. "Just one thing before we move around."

He moved closer to the wall opposite the window-wall and placed his hand on it. A seam appeared where there wasn't one and the surface of the wall rolled out like a drawer opening. Out about three feet, it stopped. Kip peered down into the drawer, reached in, and pulled out what appeared to be a space helmet.

"You need to put these on," Kip said.

"Whoa! Hold on!" Hayden said. "How come we didn't need to wear them before?"

"Nothing to see but an exhaust shaft and a fancy elevator," Kip said. "Now, there's no visor in these things, so this is the front." His finger tapped a side of the helmet.

"Oh, fine," Ora said and snatched the helmet out of Kip's hands.

Kip pulled out a second helmet and handed it to Hayden.

"Insert melon into cavity, people," Kip said. "Time's a wasting. They're safe."

When they placed the helmets on their heads, pitch-black void enveloped their sight, and then fluorescent-green lights flickered on, outlining the parallelogram room and their bodies. Nothing else appeared in view.

"A computerized blindfold," Ora said.

"Exactly right," Kip said. "You should be able to see an outline of the room, showing you where the ceiling, walls, and floor are and an outline of us. All you have to do is follow me by walking in the middle of where the walls meet the floor and you'll be fine. Oh, and don't be alarmed when the little warning arrows blink if you get to close to a wall or something."

"What about furniture and things like that?" Hayden asked.

"It'll warn you as will I," Kip said. "You'll just have to trust me and follow. Oh, and Hayden. Don't mention anything about the numbers to the eye doc. He's checking your eyes is all."

After the eye examination, the specialist shared his thoughts. "Hayden shared with me that on one of his missions his eyes were exposed to space. Keep in mind, I know you know this, but typically, space wreaks havoc on the eyes. Dust. The lack of gravity. But, in Hayden's case, his vision improved. Not immediately, mind you. I can't prove space did this, but there was a case study done on another astronaut who experienced the same thing. So, although this is rare, it's happened before. I wish I had a better answer."

"No, you answered it, doc," Kip said.

"How can you be so sure?" Hayden asked.

"Because. You were a meaningless creature in the universe and there was nothing going on around you to see. It was as if the universe gave you a gift and called upon you when it felt necessary to do so."

"Yeah. A little like Satan calling on a servant who had made a deal with him by selling his soul," Hayden said.

"Possibly. Or it could go the other way. A true miracle," Kip said to Hayden, then to the eye specialist, "Do you know, doc, if the other astronaut ended up doing anything special with his enhanced eyesight?"

"I don't believe so, no. In fact, he died a couple of years after the case study."

"*Hmm.* Not exactly what I was looking for," Kip said. "Helmets on, kids. Time for a nap before we improve Hayden's looks."

The door slid open and Kip entered a room followed by Hayden and then Ora.

Once the door closed, Kip said, "Okay. You can remove your helmets."

A stale, uncirculated air welcomed them to a new room within the cavern. Other than the idle air, the room had all of the qualities of a fine hotel suite. Instead of windows, two animated computer screens hung on the wall, strategically placed, for the illusion of windows.

"Don't get many visitors, I take it," Ora said.

"No, it seems not," Kip said. "It'll liven up as you move around." Admiring the room, he wandered and said, "This underground bunker can withstand the worst that could happen on the surface. We're deeper into the canyon, but it's never been tested. That big crack in the Earth makes me doubt, but who am I to say. Anyway, as you can see, you have everything you need. If you need help, say help or assistance or anything like that and…"

The amiable voice of a woman spoke into the room, "I am here to help. How may I assist you?"

"And there you go," Kip said, then said louder to the voice, "Just showing them their rooms."

"Very good, Mr. Stanton. Enjoy your stay, Mr. Bakley, and Ms. Frush."

"Don't answer. Just let it go," Kip said. "Okay, so, yes, enjoy your stay, but it'll be brief. Six-hour super snooze and we'll get to work. Helmet on, missy, and we'll be off."

Father-like, Kip moved to the door and waited for Ora to put on her helmet. Hayden and Ora looked at each other, wanting to stay together, but as exhausted as they were, it was probably best, so they let it go. Facing Hayden, she slid the helmet over her head and left the room with Kip.

The gears in Hayden's mind wouldn't stop moving. It was the last thing he needed. Suspicion powered unwanted thoughts of Kip taking Ora to her room and not leaving. In wearing the helmet, he had no clue where his own room was, let alone where Ora's might be. The elementary computerized outlines, inside the helmet, hadn't provided sufficient detail of distinguishable landmarks to establish his location.

When he stepped near the door, it didn't open and there were no controls to operate it. He tried his luck at speaking commands, but nothing worked. Even the hospitable female voice kindly declined his request when he asked for her help and assistance.

He put an ear to the door and listened, but didn't hear anything. It didn't surprise him; the rooms were probably soundproof.

Held against his will without hope of escape, he belly-flopped onto the bed. One-by-one, life's cares vanished from his mind and as they left, the deeper he wandered into sleep.

"Time to wake up, Mr. Bakley."

Hayden heard nothing, immersed in the deepest depths of sleep, somewhere past disturbance's power, where dreams, sleepwalking, and bedwetting exists.

Time passed and a persistent voice called to him in what felt like death itself. The voice sounded faint, distant, and his mind wandered to something specific. He felt himself spinning through space in a spacesuit and, as he rotated around, he saw a ship in the distance, none like any other he's ever seen. A woman's voice sounded in his headset, Ora's, calling out to him, while the gap between him and the ship grew at an accelerated pace. The ship shrank before his eyes and there didn't seem to be any indication of a rescue. He felt his pores open and his body tingled—a feeling he'd never experienced before. The give in the lining of his suit filled and, feeling the material tighten against his skin, he realized his body began to balloon. As his body rotated in a rhythmic cycle through space, each time the ship came into view, the smaller it became until it reduced to a dot and, eventually, he couldn't see it anymore. Disorientation, sickness, and a bloated body ganged up on him, but, at that moment, the universe seemed to know him and accept him in his state. He felt a delicate touch on the shoulder and couldn't decipher if it stemmed from a memory of Ora or if mother universe somehow manifested herself, personally welcoming him into the cosmos forever.

"Time to wake up, Mr. Bakley."

The words came through louder, clearer, closer. Hayden's mind had never spun like this before, not even during the most vigorous training or his worst intoxications. A hand touched his shoulder again and, just when he sensed his body explode within his spacesuit, he woke up, jerking up on his hands to get some air, and spewing vomit so forcefully, it bounced off the mattress onto his face.

The violent flow slowed to a trickle and diluted honey cords hung from his bottom lip, some all the way to the bed. Remembering the touch on the shoulder, he looked around the room, but no one was there. Only the sound of the woman's voice telling him to wake up in a sunny tone with the volume turned up so he would awaken.

The volume returned to a normal level as the female voice said, "Good morning, Mr. Bakley. Glad to see you slept well. The time is eleven-twenty-one."

"Eleven-twenty-one!"

"Yes, Mr. Bakley, eleven-twenty-one. Now, eleven-twenty-two. Lunch will be served in thirty-eight minutes. In thirty minutes, Mr. Stanton will be by to take you there. Would you like the TV on? Some news? Listen to some music? Some coffee?"

Listening, Hayden wiped his mouth on the bed covers and hearing *coffee* said, "Coffee please."

"How would you like it?"

"Space black, please, with some dust."

"Black with sugar. How many sugars?"

"Four."

"Black coffee with four sugars. Brewing now. Anything else, Mr. Bakley?"

"No. Just some privacy."

Not hearing the woman's voice, he assumed she took the hint.

Hayden showered and, when he walked out into the main room, fresh clothes draped the back of a chair and underclothes lie folded on the cushion. He looked around the room, but he was alone.

Almost noon, Kip walked into the room. "What is that smell?" His hand clamped over his mouth.

"I'm not trained in this sort of thing," Hayden said, "but I'm going to say a combination of Ora's dinner, wine, brandy, breakfast, and coffee."

Muffled through his hand like a mask, Kip said, "*Good, Lord.* I'm going get the chemical guys down here to see if that stuff can be weaponized. You ready. I am."

"Almost. Just a sec."

"When you're done, get your helmet on and meet me in the hall."

The odor smelled raunchy, but Hayden couldn't help smiling at Kip's discomfort.

Ordering lunch in the canyon wasn't anything Hayden or Ora had ever experienced. Instead of ordering from a menu, you just stated what you wanted, and the servers brought it out. It wasn't far from ordering through a drive-through mic and then taking a seat at a table. All foods were available any time of the day. Breakfast, lunch, or dinner, it didn't matter, and there was no limit on how much could be ordered. Coffee provided Kip his nourishment. For a big man, he had eaten the least. Fruit made up half of what Hayden had eaten for he knew he needed his share of all of the food groups and then some. All said and done, Ora packed away the most food, loading up on the heavy stuff: meats, dairy, and grains.

Winding down with coffee and dessert, Kip said, "I hate to break up your contentment, but here's the plan. Hayden, you and one of my guys are going to, covertly, go to your place and get that blood. While you're at it, you may want to grab some things you might need. Your place isn't big, so anything of nostalgic value, just set in the middle of your living room and we'll make sure it's stored away for you and let you know where."

"Are you saying I can't go back to my home after this?" Hayden asked.

"No. I'm saying you shouldn't. Whatever you don't put in the middle of that living room, I would consider abandoned."

"Well, don't go selling it or anything. Take what I put in the living room, but leave everything else be."

The meaning of what Kip had said without him coming right out and saying it flew into Hayden's unbelieving ears and confirmed what he already knew himself some time ago on the unusual plane. His home had been black-marked and orange-marked. The deed handed over to the man wearing a hat on a tanned-skinned body, *Manhattan*. There was no way he could return there and realistically expect to live peaceably. Sanctuary wasn't possible there—anymore.

"I would like to go with him," Ora said.

"No can do," Kip said. "You're safer staying right here."

"With you, of course," Hayden quickly followed.

"Of course," Kip agreed, knowing his long-time friend wouldn't like it.

"*Hayden!* I want to go. Tell him I'm going," Ora pleaded.

Hayden's eyes set on Kip for a while, watching him sit there and drink his coffee, patiently waiting out an uncomfortable situation.

"Hayden," Ora said softly, breaking the silence. "Tell him."

"He's right," Hayden said. "You're staying here."

The tension between the two men moved to Hayden and Ora.

"I'm not staying here," she said. "You can't…"

"I brought you into this and I'm taking you out," he firmly interrupted.

"So that's it, huh? The man has spoken."

"The men have spoken."

Ora turned to Kip and he nodded in agreement.

"I'm going to my room," she said and stood.

The sterile room, the closed door, and the helmets hanging on the wall beside it reminded her of where she was.

Upset and about to cry, she said, "I don't know where my room is."

Kip went over to her and rubbed her arms. "I'll have someone take you. I'll come to see you later and take you to get disguised. It's for your own protection. I'm sorry."

He took a helmet off the wall and handed it to her. Now was not the time to tell her that her own affairs needed taken care of to erase any tracks that may lead back to her, so he let it go. As she put on the helmet, the door opened. An escort guided her to her room and Kip walked over to Hayden.

Hayden hadn't heard everything Kip had said to her, but he had overheard him say he would see her later. Once again, thoughts he didn't want to think, he thought. How this could be mystified him. Purposefully concentrating on other thoughts made it worse, almost fueling scenarios of how Kip might weasel his way in with Ora. Vulnerability could lead to irrational behavior. Need could lead to expeditiously filling a void. Similar to a nagging injury, those unwanted thoughts hung around. Behaving like a virus, those unwelcomed thoughts multiplied, invaded, and consumed all others until all thought suffered disease.

Kip finished his coffee and said, "You did the right thing by her, Hayden. She doesn't see it now, but in time."

"You're fooled, too, huh," Hayden said. "Time is a conundrum. It's not a friend and certainly not a healer. While you're being healed, time is taking your life. Man sees time as precious and they should while they still have it. Most don't know how much time they have, so they don't think about it. Dying, now that they get. They're told how much time they have and all of a sudden they live like someone on the clock." Hayden chuckled. "Stupid, isn't it. We're all on the clock."

"Man, Hayden. You're a gassy butt-face today. You open your mouth and only stink comes out. And I got to tell you, it's raunchy."

"That's what I'm saying."

"I'm sorry. My eyes are too watery to see where you're going with this."

"Nothing complicated. Just that life stinks."

"Well, can't argue with you there. But don't be fooled. A fart is complicated."

Hayden sighed, plucked one of the last grapes from a vine, and ate it.

"She'll be fine," Kip reassured. "She's in the best place

she can be." Kip's hands slapped his thighs. "Well, we can't wait anymore. You need to be made over and must get into the air. Transforming a butt into a face won't be easy."

Overall, the non-surgical procedures in altering Hayden's appearance had been easy and most of it done with the goal of hiding the scars on his face. The stylists lengthened his hair so it hung down over his forehead and dangled the sides of his face. They shaved his face and then added as much facial hair as possible without going overboard, giving him a healthy beard, mustache, and sideburns. All the hair, including his eyebrows—a detail usually overlooked in amateur makeovers—was dyed a dirty blonde, quite a contrast from his natural-born dark hair, but it worked. The rustic, not NASA-like makeover gave Hayden a glimpse of his retired future if he did decide to let himself go a little.

Most important, very little skin remained exposed on his face, allowing the dermatologists to hide the scars in such a way no one would ever know they were there. Hand-picked clothes completed the look and gloves were to be worn to cover the cut on his hand, which fit in with the winter season, and when inside, Hayden just needed to remember to keep his hand cupped to hide the palm and avoid bandaging his hand altogether.

When Kip saw Hayden, he couldn't believe the transformation.

"Wow!" Kip said. "Hayden Bakley's in there somewhere?" He pointed at Hayden. "Don't answer that. No, he's not. You don't know a Hayden Bakley. He's missing somewhere, but you don't know that, because you've never met him." His hand gestured to himself. "My name is Pik Notnats and you are?"

"Bo Arden," Hayden answered.

"That's right! Bo Arden. And you're at Hayden's place because?"

"I went to high school with Hayden back east. Visiting the Pacific Northwest, I thought I'd drop in and surprise him."

"Not terribly convincing, but perhaps that'll be to your advantage. I mean, who would be ecstatic to see Hayden Bakley."

"Go ahead and laugh. Your boss said you're going on this trip, too, and to use you as a human shield if it came to that."

"Oh, I would never risk going on a trip like this," Kip said. "*He's* your escort."

A big, burly man dressed in all black head-to-toe walked toward Kip and Hayden, carrying a helmet.

"What a gentleman," Kip said. "He brought you a bigger helmet so you didn't mess up your new look."

The cordial woman's voice spoke into the room, "Sorry, Mr. Stanton, but I'm afraid Mr. Arden won't be using the helmet due to the impermanent nature of his makeover."

Relief came over Hayden at the news.

Kip pointed to the ceiling and whispered to Hayden, "She called you Mr. Arden." Louder, he said to her, "Thank you. We know what to do."

"Man, I'm glad I don't have to wear that thing anymore," Hayden said.

"I'm sure. But that means we need to blind you for a few minutes to get you out of here."

"Don't you mean blindfold?"

"Did I stutter? Blind."

"*Blind me!* On purpose? How?"

The same nurse, who had cared for Hayden last night, entered the room, carrying her black bag. As Kip and Hayden watched her walk, the man in black slid his arms under Hayden's armpits and clasped his hands behind his head, securely seizing him.

"Don't fight it," Kip said. "You don't want to ruin your hair or makeup."

The nurse opened the black bag and pulled out a needle.

"You'll feel a little pinch," she said, "and this will work quickly, so don't be frightened. After a few minutes, it will wear off and your eyesight will be fully restored."

"You're serious about blinding me?" Hayden spit out.

"Feel a pinch where?"

"Remember, get that blood. At all costs," Kip said to Hayden. Then, he said to the man holding him, "Even if that means using him as a shield."

"Yes, Mr. Stanton," the man said.

"See you soon, Bo Arden," Kip said to Hayden as he left the room.

The gorgeous nurse didn't look so beautiful as she separated the eyelids of one of Hayden's eyes with her fingers and advanced the point of the needle toward his eyeball.

Over the North Pacific Ocean, NASA's un-aerodynamic-shaped aircraft approached the Gulf of Alaska from the Southeast.

Buckled into a seat, Hayden felt a shove on his shoulder.

"Wake up," Hayden's muscular escort, dressed in all black, said.

Groggy, Hayden looked around. What he could see wasn't much: the interior of the plane, seats, blocked-off windows, and his accompaniment, but his vision had returned. *Bodyguard* had entered his mind first, but he knew that wasn't accurate. Without question, this guy would use him as a human shield to save his own derriere.

It was up to Hayden to guard himself against harm. Once he led the brute to the blood, who knew what this guy would do. Dispose of him and concoct a story so when he returned to the cavern and reported to Kip, it came out sounding genuine. It wouldn't surprise Hayden if the man had already formulated his story on the way to pass the time. Oh, how torn up Kip would be at the news, especially in front of Ora, who he would console in her darkest hour as he had consoled her fear of space on previous missions.

"Up! Now!" Hayden's potential cause of death said.

"Why? What's going on?" Hayden asked.

A wad of black cloth hit him in the face and rolled down to his lap.

"Put that on," the man said.

Holding it lumped in a hand, Hayden asked, "What is it?"

"Now!" the man yelled. "We miss our window, I'll kill you myself."

"I hate being right about the worst things," Hayden mumbled.

"Shut up and move."

Hayden slid into the suit and, with one arm still to get into a sleeve, the man grabbed the material behind Hayden's neck, as if pinching the skin on an animal to pick it up, and pushed him forward.

"Damn you!" the man said.

"Where are we going?"

The man reached around Hayden.

"Through this door," he said and pushed him through.

"Work with me," Hayden pleaded.

"Don't look around! Eyes straight ahead!" The man in black yelled, rushing him through the aircraft.

They moved too fast through an enclosed hallway for Hayden to make heads or tails of anything. The hallway seemed much longer than he would have suspected and if he had to render a guess, he would bet they were moving toward the back of the plane.

For a second time, the man reached around Hayden to open another door and shoved him through by the neck. Pinched pain in Hayden's neck subsided upon the large hand's release.

In front of Hayden was another aircraft, a small, two-man glider, ironically, or perhaps not, in the same shape as the plane they were in, having a thick round belly and short, stunted wings.

"What's wrong with the plane we're in?" Hayden asked. "Why aren't we landing?"

"You, right. Me, left," the man said, lowering himself

into the craft.

Throwing a leg over the side, Hayden said, "You thought this through on the way didn't you?"

Once Hayden sunk into the seat, domed glass windows closed over both men. Controls blinked, beeped, and clicked as the man operated them.

"Mother snake, this is sea snake," the man in black said. "We are ready to strike."

"Sea snake? Isn't that a water animal?" Hayden asked.

"Sea snake, this is mother. Opening the mouth," another man's voice said into the vessel.

"They're found in the Pacific Ocean," the man, sitting beside Hayden said. "You're not as dumb as you look."

A humming sound came up from the floor of the small ship. The sound stopped and the front of the craft tilted forward, forcing into view an opening in the large plane's floor as big as the small ship itself. They had departed during the day, now it was night, and Hayden had a feeling there was more to that blinding needle than what the nurse had explained. Facing down into black nothingness, he assumed they were over water not seeing any lights, but they could be over a remote location. If true, they weren't in the state of Washington.

A man's voice entered the cabin of the small ship. "Sea snake, this is mother. The mouth is open. Strike when ready."

"Sea snake acknowledges we are clear to strike," the man about to lead Hayden to his death said.

"Alright, NASA astronaut, maintain your gravity legs," the man said to Hayden, then barked, "Strike!"

Released like a bomb, the craft quietly freefell through the opening and into the cold night sky.

A voice said into the craft, "Sea snake, this is mother. We're abandoning our young."

The plane that brought them to this point raced away.

"Roger that, mother," Hayden's pilot said. "Sea snake entering a tight coil."

"Roger that, sea snake. Don't strike too hard," the voice said into the vessel.

"Tight coil. To pick up speed?" Hayden asked.

"Exactly," the man in black said.

The vessel corkscrewed toward the Earth like a leaf spinning to the ground only much faster. Hayden's eyes adjusted and he thought he saw the surface move below. In view now, the surface was moving, there was no questioning it. They were above black, turbulent water, which did not look inviting.

Spiraling with its nose slightly tilted down in a constant right turn, the craft descended in a controlled manner.

Based on their distance to the water, Hayden anticipated a pull-up and leveling of the ship to avoid the water and fly through the air. But the pilot remained on course for a nosedive into the ocean deep.

Hayden didn't like this at all. Despite being much closer to Earth, it reminded him of reentering the Earth's atmosphere, which had a specific, narrow window for success and everything outside that window resulted in failure and death. He would much rather be in a Soyuz ship, returning to Earth over the dry flatland of Kazakhstan, than being in this one about to enter the massive body of water below, in his estimation, at too high of a speed. A belly flop here would undoubtedly break the tiny ship apart.

"Pull out of it, man!" Hayden yelled at the pilot.

The black ocean grew closer and closer in the domed windshield.

CHAPTER **EIGHT**

"**Y**ou strapped in?" the pilot asked Hayden.

Hayden's eyes didn't need to, but they looked down at his unsecured, tense body fighting to remain in the seat, then they flashed over to the pilot and coveted the straps crisscrossing the man's chest. Perhaps, the man next to him had been too busy piloting the craft to notice, but Hayden had been holding on for dear life the entire trip down, being careful not to touch any of the controls around him. If he had to guess, the pilot *had* noticed and enjoyed it too much to say anything until now. The fact he had said anything made Hayden recant a little that maybe the man wasn't out to kill him.

"Last chance," the pilot said.

Hayden located the straps attached to his seat and buckled himself in just before the nose of the small ship tilted lower, heading straight for the water.

"You're too steep!" Hayden yelled.

"You don't do much diving do you?"

Despite being strapped in, Hayden held on where he could. Frantically, his head moved on a swivel and his eyeballs rotated in their sockets at angles normally not reached. Out of the domed windshields, all he could see was black water. That's how close they were. Not wanting to see the impact, he turned his head to the right. It wasn't planned, but probably best. Otherwise, the last thing he would see in this life was the numbskull pilot on his left being sliced apart by the craft at the hand of the ocean.

A view of the stunted wing on his side of the vessel might be his last image recorded. Before closing his eyes, the truncated wing shorted and he realized it was retracting inside the ship. His head snapped left, but he couldn't see if the same was happening on the other side.

"What's going on with the wings?" Hayden asked. "Aerodynamics again?"

"Hold on," the pilot said.

With the wings withdrawn inside the ship, their vessel had turned into a rocket. The nose of the craft touched the ocean with an endurable amount of impact and very little splash. Water slapped against the domed windshields and once the rocket submerged, the whole experience was over. An experience Hayden knew could have been a lot worse.

A dim light flickered on inside the cabin, while brighter lights flickered outside on all sides of the ship, creating an angelic-like aura around its perimeter. The domed windshields, now water shields, pressed against the murky water as the craft advanced. To Hayden, the lights seemed as useless as turning on automobile headlights in a thick fog. As in space, he knew instrumentation was critical in an environment like this.

Based on feel more than sight, Hayden figured they were still diving. They were and although the craft sank to depths he never expected, instead of asking or saying anything, he let the man to his left alone. Getting them this far, the man deserved it, not that the pilot needed Hayden's approval.

The nose of the ship rose to level out the vessel and Hayden felt the straps relax across his chest. Without his knowledge, the wings extended out from the ship once more. In complete concentration and control, the pilot busily pushed buttons, flipped switches, and checked gauges.

"King snake, this is sea snake on the slither," the man in black said.

"Roger that, sea snake," a man's voice said into the vessel.

"Crawling under a rock, but tell mother her baby's alright."

"We'll do."

Spaceships of the highest caliber money could buy were something Hayden was familiar with as an astronaut. However, this piece of machinery might take the cake. A multipurpose vehicle that had the capability of uses as a glider, plane, and submarine made it versatile and who knew what else it could do? Perhaps, launch into space or drop wheels and drive on land.

Something hit the domed windshield, ricocheted off, and disappeared into the blackness.

The pilot saw it had startled Hayden and said, "Ice."

Ice. In all of the excitement, Hayden had forgotten about one thing—the weather. The oversight worked to his advantage because the anticipation of entering the water had been bad enough without the thought of ice. Colliding with a sheet of ice or an iceberg could have been disastrous. He didn't know what kind of instrumentation exactly the pilot had at his disposal to work with, but hoped ice detection was one of them.

All of this talk of instrumentation and environment resurrected Hayden's training to the surface. For the last two years, he had been on the ground, such unused knowledge had buried itself a little deeper each day. If called again for a mission, most of it was still there for recollection, but even knowing what he knew and as more recalled, he still decided to ask the man next to him some questions. Surprisingly, the pilot answered with as much detail he knew, occasionally, interrupting their talk to provide updates of their whereabouts.

They had entered North Pacific Ocean waters one-hundred and twenty-five miles away from the coast of

Vancouver Island to avoid the ridge supporting it. Then, the submarine entered the Strait of Juan de Fuca, teetering the waters bordering Canada and the United States. Approaching the likes of Whale Rocks and Mummy Rocks, the watercraft turned left, going between Goose Island and Deadman Island into Griffin Bay. The sub negotiated another left turn around Turn Rock, of all places, and navigated into Friday Harbor.

The submarine's momentum slowed and Hayden felt it in his body. One-hundred yards out from Hayden's floating home, the pilot stopped the sub and checked the controls.

"Not bad time," he said, interrupting Hayden mid-sentence. "Should be picked up by daylight. There's gear under your seat. Put it on."

It occurred to Hayden the pilot had talked so freely not only for Hayden's sake but also for his own—to pass the time.

Hayden reached under and pulled out a vest and full facemask. Looking over, he was surprised to see the pilot already had the mask over his face and was, now, working on his vest. The big guy appeared comfortable operating in tight quarters.

The pilot's words came out of a speaker at the mouth. "Facemask—face. Vest—body. Small tank in vest. Careful of your failed beautification."

At first, Hayden didn't follow the last part, then he remembered his makeover. The excitement of the ride out of the plane had made him forget.

Both geared up, the pilot checked Hayden's equipment and gave him a thumb up.

"We're a hundred yards out from your house. I'll navigate and lead. You'll have ten minutes to stack your shit you want in the living room for pick-up. *Ten minutes.* Clear on that? Get the blood and," the man handed Hayden a container, "put it in here. It's air and water tight. Eleven minutes, we're out of there. Agreed?"

"Agreed," Hayden said. "Any flippers?"

"You should be slapped for that. Now, look. When I open the glass, let the water come in. Don't fight it to get out. Once the water settles, follow the beacon light in my vest. Got it?"

Hayden nodded.

"Oh, and one more thing. Some ocean life is attracted to shiny things so you may feel some visitors press in and around your body. Just keep moving like a floating piece of driftwood and they may not bother you."

When the man's black-clothed finger pushed a button, the windshields unsealed and retracted. Frigid ocean water rushed into the sub; its force nearly knocked the mask off Hayden's face. Immediately, blackness pressed against his mask, blinding his vision and the body of water pinned his body against the seat. Feeling helpless, he fought to move, but couldn't, and then remembered the pilot say not to fight it. At the mercy of nature, there wasn't a choice but one and that was to trust his gear as he would in space. Everything seemed to work and he had oxygen. His breathing slowed and he relaxed.

Once the water had settled around them and the windshields had disappeared into the ship, the man swam out of the submarine. A blue light, blinking intermittingly, moved away from Hayden and he followed. Occasionally, a dim light from the screen embedded in the man's forearm could be seen. If it weren't for the lights, Hayden would be lost in the murky water, because there was no sign of the man in all black swimming ahead in darkened water, even though mere feet separated them.

Looking down at the navigator, the man stopped swimming and waded under water. Hayden's face ran into him and he almost lost his mask a second time. He felt a large hand cup his head and push off. The blue and screen lights moved toward the surface.

As Hayden gathered himself and waded, his dirty-blonde hair fanned in the water as if in a static fit. A few strands pulled tight on his scalp; from what, he couldn't see.

Something else slithered across the back of his neck and up the side of his head over the ear. Whatever it was, felt scaly, muscular, and large. Feeling exposed and inferior, he headed for the surface while he could still see the lights above him.

When Hayden surfaced, a wooden structure above his head surprised him, expecting to come up to open sky. He turned and a masked head above the water startled him, the man shaking his head in disgust. They were under a floating house and, after locating a dock ladder, the man climbed up first, then Hayden followed. As soon as Hayden's eyes cleared the deck, there was the window-wall to his bedroom.

The sliding glass door was open and the lights were off inside. On his hands and toes, the man in black crabbed over to the wall and stood. For a big man, it couldn't have been done stealthier. He drew his laser and motioned for Hayden to come.

When Hayden reached the man and stood, the man's arm steered Hayden like a shepherd's staff behind him and against the wall. Everything the man did, Hayden mimicked. They removed their masks and set them on the deck by their feet. Wet long hair matted the sides of Hayden's face and he wasn't sure he could get used to having long hair. The man's black-gloved fingers reached into a small pocket in his vest, pulled out a black hair tie, and handed it to Hayden. The gesture surprised the hell out of Hayden.

After peeking inside and not seeing or hearing anything, the man leaned his back against the side of the house and operated the screen lodged in his forearm. His arm straightened across the opening of the door so the screen faced the bedroom. No more than a couple of seconds passed and the arm retreated back behind the wall. When the man checked the screen, a layout of Hayden's home appeared. At first, only general blueprints lined the screen, then, an orange dot blinked, which meant an orange-cloaked warrior was nearby, whereas a red dot would have appeared for any other foe.

"We're not alone," the man whispered to Hayden.

"Other end of the house."

"Shouldn't I have a gun or something?" Hayden asked.

White filled the man's eyes as if he were a zombie from rolling them up. Business like, he raised his laser and took his time entering the house, while Hayden followed closely behind. As they crossed the bedroom and entered the hall, the orange dot tacked left and straightened as if moving away from them. The man in black stopped and showed Hayden the screen.

"Outside," Hayden whispered and pointed.

"Moving to get behind us," the man agreed.

They backtracked toward the bedroom and the orange dot changed direction, moving toward the front of the house again. A handheld laser appeared in front of Hayden.

"Here," the man whispered. "These are powerful, so a strong arm, point, squeeze, and hold. Got it?"

Hayden took the laser and whispered, "Why didn't you give me this earlier?"

"Quiet. You continue to the front because he'll come back this way and I'll be waiting for him."

Hayden nodded and then moved through the hall and into the living room. Wood ash from a burned-out fire lingered, no doubt containing some ash from Kip's overcoat and gloves. Even in the darkness, the place appeared trashed, worse than the last time when someone had disconnected the house and moved it out farther into the harbor. Some cleanup by Ora and she had the place back in order.

Not this time. No, he would need the skill of an experienced carpenter to whip the house back into shape. Furniture moved, cabinets and closets smashed in and emptied, most knickknacks shattered and the rest tousled, bookshelves destroyed, permanent rugs lifted and throw rugs tossed aside, and wood planks in the floor raised. Orange warriors had thoroughly checked under every rock and left them lie there, overturned. Even in the dark, the damage appeared extensive and the coming daylight would shed more light on just how bad. His home and life had been turned upside down and inside out, all because of some stupid briefcase.

As much as Hayden wanted to start rebuilding, he stayed on task, hunkering down behind the couch flipped over on its backside, and facing the opened front door.

Inside the bedroom, the man wearing all black quietly slid the mattress back onto the box springs and hid behind the bed, facing the sliding glass door. The orange dot on the screen blinked along the side of the house and then stopped at the corner. Time passed and the indicator held there.

It seemed strange to Kip's man for the orange enemy to remain at the corner, thinking they would have slowly moved across the back deck to advance to the back door to bring this to a head. Those in cloaked orange tended to operate on the aggressive side.

It was the job of the man in black to be equally as aggressive, so he stood slowly from behind the bed and advanced to the sliding glass door. After peeking out toward the corner, he retreated inside the house and checked his screen one more time. The orange dot was still at the corner of the house.

Both arms extended with the laser at the ready, Kip's man stepped out onto the back deck and, hugging the wall, moved quickly and quietly toward the corner. A flash of pain cramped across his stomach and, when he looked down, the bottom half of his body from the waist down had begun the process of dissolving away. As if eaten by acid, his form dissipated to losing form. A man who studied the enemy and their weapons, he knew exactly what had hit him.

His black-covered head turned on the black-clothed torso toward the water. A cloaked figure in all orange approached the dock on an individual water ski few men had ever seen, but the man in black had on a couple of occasions. Kip's man had no choice but to die with the mistake, knowing the cloaked man had identified them at some point. It was also possible that during the man's post at Hayden's place, he figured someone would return eventually and had planned appropriately. Either way, it was a mistake. Even sending Hayden alone wouldn't have solved anything. No matter who entered the house, they would have had to deal with the orange man.

By the time the figure in orange debarked the ski and stepped onto the dock, the man in black's body from the waist down had entirely disappeared into the ghostly invisible. His hands waved under his own torso, suspended in the air, and felt nothing. As if on an amusement ride, he felt what remained of himself drop out of the air. The downward momentum launched his centering balance from his belly to his head and, in no time, a sticky thud sounded when the innards of his exposed torso hit the deck.

Intimidatingly, the faceless man, hooded in orange, towered over the head and armed torso as if death itself. After setting his laser to another setting, he pointed it at the half of body and asked, "Where is the briefcase?"

"I ran away with it," the man in black replied.

"Funny. But not as funny as how you look down there. Midgets always make me laugh."

Holding the laser indifferently at the enemy in black, the man in orange would have asked again where the briefcase was but knew the half-dead man would never answer. Finishing the job, more than pity, he disposed of him into oblivion without a trace and stepped through the sliding glass door into the house.

In checking his own tracking system on the screen nested in his forearm, a red dot in the living room was still there. Ingeniously, the tracking system in his forearm worked properly, while the one in the man in black's forearm had been manipulated remotely so it tracked Hayden's movement, instead of his, casting Hayden's location away and opposite from the man in black's location, creating the illusion of the orange man's whereabouts, when, really, it tracked Hayden.

It had worked beautifully, making the man in black

believe that when he and Hayden had proceeded to the living room earlier that the enemy moved toward the back of the house. Working better than planned, when the man in all black and Hayden split up, the orange dot was Hayden in the living room, but cast opposite, so it appeared as if an orange warrior was at the back corner of the house.

Something the orange man had learned on another job, this was mirror imaging at its best, and the invisible collaborator carried out the deception flawlessly from the safety and anonymity of a secret location. It didn't appear to him the seasoned enemy in black knew it could be done and it certainly wasn't something to be divulged, even before death.

Standing in the hallway, the man in orange saw the backside of a man dressed in black, wearing his blonde hair in a bun, and crouched behind the couch, keeping an eye on the front door.

"Knew you'd be back," the assailant said.

Startled, Hayden turned around and aimed the laser at the orange figure. A faint light from the dock entered the house through the opened door and living room window, casting a soft sheen on the intruder's orange outfit. The outline of the hood appeared as a ring of glowing embers compared to the black void it surrounded where a man's face should be, which appeared depthless and darker than the early morning itself.

"Go ahead, fire," the man said confidently. "You've never fired one. They handed it to you without any training."

Hayden stood and, as his body rose above the couch, a golden hue from the dock light outside surrounded him and all of the detail of his front shadowed over, leaving only a black silhouette for the man in orange to look at.

"At this distance, no problem," Hayden said.

"Where's the briefcase?"

"Sorry. I didn't pack for the trip."

"I don't blame you. The dead in this game don't wear

clothes. There's nothing to bury."

"True. The body without life is nothing."

"Then make your final act count. Tell me where the case is."

"My life has already been taken from me."

"Tell me," the man in the orange outfit said, "and I'll make it official."

Something seemed off to Hayden.

The orange man raised his hands in the air and said in a surprised voice, "You're not alone."

Oh, thank God, Hayden thought and snuck a peek over his shoulder. "About time you got here."

The assailant lowered his arm and fired the laser. A tingle vibrated Hayden's hand as if he held onto an electric wire. The laser in his hand illuminated into many colors and, seeing some of it dissipate, he threw it over the couch behind him and retreated to the floor behind the couch. In mid-air, the hand-held laser disintegrated and a multi-colored explosion occurred there in its place. As in Manhattan, nothing else in the house had been damaged.

While changing the setting on his laser, the orange warrior briskly walked up to Hayden, jabbed the tip of the laser against his forehead, and pressed it there.

"Try me, asshole!" the laser-holder said. "This does much worse. Lay your hands flat on the floor. Palms down."

Hayden abided and the man stepped on the back of his hands with his full weight.

"Now, tell me where the briefcase is and die," the man in control said. "Or don't and still die."

Hayden's eyes crossed, looking down the laser barrel. "I don't know," Hayden whispered.

The muscular man in orange grabbed the back of Hayden's head by the bun in his hair and pulled as the tip of the laser dented the skin on Hayden's forehead. "Your friend is dead because he couldn't help. Take a guess if you can't either?"

"I don't know!" Hayden screamed. "You fucking

hemorrhoid! I don't know."

While the man stood over Hayden, his hand relinquished Hayden's hair and a finger on his laser hand tapped the screen inlaid in his forearm, removing the laser briefly from Hayden's forehead. When he finished, the laser tip rammed into the bridge of Hayden's nose between his eyes.

Warm blood tickled the outside of Hayden's nose and collected on the mustache of his upper lip. Some relief came when the laser barrel left his nose, but new pain arrived when it struck the top of his head. Another unsuspecting blow banged down on his forehead and the bridge of his nose from the screened forearm swung down on him like a club, nearly knocking him out. Blood rushed freely from the contusion and uncomfortably clogged his nose.

"Look into the screen!" the brute barked.

Dazed and in pain, Hayden obeyed; his eyeballs rolled free in their sockets.

After a few seconds, the hard screen left Hayden's face and the man in orange checked the monitor. Nearly an impossibility, the tip of the laser barrel pushed harder and farther down on Hayden's head and the screen banged against his face in a glancing blow.

"Look, again!" the enforcer commanded. "Open wide and keep your eyeballs still. Show me how scared you are."

Hayden widened his eyes as far as he could in a stare and the screen beeped almost immediately.

The man checked his forearm and, dejected, hammered the butt of the laser down on Hayden's head and yelled, *"Fuck!"*

Orange soles on the bottom of his boots twisted the skin on the back of Hayden's hands and crunched some bones as he stepped off and moved away.

Even though the man turned his back toward him, Hayden sat still, letting his body be for a moment, hoping it would work out the pain.

The man's forearm with the screen dropped to his side and, when it did, Hayden noticed the word truth on the screen.

"Truth," Hayden said. "You know I'm telling the truth."

"I know," the man said. "Lie detector."

Gingerly as possible, Hayden lifted his right hand off the floor. He tried fooling himself it was stiff in a cast, but working to hold his hand still in restricted movement brought on pain anyway. Wincing, he said, "So, now what?"

"Why do people like you ask when you know?"

Hayden's fingers could only bend so far. Through pain, Hayden said, "I guess we're hoping for a different answer."

"Hope," the man wearing orange said in a low voice.

A flicker in the darkness and Hayden's eyes went to it. Truth had disappeared from the face of the screen embedded in the attacker's arm, replaced by numbers. The same numbers Hayden had seen on the orange assailant's screen when they were flying on the unusual aircraft. These, too, counted backward in a countdown and he knew the orange warrior in front of him would be no more once time ran out.

This was more than any payback Hayden could have laid on him, although some pain, breaks, and blood by his own hand sure would feel more satisfying. Doubtful his hands at the current moment could deliver what he sought, he would just have to live with the man blowing up to smithereens. Either way worked and the result would end the same. There was no use in getting caught up in technicalities. Death awaited the man in orange and justice would be served. Unless the man took Hayden with him.

"You're counting down," Hayden said as he stood. "Six minutes and change."

The man raised his forearm, looked, and let it fall. "They must have given me seven. I must have done a decent job. They give more time to those who have served well."

"If you served well, why kill you? Seems like you would be a good asset."

"It's what happens when we fail."

"Not getting the briefcase?"

The man's head nodded under the hood it was the reason.

"Under this system, wouldn't you run out of men?"

"You're on the losing side of this."

"Of what?"

"Yes. Of what?" the man said.

As the numbers ticked down, the man's muscular form relaxed under the orange material as if deflated. He pushed the couch upright, collected a cushion, placed it on the couch, and sat on it. The man seemed defeated, but also calm and at peace.

Under six minutes, now, Hayden said, "I can cut it out, chop it off, or something."

"Can't," the man said. "Any tampering and it defaults to zero and it blows. Besides, I'd only be a walking dead man. As you are."

"It just destroys you, right? Nothing else?"

"I'm afraid not."

"Then, I'm sorry. You have to get out of my house."

"Your house?" the man said.

Slowly, he raised his hands, as if he had all the time in the world, and removed his hood. Unveiling his true self in his final moments seemed to make the man reflective. Perhaps, he saw his life flashing before his eyes. Reflection had only moments to live, same as the man who reflected, and would show itself only for a brief time in vain, because the man's life was what it was, and there wouldn't be a chance for him to change, improve, or reconcile anything.

"What are you waiting for?" Hayden yelled. *"Go!"*

The man turned toward Hayden. A glint of hope twinkled in the midst of despair in the man's eyes, but then, the oblivion-vacant erased it and he answered, "My death."

"Leave! You don't have to do this," Hayden pleaded.

"It is a nice place. You like your neighbors?"

"Yeah, I do. So much so, I want you to leave. Jump in the water and swim away."

The time remaining ticked under five minutes. Behind

the windows to his soul, the man's mind raced, as happens in the final moments of life when the person knows how much time they have, and, in that time, death had deceptively moved so close, that it, now, sat next to the dying with its arm around the body.

"No," the man said flatly. "You should be going." A shocked kind of snicker winded out of him. "Funny. I was supposed to keep my mouth shut and take you with me." Ensuring his eyes met Hayden's, he said, "I don't have to kill you to know you're dead."

Just over four minutes remained and Hayden said, "But, my neighbors."

"I spared you. That should count for something."

"All of them for me! That doesn't make any sense."

"It's better to die doing one's duty than to fail again."

"But I'll be gone. Isn't that failing?"

"You don't understand. My mission changed when they started this," the man in orange said, as he raised his forearm—the countdown just above three minutes. "Sacrificed. Like the Lamb of God."

"Enjoy Paradise," Hayden said. "I plan on staying here for a bit."

As the man sat there, his eyes performed a slow blink and he said, "That's right. You are pardoned. Now, go, and sin no more."

With two and a half minutes to detonation, Hayden ran out of the house, yelling his fool head off. *"Wake up! Get out! Everybody out!"*

Adrenaline pumped through him and hid the pain in his body. His heavy feet banged the dock as he ran toward land.

"Come on! Get up! A bomb's going to go off! Let's go!"

Through the window of one of the homes, an upstairs light came on and a woman appeared, looking down at Hayden.

Seeing her, he yelled at her specifically, *"Your house is going to blow! Get everyone out!"*

She moved away from the window slower than she had

appeared.

In a different house, an older gentleman opened a second-floor window. "What the hell are you yelling about? You're waking…"

"Yes, I know," Hayden interrupted. "Someone inside my home has set a bomb to go off in less than two minutes. Maybe less. You've got to get everyone out."

"Well, where are the cops? The fire department? Didn't you call them?"

"No! Look! Time's running out. You're going to die if you don't listen to me."

"Alright. Alright," the man said as he waved a hand and closed the window, not in a rush.

Hayden moved on, yelling and screaming. He picked up a neighbor's shovel and banged it against houses, trash cans, whatever would make the loudest sound.

Thirty seconds—a minute, Hayden thought. He threw the shovel up against a neighboring house and, out of breath, bent over hands on knees. A sound diverted his attention toward the woods and he saw an orange dot appear out from the snow-covered trees. Another orange dot appeared, then another.

Hayden stood. *Thirty seconds*, he guessed and ran down his dock and back into his house. The man in orange sat in the middle of the couch with his eyes closed as if meditating. Hayden checked the time and there were twelve seconds left, less time than he had estimated. Messing around yelling to others, he easily could have entered the house just in time for it to blow. Turning in place and frantically looking around, it occurred to him he was going to die if he didn't move.

Eight seconds and a process of elimination sped through his mind. *Woods out. Car out. Help out. House out. The water.*

Six seconds left, he ran down the hall, through his bedroom, and onto the back dock. He started toward the water and then saw the masks and vests. He grabbed both sets and jumped into the water.

Orange figures in pursuit ran into the house in time to see their comrade, sitting on the couch with his eyes closed, and only two seconds left on the timer as he said, "It is finished."

Violently, the orange man exploded into fragments, which blew out from where he had sat with such force, the blast destroyed everything in its path, eating through the other orange warriors and the materials of the house as if a hoard of hungry locusts consumed everything in their path in time-lapsed speed.

In no time, the neighboring home beside Hayden's blew out and disintegrated, as did his neighbor's neighbors, and so on in succession, until that dock of floating homes and the flanking docks on both sides, running parallel, were no more. A rainbow of light within white smoke, resembling the Northern Lights, covered the decimated area in mercy with something beautiful.

While Hayden slipped into one of the vests and cleared his facemask for oxygen under water, debris slapped against the water above him and he knew he had to dive deeper. His only choice was to return to the sub—if he could find it.

CHAPTER **NINE**

How hard could it be, finding a sub one-hundred yards out from the dock? Not having a navigation system in his forearm, Hayden found it damn hard. In every direction, the murky water looked the same and visibility lessened from about a foot in front of his face near the surface to none as he dove deeper. He didn't want to ascend and raise his head above the water to gauge where he was, but he didn't have a choice. A land marker was necessary to try to locate the sub.

The top of his head peeked out of the water. At this moment, it occurred to him that his hair was blonde and wished it were dark again. Through the water beads on his facemask was Brown Island. Turning himself in the water, he saw what he didn't want to see. Within the clearing white smoke, a gap between surviving docks told him what he didn't want to know. Only remnants of the two docks, which had once flanked his, remained, slanted and clinging to the shoreline where they attached like clawing hands in desperation. A gentle moonlight reflected off the wet wood, creating a pale sheen after escaping death. Nothing remained of *his* dock. Even where it had once anchored to the land, there was nothing. All that wood and material had to go somewhere. There should have been more debris floating on the water, but there wasn't. Nor were there any screams or cries for help. Three docks of death, his own, and the two adjacent docks, and those who lived along them in floating homes were no more.

How he wished they might be away, visiting family or friends for the holidays. Perhaps that's why there was such a small response to his carrying-on. But some were home. He saw them peeking out. Probably too frightened to open their window or door. A lunatic loomed outside, don't let him in. The woman in the window. And the old man he had talked to. Hayden had been the deliverer of death, a message sent by the man in the hat, who sported a vacationing tan in the middle of winter—*Manhattan*.

Mentally, he envisioned a football field on the water and figured he might be a little long. His adrenaline may have had him swim a little faster than usual. If he swam toward shore, maybe another ten yards or so, he would probably be okay. Then, it was just a matter of diving the right depth and branching out until coming upon the sub. The only idea he had in trying to figure the right depth was to remember, approximately, how far he and the man in black had ascended until they were under the house. It wasn't perfect, but it would have to do.

This go around, Hayden found the submarine. Ran into it, actually, hitting one of the stubbed wings with his hand as he waded. The lights were on when he had exited the vessel and now they were off. Maybe like a car, they timed out, but he still didn't like it. Who knew what creatures had entered the sub and claimed it for habitat?

It didn't matter, because he needed the sub. While situating himself into his seat, breathing had grown laborious and he figured he had used most or all of the oxygen in the tank. If it hadn't had taken him so long to locate the sub, he would have been alright. Pleased to feel nothing under him as his behind touched the seat, he sat as best as one could in deep water. It occurred to him that maybe he should sit in the pilot seat, so he changed.

The controls in front of him were hard to see and acclimating himself took longer than he had hoped. The oxygen tanks needed changed. There was no way around it. Instead of disconnecting the mask from the tank in the other vest and attaching the tank to the mask on his face in hazy conditions, he held his breath and changed masks and vests. In a life or death situation, there was no use in being meticulous. Besides, he didn't know which was his originally anyway when he picked them off the back deck of his place.

Based on how long the last oxygen tank lasted, he guesstimated he had equally as long with this one. Which was? He didn't know. Other than short.

Not wasting any time, Hayden thought he remembered the control his pilot had used to open the domed windshields and took the gamble and tried it. At first, nothing seemed to happen. Then, without warning, the domed glass closed over him. The idea ignored before, it occurred to him he might have just entombed himself with water still trapped inside, but then reason kicked in that the same button would open them to get out. He hoped.

A good part of his space training had taken part under water, but that was many years ago. Although he had been in a pool since then, this depth and duration was another universe, and it was getting to him.

Hitting a bunch of buttons and levers to see what would happen awaited his future, but could be held off a little longer. Knowing what to do now never came, because he didn't have the knowledge. He wished now he had watched the man in black pilot the ship more closely instead of thinking about dying. Controls weren't labeled as they sometimes were in spacecrafts and even if they were, they were hard to see. Manuals wouldn't do any good in this wet environment. So now what?

In space, he would call mission control. Communication went black some time ago, like being on the dark side of the moon in the old days, and he didn't know if the pilot had done anything or if mother snake had handled it. Usually, maintaining communication ranked extremely high to mission success, so Hayden leaned that way and spoke into the mask.

"Mother snake, this is sea snake. Do you read?" Hayden said. "Mother snake, this is sea snake. Do you do read?"

Nothing, but he knew not to quit.

"This is sea snake. Come in."

Repetition was important in maintaining contact, so he repeated himself numerous times, hoping for the best. Just when he was about to go for broke and start hitting buttons, flipping switches, turning dials, and sliding levers, static crackled into his facemask.

"Sea snake, this is mother snake. We read you," a man's voice said.

"Roger that, mother snake," Hayden said, his astronaut experience kicking in as if he were in space rather than under water.

"What's your status, sea snake?"

"Lost my pilot," Hayden reported and he realized he never retrieved the blood he had collected from the skylight. "And I don't have the blood. I hate to be short about it, but I'm in the ship a hundred yards away from where my house used to be and short on oxygen with the cabin full of water. How do I get the water out? Over."

"Copy that. Mother will walk her young through it." More static, then the man said, "Ah, sea snake. It looks like there's an infestation of mongoose in your area, so I'm going to need you to read into what I'm saying. Copy?"

Saying little without saying anything would be coming Hayden's way and he knew it. His ears and mind were perked to survive. "Roger that. Sea snake's a fast learner."

"Mother says, before it gets too late, make sure you walk the canine. Don't wait or suffer a gruesome fate," the man said.

A bunch of words rhyming with eight had tipped Hayden that mother had spoken in numeronyms, elementary ones, but there were only so many controls on the panel of the ship. Ten rows and an almost equal number of columns were still a lot, especially unmarked and in dirty water.

Hayden tried remembering what mother had said, recalling late (L8), wait (W8), fate (F8), and canine (K9) came to him later. The four numeronyms were verified with mother without coming out and saying them.

"ABC—123, mother?" It was the best Hayden could come up with at the moment.

"Uh, roger that, sea snake. You know your alphabet."

In number order, Hayden carefully fingered the controls and located the first row. Needing the eighth row, he brushed his fingers lightly down the controls until he got there. His hand moved to the right, as he mentally followed the alphabet to *f*, and he flipped the switch. The control panel lit up, making it easier to see what was where in the dark water. Six more moves over to *l* and, when his finger flipped the switch, the inside lights in the cabin flickered then steadied on. On over to *w*, the columns ran out—there wasn't a *w*.

"Mother snake told sea snake waiting wasn't an option. Verify, over," Hayden said.

"Roger that, sea snake. Waiting not an option."

Down one to row nine and back one to *k*, Hayden flipped the switch and the outside lights flickered on. A tinge of orange through the water and two silhouettes looked down on him through the domed windows.

"Sea snake, mother's not pleased. You're walking the line and forgot the canine," the man's voice said.

Hayden knew what mother had meant. "Going back and getting him, but I have company outside." His fingers had gone straight down from L8 to L9 (line) instead of moving back one to K9 as he thought he had done. The oxygen in his last tank must be running out. Once he flipped the K9 switch, the submarine rumbled and, a few seconds later, the water inside began to recede. His own reflection and that of the inside of the cabin filled the domed glass, rendering it a mirror, hiding the orange divers behind the dark water outside.

Orange fists emerged out of the murky water and banged on the windshields before disappearing again. With that kind of effort, as long as he had oxygen, he could sit there for a long time and not be in any danger. It occurred to him then, the orange man that blew up his house hadn't acted in mercy, but in tactics—the orange people wanted him alive. That's why those outside had banged on the window instead of vaporizing him and the sub into oblivion. Perhaps, they wanted the submarine.

When the water receded to Hayden's nose, he tilted his head back so he was looking straight up and removed his mask. A desperate gasp sucked in air and he coughed because of the moisture.

"Hold on, mother's got you," the man said.

As Hayden faced up, two orange-masked faces appeared in the domed windshield above him.

With water still inside the cabin, the sub began to propel forward, taking the two divers outside by surprise. Their faces and bodies made a dull thud sound when they banged against the glass and, as the sub picked up speed, they disappeared somewhere in the dark water.

By this time, the water had receded down to Hayden's waist and he asked to make sure, "Mother has sea snake?"

"Mother has reclaimed her young," the man said into the ship with the water level dropping inside.

For a while, the two divers in orange swam behind the sub, but once all the water drained out of it and it navigated into deeper waters, the submarine left them in the backwash. The only thing now, they probably had a bead on him, figuring the sub headed for the ocean.

Hayden wondered if he would make it that far, or, instead, be hauntingly greeted by orange-costumed hellions and black-dressed devils in disguise somewhere around Deadman Island and Mummy Rocks, in what was sure to be one hell of a Halloween party.

Mother snake had decided not to take Hayden to the Halloween party. Rather than backtracking toward the ocean, she had remotely piloted the submarine to swim east toward Obstruction Island. Not another word came from mother snake and Hayden was at the mercy of the controller of the sub. Ignorance of his destination, if danger still followed, or what the plan was, if there was one, made him an unknowing prisoner in transport.

As the submarine approached Obstruction Island, it dove as deep as it could, picking up speed. The acceleration through the water surprised him and it had reached a point where the force against the front of his body was so great, it drove him back against his seat. Ripples waved through the skin on his face as the pressure increased against him. This was worse than launching into space, but for the life of him, he hadn't a clue how the tiny two-man sub could move that fast under water.

A quick, smooth swoop and Hayden's back bore all the push. The position felt familiar to his experiences inside a launched rocket ship and he knew he now faced the surface of the water, behind it, the sky, and behind it, outer space. Impossibly, the submarine picked up speed as it approached the surface. The water lightened in the domed windshields and, completely surprising him, the submarine broke through the water, out of the darkness and into the pre-morning light.

The submarine continued to ascend through the air and, based on his journeys into space, he wondered if a thruster had been responsible for moving the vessel that fast through the water and now higher into the atmosphere. A turn of the head for a quick peek out the window and the land and water below were shrinking. The craft slowed as if an engine died, peaked, and began to descend toward Earth.

"Oh, mother!" Hayden said allowed, hoping she would hear him.

The domed glass windows unsealed and started to slide open.

"Mother! Mother snake! I have a huge problem," Hayden yelled.

Remembering how this craft had descended out of the offbeat plane, he hoped the submarine out of its element would adapt to its new one, because he didn't know how to operate it. With the domed windshields fully receded, it didn't seem likely.

As the plane freefell out of the sky, Hayden yelled, *"May…day! May…day! Come…in, mother…snake!"*

The wind gust inside the cabin made it difficult to talk. *"May…"*

That was all Hayden could get out because he and his seat ejected out of the ship.

Sloping toward Earth as if in reentry, he could have thought about many things, but he thought of Ora. For a moment. The resolver in him had to give it a go before giving up. Which might be soon. The water below came at him awfully fast and him strapped into a seat not attached to a flying machine screamed surrender. The white flag dangled halfway out of his pocket.

This thing had to have a parachute, right? Sprout wings or something crazy like that. Just had to. Time was running out. Air, too. He could fall through the air, and water, but not at this height and velocity. Hitting the water would be like hitting the ground. And, then, his limp body would fall through the water. No wings sprouted out of the seat and, at this ever-decreasing height, a parachute wouldn't do him much good. His eyes closed and, mentally, he tossed the white flag, and checked out.

An unexplainable whoosh of wind encircled around him and startled him out of his ready-to-die slumber. His bugged eyes no longer saw the sky or on-coming water. Perhaps this was the afterlife and his death had been so painlessly quick that he wasn't aware it had happened.

His wind-irritated eyes focused and eternity resembled the inside of one of those offbeat penguin-looking planes. For sure it was because he had spent so much time in one. The peculiar flyer had sucked him out of the air as it had snatched him, Ora, and Kip off his back deck.

Reclamation was nothing like Hayden had ever experienced. Tough to say for an astronaut, who had experienced reentry on many occasions, but it was true.

Inside the same parallelogram room, buried inside an undisclosed canyon, Hayden paced the floor with a clean white bandage encircling his noggin—under the chin, over his ears, and holding an ice pack on top of his head—a bandaged nose, and wrapped hands, one of them holding a plate of de-leaved strawberries. He ate them while giving Kip an earful, who sat leaning in one of those brown leather chairs with his elbow on the desk and two fingers on his temple.

"Your elite, trained man died," Hayden said and interjected himself in a lower voice, "I don't know where his bottom-half went." He continued. "I didn't get the blood out of my coat pocket. All I got was my own blood on me." Hayden brought his dressed face close to Kip's and raised his mummied right hand. "Look at me. Every time, I get injured. You're trying to kill me. Don't deny it."

Eyeing Kip, Hayden stood and took a bite of a strawberry. Only when it was finished did he walk away.

In the same position, Kip watched.

"Speaking of death," Hayden went on, "After getting my ass kicked, the suicidal carrot told me to *'Go and sin no more'* then blew up my house and all of my neighbor's houses on three decks. *Three decks, Kip!* This wasn't like Manhattan. This was murderous havoc. You wanted blood, now you have plenty of it. Including mine."

Hayden's bandaged face moved in close to Kip. "Are you hearing me?" he asked.

"I thought you were a fruit guy," Kip said.

Hayden's face contorted as he said, *"What?"*

"You said carrot instead of any number of orange varieties, or peach, or apricot, or cantaloupe."

"So?"

"Carrots aren't a fruit, they're a vegetable. I'm going to have them reexamine your head again."

As if Kip never went down that road, Hayden paced again and moved on. "Then, I get spewed out of the sub or plane or whatever it is and my seat is holding onto me like a drowning victim and I'm falling through the air, Kip, toward the ground at a," he accentuated each word, *"very … high … speed!"*

Kip's fingers came off his temple. "Well, you got out of there, didn't you? That should count for something."

Hayden stopped pacing and stared at Kip. The plate with only a couple of strawberries remaining and strawberry leaves dropped toward the floor as Hayden ran over to Kip and picked him up out of the chair by the lapels of his jacket.

"How about I spill some of your blood, huh?" Hayden said, his face grimacing from anger and the pain in his hands. "Or maybe it was your blood on my skylight. Watching Ora and me. You sick pervert. And you wanted it back so you could destroy the evidence." He pushed Kip back into his seat.

Re-straightening his jacket, Kip said, "So, there were a few setbacks. That happens in this business."

"I'm not trained for this," Hayden said. "Hell, I'm not even in shape for this."

"What do you mean? You've had extreme altitude testing. Underwater training. Survival skills. Physical tests, not to mention mental and emotional. You're even instructed how to kill if a fellow astronaut loses it up there." Kip's shoulders slouched. "Listen. You were born for this. Same as me. For all the same reasons I was brought on."

Hayden shook his head. "And a lot of good the makeover did. They still knew who I was."

"I figured as much."

"Wait a minute. You figured as much?"

"They have your DNA code mapped. There's no hiding now."

Hayden's bandaged head bobbed up and down. "No hiding now. Really. That's comforting."

"Mr. Stanton," the same pleasant woman's voice as before said into the room. "Would you like to see the news coverage of the explosion on Friday Harbor?"

"Please. Not all of it, though" Kip said. "There's so much news, I'd grow old sitting here watching every take of it. Can it be sorted or something?"

"Already have," the woman said, sounding pleased with herself. "All redundancies have been removed."

Kip sighed. "Alright, then. Let's see what kind of damage control we need to employ."

He and Hayden looked at each other.

Kip tapped the leather chair beside him. "Come on. Take a seat."

As before, a narrow beam of light from the screen lodged in Kip's forearm widened into a large projected hologram screen, hanging in mid-air. A newswoman started the string of news coverage.

"The scene behind me is beautiful. But Friday Harbor, a small community of only a couple thousand people on San Juan Island in Washington State, is in a cold state of shock. Over here," (the camera's focus moved off her and onto the embankment) *"used to be three docks, each lined with floating homes, a trending choice of residency here in the United States. But, as you can see, they are no longer there. A horrible explosion occurred this morning on most likely the middle dock, destroying the other two with it."*

Every television and radio broadcast that had covered the tragic event had been spliced to create a unified, coherent report minus the redundancies. Kip and Hayden watched; Kip's eyes glued, Hayden would have looked away, but he couldn't, because even though he was there, he hadn't seen everything that had transpired.

All of a sudden, there was no picture or sound.

"That it?" Kip asked in the air.

"Yes, Mr. Stanton," the smooth female voice said.

"Would you like to watch it again?"

Kip began to say that he did until he saw Hayden shaking his head no.

"No, that'll be all," Kip said.

"Now what?" Hayden asked.

"That'll be all for you, too. It's over. For you anyway. We'll fight the good fight on your behalf."

Hayden stood out of his chair. "They ruined my life. Blew up my house. Took all I owned away from me. As much as I want to, I just can't walk away from this."

Kip stood; his nose mere inches from Hayden's. "They know who you are, Hayden. Down to your DNA. They'll find you, try to get you to tell them where the briefcase is, and, either way, kill you. I'm trying to protect you by keeping you in the dark. Listen to that small voice that wants to walk away. It's right. It's the right thing to do."

"Walk away to where, huh?" Hayden's hands rose then flopped against the sides of his body, stinging his hands.

"I'm working on it." Kip turned away from Hayden, walked, and then turned and faced him again. "First things first. We have to get you out of dodge."

"Where? You just said they'd find me."

"I'm working on it. It'll only be temporary until we figure this out. You still have cash, right? Savings? Retirement?"

"Yeah. What about everything I've lost?"

Kip's hand waved. "Don't worry about that. You'll get everything back and more. Eventually. I promise."

"Eventually?"

"For now, we'll have to use what funds you have. We can pitch in a couple of bucks. A sloth could learn how to use an ATM faster than our reimbursement department can process what they do all the time—reimburse. I'm still waiting on funds from when I joined this outfit."

"Forced retirement. Far from the way I wanted to go out."

"Going out's much better than going under. Besides, if NASA wants you, they'll find you."

"Fine. Whatever."

"Now, let's see. Germany's out," Kip said.

Hayden looked confused.

"The whole, your bullet found in their President's melon thing."

"Oh, that," Hayden said.

"Yeah, that. Right after my plane crash, I was called into a meeting to be told that before they made sure I was okay."

Thin lips pursed on Hayden's face and his eyebrows raised.

"I guess you're right," Kip said. "A plane crash or discussing things to death really aren't that different, are they? Which reminds me, you can't go to Niger either."

"*Niger*. I would never go…"

"Their president was assassinated. Found dead with your bullet in his head."

Hayden's eyes rolled and his head followed. "Another one? Who can be doing this?"

"I'm working on it."

"Well, get some help and work a little faster. Someone's setting me up."

"Okay," Kip said. "I got your back."

Hayden cupped his hands on his hips and looked down at the floor, shaking his head.

"*Now,*" Kip said. "It's always about the *now*. This is serious enough you should get out of the country. Someplace remote. Have you enter NASA's version of a witness protection program. That'll give us more funding so you don't have to touch much of yours."

"You're sure concerned about money matters. I have a feeling more than my life."

"How can you think that way? I'm trying to save you. And, make sure we exist going forward."

"Well, why can't I just stay here?"

"Every second you're here, you're a risk to our existence. I have no choice. You have to wait it out someplace else. We'll come up with a plan. Together."

"Exactly. *Together*," Hayden stressed. "Something better than your plan in having me return to my place."

Now, it was Kip's turn and his eyebrows raised and his lips pursed because of the comment.

"Where's Ora?" Hayden asked. "I want to see her."

"Hayden, I don't think…"

"I don't care what you think. *Now!*"

Kip's eyes locked onto Hayden's. "You know she can't go with you, right? Not now, anyway."

"I know. That's why I have to see her."

"Fine," then louder, Kip said, "Please have Ora Frush escorted to the canyon room."

"Right away, Mr. Stanton," the woman's voice said into the room.

In a short time, Ora entered the parallelogram room and removed her helmet. Hayden remained seated in the fifth brown leather chair among the row of twelve. It took Kip going over to her and having her come to sit beside Hayden. Hesitation and estranged avoidance exhibited in her every move.

"I'll leave you two alone," Kip said and reluctantly left the room.

"I'm surprised you came," Hayden said.

Ora's face twisted as she said, "*Surprised?* The men have spoken. I had to come. Or maybe you missed my escort."

"I saw."

Hayden reached for her hands. Uncertainty made them tremble in his as he held them. He may as well have been a stranger.

"Ora," he began. "Before I leave. I have to know something."

"Well, so do I," she said with attitude.

"That's fair. But I go first."

"Someone has to go first. It might as well be the man."

Hayden shook his head that wasn't the case, but not wanting to waste any more time arguing who should go first, he asked, "I have thought about this many times and I'm tired of asking myself because I don't know the answer. I should have asked you a long time ago. Did Kip ever, ugh, *help* you with your Astrophobia on any missions I wasn't on?"

Glossy eyes stared back at him. She'd only looked at him one other time like that and they didn't see each other for a while afterward. It always amazed him how two nearly inch-round eyeballs could cast all the feeling behind them through and into someone else's eyes. Especially unconditional love and, of course, pain, which, now, reached out through Ora's eyes, into his, and down to his heart, where pain begot more pain, with one eye's glare squeezing and seizing his heart, while the other, simultaneously, seemed to slice his heart from the inside out. Looks could kill and, like trained assassins, they were doing a thorough job.

"By *help*, you mean did I sleep with him?" she asked.

A slow blink of his eyes told her that's what he meant.

Her eyes relaxed and love joined the assault. "Yes. Once."

The breath held in Hayden's lungs blurted out of him and emotions caused all kinds of unwanted reactions in his body. His chest collapsed. Spittle came out of his mouth. Clear snot collected in his nose. His eyelids reddened around glassy eyeballs. When love and pain joined forces, there wasn't anything more lethal in this world. This couldn't be happening. But it was.

"It happened longer ago than you would think," she continued. "It was one of my first missions and I was really struggling. I needed to escape or probably die. There wasn't any alcohol. I thought about raiding some drugs from the stability kit but didn't. He was there, Hayden. That was all. To be honest, it could have been any man aboard the ship. This was all before you and I ever got going. He always held onto it, like there might be a chance it could grow into something more. It didn't. It couldn't. Because you came along and that was that."

"Sounds a lot like how *we* met," he said. "I was a remedy, that was all."

"*No! Stop!* My turn. Same question back at you."

"No. I never slept with Kip."

"That doesn't count. You know what I mean. Female Astronauts. And all of those young office girls on the ground. *Hi, Mr. Bakley*, or, *Hi, Hayden*. Pathetic."

"Yeah. And Kip isn't?"

"Yeah, what? A lot of them?"

"Yeah," Hayden whispered.

"While we were together?"

"Between us being on and off. I thought you and Kip were … That's three by the way."

"Ask away," Ora said.

"Was there anybody else?" Hayden asked.

"No. Not even in between our breaks. There was this one guy once I came close to … but I spent the night alone. You know I went to your place for you, right. Only you. To spend the holidays with and see if …"

She choked up.

"What?" he asked.

"If you were the one or not," she said.

"And?"

"We're even now," she said, keeping score. "I don't know. I honestly don't."

"I figured. After you sliced my hand up." Hayden raised the hand she had cut with the scissors, but it was bandaged because of the fractures.

"I don't know what you did or didn't do…"

"Like chopping up people with my tomahawk? Traveling all over the world and shooting presidents in the head? That kind of stuff?"

"I know what I want to believe. You're one up. So, is this goodbye?"

"I guess for a little while." His fractured hands squeezed hers the best they could. "If I knew I wouldn't place you in danger … I wish you could come with me."

"Maybe taking me with you would place you in more danger."

His head hung. "We're even. You want to stop?"

"I wouldn't say we're even. I would say, don't tell me where you're going. You don't need to keep an eye out for another pursuer."

"I don't know where I'm going, yet. But, I'm sure if you really wanted to know, Kip would not only tell you but take you there himself and hand you a weapon."

Reclined in his black leather chair with his ankles crossed and feet on his desk, Kip listened, having the conversation piped into his office.

CHAPTER **TEN**

Eight hundred feet in the air and seated at a table, Hayden stared out a window of a rotating restaurant, having a bird's-eye view of Sydney, Australia. Clear skies, seventy-six degrees, and a view of water in three directions, he couldn't help but think maybe he should have come here for the holidays instead of Manhattan. Maybe his life would be intact instead of being in danger. It had all of the makings of a nice vacation, the only problem was, it wasn't.

Before arriving in Australia, his two-week expedited orientation into NASA's equivalent of a witness protection program hadn't gone well. Everyone agreed he had a hard time adjusting. Living inside the canyon in close quarters to Ora and Kip certainly contributed to his inability to cope; mainly things hadn't gone as he had hoped with Ora. Playing the game of wearing that damned helmet every time he left a room and everyone being so careful and secretive had grated on his nerves. Not enough, apparently, because he figured at some point, there wouldn't be any nerves left and, therefore, no feeling.

To his utter disappointment, feelings remained. The last thing he wanted to do was deal with them, let alone live with them. Assisting Kip in working the case ended up being a constant reminder of how his life had changed in just a few days. But the most difficult part was he couldn't accept all that had happened to him.

No one at the canyon blamed him. Pride filled the canyon just as real as rooms, things, people, and the dirt and rock itself. Few things could humble these people. In their line of business, it had to be so. Thick skin was a requirement.

Hayden was intelligent, tough, and normally adaptable, but this many things out of sorts for a guy who usually had all of his skivvies folded just so from carefully packing for so many space trips just couldn't handle seeing them out of the drawer where they belonged, unfolded, and lying across America, coast to coast, like dirty laundry for all to see. It felt that way, when, really, only a minuscule number of people knew he existed. Fewer, yet, knew the true meaning behind what had happened. Still, even though he knew it wasn't true, everyone else's life seemed to be calm and in order compared to his.

Now, a trail of Hayden's dirty laundry went across the ocean to Sydney, Australia. He hoped the trail wasn't as obvious to the orange warriors as it was to him.

Give Kip and his unseen team credit. The demographics in Sydney were perfect to hide Hayden for a while. More Americans were migrating *Down Under* these days and Hayden's cover story contained many of the reasons why so many were doing so. Even renting an apartment rather than buying was a nice touch. It reduced the number of times his new name appeared in documents.

The plan was for no contact with Kip for six months and no job to avoid further documentation. Passports and the like couldn't be avoided, but at least they all contained his cover name. Oh, how he wanted to use Kip Stanton as his alias. A delicate balance between maintaining a low profile, mixing it up a little by getting out among the populace, don't get into trouble, and above all else, avoid the outback had been suggested to him. Everything would be paid in cash, including this meal, which he did.

Hayden understood why he was in the witness protection program, for he had witnessed something otherworldly. He tried thinking back through his life and wondered why he had never seen lasers, the atomizing of a man, and bombs that destroy only what they want destroyed, leaving everything else in their path intact. The world, dangerous as it was, grew more dangerous and he realized just how little he and the general public knew of the affairs happening in the world.

Protection was a different matter. Due to his shaky orientation, some person, or persons, above Kip's paygrade, had decided he would never meet or know those who protected him. Knowing Hayden, they figured if he had spotted one of them, he would approach them and demand answers. Not only could this blow the guardian's identity, Hayden might find out information he shouldn't know and do something foolish like taking matters into his own hands or not be able to handle how many attempts on his life had failed because his life preservers took care of it without his knowledge.

As far as the program, he would have to wait and see if it worked or not. Absolutely binary, if he lived it worked, if not it didn't.

As he rode the elevator down, dots on a monitor showed him his exact location in the tower. On the ground floor, he exited the elevator and headed toward the parking garage where he had parked his car. It was only a block away, but with temperatures here much warmer than in Washington State this time of year, Australia's early evening sun toasted him just enough that tiny sweat beads broke out on his skin. As did goose pimples, because he sensed someone was following him. Bay and river breezes cooled him and dried any perspiration, but the pimples remained in his heightened awareness.

Opening his car door, he paused and looked around. Only a couple exiting a car and closing their doors were in view. Their laughter turned into concern and they both got back into the car. For a moment, the un-started car remained parked, so Hayden waited. The car started, backed out, and began its descent down the garage, presumably to the exit.

It didn't mean he was alone. Anyone tailing him could have hidden in or behind vehicles, columns, or in the shadows. If they wanted him, they could have had him. He stood there long enough.

Hayden peeked into the back seat and, all clear, he got in, and started the car, figuring if it was going to blow, it would be too late to care, and the program failed. The car started without incident and the program, still alive, as was he, had a chance to succeed. Navigating down the parking garage, he was happy the brakes worked—at this speed, anyway. Who knew if somehow speed regulated a failure? Thankfully, his speed would remain under highway speeds through downtown Sydney to his hotel.

As he drove inland away from the water, he wondered if his life would be lived this way in pent-up paranoia. The hotel where he had been parking appeared up ahead. It wasn't where he was staying. His hotel sat behind this one and they shared the underground parking. Kip and his crew nailed it. The more confusion, the better. Even the hotels were different. The one above the parking was a hotel in its truest sense. Where Hayden had been staying was actually an apartment hotel. This gave him access to all the comforts of an apartment, including a fully equipped kitchen, which he hadn't used to cook anything yet, laundry, and twenty-four-hour room service. The room had been booked on an extended-stay basis without leaving a contract trail and he could check out whenever he wished.

Entering his apartment, he didn't want to be there, but locked and bolted the door behind him. A white-collar prison laid before him. The décor wasn't his taste, but maybe it's best to say if he had one it wouldn't be this. The floor-to-ceiling window-wall reminded him of home, but the lights of downtown Sydney on the other side reminded him of Manhattan.

As he walked farther into the open-spaced room, he slipped out of his shoes and let them lie there, let his jacket slide off him onto the floor, untied his necktie and let it fall like a ribbon to the floor, unbuttoned the top button of his shirt, and pulled the belt out from the loops in his pants; the buckle dropped to the rug like a bobber weighting down a fishing line. A trail of clothes laid behind him as if he had an affair with himself.

Living a life of purely existing wasn't the norm in today's globally-connected world and, quite frankly, hard to do. When time applied its pressure during life's busy times, the argument was always there wasn't enough time. Now, there was too much time. Each passing second ticked in his head. However, a resolver could fix anything and he would. He already knew how.

A chance of a lifetime lay before him, no matter how long it might last, and his intelligence wouldn't allow him to miss it. With time to pursue other interests, now was the time to feed his inquisitive nature. And with any luck, the knowledge and know-how gained just might fill any holes in his being and he would become fulfilled and complete.

Since Hayden moved Down Under, mental pep talks in the evening had become the norm. And as usual, before he began his quest, he would settle for existing a little longer. Near the window-wall, a small table made out of a sturdy plastic material had more purpose than he did, a very important purpose: to hold a brandy glass and a wooden tilting pouring stand, which also had a purpose in housing a bottle of Australian brandy that had aged nearly as long as he has been alive. He poured himself some brandy and sank into an uncomfortable black leather chair he had moved closer to the window the first night he arrived so he could look out over Sydney. The chair would become comfortable soon enough.

With the lights off, a gradual luxurious transition and

transposition occurred, where, as the apartment darkened around him in his chair, the city below speckled with light. Previous nights, the moon had added its own coloring on the structures and water below, but not tonight.

Still, the backdrop suited to share a drink and talk with Sydney, who knew the man who wore a hat and had a tan from Manhattan. Sydney's tan was darker, but he had the benefit of more beaches. Their conversations had run the gamut of possible things to discuss, but Hayden's situation had come up the most.

This evening, they listed the holes in Hayden's life and named them as one names hurricanes, stars, or black holes. Before they went any farther, they had to decide on which name to use for the naming. Should they use Hayden, his real name, or his new alias name, Darrick Cardull, which Hayden had only grown to know because of making reservations and dealing with the hotel staff? Otherwise, he doesn't talk to anybody.

Cardull. He knew Kip had something to do with coming up with that name. His previous alias, Bo Arden, hadn't lived very long and he would have preferred that over Cardull, but Kip's people came up with a new one just in case Bo Arden may have been compromised. Doubtful the short time he had it, but anything was possible. Hayden argued for using Kip Stanton, but Sydney wouldn't allow it, reasoning Hayden wasn't Kip, nor were the holes they listed. When he asked Sydney if that meant Kip's life was more complete, Sydney just stared back at him.

After some spirited discussion, they settled on using his birth name. The first black hole in Hayden's life was losing Ora, designated Hayden1. The fact he would never launch into space again became Hayden2. In disagreement, they stopped there for a while and argued which one of these two should be first. At the end of the discussion, Hayden didn't quite know himself.

Many hours had passed. As he sat there in the dark, about to pour himself another brandy, the bottle in his hand felt lighter. Sure enough, night's light coming in through the window-wall glazed nearly the top half of the bottle's clear glass while the brandy in the bottom half blended in with the dark room. It had occurred to him the animation in the window, seemingly floating over Sydney, was his own reflection and that he had been arguing with himself the entire time.

People do it all the time, the unspoken conversations of the mind, so concern over his mental capacities and overall wellbeing at this point would be premature. With that settled, his quest for life and experience would start tomorrow with a ferry ride to Manley Wharf to spend the day, eat, and, admittedly, drink a little. Planning ahead, perhaps the next day, he would visit Cockatoo Island, and so on, until he rode every ferry route out of Sydney. That should keep him busy for the next couple of months or longer.

Early afternoon, after sleeping in, Hayden had purposefully sat outside near the center of the ferryboat, heading for Manley Wharf, to curb from getting sick. With the Sydney Opera House and its distinctive multiple quarter-circled top only minutes behind, the first humpback swell caused the ferryboat to rise and fall. After last night's drinking and this morning's breakfast, he second-guessed his decision on taking the ferry ride. Drinking came off the list of things to do while visiting the wharf. Lemon water would have to do until he returned to his room.

Returning to the room seemed like a good idea. He would have to ride it out, of course, but he could reach the wharf, catch a ferry back, and call it a day. Besides, what's one more day of slothfulness and gluttony before truly living again?

Waves, this early in the trip, weren't a good sign and he wondered what awaited the ferry when it hit the open water of the harbor. Continuous swells would be bad for his head and stomach. It would be equivalent to driving a car over a series of speed bumps.

White sailboats contrasted against the blue water. In the distance, multicolored structures, built close to one another, covered a small hill of land as if a knitted quilt blanketed a protruding stomach. Wavy water stretched farther out to gray rocky cliffs, which supported lush green land as gray and white clouds stained an otherwise blue sky above.

The ferry approached Pinchgut Island. Hayden only knew it from studying an area map in his room before he left. *Pinchgut*—how timely. That's how his gut felt—pinched. Not by two little fingers, no his whole stomach felt squeezed. Yet, determined to make the best of his new life, he stood out of his seat and cut through the cabin of enclosed seating with large windows to get a better view of Fort Denison. Outside once more on the other side of the ship, he sat down, facing the fort. He would have taken some pictures, but he wasn't to give himself away as a tourist by doing such things—as if locals never snapped pictures. His memory would have to do and, if he forgot, he could always go online and view pictures and videos there.

The old fort gave Sydney Harbor an Alcatraz Island in San Francisco Bay kind of feel, only on a much smaller scale. Still, it was worth the look. A chilly morning on the water, he could have sat inside and still had a nice view of Denison, while dousing the smell, but the cool air felt good on his nearly healed face.

A gasp of surprise came from those outside near the back of the ferry. Hayden turned to see what initiated the commotion. People who were sitting, stood, and moved inside. Those standing near the railing backed away. Some went inside, but many moved to the far end of the ferry. To Hayden's surprise, an arm reached up from the side of the boat and grabbed a railing. A second arm appeared. They were orange.

Hayden stood and stared, too shocked to move.

A man, dressed in the same orange outfit as the divers who had chased him in the tiny sub, appeared behind the railing and looked around. When he faced Hayden's direction, Hayden turned away, and, keeping his face toward the deck, moved toward the front of the ferryboat. Not seeing a hook on the railing, a dangling rope, or anything, he wanted to know how the man had climbed the side of the boat and if there were more, but he had to choose between satisfying his curiosity and being hurt again or possibly killed, or let his curiosity die. Curiosity died a swift death and he no longer cared how the man had boarded.

With Hayden's back turned on his way to the front of the ship, he missed everything going on behind him. Rounding the corner of the cabin at the front of the ship, he stopped and peeked around. There was no sign of the man in orange. The large passenger windows, running the entire cabin, came in handy to peek through, until people inside backed into them, apparently staying out of the questionable man's way.

There was no way Hayden was going in there. A flurry of screams erupted, and then eerie silence, followed by more screams and then silence. He tried peeking in through the windows, but for those who couldn't make it to a door, hugging the windows seemed to be the last resort. It would have been helpful to see what was happening, but just as long as it wasn't happening to him, everything was good.

Hayden crossed the front of the ferry and peeked around the corner. Nothing happened there. Then, screams erupted through the windows from inside the cabin and a woman barged through the side door onto the outside deck. A briefcase handle secured in her grip, she continued toward the railing. Hayden's eyes bugged. The briefcase appeared to be the same one that flew through his car window in Manhattan.

The orange man pushed both glass doors open and briskly caught up to her. Orange-gloved hands grabbed the back material of her clothing, stopping her from climbing over the railing. He yanked her back and she stumbled in her high heels onto the deck; her hand clutching the briefcase handle. In a purely dominating fashion, he walked over to where she lay and stood over her, apparently not concerned about her high heels and his vulnerably-exposed crotch.

Decision time bum-rushed Hayden to make one. Does he risk himself to help her in exchange for answers or does he lay low as planned?

The man took his eyes off the woman underneath him to observe everyone staring at him, mostly through the cabin windows. As his eyes scanned, passenger's eyes turned away like weaker animals not wanting to make eye contact to challenge. This seemed to please him, as he relished in the power.

Witnessing this, Hayden figured the guy wouldn't waste her right in front of so many witnesses. Then again, how could he be found when no one knew who he was or what he looked like underneath the orange mask covering his entire head?

The assailant must have understood this, too, and without hesitation, he pulled a laser out from somewhere of the skintight orange suit and pointed it down at her.

"He's got a gun!" a couple of people yelled in their own way.

Apparently set to where he needed it, the laser fired and an orange beam extended out of it and reached her forearm. People screamed, fainted, and reacted as any hysterical person might seeing that. Sparks flew in and around her forearm as if being welded and Hayden knew it had to be from a screen or metal inside her forearm. In only a few seconds, the laser beam had severed the forearm from her body; the briefcase handle still gripped by the hand.

Winces of pain expressed on the woman's face and then toughness set in when she gritted her teeth, unwilling to give him the satisfaction. Arrogance slowed the man in orange, who took his time using an orange-booted foot to slide the case away from her—her hand and forearm followed. The distance was too far for Hayden to make a run at the case and get around the back corner of the ship before being lasered down, which would have been this guy's first instinct.

While Hayden thought, the man quickly changed the setting on his laser, pointed it down at the woman lying underneath him, and fired. This time, the beam entered her chest. Witnesses reacted.

Where the laser had hit, blotches of her clothes and chest appeared invisible within what had remained. Chunks of flesh and remnants of clothes seemed to hover in mid-air. More of her disintegrated, gradually erasing from existence, until she disappeared. Only her severed forearm and its hand, still gripping the handle of the briefcase, remained.

Decision time had run out on Hayden and he had to live with standing by and doing nothing. Not alone, so did everyone else aboard the ferry. No question, if he went for the case, the killer would vaporize him. The only decision now was to revert to the original plan of laying low and not drawing attention to himself.

The man in orange toyed with the passengers by turning at the waist and pointing the laser in their direction. Screams, wails, and supplications erupted from each pocket of people at whom the laser pointed. The laser returned somehow, somewhere into his form-fitting suit. No one chanced challenging him and he moved freely and unthreatened as if he knew it, grabbing the briefcase and forearm off the deck and casually walking into the enclosed cabin.

Looking through the windows, Hayden crossed the front of the ship to the other side and peeked around the corner. No sign of the orange man yet, then the glass doors opened and he appeared. It was easy to imagine him milking the trip through the inferior crowd inside the cabin. Nonchalantly, the orange figure returned to the rear side of the ferry where he had first appeared, tossed the briefcase and forearm into the harbor, climbed over the railing, and dove headfirst into the water.

By the time Hayden ran to the back of the ship and

searched the water, there was no sign of the orange pirate or the loot.

As the ferryboat circled Pinchgut Island to return to Sydney because of the incident, Hayden studied the island, looking for any sign of orange, thinking he must have come from there to board the ferry. There was no sign of him.

Once the ferry docked at Circular Quay, all passengers and crew were escorted to the Overseas Passenger Terminal for questioning. The hours passed and the number of people dwindled, as did Hayden's patience. Finally, they called for him and escorted him to a room. Only the facts of what he saw were reported, talking through his eyes, and avoiding any insight that might spur more questions or even suspicion. When they finally let him go, he went back to his apartment and had a brandy.

The plan called for no contact with Kip for six months. Keeping that promise would be easy because Hayden had no clue how to get a hold of him. His old cell phone that had Kip's personal contact information had been taken from him and they didn't give him a new one to avoid being tracked.

Ora's home phone number escaped him entirely. Not that he used it much, nor could she probably remember his home number either. If either of them needed to get a hold of each other, all the information had been stored in each other's cell phones. On the go, as they were, cell phones were how they stayed in touch. It was a risk against established protocol, but with a few brandies in him, he dialed Ora's cell phone number from memory.

It rang without an answer, then, an annoying beep, and then a recorded voice said, "We're sorry. You have reached a number that has been disconnected or no longer in service..." It may or may not have been the right number. He hung up.

The only choice now was to ride it out and wait until Kip contacted him. With what had happened on the ferry, it seemed reasonable that Kip might reach out sooner than later. But with Kip, who knew? There was only one thing Hayden could do now—drink the rest of the brandy.

The next morning, Hayden didn't know what to do. Yesterday's attack on the ferryboat had squashed his plans of riding every ferry out of Sydney. The plan was tentative, of course, but still a plan.

Australia's morning sun, coming into the room through the windows, told him he should get out of bed. However, was there any better way of laying low than lying in bed all day? The only problem was the tired room and apartment had sickened his head a little. He knew that now. Staring at the ceiling would be like a vampire staring at the back of his own eyelids as he slept the day away, or the lid of the coffin if he actually slept with his eyes open.

As far as an agenda for the day, only one item truly needed done and couldn't wait and that was requesting another bottle of that fine Australian brandy for the room. Getting himself cleaned up would waste some time, but not a must. Eating would chew more time away, especially, if he ate three meals and milked each one. Maybe a few snacks of fruit throughout the day. Pathetic, existing like this.

Gumption to stay committed to living a new life and take advantage of the downtime could show its perky little head anytime. While Hayden was in the shower, it did and energized him to try something new today.

Standing outside the Sydney Opera House, Hayden perspired in his tuxedo. He was one of the few people who had dressed up for a nice meal and a show. The big inspiration that hit him in the shower this morning was to buy one of those packaged combos for the Opera House that had a tour, a meal, and a show. Climbing stairs and moving around on the tour earlier had made him perspire, so laundry and dry-cleaning awaited the worn-in tuxedo. The nice thing was the hotel would handle it for him.

Compliments of the witness protection program's

budget, Hayden splurged on a box seat, hoping some of his expenses would cross Kip's desk. He could hear him now, complaining about it. Purchasing a single ticket made it easier to obtain a balcony seat. There were only two seats next to each other left, so he selected one of them before they were gone.

The row had three seats; his was the middle. The view of the stage from his seat was fine. Until this morning's tour, he never knew there were numerous performance spaces within the Opera House and now understood why there were so many quarter-circled roofs in the design of the building.

As he thought about comfort and space, the seat to his right, nearest the walkway, would hold the body of the purchaser soon. The one on his left still might be open, he never checked. Later in the program, if no one sat there, he planned to move into that seat so there would be a seat between.

Just as he settled the plan in his mind, a beautiful woman entered the entrance of the balcony and made her way to the end of Hayden's row.

"I'm pretty sure that's my seat along the wall," she said.

All he could do was stare. Her beauty apprehended him. Green eyes on clean whites spellbound him. Crisp facial features contrasted against her light fair skin. A thin nose went to thick rosy lips that glistened, probably from a gloss rather than lipstick. Dark auburn hair framed her face and clothed her shoulders, which, otherwise, would have been uncovered in an open-shouldered black evening gown that hung on her perfectly to the floor. Long black dress gloves reached above her elbows. Sparkling diamonds around her neck and wrist contrasted against the black she was wearing. Rendered a complete buffoon, he sat at the edge of his seat, staring.

Her dark eyebrows raised and her mouth opened. "My seat."

Her voice and mannerisms had him bewitched. Ineptly,

he stood and moved into the walkway to let her through. She didn't leave much room for him and smiled when they brushed against each other.

"Sorry, I ... *uh*, took the tour this morning in this and have been in it all day," he explained, figuring if he could smell himself, so could she. In space, he learned to live with it. On Earth, maybe he should have thought about sitting beside others in tight quarters and done something about it.

Elegantly, she entered the row and sat in her seat.

"Excuse me, I'll be right back," he said.

Hayden found the nearest restroom. Inside, he had hoped there would be an attendant with cologne, but there wasn't, so he tried cleaning himself up a little. How embarrassing it would be to have those around him smell him and either get up and leave, say something, or have him escorted out. It wouldn't surprise him if the beauty would be gone when he got back.

As Hayden came out of the bathroom, a large squared-off man bumped into him and nearly knocked him over. Hayden wasn't a small guy himself, so it took a low-center-of-gravity to do it. The man stared-down Hayden for a moment and then went into the restroom.

As Hayden entered the balcony, more people were in their seats, waiting for the show to begin. To his surprise, the beautiful young woman was still in her seat.

Watching him sit, she smiled at him.

Noticing, he smiled back and said, "I see you got the other seat."

"What's that?" the woman asked.

"The other seat. When I ordered this morning, there were two seats and you must have ordered the last one after me."

"It was the last one," she said and shrugged her shoulders.

Hayden looked around the balcony. "Seems we're a bit overdressed."

"Perhaps, everyone else is underdressed."

He laughed. Beautiful and smart, he thought. Gradually, the laughter on his face changed to annoyance when a person bumped into him while taking their seat. Hayden turned, about to say something, when he saw it was the burly man from the restroom.

This guy didn't look like the take-in-a-performance type and his shoulders were wider than the seat. There was no way Hayden could remain in a seated-tilt the entire show, but there were worse things than leaning toward the woman.

"Sorry," Hayden said to her and thumbed to the guy sitting next to him.

So far, she didn't seem to mind.

Feeling a poke in his back the size of a broom handle rather than a finger, Hayden turned around.

Showing a printed piece of paper, the man pointed and asked with an accent, "Right zeat?"

Hayden peeked and said, "Yeah. Right seat."

"Zank zou," the man said, folded up the paper, and slid it in the pocket inside his casual jacket.

Flying on shared space stations and missions with other countries, Hayden knew the man was German.

Hayden had been one of only mere thousands of all the people who had ever lived to enter space. His own eyes had seen the Earth in its entirety. Many times, his heart had shut it out. Although he was adaptable, he was also easily annoyed, as he was now. Any inconvenience to his ease and comfort, as sitting this way, would have normally resulted in a confrontation. Tonight, for some reason, instead of complaining about it, he let it go. The woman's proximity and perfume helped.

The show ended and Hayden's left butt cheek couldn't wait to stand and relax after bearing the brunt of his weight throughout the performance. The German didn't clap, show any appreciation or enjoyment, or say anything. Mechanically, he stood out of his seat as expressionless as a robot with a fixed face.

"Must be in a hurry," Hayden said to the woman.

"Come on," she said. "There's a bar in here."

When they got there, the hostess asked if they would like to sit inside or outside. The woman answered, "In," and explained to Hayden that it was because she wanted to smell what she was drinking. They were seated at a table for two, she ordered a drink that sounded complicated, and Hayden ordered a brandy. The drinks came and hers looked as complicated as it had sounded when she ordered it. Of all the colors it could be, it happened to be orange.

"What did you order, again?" he asked.

"An X-Rated Tangerine Touch," she answered.

They talked. Hayden found himself monitoring how much he said compared to her. It's been a long time since he'd sat down and talked with a real live person over a drink and the conversation was much more interesting than the ones he had with Sydney in his apartment. As she spoke, he listened, but also thought of his time in space. How he had shut out the world. Perhaps, now, it was time for him to join Earth's inhabitants and be worldly for a while.

"We're on our second drink and I don't even know your name," he said.

"Well, I don't know yours," she said a little sassy. "I mean, what kind of man has a drink with a woman and he doesn't even know her name?"

"Any breathing man, that's who. I know it sounds desperate, but the same can be said of you."

"Sounds like you're ready for the next step."

"Baby steps. You mean *names*?"

"If I said bed, would that be a shock?"

"You and me, *yeah*. That would shock anybody. Mostly me."

"You don't find yourself attractive?"

"See, there you go, leaving the nursery again."

"I think you're attractive," she said with playfulness on her face and in her body language.

Her gloved hand stretched across the table, removed the

brandy glass out of his hand, set it down, and caressed his hand.

His gulp sounded as loud as a massive gurgle in Sydney Harbor.

"So, what's your name?" she asked.

"Hay, Hay … hey, Darrick. Darrick Cardull."

She pulled her hand away. "You don't sound so sure."

"No, I'm sure. It was just your hand touching mine jumbled me all up." He wasn't an actor, or a salesman, or a con man, but he sure hoped his explanation worked.

"I told you I find you handsome. You find me beautiful?"

"Oh, yeah." It wasn't the smooth answer he wanted. But it was honest.

"You're honest. You have an honest face. I like that."

A funny feeling like a tiny alarm going off made him think she could go all night without telling him her name, so he pushed.

"Darrick Cardull," he said convincingly as he gestured to himself. "And you are?"

As if she had thought about going as long as she could without telling him or was busy making up a name, she finally said, "Ara. Ara Bok."

"Ara Bok. There you go. Pretty, but as unusual as your drink."

"Pretty. Unusual. Quite the vocabulary you have there for a—what do you do?"

"I'm an *aaa*-countant. I'm an accountant. I deal in numbers all day."

"I thought you were going say you were an attendant, as in a gas attendant or a restroom attendant. An accountant. Sounds boring. Are you boring?"

"Am I boring? I've been to the *mmm, uh*, zero to a million and back." He bobbed his head. "Yes. Yes, I'm boring."

"Maybe you aren't as honest as you look."

"I'm honest. Everything I said is true. What about you? What do you do?"

"You're seeing it," she said. "Where are you staying?"

"Forthcoming," he said. "So, what exactly are you doing?"

"Arousing you. How am I doing?"

"Excellent. Excellent. But you should know I'm not rich."

"This isn't a scam. Besides, I am."

"You're beautiful and rich and this isn't a scam?"

"Ask me where I'm staying?"

"Okay, fine. Where are you staying?"

She leaned over the table and waved a long, gloved finger for him to meet her. When he leaned in, she said, "With you," accentuating her lips. "Just lead the way."

Somehow her thick lips remained rounded when she spoke and the name of his hotel and apartment number almost rolled right off his lips before asking for the check and being on their way.

"No, I, *uh*, just met you," he said. "I told you baby steps and that's what I'm going to do. I should go."

"I don't do this all the time," she explained. "When I said this is what I do, I didn't mean what you're thinking."

When he stood, she reached over the table, grabbed his hand, and squeezed.

She winced.

Hayden noticed.

Desperation contorted her beautiful face as she looked up at him. "*Please!* I don't want to be alone."

"A waiter came to their table with a brandy on his tray and said, "Compliments from that gentleman over there. I think he said, *'For all the trouble.'*"

Hayden looked and saw the German looking back at him. When he pulled his hand out of Ara's, she winced again.

"I'm out of here," Hayden said to her. "You're rich— you pay. And I'm taking this."

He picked up the fresh brandy off the waiter's tray and carried it out of the Opera House.

Unsure of what was happening, Hayden had decided to walk to his hotel; a no-no in the realm of his protection, even if it was only a twenty-minute walk. He could turn around and get the car, but why? It could be retrieved tomorrow, or the next day, or the next. Kip would love being asked why his man incurred so many parking bills.

The farther he walked away from the water, the number of lights dwindled and the darker the city became. About two-thirds of the way to the apartment, he stopped on the sidewalk to sip his brandy. Before the glass touched his lips, a gloved hand forcefully covered his mouth, while a forearm braced the back of his neck. The glass shattered on the sidewalk.

The assailant drug Hayden on his heels into an alley. Nothing Hayden tried could get the man to let go: stomping on his feet, swinging a balled fist back to whack him in the nuts, bending over to get the man on his back. It wasn't that it was a hold he couldn't get out of more than this attacker was tough. Balls of steel.

"Quiet!" the man whispered in Hayden's ear. "Calm down. If you would just … stop, I can let you go."

"Eally," Hayden said, muffled through the gloved hand.

"Yeah, *really*. Now, are you going to be quiet? Not talk, yell, or run off? Nod your answer."

Hayden nodded he would cooperate.

The man slowly removed his hand, ready to reapply it at any moment for any reason.

"Now, turn around," the man said.

When Hayden turned around, the man before him was wearing one of those all-black outfits that Kip's men wear.

Hayden started to say something, but the man cut him off. "I said, don't talk. Now, this is what you're going to do. You're going to return to the sidewalk, pick up only the big pieces of your glass, and toss them into the patch of weeds twenty or so feet ahead. Second, instead of going down Riley Street, you're going to cut across to Crown and follow it all the way over to Campbell. That'll bring you in behind your hotel. Got It? It'll take you a little longer and you'll be exposed a little longer, but you'll be covered. Now go."

Hayden did exactly as the witness protector had said.

Safely making it to his apartment, he unlocked the door and went inside. In the window-wall, there was a blurred reflection of a man sitting in his chair. The lights came on and the man stood and turned around.

"You sat there a lot, didn't you?" asked Kip. "That chair's broken in."

"What's going on? What's happening?" Hayden asked. "Your man attacked me out there."

"*No.* My man saved your ass. Now, come with me." Kip waved a finger as he walked for Hayden to follow.

The lights turned off and, as they moved through the dark apartment, it became obvious Kip wasn't alone. Some of his black knights were present. Kip entered Hayden's bedroom and Hayden came in after.

"Do you know this man?" Kip asked Hayden.

The lights in the bedroom turned on and a man in black pulled the covers back on the bed. A man lay there where Hayden had laid this morning. Hayden moved closer and knew exactly who the man was. It was the sturdy German.

CHAPTER ELEVEN

"So, do you know him?" Kip asked.

"I don't know him. I've seen him before. I sat beside him at the Opera House," Hayden explained.

"You two go together? Fruit got to you and you switched teams?"

"No!"

"I know. I'm just messing with you. A little comedy relief goes a long way when you're staring down a dead body. It helps me."

"No, really. You should have seen the young woman coming on to me."

"Young? You? *Please!* She didn't happen to order a drink, a, *oh*, what is it, a triple X-rated something or other, did she?"

"Yeah, something like that. How do you know?"

"Do you know her?"

"No. Just met her tonight."

"Was she your date?"

"No. She sat beside me at the show."

"Wait a minute! Hold the lettuce on that salad. Are you telling me you sat between X-rated and the kraut?"

"Well, yeah. And among a full balcony of other people."

"You overdressed, didn't you? The tux. It happens to everybody their first time there."

"Kip! What is going on?"

"Not what—*who*. As in all of us. We're getting out of here." Kip pointed to two men with his index finger and pinky on the same hand as if giving the sign of the horns or digging some metal music. "Except you two. You have body disposal and cleanup detail."

"Why won't you tell me what's going on?" Hayden asked.

"Later. We made it here just in time and I have a feeling we're going to get out of here just in time. Our tangerine friends and the Germans got way too close to you."

"Wait … what?"

"Our witness all packed up?" Kip asked his men. "No prints? No trace?"

"Ready to go, Mr. Stanton," one of them said.

"Then, lights off and let's roll."

Walking in the dark toward the door, Kip said, "Someone grab that newly replenished bottle of brandy. I don't want to walk out of here empty handed."

"Well, what am I?" Hayden asked.

"Costly," Kip said. "I've been asked about some of your expenditures."

On the flight back to the canyon in one of those oddball planes, one of Kip's operatives in civvies checked Darrick Cardull out of the apartment and paid in cash. Once away from the building, she saw orange dots crawling on the outside walls of the upper floors of the hotel and contacted Kip. He told her, "You may have paid for the party, but you weren't invited," and she vacated the area.

Shortly after, Kip's men, inside Hayden's apartment, contacted Kip to inform him of their situation. It wasn't good. Employing the screens nested in their forearms, they tracked a number of orange warriors now inside the hotel. Kip ordered them to "Cremate him," meaning to vaporize the German's body with their lasers to get rid of the body, "Cable's out," meaning shutdown their screens before they were detected, and then, "Get out," of the apartment without leading them there. If they couldn't, Kip simply said, "Make yourselves scarce," which meant the two men would fire their lasers at each other simultaneously to not leave a trace. He ended the communication with "I've filed divorce papers," meaning there would be no more communication between them and the men were on their own.

"Is it bad?" Hayden asked.

A sigh escaped Kip out of necessity. "Yeah. The good news is Darrick Cardull is officially dead."

"Cardull. Your brainchild?"

"All me. I hate eating my own children."

After Kip said it, he turned his head as if to look out the window of the craft, but it was already blackened out.

Inside the parallelogram room entombed in the canyon, Kip had strategically fed Hayden some fruit and then asked him to recount, from his perspective, what had happened on the ferryboat and at the Opera House. As both men sat in those brown leather chairs, vivid details that had been captured in Hayden's mind verbalized. When asked if, upon recollection, there were any clues leading up to the incidents, Hayden couldn't think of anything.

"Cardull lived up to his birth name, because, up to the ferry ride, he lived a pretty dull life," Hayden said.

"Well, I had high hopes he would," Kip said. "You think you know someone, then *bam!* Surprise!"

"Well, the same can be said of you," Hayden said. The memory of his conversation with the beautiful young woman stopped him there, just as her beauty had. "She winced," he added.

"Why wouldn't she? She was with you," Kip joked.

"No, you see, when I got up to leave, she squeezed my hand and winced."

"Again, only natural."

"She winced again when I pulled my hand away. She must have been injured or something. And as I described, she wore gloves that covered her…"

"Forearms. *Shit!*" Kip interjected. "Sorry. Keep going."

"So, did she have a screen in her forearm? Maybe the orange person that wanted the briefcase in Manhattan was a woman. The hood and cloak concealed the shape some, but the person wasn't very big."

"It could have been a small man. Asians are small."

"Maybe. And my attacker didn't move like the beauty in Sydney."

"Your attacker hung onto your car," Kip raised his hands and pretended to grip something, "by a broken out window with some glass still in it. Is that right?"

"Yeah."

Kip sat forward and opened his hands with the palms up as if giving or receiving something. "Because that's not what she wanted you to see. This business is theatrical. Let me run this by you. Let's suppose she was your New York attacker. Her hands would have been butchered by hanging onto the car. Yes, they would have healed some, but you had small cuts compared to her gashes. Now, whoever it was had shown great strength in just hanging on. Did she appear to have that strength?"

"She looked as feminine as feminine gets."

"*Okay*, maybe a gymnast or martial artist. Whatever. But picture her not entirely healed hands. You didn't see or feel any bandages, right?"

"None."

"So the bandages are off to get into costume and character. The air is stinging them. The fabric of the gloves rubbing them the wrong way. An un-expecting, but necessary grip of your hand. You pulling out—more rubbing."

"Maybe. You seem to know a lot about it. She wasn't one of yours, was she?"

"No. If she was injured, I would have sent another, if there was another. Seems like her beauty for the assignment overrode her injuries. Now, the woman on the ferry was mine."

Hayden stood out of the chair. "*Geez, Kip*! And the German?"

"No. He belonged to Germany."

"Well, how was the woman yours?"

Kip sat back in the leather chair, making a calculated decision. Once made, he sat forward and clapped his hands. "This is highly confidential, but it's fair for you to know. Since you've brought that briefcase in here and images were sent to my team, she thought she saw another one while on assignment in Asia. She seized it by force and, just by happenstance, resistance forced her south to Australia. She tried avoiding your location, but she didn't have a choice. As badly as we wanted that case, the idiot in the orange onesie botched up our asset retrieval attempt."

"You mean rather than rescuing her, you let her die?"

"Had to. It was more important we remained under the radar."

"More important than a human life?"

A hesitation paused the discussion and then Kip answered, "Yes. The spheres are that important."

Hayden's head collapsed back so he looked up at the ceiling. "What's this world coming to?"

"War. For the spheres." Kip pointed up. "That air up there is the battleground. It's been coming for a while. Now it's here."

"Was the briefcase the same?"

"From the pictures she sent, it appears so, yes."

Hayden straightened his head. "You obviously knew about the German, because you took him out."

"Just because we couldn't save her on the ferry, didn't mean we couldn't save you."

"Would he have killed me?"

"No doubt. Retaliation for you assassinating their

president." The screen inlaid in Kip's forearm illuminated and, after he studied the information, he looked up at Hayden and said, "In fact, I just got word the Germans want to know where their man is."

"So, they're admitting they tried to kill me?"

"Of course not. They'll battle it out with the Australian government as to why a German went missing on their soil."

"Will you help them out?"

"Indirectly, since we're responsible. We're working on it."

"You're always working on something. So how did the German's find me?"

"We think they tracked the orange imbecile to the ferry. They wouldn't have if our adversaries had sent a more intelligent assassin."

"Well, that's reassuring. What else have I missed since being in hiding?"

"Oh, nothing much. Trying to get that damned briefcase opened."

"Still no luck?"

"Luck doesn't have anything to do with it. These things come in waves and we're just waiting for the next one. When it comes, we'll be ready."

"In the meantime, what now?"

"We have another briefcase to go get. And, we need to find you a new location."

"Mr. Stanton," the composed female voice said into the parallelogram room. "I have a complete, sequential, and non-redundant recording of all coverage to date of the incident on the ferryboat. Would you like to see it?"

"Sure. I don't know what I would do without you," Kip said, as he positioned the screen in his forearm to project the images into the air as he had done before.

"Not much it appears," she said.

The spliced videos began to play and an announcer on TV, caught mid-thought, said, "We're about to show you a homemade video of what happened on a ferryboat on

Sydney Harbor. Once you watch it, text the number on your screen and let us know if you think it's an elaborate hoax or real? Without further delay, here it is."

Someone had videotaped from inside the cabin of the ferry the man in orange standing over the woman on the deck. It had captured the man severing her arm with the laser and then footage was shown of her disintegrating until she disappeared. Shaky, unfocused video bounced around until it zoomed in and regained some focus on a partial forearm lying on the deck with its hand gripping the handle of a briefcase.

"They're getting sloppy," Kip said. "First, the blood on your skylight and now this. I mean look at him. The arrogant bastard's not even wearing civvies to blend in. He shows up like some orange villain and lasers my agent in front of the whole world."

"Did she have any family?" Hayden asked.

"Yeah—us."

"Sorry. I feel like a bigger ass than that orange guy."

"There's one thing for certain from all of this. We won't have to deal with this moron anymore, guaranteed."

"Why is that?"

"Because after this display of stupidity, he's a dead man. There's no way his own kind is going to tolerate that."

The rest of the accumulated coverage played on the holographic screen and the men watched in silence.

The same room Hayden had stayed in before in the canyon was where he lied on a bed now, looking up at the ceiling. At least, it seemed like the same room. Kip had him wear that stupid helmet again that only provided an electronic outline of where the ceiling, walls, and floor connected. The staff had fed him a nice meal and even supplied him with a bottle of the Australian brandy he had become accustomed to; probably the one Kip had ordered one of his men to take on their way out of the apartment. The bottle sat beside a self-chilling tray of cheese and fruit. Quandong, an

Australian peach, had been included on the fruit tray, most likely a Kip request, knowing his sense of humor, as was the Australian aborigine music piping into the room. Despite the occasional wail of singing in an ancient language, which annoyed him, the music itself sounded quite relaxing. As time passed, even the singing didn't bother him and he flirted with sleep.

The door to his room slid open and Kip entered.

"Wake up, Hayden!" Kip said. "Come on, buddy. Big moment. Big moment."

The intensity in Hayden's voice grew as he said, "You don't sound like Ora. Or the Aussie beauty. You don't sound like a woman at all. So why are you in here? I'm only trying to get some goddamn shuteye."

"You don't sound grateful at all. You can sleep after. You're going to want to see this. Hell, I want to see this. We're holding up the presentation for you, so come on."

Kip reached for Hayden to help him out of bed, but Hayden slapped his hand away. "I can sit up myself!"

"Faster!" Kip said. "I want to see."

"I was so close," Hayden said, sitting on the edge of the bed. "So close to dozing off on a warm, sandy beach."

"That's it. I'm helping."

As Kip helped Hayden to his feet, the smell of brandy whispered from his mouth.

"Are you drunk?" Hayden asked.

"I'm more sober than your sobriety. Now come on."

Kip pulled Hayden toward the door. The helmet hanging on the wall made an otherwise cooperative Hayden hesitate liked a trained animal used to a leash. Despite the moral dilemma, there was no way he was going to say anything about it. Freedom came over him as they moved out of the room and into the hallway. What he might see excited him and he no longer wanted to sleep.

As they walked, Kip talked. "It's a short walk, so just listen. Remember when you saw those numbers under the fingernails of our enemy's hand? Turns out you were right.

But let's keep your number-seeing abilities under wraps, *huh*. The less who know about it, the less likely it finds its way floating out there and someone, we don't want to know, learns of this intel. Your services might be requested and, honestly, I would like to keep this in our back pocket if it's ever needed."

"Fine. But I want something."

"We humans condition ourselves so easily don't we? The poor get used to being poor. The loser gets used to losing. Anything otherwise becomes uncomfortable. Sad, really. But you, my friend, are learning, so shoot."

"What goes on here? Specifically, behind all these doors."

"Soundproof doors," Kip pointed out. "Sure. I'll play along for a bit. You're aware of the renewed desired for more space missions, especially to Mars and beyond and the challenges we face with such travels. Well, let's just say, NASA does some testing, the ones people interested enough read in articles and so on. And I'm not discounting them, they have their place. But let's face it. When you want to know the impact of extended radiation exposure on a human, the best way to know is to test on a human. We're talking maximum exposure to see what happens real quick like. That's what happens here."

"Like what?" Hayden asked. "Can you show me?"

"For your cooperation in remaining quiet about your space-enhanced eyeballs, sure, we can all wait to see what's inside the briefcase. But, we're going to skip these doors. We're not a hospital, but our cancer patients are in there. I've seen live video feed and it's brutal. I know you're going to ask, so I'll just tell you now, those being tested aren't ours. They're not our group. They're not NASA. They're not volunteers. They're enemies we captured and are no longer useful to us."

They walked a little farther down the hallway to a long section without doors. When doors started appearing again in the walls, Kip passed a few, then stopped at one. Without him doing anything from what Hayden could tell, the door opened.

"Awesome science and technology," Kip said. "I can't tell you how it works, but it steers away from the typical security where anything physical is read by a scanner. Not very secure when someone can chop off someone's hand with clearance, pluck out their eyeballs, full-body scans, you get the idea."

Once inside, the door closed behind them and the room didn't appear as a room. In fact, so much so, Hayden didn't believe he was in a room himself. The environment could have passed for outer space. There was, but didn't seem to be a floor under their feet. Walking on the darkness of space away from the door where they entered, Hayden found himself losing reality. Weightlessness, disorientation, nothing underfoot, all crept in on him as if he really were in space. Whispered reassurances by Kip helped, who admitted he still experiences vertigo even after seeing the structure of the room in full light and it was explained to him how it worked.

They approached what appeared like nothing more than a dot in the distance.

"What is that?" Hayden asked. "A planet?"

"In a canyon? Just keeping the reality of where we are and what's happening home."

Kip stopped and held out a straight arm across Hayden's chest for him to stop, too. His hand on that arm moved forward a little and tapped on what sounded like glass. A screen came on in front of them.

"Look closer," Kip said.

The screen zoomed in on the dot, which wasn't a mere dot, but a man, suspended in the center of the blackness as if he were the sun without any orbiting planets. How he remained there, Hayden didn't have a clue, for he couldn't see anything holding him in place. Without any movement, Hayden began to think that the person was dead. A hand moved. The otherwise still body didn't speak a language unless the stillness itself spoke of defeatism.

"How long has he been out there?" Hayden asked.

"You mean in here," Kip said. "It's important to remember where you are. Weeks. He can't see us or hear us. Seems like he won't be doing either very long. He's dying and he longs for it."

"Isn't that torture?"

"Officials would say it's isolation testing. Which it is. That's what we're doing. It doesn't get much more isolated than being the only one or thing in the universe."

"Weeks don't seem long enough."

"In this environment is it. We used to provide nourishment through intravenous, but the needle was counterproductive because it told them they weren't alone."

"*Oh, Kip!* No food. No water."

"Yeah, but the guy's a dirtbag. Look at it this way, it's capital punishment and educational."

Kip turned off the screen, turned himself and Hayden around, and as they proceeded toward the unseen door, it opened.

Kip led Hayden down the hall. "We're skipping the muscle and deterioration lab and the diet lab. I don't think you want to see decomposing people who are still alive or people eating shit and piss because they want to survive." Pointing to a door with a finger, Kip continued, "We're going to skip the hostile-closed environment area. I don't think you want to see how small the human body can get with careful packing and once they're packed, having things crawl and slither on them and there's not a damn thing they can do about it."

A finger pointed at another door and Kip said, "For the sake of time, we'll skip the distance test, too. Picture the isolation room, only this guy housed on a pretend spacecraft has a window view of a dot he knows is Earth thirty-four million miles away." A wave at another door as they passed and Kip said, "Definitely not that one either. It's the near-weightless test. This guy's body has been floating upright in there so long that the fluids and all that crap rose out of his feet and legs into his head and shoulders to where the guy's body looks like a top-heavy fat exclamation mark."

"Here, we'll do this one," Kip said as he opened the door like magic and they went inside.

This room appeared to be typical, complete with a ceiling, floor, four walls, and shaped like a box. The poor guy behind a window-wall stumbled all over the place, unable to keep his balance.

"Geez, Kip. He thinks he's tumbling all the time, doesn't he?"

"Very good," Kip said. "This is one of the balance tests. So, you see enough?"

"I guess so. I wish you showed me something else."

"You wanted to know what we do here, so I let you in on a little. Being an astronaut, I thought you might find this interesting."

"Just goes to show, you don't know me very well. Reading theory and about NASA-controlled studies, sure. Not the real deal."

"I like that. *The real deal.* Speaking of which, let's see what's in that briefcase you stole in Manhattan."

As they entered a laboratory, many people, men, and woman, Ora among them, stood around a large, glass working table. A screen hovered over the table like a scoreboard hanging from the ceiling of an ice arena; the bald man looked out from it. All eyes were on Kip as he made his way to the table. Ora's eyes left Kip and moved onto Hayden, who peeked just enough to make eye contact, then cowered away. Lying on the table was the briefcase that had brought so much unwanted change to Hayden's life and, most likely, Ora's.

"Alright, people. Settle down," Kip started. "Some in here would say we know of at least two briefcases. Get that out of your head right now. In my estimation, we have none. For all we know, the other one may have been a decoy to send us on a wild goose chase. All of us who knew Anne hope she hadn't died in vain. To be clear, our carroty enemies would kill to sell the head fake and make us believers. I urge you not to believe until there's something to believe. As far as this one, well, we don't know what's in it. But, in a few moments, we will. Because we know how to open it."

Kip's hands caressed the black shell of the briefcase as he continued, "I'm itching to see what's in here, too. But first, I would like to introduce you to the one who figured out the combination sequencing so quickly, a feat that would have taken an unh*um*anced being much, much longer. So, without delay, from our enh*um*anced department, please welcome Robman Cross."

A man, standing among them, made his way around the laboratory table and stood next to Kip. Some clapped, while others didn't. Robman unbuttoned the left cuff of his shirt and rolled it up just below the elbow. There was a screen inlaid in the forearm. The forearm itself sure looked familiar to Hayden, like the one that had been chopped off with an ax in Manhattan.

Kip looked at Robman and said, "Okay then. Mixed crowd." When no one reacted to the pun, he continued. "Anyway, this guy produced amazing results in getting the case open. As his name suggests, Robman Cross here is a robot-man crossover. Mostly man, so be careful what you say. Besides there being some brain-computer codependency in his egghead wired down to his forearm and hand, he's just like you and me." Kip raised his left hand. "And don't forget, many of us in here have screens in our forearm, so we truly are a mixed crowd." Disappointed by another failed attempt at the pun, he moved on. "Now, he already knows the combination, but for demonstration purposes, he's going to pretend he doesn't know it." He gestured a hand toward the briefcase. "Robman."

A Caucasian-skinned human hand reached out and gripped the case's handle. The hand itself appeared normal: wrinkles at the wrist and joints, veins visible under the skin, healthy groomed nails. Reattaching the dead limb to a live body had done wonders for its health and appearance. When he tightened his grip into a squeeze, the skin smoothed and the veins flattened. Other than the tension in the hand and forearm, the rest of the man appeared relaxed. Greenish-yellow light appeared under the fingernails, possibly triggered by the squeeze. The hand loosened around the handle and four fingers moved in a fidgety motion, sometimes one finger at a time, and any combination of two to four fingers simultaneously. The speed with which the fingers moved increased until they became a pale blur around the handle.

Kip explained, "As you can see, his fingers are rapidly moving around the handle as if playing an instrument, in search of the right combination. You might find it interesting to know that his brain and hand worked continuously like that for weeks, while the man used his other hand to eat, drink, and, yes, he even slept while his fingers worked to the metal. His dedication to this assignment was phenomenal. Let's find one, Mr. Cross. I'm sorry, make it two."

Robman played along and found the first number and then the second.

"Now, you all have been watching him and I don't blame you," Kip said. "But's it's hard to see. So, our beloved bald man will slow it down for you on the screen above the table."

A close-up of Robman's fingers, which had belonged to the man in the brown over-coat crossing the street in Manhattan, slowed down to catch the last two finger movements. It meant nothing to anyone. Other than seeing the fingers move, there wasn't anything to see.

This was Kip's opportunity to make sure of that. "Anyone see anything?" he asked, looking around the group. "Anything at all? Symbols? Letters? Numbers?"

No one had and relief came over him.

Hayden saw things as they truly were, for he knew how

the fingers were numbered one to four, starting with the index finger to the pinky. When Robman's fingers had moved together around the handle, a greenish-yellow number two illuminated under the middle-finger nail and a three under the ring-finger nail. It had occurred to him that the combination didn't simply entail single numbers one through four, but could contain any number using up to four fingers simultaneously, which had made Robman's task more complicated than he had imagined. The combination could contain numbers in the thousands, say if all fingers were used simultaneously; one number could be one thousand two hundred and thirty-four or even four thousand three hundred and twenty-one. But who's to say each number couldn't be used more than once in making a number or any other countless ways to make a number.

An agent asked that very question. "Kip, you said Robman's working on cracking the combination, but what goes into that combination? You asked us if we saw anything, symbols, letters, or numbers, so what should we see?"

"That's a very good question," Kip said. "We only know it's a finger-sequencing. So, for now, any case-cracking will be done by Robman."

"Kip. Any pattern to the sequencings?" another agent asked.

Kip shook his head. "Man, are you guys good. We think so. This combination had twenty or so movements. More than half of those entailed an index finger. We don't know exactly what it means, but ..."

"Wouldn't that have made cracking the code easier?" a third agent asked.

"No," Kip answered. "For two reasons. One, some of the finger sequences were short, while others were quite lengthy, and two, we thought there might be a pattern, but wasn't sure until, well, we're still unsure."

Kip looked around and asked, "Any other questions? I hope not, because I don't have any answers." When no one did, he said, "Good. It's important to keep your boss happy. So, now, let's assume Robman cracked the combo," he visually checked with the robot-man crossover to ensure he had, "which he did, and, now, the moment we've all been waiting for. Let's open this thing. Drumroll, anyone?"

As Robman let go of the briefcase handle and Kip situated it in front of him so when it was opened, everyone could see what was inside, one of the agents tapped his index fingers on the lab table, providing a drumroll. Others followed suit.

Anticipation had everyone on edge, including Hayden, who understood in part what Kip had glossed over because he knew the finger-sequencing was really numbers. *Why would more than half of the numbers be the number one—the index finger*, he pondered.

"Maybe we should have had the bomb squad open this thing up?" Kip said. "Robman, here, calculated a ninety-seven point three percent chance it was safe to open, so here it goes."

Kip opened the briefcase and the unified drumroll stopped.

CHAPTER **TWELVE**

Nestled in foam in the bottom of the briefcase were twenty balls about the size of golf balls, evenly spaced apart, in four rows of five. Not dimpled like a golf ball, they resembled tiny soccer balls, having black, reflective, pentagon-shaped solar panels connected together. Electronic as they were, they appeared fragile, but their short circumference might prove durable, but certainly not for sport.

"If I weren't standing, the mare in my daymare would have scooched from my chest onto my face and farted," Kip said. "So they went with mini-soccer balls. If these do what we think they're supposed to do, they did it. They really did it. And we're fucked."

"Unless, it's a head fake," an agent chimed in.

"True. Very true," Kip agreed. "My own words thrown back at me. These might be something else entirely. At the risk of breaking my own don't assume anything rule, I'll say right now, based on intel received about these briefcases, I think these are the real deal. All scientists, researchers, technicians, assemblers-dismantlers, and everyone else who would handle these things, how quickly can we decipher what we have here?"

No one wanted to answer. All around the lab table, who

fell into such categories, looked at each other.

Finally, a technician offered, "Well, it's hard to say. If we knew they were all the same, that would cut down the work, but we won't know that until they are all checked. Also, their size doesn't automatically mean easier. In fact, smaller scale tends to mean longer, more careful handling."

"Tomorrow, then?" Kip pushed.

Most in the groups, who would examine these balls, laughed.

"No," an assembler said. "Not tomorrow. Or the next day. Or the next. With that said, there are twenty of them, which means no one group would have to wait to get started. We can all start on one and rotate them, keeping track by numbering them as they are presented in the case."

"Sounds like a plan," Kip said. "You all can at least start today, right? Before you answer, this takes priority above anything else you're working on."

Those working together in the same department made eye contact with each other and within a few seconds nodded they could.

"Great!" Kip said. "Research gets the kit-and-caboodle first, pictures, documentation, description, the whole nine. They're going to be control on this. Once they're done cataloging, they'll let the dismantlers know so they can open them up for you and then your group can go and sign out a ball. That way, you're working at your own speed. One ball per group to spread the wealth. So, let's get to it. Time waits for no one."

The group disseminated in pockets out of the lab, animated about the assignment ahead of them.

Back in the parallelogram room, Kip, Hayden, and Ora discussed what they had seen in the briefcase. Knowing his personnel was good at what they do, Kip didn't want to divulge too much intel his agents had gathered to the scientists, researchers, and assemblers, who also do the disassembling, not wanting to lead their findings in any way.

Before the meeting, the agents had been ordered by Kip not to share what they knew, even if asked.

Hayden had thought many times about confronting Kip in reference to him saying he was just an agent. After the way he had led the meeting and gave orders, there was no way Kip was *only* an agent. Perhaps, a lead agent or some other title, but, without question, he served in some kind of managerial capacity. Nothing wrong with that. It's not like the guy avoided danger, flying out to Hayden's home and down to the apartment in Sydney. Probably ordered there, it might be safe to say that Kip wasn't high enough in the chain of command to remain safely snug in the cavern or one of their other locations and direct people like play-pieces in a chess match. That power rested with Kip's boss.

The time seemed appropriate, so Hayden asked Kip what official role he filled in the organization. Kip stood by his earlier claim that he was indeed an agent and if Hayden wanted to think of him as a lead, it was close enough to be accurate. His ascension to his current role had been paved by unfortunate events, namely the deaths of those who preceded him. This truth had a humbling power over an otherwise prideful man.

"Mr. Stanton," the pleasant woman's voice interrupted over the speakers into the room. "You're presence is requested in the nearest intel room for a reported WDU."

"I understand," Kip said. "Thank you."

"They found something already?" Ora asked.

"No. My people are good, but they're not that good. Besides, they would have tested and tested again to confirm before pulling me in on it."

"What's a WDU?" Hayden asked.

"Oh, that's just code for us when we're with people who shouldn't know what a WDU is," Kip said. "However, since it's you two, it's a *World Development Update*. In short, it could be anything."

"Sounds fun," Ora said.

"It's not," Kip grumbled. "It usually means something

bad happened and not in our favor." He looked at Hayden, then Ora, and said, "You two keep each other company. I'll be back."

"Didn't a famous cyborg say that once?" Ora said.

"Famous is what kills the comparison," Hayden said.

"*Ha, ha.* Very funny," Kip said and exited the room.

When Kip left, it was as if he had taken the warmth of life with him. Ora stood out of a brown leather chair, moved to the far side of the room, and stood, facing the window-wall with the dirt behind it; the canyon view hadn't been displayed since their arrival some time ago. The room was quiet for a long while and both had time to kill.

For the first time, the unusually-shaped room, buried within the canyon, seemed like a cold, damp, and earthy cave to Hayden. Anything civil disappeared around him and became natural. The smooth man-made walls turned to rock. The brown leather chairs became mounds of flowstone. The dim lights were from the sunlight prying into the cave's opening, no longer powered by generation. Even Ora's appearance transitioned into a lone stalagmite column fixed to the cave floor. Because she formed so quickly in his mind, she must be an ice stalagmite—cold and immovable. They had shared so much together, on Earth and in space, so he went over to her to try to melt her a little.

"Hey," Hayden said.

It took Ora longer, but eventually, she replied, "Hey."

His shoulders shrugged. "I just wanted you to know that I'm glad we cleared the air before I left. Knowing now, I stopped wondering about you and Kip." Fumbling over his own words, he clumsily added, "Or anyone else."

"What a relief for you."

"You make it sound like I took an antacid."

"Well, you're settled, aren't you?"

"*Settled?* No. Far from. How could I be?"

Her hands went into the air. "*Oh, no!* That's right. You couldn't settle on me or anybody. You had to go exploring, sticking your space probe into all kinds of galaxies."

He knew she was heating up. Soon, a savage woman from the ice age set on survival would emerge out of that hunk of ice stalagmite. A stubborn caveman, he pushed on, despite what faced him.

"What about you?" he asked. "Earth wasn't good enough for you, so you went looking for another planet."

"Your Earth had nothing but women on it and they were depleting your resources."

"I'm not drained, yet, honey. Far from it. We both know your well's been drilled way before we met."

It didn't seem possible, but Ora's eyes narrowed more than what they already were. How she could see out of them, Hayden didn't know. Seething, she inhaled long, almost too long. The air never expelled out and he didn't know how her lungs could hold it all.

While she stood there, fuming, he continued. "Look. Other than the first part, I didn't want to say any of that. What I wanted to say was that our inquisitive spirits wandered a bit. I know you think I wandered more than you did, which sounds like I did, but we both still wandered. It might be an ass-backward way of getting somewhere, but I have to say, if you're Earth, then that's where I want to live out the rest of my days."

Her eyes opened, as did her mouth. The long inhale from earlier leaked out and the ice stalagmite she had stiffened into melted and, to Hayden, she looked like herself once more—just as Kip entered the room.

"Well, no luck yet finding that other briefcase from the ferry," Kip said. "But, we have a lead." He plopped into the closest brown leather chair. "And you'll never guess what world development I was just updated on." He sat forward in his chair and tapped the seat cushion of the brown chair next to his. "Hayden, have a seat and I'll tell you all about it."

As Hayden sat down, Kip sat back and talked. "The President of Niger is dead. Gunshot to the head at close range. They're still trying to figure it out, but our intelligence says it's your bullet fired out of your gun."

Ora walked over and leaned on the back of Hayden's chair.

The last Hayden had seen his pistol and the gun case was when it had hung on the wall of this very room at the center of a briefcase and two-forearm triangle. Come to think of it, he hadn't seen it since.

"Where is my gun?" Hayden asked.

"In a safe place where you can't get a hold of it," Kip said. "But, wait. That's not all. Just when you think you ordered a single cheeseburger, a double comes out instead. Sources tell me an assassination attempt had also been made on the Prime Minister of Niger but failed. You know what two out of three comes out to, right? Point six-six-six. You're the devil to the world, Hayden, and I'm afraid our witness protection program isn't equipped to guard a devil."

"But I was here," Hayden said.

Kip shook his head side-to-side. "No, you weren't. You were Down Under when this went down. As in, you were supposed to lay low. Well?"

"Well, what?"

"Did you?"

"What? Lay low? Yeah. I was so low, it was depressing. I don't even know how far Niger is from Sydney."

Kip's nose raised slightly. "Ten thousand miles, give or take a few. You had time to kill, so maybe you did."

"And time almost killed me. I can't believe this shit. You don't really…"

"No, I don't. But I had to ask."

"You had to ask. What about you? You have my pistol. And bullets—which I still don't know how you collected out of the damn river. You have those pudgy planes that fly like rockets when they want to. You're the miracle man to make something like that happen."

"*Ah*, I don't blame you. You had to ask as did I. Question is, what does all of this mean and what do we do about it?"

"I mean, how could my pistol get to so many places when it's here?"

"Obviously, someone had to take it there."

Hayden's entire body appeared carved out of stone because he sat so still. "Not if you have it. You do have it, right?"

Kip's hand waved around as he answered, "Sure. It's locked away where no one can get it."

Hayden sat forward on the edge of his seat. "Whoever has the key, password, or whatever can."

Shaking his head, Kip said, "Yeah, but no one here would."

Hayden's finger pointed to the floor in a demand. "I want to see it. Right now. You show me where it is."

Just then, the soothing woman's voice sounded over the speakers into the room. "Mr. Stanton. We have a breach on the top floor. Your guests are to proceed to the bunkers, while you get your agent team assembled and directed there."

"Alright. Thank you," Kip said. "You heard the lady," he said to Hayden and Ora.

"How could anyone find this place?" Ora asked.

"When you come and go as much as we do, you're bound to be found," Kip answered. "Everything will be alright. We'll get them."

"Well, what floor are we on?" Hayden asked.

"The second," Kip answered.

He reached into the inside pocket of his jacket and pulled out two clear plastic cards, a little larger than a credit card, and handed one to Ora, but kept the second. He rubbed his hand then massaged the card. When he removed his hand, blue lines and words appeared on its surface.

"This is a map to the bunkers," Kip explained. "Now, remember, unlike a building where the top brass is usually on the upper floors, the opposite is here. The brass is at the bottom of the canyon. All you need to do is warm your hand and rub the card and the map should appear where you rubbed. You have four seconds until the map disappears and then you have to rub it again. They work for me, but Ora's should only work for her and," he handed Hayden his card, "Hayden's should only work for him. The yellow dot tells you where you are. An orange dot is for our cantaloupe foes and red is for all other enemies. Now go. No helmets either. You're going to want to see with your own eyes. I'll come get you once the situation is under control."

Ora asked a question, but Kip ignored it and left the room.

"I guess we better get going," Hayden said.

"I guess so," Ora hesitated. "Why can't we just stay here?"

"We're one floor away from being part of this thing. I say we do as he says and make our way down to the bunkers."

Ora agreed and, together, they exited the room into the hall. With elbows tucked against their own bodies, they each held the clear plastic card as if holding a cell phone. As they alternated between looking down at the card and looking up to view the hallway, they each rubbed their other hand to keep it warm, occasionally touching the card to keep the map visible.

"Feels strange not wearing that stupid helmet out here," Ora said.

"Yeah, same here," Hayden admitted. "Like trained dogs without our leash."

Simultaneously, they both stopped, seeing a red dot appear on the map ahead of them. Before either one could say anything, the red dot changed color to orange.

"What do you think?" Ora asked while holding her card so Hayden could see where she pointed. "Cut down this hallway?"

Hayden nodded and they proceeded down the hall and took the first corridor on the right. The yellow dots, indicating them on the map, moved right along with their movements. Taking the hall was the right call in avoiding the orange dot and the navigational cards recalibrated their route to the bunkers. At some point, they knew they had to take an elevator or some other kind of transport, which could be anything in this place, to descend them to the bunkers. Good old-fashioned stairs might await them, but Hayden remembered Kip's boss saying about the rocket ride up, *'You don't realize how far we traveled.'* Which was true, because no one ever told them.

Unless Kip's boss was offsite, he had to be part of the brass below. Outside of him welcoming them to the canyon, he's been missing-in-action, nestled somewhere safe in the base of the canyon.

Black lines in varying widths appeared on Hayden's plastic card, fragmenting the map. The entire face flickered as if a television set losing clear reception. Even after placing a warm hand on it, the map content lessened until there was nothing left and the lines broke up into tiny black and white squares of quiet static.

"Look at this marvel of shit," Hayden said while holding it out so Ora could see.

Showing him her card, she said, "Mine's still working."

It had occurred to Hayden that maybe the glitch was purposeful on Kip's end. Do-away with him, so Kip had a chance at the girl. Who was he kidding? Kip didn't need any help. Hayden knew he had botched things up himself. So good, in fact, the damage might not be repairable.

"Well, that's good," Hayden said. "I can't say it's a sup…"

Static sounded out of his card, interrupting him.

"We need to turn here," Ora said.

They rounded a corner into another hallway.

"Apparently, there's an elevator up ahead," she said.

"How do you know that?" he asked.

"Because a note popped up saying so."

"The statics getting on my nerves."

Hayden slid a finger around the front of the card. To his surprise, a volume bar appeared and he was able to mute the sound. The screen scrambled and images began to come into focus underneath the interference. Then, a perfectly clear picture showed through the card of a head and shoulders view of an orange-hooded person. The transmission appeared to be live.

Hayden stopped in his tracks and showed Ora.

A near-oval shadow concealed the person's face.

"Turn it up," Ora said.

When he swiped a finger across the card, a distorted voice was speaking.

"Where are you?" the voice said, sounding demonic.

Hayden looked at Ora's card and it appeared they were clear of all assailants. His and Ora's eyes snapped back to his card when the hooded person said, "Hayden. Tell me where you are."

"How do they know y…" Ora began.

"My DNA," he interrupted. "They know me by my DNA."

"They're tricking you, Hayden," the sinister voice said. "They covet what's inside the briefcases for their own ambition."

"I don't know if you can hear me," Hayden said, "but who's they?"

"The perverse you've been working with."

"To be clear, I'm not working with anybody. What is the group's ambition?"

Waves distorted the picture and the sound crackled as the orange-hooded person spoke.

"What?" Hayden asked. "You're breaking up."

Garbled speech came through the card and, then, as if an antenna been adjusted, the pictured cleared, as did the sound when the veiled person said, "To control the spheres."

"*Uh*, Hayden," Ora whispered as she looked down the hall.

Hayden looked up. A person in the distance walked toward them.

"Come on," he said as he grabbed her elbow and headed

back the way they came.

The hooded figure continued to talk through Hayden's plastic card, so Hayden swiped his finger across it to mute the sound.

"How did they show up?" Hayden asked.

"I don't know, I didn't see. Maybe out of the elevator?" Ora offered.

"Did you pick them up?"

"No."

"Tell me they're not red or orange."

"Orange."

"But that person's in all black."

"I guess we know now how they got in."

"Or they've been here all along."

"Maybe they're one of Kip's agents?" she asked. "Maybe they can help us?"

"You said they're showing up orange, though," he countered.

"These things might be all screwed up. I mean, someone hacked into yours."

"I think it's best not to trust anyone."

When they backtracked to the previous corridor, Hayden stopped and said a little winded, "Here. Let me see your card." After orienting himself, he said, "On here, it looks like they're going away from us."

Ora peeked down the hall they came from and said, "Still coming this way. The tracker must be wrong like I said."

Hayden hadn't picked up on it in his house before it blew to smithereens and didn't entirely understand what was happening here, but the same tactic of mirror-imaging was being utilized by the enemy to trick and deceive.

"They're coming, Hayden," she said. "Do we go back to the room?"

"I don't see any trouble that way, but who knows for sure. I guess so."

He handed her card back to her. "Keep yours. Maybe it's not entirely wrong."

"Hayden, come on! If they see us entering the room, what would be the point?"

As they trotted down the hall, it occurred to Hayden that just because he turned down the volume on the orange-hooded individual who had hacked his card, didn't mean they couldn't hear what Hayden and Ora had said on their end, in particular, about returning to the parallelogram room. As he held out the card in front of him as he trotted, the faceless figure was still there on the screen. With all his might, his thumbs pressed against the plastic card to snap it in half. It was tougher than he thought. Plastic could be a strong material, especially when it took on a slight flexible quality that would bend but not break.

A grunt expelled out of his taxed body and his face reddened from exerting effort. To his surprise, the card snapped in half. The colored live feed on the card shrank into an ever-diminishing circle until only the clear plastic remained and the communication was cut off. Sparks flew, snapping, crackling, and popping as if a larger machine had malfunctioned and gone berserk. Electronic shocks tingled his fingers and the heat generated made him drop the bifurcated card onto the floor. From the inside out, uncomfortable itches pricked his charred fingers from the greater than anticipated explosion from the tiny device. He wanted to scratch, of course, but thought the better of it, reasoning it would probably make it worse.

"Hayden, you okay?" Ora asked. "Your fingers are black."

Nothing like stating the obvious, Hayden thought. He always wondered why people do that, especially when it was obvious the person saw it before they did.

"Hold on a sec," Hayden said and he stopped and backtracked.

For good measure, he stomped on the card pieces, ran back to Ora, and grabbed her by the arm to pull her into a sprint.

"They may think we're going to the room if the orange-hooded hacker heard us, so we can't go there," Hayden said.

"Where are we going to go?" Ora asked. "We don't know what's beyond that room the other direction."

"I know. Come on, we have to run."

What he really wanted was one of those experimental rooms to hide in, but this hallway didn't have as many doors as the ones Kip guided him through that had all of the testing rooms. A viable option might be the room Hayden rested in after Australia. If the brass was buried lower in the canyon, then what do you do with secrets like the testing rooms? You bury them as deep as you can. Hayden guessed the room assigned to him after Australia had to be located lower in the canyon.

Stairs would do. An elevator would be better. Anything to get them down to the bunkers.

An elevator! It occurred to Hayden that among the confusion of their ascent when they had first arrived, they had stepped out of the elevator and saw Kip's boss standing at the end of a row of brown-leathered chairs, which meant there was an elevator in the left angled wall of the parallelogram room. The entrance to the elevator must somehow masquerade in with the wall like a chameleon blending in with its surroundings for them not to notice it or think of it after all the hours they had spent in the room.

"In here," Hayden said.

"That's the room," Ora said.

"I know. There's an elevator in here."

"There is? *Oh yeah*, there is."

They went inside and, immediately, Hayden gravitated to the left wall. His eyes didn't pick up any indication of an opening, let alone elevator-sized doors. The dim lighting didn't help in finding it, only concealing it, if it was there at all. Let down by his sight, his hands glided across the smooth olive drab wall. Its surface felt cool and, as suspected, most likely metal, seamless like a large sheet on the hull of a battleship. But it had to be here. It's where they entered the room.

Hayden turned so his back was against the wall and looked into the room.

"We entered here, right?" he asked and then pointed. "Kip's boss stood right by those chairs."

"Yeah, I think so," she said.

"You think so?"

"*Shh.* Keep it down."

Discombobulation froze Hayden for a moment until he turned back around and touched the wall again. Thoughts of what to do now all led to one conclusion: wait it out in here. The room's walls were their only protection. Not bad, being a canyon. However, the door could be problematic. Any intrusion, there was nothing in the room to hide behind. The chairs wouldn't do, neither would standing in a dark corner.

All of a sudden, the opposite wall opened up and Ora, seeing it, urged Hayden to turn around. He did and got his answer as to how a solid sheet of metal could separate and open. It couldn't, of course, it moved and behind it were elevator doors and an opening. When they had followed Kip's boss into the room the first time, the metal wall had already been moved and, in their exhaustion and paralysis, they hadn't seen or heard it close. Here, he thought they had spent their time in the same parallelogram room but now wondered if he had been wrong about that, too.

A light in the elevator revealed a woman, standing alone and wearing a black blouse, gray skirt, black nylons, and gray high heels. She was the same woman who had greeted them upon their arrival at the canyon and had led them through the dark corridor to the elevator, which had really been a rocket.

"Her clothes are opposite than when we first landed," Ora said. Her observation was something only another woman would notice.

"Come with me," the woman said.

"And that's exactly what she had said when we landed," Ora said.

Hayden looked at Ora and shook his head.

Motioning for them to get into the elevator, the woman said, "Come. I'll take you to the bunkers."

An unpleasant sound behind the door to the room made up their minds for them and Hayden and Ora entered the elevator without any further nudging.

"You don't need that anymore," the woman said, holding out a hand.

Ora knew what she had meant and laid the plastic map card in her hand.

The woman slid the card into a tiny pocket in the skirt. As she had done before, she pushed a lever up on the control panel and pressed a button.

Again, Ora noticed. She tapped for Hayden's attention and nodded her head in the direction of the lever. "She pushed it up," she whispered.

Hayden shrugged.

"Shouldn't it have been pushed down?" she said discreetly.

As before, there was no indication of movement. The floor under their feet felt equally stationary as a solid foundation.

"This won't take long," the woman said.

The comment by the talkative woman seemed out of place and Hayden and Ora looked at each other.

"That's good," Ora said. "We're glad you came for us."

The woman didn't respond and it had always confused Ora how such a beautiful woman on the outside could be so ugly on the inside.

Just as Hayden's eyes returned to the controls, he saw an orange laser lying on the flat part of the control panel. Mechanical as it was, it blended right in. If he hadn't looked there, he would never have seen it. An idea of how the canyon base may have been breached formulated in his mind and the woman before him just might be who had let them in.

"Aren't the bunkers bel..." Hayden started to ask when

he thought, perhaps, the elevator had stopped.

The woman casually reached for the laser and when she turned around with it, pointing it in the direction of her passengers, Hayden had already moved toward her and lunged for the lever, able to pull it down before the doors opened.

"Get off me!" the woman demanded, as she pushed against him, trying to get her arm free, and a little space between them to use the weapon to regain control of the situation.

Ora pushed her way around them enough to push the button. The elevator didn't give any indication of movement.

"What do you want with us?" Hayden yelled at the woman while trying to pry the laser from her.

For a petite woman, her strength surprised him and he couldn't budge the weapon from her hand. A voice sounded into the elevator. It wasn't any of the passengers or the silky-smooth woman's voice that would invade the parallelogram room to talk with Kip. It didn't even sound human, other than it spoke English. It had a perverted, demonic cadence.

In mid-struggle, Hayden looked into the woman's eyes, shock in the very fibers of his face. He released his current grips and, with both hands, grasped her arm holding the laser. The woman beat on him with her free hand, but the blows landed weakly. A sleeve button on her black blouse popped when he slid the fabric up her arm and, now, knew why he struggled to get the laser away from her. Implanted in her forearm was a screen and the inorganic metal hybridized with the otherwise organic limb was what gave the woman strength.

The disturbed voice, from an orange-hooded person, televised through the monitor, breaking up and crackling. In the midst of the garble, "Bring him in alive," came through loud and clear.

The directive had changed everything. Assuming he was the *'him,'* Hayden let the woman go and backed away.

"You can't kill me," Hayden said.

With a nod, she flung her hair back and said, "Things sometimes go wrong on assignments like this." The laser pointed in his direction.

"Be careful," he said. "They're listening."

Humbly, her eyes gradually observed the screen nested in her forearm. As her eyes rose from there to Hayden, contemplation filled them, supplied by the working brain behind them.

"Maybe not. But I can kill her."

Without hesitation, the woman swiveled on the soles of her high heels and fired the laser at Ora. In anticipation, Hayden moved toward Ora, but only managed to get his left arm in front of her. The laser beam hit him about mid-forearm, maybe a little closer to his wrist. It had happened so fast and no pain, yet, he wasn't exactly sure where it had hit. Stumbling in front of Ora, he tried regaining his balance from the lunge and when he reached down to catch his fall, his left hand and part of his forearm weren't there to brace him.

CHAPTER **THIRTEEN**

Even after all the weird things space had done to Hayden's mind and body, this experience topped them all. It was the strangest thing. His senses told him that his hand and forearm were still there, while his eyes registered to his brain they weren't. A clumsy collapse to the floor and he landed face-first with his other arm twisted awkwardly out from his side. With the laser set to disintegrate, it was obvious the woman had every intention of killing Ora.

The elevator jerked as if an earthquake quivered through the canyon. Ora's hand pressed on a red-lit button. Being on a number of spacecraft, she assumed it had something to do with an emergency. Whether the elevator-rocket had slowed or stopped, they couldn't tell.

Without warning, the elevator doors opened and Ora tucked her body against the control panel, making herself small; only a sliver of wall kept her inside the elevator. Already on the floor, Hayden flattened himself and turned his head away, feeling the unsettled wind in the shaft outside pull on him.

The woman turned around and stumbled toward the door, stepping out of one of her high-heeled shoes; the wind's invisible arms pulling on her.

The outside draw summoned them. Ora struggled to remain inside the elevator, as did Hayden, who continued to grasp at the floor with a hand that no longer existed.

The force was so strong that the woman couldn't turn herself around and, standing near the middle of the elevator, there was nothing close for her to grab onto with that strong composite hand. Now, near the door, she reached the bionic hand out for Ora, who was shielded behind a narrow section of wall. Determined eyes on the woman's maddening face met Ora's fearful ones and when her fingertips touched Ora's flapping sleeve, flames belched into the elevator and consumed the woman; a small detonation exploded at her waist from the plastic card in her skirt pocket. One moment she was there, the next, gone into oblivion.

The torched flame persisted into the elevator. Although within reach, Ora struggled to move her hand to press the red button. The continuous blaze weakened to occasional bursts of fire coming through the doors as if someone stood outside with a blowtorch and intermittingly sprayed into the elevator. From Ora's view, it appeared that the elevator continued to descend. Swirling fire ceased and only a whirling wind remained, circling inside the elevator like a tornado. Initially, it pulled Hayden's body toward the open door like invisible hands dragging him by his legs. That's how it appeared to Ora, something supernatural happening, instead of it explained by physical science.

Circling wind eroded space between Hayden's body and the floor and he felt his body, momentarily, lift off its surface. If he remained airborne, there was no way he could stop himself from being sucked out the door. Even spreading his legs wouldn't work, because the door was too wide.

Grunting with effort, Ora reached toward the red button and pressed it. The doors closed and Hayden's elevated body dropped to the floor, while a last spiral of wind knocked Ora against the control panel. Careful as to not hit any more buttons, she stood very still, waiting to see if the air had settled. Hayden still laid flat on his stomach, but it wasn't because he waited. It was because he struggled to get to his feet, still wanting, believing, he still had the use of his left hand.

When he got to his feet, the elevator door opened and it scared him enough that he moved away from it to the opposite wall. As he turned around, Ora nearly tackled him in a bear hug; her head pressed against his chest as if she wanted to crawl inside of him. Her warm damp body felt good against his, but only being able to feel her with his right hand disoriented him and the un-equilibrium state made him feel queasy.

He took a step forward and she took a step back. They danced that way until they were out of the elevator and inside a corridor.

When he rubbed her left arm, she winced but didn't move away, remaining tucked into him. Her arm felt hot as if sunburned and the sleeve of her shirt had holes running the length of it as if moth-eaten.

Her touch felt the same thing, only it was his back that felt warm, and his shirt had many holes in it as if it were a slice of Swiss cheese.

When she unattached her cheek from his chest to look up at him, the left side of her face appeared sunburned, while the other half was as pale as he usually noticed about her, especially during the winter months, and the left side of her hair appeared shorter than the right.

One of her hands reached up to the back of his head and, after taking a quick peek, she noticed the hair there had been singed. In her own need, she coveted his embrace. Being that distressed scared her because she believed she might have latched onto anyone or anything.

Her composure regained, she stepped back and said, "I'm sorry."

Hayden's shocked facial expression communicated much, which was good because only a single-syllable sounded out of his mouth.

"I'm okay," she reassured him, her eyes filling with tears. "You saved me."

His mouth opened, but nothing came out.

"Here. Let me take a look at your arm."

Undecidedly, she didn't know where to grab him. After she settled on his elbow, it had occurred to her the awkward search had probably made him feel worse.

"It looks like it was cleanly severed," she explained what she saw. "Cauterized with minimal bleeding."

The elevator door closed and, unsure if the rocket-elevator would blast off again, Ora said to Hayden, "Come on! We need to move."

His hesitation spoke volumes about how he felt about what had happened to him and she knew his mind thought through his life without a hand, mainly he would never enter space again and, in a selfish way, she hoped he wondered about their relationship and intimacy. As far as she was concerned, it didn't matter to her if he had lost both hands.

"Oh, no you don't!" she exclaimed. "You need to toughen up."

She grabbed him by the hand and led him down the corridor. At first, they started with a brisk walk that turned into a run. This corridor may or may not be the same one they had used when they first arrived. A major difference was the first one was dark with a light that illuminated where they stepped, while this one had overhead lights, running the entire length of the corridor. Doors lined this corridor, where, in the first one, the doors may have been hidden behind the darkness and even behind spotlights that followed them as they proceeded.

"We need to split up and try doors," Ora said.

Nudging him right so he could use his right hand, she went left. There weren't any handles on the doors to try. They were blank metal slates—not even a peephole. The frames sure looked like doors, but down here, who knew if they opened at all.

A sound, she wished she didn't hear, came from the

elevator-rocket behind them.

"Just run Hayden," she yelled over to him.

As far as she knew, no one had entered the elevator after they had exited, but it sounded like the elevator-rocket might be gearing up to blast off. Winded, she looked over at Hayden and he had already stopped running, walking along the wall as if on a casual stroll through a park. She crossed the corridor to the other side to get him.

On her way to him, as she passed one of the doors, it opened as if an automatic door. The soles of her shoes gripped the metal floor and she almost fell forward from balancing herself to stay where she stood, hoping the door remained open.

"Hayden, come on!" she pleaded, waving for him to come, afraid to move.

The door started to close and she placed a foot inside the frame as a doorstop.

"Hurry!"

Sounds from the elevator at the end of the corridor increased. Hayden trotted, then ran. The gap between the metal door and its frame narrowed, so Ora stepped into it and held out a hand.

"Come on, dammit!"

He reached out his right hand and she grabbed it and pulled. When his body slid through the opening, the edge of the door touched his chest and the frame his back. In another second or two, there was no way he would have fit through. When the door closed, it soundproofed the room and they didn't know whether the elevator-rocket had ascended or not. It didn't matter, because no smoke or fire came through the door or its frame, nor could they feel any temperature change in the door itself.

"Do you think this is the bunkers?" Ora asked.

Hayden only shrugged.

"We have to get you to a doctor," she said.

"Let's see where we are," Hayden said.

They were the first words he had spoken since escaping

from the elevator. She smiled, glad he finally emerged out of his funk.

He led her through the lit area to the edge of darkness. Before he entered, his right hand reached back for her and she grabbed it. Together, they entered the unknown.

They proceeded slowly and carefully. With each step, his foot tapped the floor in front of him first and, if it seemed solid, he stepped. So far, every step had felt secure.

Unsure of how far they went, it must have been a distance. Darkness deepened the farther they ventured away from the light and, without it, they lost all visibility, including each other. Both maintained continuous contact, afraid if they lost it, they might never get it back.

Other than the firmness under their feet, there didn't appear to be anything near them. Not once did they run into anything during their processional. Walls didn't seem to exist here, nor a ceiling. A vast void forgotten in the formation of the cavern.

The temperature cooled, but not enough to see their own breath, let alone each other's. Strangely, there was no echo or sound and when they talked, it sounded clarified and amplified in a nearly perfect acoustic environment.

They stopped and stood still. While Hayden remained facing forward to not lose their orientation, Ora turned around, keeping a firm grip on his hand. She no longer saw the light near the door where they had entered. So far, they had moved consistently in a direction away from the door. Doubt crept into Hayden as to whether he had maintained a straight line or had veered along the way. Either way, what was done was done, and they kept moving forward in the direction Hayden walked.

In a strange way, this place may have served a better hiding place than the planned bunkers. There was no way they would be found down here. They had to be deep in the base of the canyon and near the brass, maybe below. The darkness also served another purpose. As long as Hayden didn't use his left arm to reach out or back toward Ora, it concealed his missing arm. To him, it felt like it was still there and this normal-state eased his queasiness. The only way of ruining the illusion would be to try to use it. All of that was great. The only question, now, was would they find their way out?

The last thing he needed was his pretending ignorance to be the cause of Ora's death. They had hurt each other enough and he vowed, then-and-there, to stop generating pain on his end, in actions and words, and inflicting it on her. This was a dream, of course, because he wasn't perfect. If they got out of this place alive and they chose to traverse through life together, eventually, he would do or say something that would cause her pain.

He didn't want to be hurt either but knew she, too, would reciprocate. Maybe on purpose or maybe not, but her actions or words would bring misery just the same. Pain can be administered by many sources, some living, and some inanimate, but mostly stems from people, whether they hurt themselves or others, purposeful or not, in any case, it hurts.

They must have walked for hours, maybe longer. At least it seemed that way. Food, water, shelter, a change of clothes would be nice—more than nice, a necessity. And light. Wandering in total darkness without any change of scenery or sign of escape had already warped their minds some. When there's no difference between having your eyes open or closed, it's only a matter of time before all workings of a human become confused.

Don't forget rest. Not once did they bend down and touch what they walked on. Part of them didn't want to know.

Assuming the breach had been dealt with, they had to get out of here, wherever here was.

"What's that over there?" Ora asked.

In the distance, a faint yellowish-gold light, an aura really, hovered in the darkness.

"You see it, or am I seeing things?" she asked.

"No, I see it," Hayden answered. "Unless I'm seeing

things, too."

It might be a mirage in the nighttime desert, but what choice did they have? Heading in that direction, toe-touch and step, toe-touch and step, their progress was slow but steady. So far, they hadn't fallen into an abyss or met any unwelcomed critters. Nor, had the canyon collapsed on them, which, unless they happened to miss every support structure, the vastness of their travels made them question how such a spacious floor, or cave, was possible this deep in the canyon.

The yellowish-gold light grew larger and brighter as they approached.

"You're thinking you're dead, aren't you?" Ora asked.

It had crossed Hayden's mind, envisioning their ascent to an eternal gate, but he answered, "No. Why are you?"

"*Liar.* I know you were."

"Like I know *you* were. Otherwise, you wouldn't have asked."

"What do you suppose is over there?"

"You mean like heaven?"

"No. Just in general. It might be a mistake."

"The light may be natural, but if it is, what the hell would cause it?"

"That's my point. Deep in the ocean, the angular fish has a light that lures its prey to it."

"I don't think the light's moved."

"Me neither. I don't think we have a choice."

"Let's keep going then."

The closer they came to the yellowish-golden light, the more it started to take on the shape of a square. Even closer, now, the square had elongated into an upright rectangle with the light at the shape's edges.

In reaching the light, it was bright enough they could see each other and for Hayden to notice his missing forearm and hand. Ora let go of his hand and grabbed his pant waist so he could use his hand to feel around and she would do the same. The area where the light emitted from felt solid and metallic and the area outside the light's boundaries felt like rock.

"It's got to be a door," Hayden said.

"I think so, too," Ora agreed. "But how do we open it?"

"Maybe something on the wall, in the floor, or on the door itself … wait a minute. What's that? Here, switch sides."

They switched and he said, "See that dull crystal-like stone right there? What's that?"

Her hand caressed the smooth jewel, getting orientated, then tried to push and turn it, but nothing happened. Pulling her hand back, she thought she felt some give to it on her fingers, so she pulled on the stone.

The jewel came out away from the rock-wall on a rod-like ball shooter on a pinball machine. A whooshing sound of air released, like something depressurizing, and the yellowish-golden light clouded with white smoke. After being in silence for so long, other than their own voices, the sound surprised them. A distinct smell of stale oil permeated the smoky light.

As the smoke dissipated, the richness of the honey-buttered light returned, but the factory-like odor of lubricated working machinery exuded through the perimeter of the door. Unexplainable clinks, clangs, and friction-rubbing sounds came from the door as if a complex interworking of some sophisticated unlocking mechanism unwound itself.

Patiently, they waited. There was no place else to go.

Loud bangs sounded recessed as if they came from beneath where they stood. In a jerking fashion, the door began to lower out of its frame and into the floor. Strangely, the yellowish-gold light extinguished where the door no longer touched its frame and more darkness awaited them on the other side.

"Well, ain't that a crock," Ora said.

"Yeah. Some light would have been nice," Hayden said. "But, let's go in any way. Maybe in there, we'll be protected from what's out here."

"We haven't encountered anything out here. I'm worried what the door kept locked up in there."

With the metal door fully receded into the floor, the honey-buttered light had extinguished entirely, leaving them in pitch-black once again. Hayden felt Ora's hand tightly grab the waist of his trousers. Reaching out and feeling the edge of the doorframe, he led her inside.

After some wandering, a white light flared in an arc out of the floor in the distance. Seeing it, they couldn't lie, desperate now for some light, water, food, and rest.

At the light, it indeed did come through slats in the floor, reaching high in this extremely dark environment. Far from a phenomenon, this light was artificial. Hayden dropped to his knees, while Ora got on her hands and knees. Peeking through the slats, she saw a man seated at a desk in a brightly lit room.

The light pained her eyes, but through it, she yelled down, *"Hello! Hello!"*

The man's head tilted back on his neck to look up. "Who's there?" he asked.

"Oh, thank God! How do we get down to you?" she asked.

"You can't. Unless you can get through that grate."

"What do mean, we can't?" Hayden asked. "You're down there."

"Bakley, that you? It better not be." The man said.

"Here, help me down on the ground," Hayden said to Ora.

She helped him and when he looked down through the grate, it was like looking straight into the sun. But the guy below knew his name. His eyes adjusted and the brightness lessened. He couldn't believe his eyes.

"Baldy?" Hayden said. "So this is where they hide you." Then to Ora, he asked, "Why didn't you say you saw a bald head? Remember, from the screens?"

"It blended in with the light," she explained.

Stabilizing himself on one arm, Hayden looked through the grate and yelled, "We've been trapped up here for a long time. We really could use some food, water, and a breather."

"*Ah*, the inhibitors of the living," the man below said. "You're in no-man's-land, Bakley. The only way down here is through that grate. Once you do that, there are ways of getting you out of here. But, not on your own. I'll call for help."

"We don't have any tools or anything," Hayden said.

"Don't need them, Bakley," the man said. "All you got to do is lift the grate out of its hole and climb down."

"All right," Hayden said. "Look out below."

The bald-headed man lowered his head to protect himself.

"You grab the grate with both hands and I'll use mine," Hayden instructed Ora. "On the count of three, we'll pull, evenly, together."

"Okay," she acknowledged.

They grabbed the grate and pulled. At first, it didn't budge and then it slid right out. It clanged on the floor when they tossed it aside.

"I'm going to need some help getting Ora down," Hayden said to the man.

There wasn't a response from the man and when Ora looked down, the man was busy communicating with someone, most likely through one of those forearm screens.

"It's okay," Hayden said to Ora. "I'm going to lie on the floor and lower you down with one hand. I won't be able to hold you, so it's going to be quick and jerky, but I should be able to slow your descent."

"What about you, with your..." she started.

"I'm going to grab the floor here, hang, and drop. What else can I do?"

"I'll grab your legs."

"No, don't. Just let me fall and land. I wouldn't want to crush you."

"Like when you lay on me?" she asked with a smile.

The comment embarrassed him with the bald man below and the glaring light, coming up through the hole in the floor, shown like a spotlight on his childish demeanor.

Hayden lowered Ora down into the room and when her feet hit the floor, her body collapsed and she laid there. Then, he lowered himself. His strength, under the circumstances, surprised him, but when he dropped and hit the floor, he, too, tumbled onto his side.

Preoccupied with the bald man, she had missed Hayden's fall. Hayden rolled over and, at first, saw Ora's blank face, then followed her eyes to the bald man, in particular, his legs, at least where they should be. He didn't have any.

Instead, the bottom of his torso merged into the seat supporting him. The bald-headed man, who broadcasted from this room, wasn't a man at all, or maybe he was, partially, a robot united with organic material, having a torso, arms, hands, neck, and a bald head. The freaky sight of the top half of a man abruptly stop at the waist and transition into robotics nestled into a chair had stunned them. When they had seen him on the screen, there was no indication he wasn't human. Light hair in all the right places on the face and neck, a little hair in the ears, eyelashes, and eyebrows all seemed impossible to duplicate. But someone had—or something. Even a little perspiration on the forehead and top lip would fool anybody, as it had them.

Unless he was real. A true hybrid: his top half human and the lower not.

Few secrets were buried as deep as this one.

After the transmission, the bald-headed man contacted Kip, who personally went to the bald man's location to escort Hayden and Ora back to civilization. As Hayden and Ora waited, they had so many questions for the bald-headed man, but a string of communications with field agents came in and went out one right after the other. Some of which were extremely intense to listen to.

Kip stormed into the room.

"I thought I told you two to head down toward the bunkers!" Kip chided.

"Well, if your plastic cards had worked, we would have," Hayden countered. "We were on our way when…"

"Not here," Kip said. "Get refreshed first."

Others arrived with Kip, carrying water, food, and even some fruit to subdue Hayden. Hayden and Ora greedily drank water and splashed it on their faces, then gorged themselves on food. Their faces were a mess, uncivilized, but they didn't care. Only watching the others serve the bald-headed man slowed their gluttony.

"You had your fun," Kip said to Hayden and Ora. "Some napkins over here, please. Wipes, whatever." He pointed at the bald man and said, "And reroute his incoming calls elsewhere."

Intermittent bites between captivated staring amounted to Hayden and Ora's movement. Other than a hand or hands moving sustenance to their mouths, chewing, and engrossed eyes roaming about as to not miss anything, they were motionless statues.

Helpers placed a food tray on the desk in front of the bald man and removed the metal cover from over the plate. It had smelled good coming in, but now, the aroma of surf-and-turf, perfectly prepared seafood and succulent steak filled the room, overpowering the machine oil smell that lingered so potently. Since the bald-man had functioning arms and hands, he fed himself. His mannerisms were prim and proper. A clean eater he was and he didn't rush. His taste buds worked fine because the simple enjoyment of eating a good meal expressed subtly on his satisfied face.

A bottle of red wine was placed in front of him along with a glass and an opener. The man-machine set down his fork and knife and went to work on the bottle.

"Here, let me help you with that," Ora offered.

The bald man looked at her for a moment, then continued opening the bottle.

Kip moved near Ora and whispered, "Let the man have

his dignity."

"He's a man?" Ora asked.

"Mostly, yes," Kip answered. "Eating is the best part of this man's existence."

"He eats like this every day?" Hayden whispered.

"Every meal," Kip said. "Whatever he wants. He deserves it."

Contentment made the man appear different, less intense as he enjoyed his meal. No food or drink dropped out of him, so the bald-headed man's stomach or something stomach-like must be intact.

"Let's get out of here and let him eat in peace," Kip said. He pointed at the man behind the desk and said, "You're the best, Baldy. We couldn't do what we do without you."

A fork with half a scallop on it rose in a gesture to Kip's words as the man's mouth chewed a bite of steak.

"Alright, come on, "Kip whispered to Hayden and Ora. "You don't want to be here once all of that is digested—if you catch my drift. I've never seen it, nor do I plan to."

Only Kip, Hayden, and Ora left the room, while the others stayed behind for what Kip had called "cleanup duty." They stepped into a hallway lined with doors and started walking.

Immediately, questions flew at Kip and he squashed them by saying, "What I'm about to tell you, most people in this canyon don't know."

That got Hayden and Ora's attention and they settled down, ready to listen.

"When our military engages or our agents are out there in the field, a lot of bad stuff happens. Even more than what's reported in the news. Although it's true most don't see war, they all still put their lives on the line. War doesn't own the rights to death. Nor serious injury. It can happen anytime, anywhere. So, for the vets up to it, who don't want to spend the rest of their lives lying in bed, feeling sorry for themselves, and being fed pudding, there are opportunities to still serve and be an integral part of a team. Many come here and other facilities, serving in roles like Baldy back there. And for their service, their lives are extended with technology not available to the public. They are fed, cleaned up, shaven, and cared for."

"Do they sleep?" Ora asked.

"They powernap," Kip said. "While they're resting, eating, being cleaned up, repaired, their work is temporarily handled by another."

"How many?" Hayden asked. "I mean, how many are here at this location?"

Kip's lips pursed and his mouth contorted, then he said, "All these doors," as his hand pendulumed wide by his side.

"That many?" Ora couldn't believe it. "There's got to be hundreds."

"On this floor, yes," Kip said reverently. He sighed and said, "I'm near this every day. Let's change the subject, shall we? So, your injuries didn't get past me. Hayden's missing the lower half of his arm, you're both wearing burned through clothing, burns, singed hair. Anything internal?"

After hearing about the bald-headed man and others who had suffered much worse, Hayden and Ora shook their head no.

"Okay … so what happened to the cards?" Kip asked.

"My card was hacked and an orange-hooded person came on and said that I was being tricked," Hayden explained.

"Tricked?" Kip asked. "By whom?"

"I guess you. They never said. There's more. Something about your group wanting what's inside the briefcase for your own ambition."

"That's rich coming from them. They're preaching the same gospel. I don't know what to say other than I'm sorry your plastic was rejected at the register. It should have worked and certainly shouldn't have been hacked into." Kip held out his hand. "I'll turn it over to my people to see how it was done."

"I don't have it. I destroyed it."

"You what? You realize how much those things cost to produce?"

"You should get your money back."

A dejected Kip turned to Ora. "What about yours? Any problems?"

"Just one," Ora said. "It wasn't hacked or anything, but it didn't seem to be tracking right. We would see dots on the screen a good ways off and we thought we were okay and then, boom, they were there."

"Patty, Peggy, and Polly piping the same prick!" Kip exclaimed. "They beat us to that, too."

"What?" Ora asked.

"Mirror-imaging, that's what. Objects on screen are closer than they appear. They manipulate the tracker so it appears they're far off when really, they're so close, their lasers are inches away from your sphincter. One false move, it's going in and you're fucked."

"Seems to me, you're losing this *war for the spheres,"* Hayden said.

"Yeah, yeah. We're working on it," Kip said to Hayden, then held out his hand and asked Ora, "Where's your card?"

"It got torched in the elevator," Ora explained. "Your elevator-girl had it in her skirt pocket."

"Mm, two cards down the drain. I was told about it, but didn't see it."

"She tried setting us up," Hayden said. "Did you know about her?"

"By the way, a hand can't stop a laser," Kip said. "I hate to admit this, but no," he answered, concern in his voice. "After the nurse, she was my second favorite employee."

Ora rolled her eyes. *"Oh, brother."*

"How many breached?" Hayden asked.

"A patrol, that was it," Kip said. "Initially, I thought, maybe, they had accidentally stumbled onto us. That was until news about the elevator-girl."

"She let them in?" Ora asked.

"Apparently," Kip said. "I'll have to review that, too.

Problem is, we may never know why."

"Well, the word's out," Hayden said. "The hooded one seemed remote on the calling card."

"Yeah, but we can't be too sure," Kip said. "You thought Baldy was a whole person. But, I agree. More are on their way. I'm afraid we'll have to abandon this place." Fondly, he looked around.

"Could she have reached out to them?" Ora asked.

Kip sighed. "Maybe. We're looking into that, too."

"What about all of the baldies?" Hayden asked. "Is there enough time to move them all?"

A second sigh came out of Kip and he stopped and looked around at all the doors.

Hayden and Ora also stopped.

A longer exhale expelled out of Kip and he said, "No," and started walking down the hall.

Hayden and Ora looked at each other and then around at all the doors. They envisioned all the baldy types, faithfully working with the agents out in the field.

Hayden wasn't an agent. He was a nobody that just happened to get caught up in all of this when the briefcase came flying through his car window. *A rental*, he remembered. Baldy had saved his life and got him out of Manhattan.

Tears welled in Ora's eyes as she squeezed Hayden's hand and held it tight. Solemnly, they ventured down the hallway—a good distance now behind Kip—together.

CHAPTER **FOURTEEN**

After much haste and controlled chaos, one of those pudgy planes had carried Hayden, Ora, and Kip to another undisclosed location. As usual, the windows in the craft had been blocked out so no one aboard could track where they were and any devices carried on by staff had to be shut down and stowed in another part of the plane.

Other than the extreme circumstances, the flight felt like a regular flight with all the seats filled to capacity. Most commercial flights could be categorized as quiet and this certainly wasn't a commercial flight, but this one went beyond quiet, having a dangerous eeriness about it. Everyone knew what was happening at the canyon. The atmosphere contained an air of finality to it. It was about as near to blasting off the Earth in hopes of surviving because there wouldn't be an Earth to return to, without actually being in that situation.

In some ways, Hayden had felt exposed in the air. If Kip's craft could be shot down, then they all could. Yet, the higher altitude had felt comfortable to him. There was something about it. Maybe, it could be his body was somehow wired for such heights.

What wasn't comfortable was being around Kip and

knowing what he knew. This wasn't the only quasi-NASA plane in the air, nor their only means of scattering to a new location. The varying of personnel, means of travel, and approximate arrival times had all been planned out some time ago in anticipation of having to abandon the canyon post. From what Hayden had gathered from Kip on the flight, not everyone headed for the same station.

All of that was well and good, but Hayden didn't like knowing there were some who weren't going anywhere. They had been ordered to remain behind, destroy secrets, protect the fort, and keep the orange assailants busy for a while and off their trail. An understood order was to kill as many of those bastards as they could.

As far as the canyon, it would be utilized by the United States government. Fitting, because the unnamed space agency's abandonment, working under the National Aeronautics and Space Administration, was the government's gain. Such vacated facilities were handed down to the government for their use, not only in the United States, but also in the world.

On the flight, Kip had also shared that unlike traditional war, where occupancy carried the day, in the war for the spheres, the enemy in orange had nothing to gain by claiming the canyon location. The main reason being, Kip's group would know they were there and simply attack, destroy, and subdue. The enemy knew this, too, and would never consider occupying the canyon. Swapping locales would be a waste of time and effort.

No, the secret to this war was secrecy. Any advantage one side gained was usually too late for the other and they suffered the consequences. But, now, that they know of it, it wasn't a secret anymore and so both sides must think of another advantage to stay one step ahead of each other. And so it went, until one of them or a new player entered the game with an advantage big enough to end the game. A game similar to nuclear war, in that, the only way one side could win between two equally matched opponents was for one to fire their warheads first without the other side knowing and destroying them before they themselves were destroyed. Otherwise, if both sides fired their warheads, what would be the point without a winner?

Kip's staple line was that he or his group were always *working on something.* In this context, now, Hayden could see the truth in it.

Hayden awoke to the sound of dripping water and Kip's voice. Both of which, equally, sharpened the pain he felt in his extremities.

"Where am I?" Hayden asked, groggily, lying on his back on a bed, covered up to his neck.

"Ironically for you, in another hole in the ground," Kip answered.

"No, I mean ... the actual location."

"Borders reach this far down, but you know I can't say. I can tell you that you are lying in a hole in the ground. Four dirt walls. A dirt floor. And a dirt ceiling." Kip turned to one of the doctors in the makeshift room, pointed to the ceiling, and asked, "Is this place safe?" Not waiting for an answer, he looked down at Hayden. "Never mind. No use in worrying our patient. It's home for a while," Kip's eyes scanned the exposed dirt around them, "if you want to call it that. It'll be nice when it's done, but let's call ugly, ugly. Unless you're an ant, the place is a dump. It's hard finding new secret places to retreat to."

"What ... happened? Why ... am I ... in so much ... pain?"

"You wanted to be whole again, right. You're whole."

"What?"

"Here. Do you feel this?"

Kip pinched the skin on top of Hayden's left hand.

"Yes ... stop ... my left hand. How did you…"

"Oh, I didn't do it. You would have had two left hands or two right ones."

"Both ... arms ... hurt."

"Of course they do after the procedures."

"Procedures?"

Kip waved for one of the doctors in the earth-carved room to come over. Then, he leaned over Hayden, tapped his friend's chest with his fingers, and said, "I can see you're not ready for this right now, so I'll see you in recovery. Okay?"

Slowly coming to, Hayden swore he heard the sound of an actual door opening and overheard a woman say faintly in the distance, "He's waking, Mr. Stanton, if you would like to see him." Her voice echoed in the hallway as if she had spoken inside a cave.

The door clicked closed and Hayden figured he must be inside a room—a real room. Fogged over and groggy, all he could recall of the other room was that it was dark and the sound of dripping water.

"Hey, Hayden," Kip said cheerfully. "How about this room, *huh*? I thought for sure you were going to catch some kind of infection in that nest in the ground. Maybe even pneumonia and die."

Lying on his back on a bed with the covers pulled up to his neck, Hayden asked, "Where am I?"

Kip situated a second chair beside another, plopped down in one, and put his feet up on the other. "Here we go again. You're in a nice room with all the comforts of modern living. The only dirt in here is specs of dust. Why can't you be happy?"

"What is there to be happy about?" Hayden said.

"*Geez!* You're a real bummer you know that. Plenty, my friend."

"My arms ... hurt."

"They will for a little while. Within a week, you'll feel better than you did before."

"What ... happened? I remember we landed ... unloaded ... ate MREs ... and nothing else after."

"We wanted to get you into surgery as quickly as

possible."

"Surgery? … My arm?"

"Better," Kip said.

The screen embedded in Kip's arm illuminated and the face of the woman with the sultry voice appeared on the screen.

"Yes, Mr. Stanton," she said.

As Hayden attempted to lean on his elbows to get a glimpse of the woman's face he had imagined that would fit the voice, pain shot through his arms as if millions of microbes with sharp teeth had bitten into his flesh all at the same time. Wincing, he stretched his neck to see Kip and, then, said, "Is that …"

Kip nodded to Hayden it was the woman whose soothing voice had spoken into the rooms inside the canyon and, then, he said to her, "Has any fresh fruit arrived, yet?"

"Yes, Mr. Stanton—cherries."

"Cherries!" Kip blurted. "That sucks. Who sits and picks at a bowl full of cherries?"

From a lying position on the bed, Hayden nodded cherries were fine and then asked, "Can I see?"

Kip shook his head that he couldn't as he said to the woman, "Apparently, Hayden does. When they're ready, bring them up."

"Right away, Mr. Stanton," the woman said and the transmission ended.

"Why … didn't you … let me … see her?" Hayden said.

"Not in your condition," Kip answered. "Your recovery would be set back weeks. Now, look. I should probably wait until you have some fruit, but you should know a couple of things."

A knock on the door interrupted Kip and he hung his head in frustration.

"That was fast," Kip said. "Must be the cherries." He sat up, turned his body in the chair, and said, "Come on in."

The door opened and Ora entered the room, carrying a bowl of cherries.

With raised eyebrows, Kip turned to Hayden and said, "Told you it's the cherries."

Laughter shook Hayden's body, which provoked the pain in his arms.

"Sorry to interrupt," she said. "I couldn't wait any longer."

As she walked by Kip on her way to Hayden, Kip plucked a cherry out of the bowl, popped it into his mouth, and said, "Be glad you did. You wouldn't have liked that dirt room."

Joy in seeing Ora made Hayden's eyes sparkle and when he went to reach up to touch her, he screamed in pain and she kissed his open mouth.

"Don't move," she said. "Do you want me to call the nurse?"

"For George Washington's sake, he doesn't need a nurse," Kip said, as he stood out of the chair, walked over to the door, and locked it. "Pop a cherry in his mouth so we can get on with it, please."

Looking down at Hayden, Ora moved her eyebrows up and down, picked a cherry from the bowl, licked it, and sensually placed it into his mouth with her fingers.

"You—sit," Kip said as he motioned for Ora to sit in the chair beside him.

"Now, look," Kip continued as he sat in the chair. "I know everybody here is experiencing some type of discomfort. Can we suck it up for a few minutes so I can share with you what's been happening?"

Hayden nodded and Ora said prim and proper, "Yes, Mr. Stanton."

Kip shot her a look, letting her know he didn't care for her dry humor and said, "Diarrhea is falling from the sky, hitting fans aimed at us, and getting into our mouths. And it's getting more and more difficult to clean it up."

"What's been happening?" Hayden asked.

"For starters, there's been more assassinations that trace back to you. One of your bullets was recovered from the head of the President of the Czech Republic. Another was found in the President of Slovakia's skull."

"Why two?" Ora asked. "Is it intensifying?"

"A *two-for*, I would say so," Kip said. "My people tell me the two countries were Czechoslovakia before they split in 1993."

"Why ... these leaders?" Hayden asked, grimacing. "Why ... these countries?"

"Before we get to that, you should know German and Niger leaders have met with the President of the United States, asking for his cooperation in finding you and bringing you to justice. Each is seeking two-counts. The Germans, two-counts of murder for their president and they're claiming you killed their man in Sydney. Niger, one-count murder for their president and one-count attempted murder on their prime minister."

"But *you* ... killed the German," Hayden said.

"Only they don't know there are two assholes with the runs," Kip said. "Diarrhea from one is hard to clean up, let alone two. But we're working on it. Not that it matters much. You're still wanted for three murders and an attempt. Five, counting the Czechs and Slavs. Speaking of which, with the Germans right next door, they agreed to hold a summit in Vienna, Austria and have invited Niger and the United States."

"While your ... ass is clean, there's one thing ... you're forgetting," Hayden struggled to say. "I didn't ... kill these people."

"They have proof, otherwise. Apparently, your shit smells guilty."

"Not a surprise yours ... doesn't stink. So I'm being ... blamed, but who would ... get the justice? There's only one ... of me and ... four or five of them."

"Quartered, I guess. Twenty percent each. Unless the United States wants a piece. Maybe they would, just to ensure they get your head and stop others from arguing over it."

"Are the bullets … enough to convict?"

"My sources say they have prints, eyewitnesses, and even established motive."

"Well … which ones?"

"All of them," Kip answered.

Any evidence these countries concocted would stick. No one would listen, let alone believe a madman.

The man wearing a hat and sporting a golden tan, *Manhattan*, had screwed Hayden over so bad, he knew the diarrhea Kip had referred to earlier was his and it was spreading. Cleanup for Kip was becoming impossible and options for Hayden were running out.

As was his life. Any chance of going up to space again died when those world leaders were killed with his name written on the death certificate as the cause of the death. Finding sanctuary in another home, or, who knew, maybe finding it in marrying Ora amounted to a pipedream. Normalcy of any kind would never be experienced again after entering the abnormal in Manhattan. The world of lasers, secret agents part of underground agencies, and otherworldly technology that wasn't from other worlds, but right here on Earth were things he wished he never learned existed.

Call him ignorant, for the ignorant live happily.

"I think you should get some kind of humanitarian award for bringing countries together in a unified mission," Kip said.

"That's not funny," Ora said. "When their mission is to kill Hayden."

"So, why these … countries?" Hayden said.

"Exactly," Kip said. "Was it random? A planned pattern? I don't know how well you know your geography, but Germany, Czechia, and Slovakia are all in a row right across Europe. But, Niger is south on the other side of the Mediterranean in Africa. So, why the outlier? To throw us off? Hayden Bakley's a sly devil."

"Come on, Kip," Ora said. "That's not helping."

"Just lightening the mood," Kip said, pointing to the bowl of cherries. "May I have one of those?"

Ora stretched the bowl out and he took one and ate it.

"Thanks," Kip said. "But Hayden's not so slick that my people didn't come across a working theory too coincidental to ignore. At first, we were too focused on the presidents themselves and failed to make a connection. Switching gears to focusing on the countries they governed, we began to connect the dots and guess where they led us? That's right, the Outer Space Treaty of 1967 we talked about. Come to find out, if you sort the list by who signed the treaty first and who ratified first, you'll never guess the order of countries. *Yep*, Germany, Niger, and Czechoslovakia."

"So, this … all deals … with the treaty?" Hayden said.

"I'm convinced, but if you kill the President of Hungary next, everyone should be convinced," Kip said.

"Kip, stop!" Ora said. "Last time. It's not helping."

"Did you … notify them … of the threat?" Hayden asked in pain.

"Who, Hungary?" Kip questioned. "And tell them what? The country that Hayden Bakley just happens to be from knows who he's going to kill next? *Oh, no.* Someone else needs to figure it out first and then we'll support them any way we can."

"Including … turning me in?" Hayden said.

"Possibly," Kip admitted. "If it were in our best interest."

Ora smacked Kip's shoulder hard enough it sounded fleshy through his clothes and some cherries rolled out of the bowl onto the floor.

"*Geez!* Not so hard," Kip said, rubbing his shoulder.

And there it was again. Funny how the truth keeps popping up, letting Hayden know there was no ignoring it or getting away from it. He believed Kip would turn him in if it called for it. That would open all kind of possibilities for him, namely, another chance with Ora.

A strange confidence overwhelmed him at the thought.

Not confidence in himself, or Kip, but in Ora. The choice had been hers right along and neither man could make the choice for her. Influence it, perhaps, but that was the extent of it.

"I mean, Hayden's gun is going to run out of bullets, right?" Ora said. "So, what are people going to say if another is killed and it's beyond what Hayden's pistol holds?"

"They'll say he bought more and reloaded," Kip said flatly. "Look. None of these people were in power when their countries signed and ratified the treaty, which means, they are being murdered for simply being post-treaty representatives of their countries. That is, if this is somehow tied to the treaty."

"So, someone's … against the treaty?" Hayden asked.

"We think so," Kip said. "The only problem is, many are, including our orange traffic cone enemies. It could be anybody."

"So, now what?" Hayden said.

"We're thinking it might be best if you were exiled," Kip said.

Emphatically, truth performed jumping jacks, showing Hayden it wouldn't be ignored and was here to stay. X marked the spot. X-iled indeed!

"Exiled to where?" Ora asked.

There was a long pause before Kip answered and, finally, he said, "Space."

An unhealthy laugh seeped out between Hayden's dry lips like hot air escaping through a fissure. A dry coughing-fit followed and Ora left to get him some water. Both jarred his body and pain ran amok in his arms.

Standing, as Ora left the room, Kip watched her leave and once the door closed, he stood next to Hayden's bed and leaned over him.

"Before she gets back, there are a few things I want to say," Kip said. "A few things I want you to think about. You lost your home, I gave you shelter. You lost your arm and hand and I gave them back to you. Better than you had before. You lost your life as you knew it and I'm offering another one. *Criminy*, Hayden, I'm even offering life itself," Kip said, shaking his head. "I can't protect you. Not down here. Not anymore. You prefer it up there, anyway. You wanted to go back and I'm giving you that chance." Kip hung his head, closed his eyes, and then looked at Hayden. "I even conceded Ora."

Ora returned with a cup of ice and a pitcher of water.

"And I'm about to prove that now," Kip finished and returned to the chair.

She poured Hayden a cup of water and situated it so he could drink.

"I'm ... hot," Hayden said after drinking it all.

She pulled down the covers and bandages covered both of his arms from his palms to his biceps.

She turned and looked at Kip. "Why are both of his arms bandaged?"

"Fine," Kip said, standing. "Since you're both so concerned, let's switch gears, and talk about Hayden's arms." He moved closer to the bed, looked at Hayden, and said. "You've been enh*uma*nced."

Neither Hayden nor Ora had to ask what he meant after being with him and the two forearms in the parallelogram room when he first mentioned the term.

"Both arms?" Ora asked.

The pain in Hayden's arms ailed him inside out, prickling nerves and tendons that would reach the inner flesh, but the exterior surface and skin must be numb because he hadn't felt the bandages on them, even the material covering half of his palm. As to why both arms hurt, he had chalked it up to either the pain had reached across his chest into his other arm, or, a sympathetic pain where one arm experienced it as it struck for real in the other like twins experiencing the same thing even though it's only happening to one of them.

"Damn it all to hell, Kip!" Hayden said about as forcefully as he could in his condition. "Why didn't ... you ask me?"

"You're right," Kip said. "I should have. But, you're the

first to have it done on both arms. They may come in handy up there."

"You don't know … when to quit," Hayden said. "Are you asking me … if I want to go up … or are you going to … knock me out again … and I'll wake up up there?"

Kip's lips pursed. "Hey, that's not bad."

"Kip!" Ora yelled. *"Get out!"*

"No, I'm not going to get out of my own facility," Kip firmly said. "It's not my facility, but some unfortunate things happen to some people it could be. So, everybody calm down, alright." He looked down at Hayden and said, "You sure you want her to go along? You won't be happy."

Hayden turned his head and looked up at Ora. "I'm not now … so what's the difference."

Kip snapped his fingers. "Right on, brother! Let's roll with that. Take everything I had said earlier and add to that that you are wanted on multiple accounts of murder and an attempted murder. There's only one kind of retaliation for murder and that's murder. That many countries looking for you, you will be found and killed. So, this isn't putting on a diaper and giving into diarrhea, *oh no,* this is fixing the problem and stopping the flow. You're in way over your head. Face it, Hayden. Your life sucks. Get off this Godforsaken dust ball and leave her here or take her with you—I don't care."

And there it was, Hayden heard Kip's concession of Ora.

"And when were you going to ask me?" Ora said.

"Now," Kip said. "The discussion is happening now. So, what's it going to be? Look at it like a free vacation. Think about it. No more bills. No traffic. No more lines. Hell, just thinking about it, I want to go."

Looking down at Hayden, Ora shook her head. "Don't answer Hayden. There's no rush. You have to heal first. Things need put in order and figured out. Personally, I think he's sending us to our graves. I mean the human body can't remain in space forever. Even with the current technology."

"Already got you covered," Kip said. "Without major

modifications, it's true. You would have to come down. So, with generous frequency, you two would come down, spend some time, then go back up. All, I mind you, in our protection. We do this a couple of years, who knows, maybe they'll forget all about you, and this thing will be over."

"You thought that far ahead, so have you ... thought about ... what we would be doing up there?" Hayden asked.

"We're working on it," Kip said. "Astronaut stuff. You'll try to earn your keep, but of course, you won't be able to. We kicked around some ideas, but it's still being hashed out."

CHAPTER **FIFTEEN**

A few months had passed and all of Hayden and Ora's injuries were healing nicely. Those months allowed Hayden to get used to his new forearms and hands and Kip had been right—they do feel better than his originals. They felt lighter, yet stronger. Simpler in design, he imagined, yet, all the dexterity remained. Best of all, from a functional standpoint, there wasn't anything new to learn. His new extremities operated the same as his flesh and bone ones had before.

Both forearms had screens inlaid in them, which, above anything else, took Hayden some time to get used to. The latest and greatest had been installed, which also meant the best available software and features as well. This, of course, meant more to learn, and, with many features in the testing phase, also meant there were more that could malfunction. Yet, to Kip's surprise, Hayden seemed to embrace the change and challenge of being the first to operate such software and test each of their capabilities and reliability. After the plastic navigation card had been hacked into and ultimately failed to get Hayden and Ora to the bunkers, Kip thought for sure that Hayden would reject being the guinea pig for such field-testing, which had only been on the ground. The true test would occur in space.

Also, over these months, Hayden had decided to leave the planet and Ora had opted to go with him. There was no way he could ever question her devotion to him and already had in the works a planned destination to propose to her on one of their rendezvous back on Earth.

Upon hearing their decision, Kip wished Hayden and Ora the best of luck and said, "You kids go have fun." He turned to leave, walked a few steps, turned around again, snapped his fingers, and added, "Oh, if you two happen to be the first couple to have a baby in space and there's a book and movie, don't forget old Kip. Maybe then I can retire."

Busy with getting ready for departure, any thoughts of marriage would have to wait. Not that it wasn't important, it's just Hayden's brain didn't have the room for it, and Ora didn't know anything about it. Oh, she hoped something would come of this because she had gone to his home—for him, she had told him. Nostalgia about leaving Earth, not for good, but damn near, gummed up their mental, emotional, spiritual, and even physical preparations.

Despite such feelings, they were ready to go. Under bazaar circumstances, space had become a destination Hayden never thought he would see again, except from the ground. Ora, who would have gone up again, most likely in an official capacity as a NASA astronaut, believed, this time and future stints with Hayden by her side, she would be able to conquer her fear of space and end, finally, her Astrophobia. If not, she would lean on him as she had done before.

Among other preparations, packing wasn't overlooked, but, let's just say, most people pack more thoroughly going on a week's vacation than astronauts do going into space for six months to a year. In fairness, most of what Hayden and Ora would need would precede them to the space station before they arrived. With so little to bring and meager choices of what they could choose, such as handpicking certain brands of bath items for a wash kit, neither Hayden or Ora had thought much about it, let alone start packing.

Kip called a meeting with Hayden and Ora and told them they didn't need to wear helmets in this facility, because, at the moment, there wasn't anything to see. They met in a trapezoid-shaped room, and as Hayden entered, a spearmint scent lingered from the fresh white putty patches and lines on an otherwise gray wall just erected. The floor appeared to be finished, covered with a gray, thin industrial rug. Three light-gray leather chairs, almost identical in style to the brown ones in the parallelogram room inside the canyon, were installed into the floor. Nine postholes, recessed into the floor, finished the circle like numbers on a clock where the other chairs would be for twelve in all when completed. A larger hole donned the center of the circle, sure to secure a large round conference table. Light-gray metal grids crisscrossed the ceiling, awaiting tiles. A lone tile, animated with a slow-moving sky, said this wasn't going to be your white-tiled composite-material variety drop ceiling.

Already seated, Kip said, "Watch when you sit down. I don't think these things have been tightened down yet."

Hayden carefully sat down, while Ora stood.

"I don't blame you," Kip said to Ora. "Okay, without further ado, I wanted to update you both on what is happening. No big deal, just a change of plans. So, who wants it first?"

"Want what?" Ora asked. "*News?* I guess me."

"Fine," Kip said. "NASA orders came in. You'll be doing a junket on the International Space Station. You can relax because you don't launch for another month or so. Obviously, these orders override what we were going to do."

There it was. Ora's plan to lean on Hayden as she chiseled away at destroying her Astrophobia had popped like an empty bubble that had been merely an idea. She shifted her weight from one leg to the other. "Well, I'm not going! I'm going with Hayden."

Doubt about Kip's concession of Ora earlier hadn't moved far from Hayden's mind, patiently waiting like a dog, sitting and facing the door, waiting for the owner to open it so it could go inside. The change of plans had opened the door and doubt trotted into his noggin. Kip hadn't conceded anything.

"You get yanked from this mission, my people can't send you up either," Kip explained. "We're off the record, not rogue."

"Go, Ora," Hayden said, lovingly squeezing her hand. "We'll catch up, then."

"Yes," Kip said. "This accomplishes the same thing by getting you off the Earth and, hopefully, out of trouble being associated with this guy."

"He's right," Hayden agreed. "We won't be together, but I like our chances better up there."

"Okay, with that settled," Kip said to Ora, "you'll stay here until we're told otherwise. At the risk of giving away our location, you're only about a thousand miles away from Baikonur."

"We're in China?" Ora asked, still stuck on what she was going to do when her fear of space threatened her without Hayden there and, she hated to admit it, without Kip either.

"No, not necessarily," Kip answered. "We could be in India, or Mongolia, or in any of the *stan* countries in the Middle East."

Ora shook her head.

"While she wallows in her frustration," Kip said to Hayden, "onto you, my friend. You are leaving sooner than anticipated. As in less than thirty-six hours."

"What's the hurry?" Hayden asked.

"The Chinese are launching is what. We need to get you packed and over to Jiuquan. Good thing we're only about a thousand miles or so away."

"What? The Chinese Space Station? They're going to let an American on board?"

"*Yep*. The first non-Chink to see the inside of the CSS."

"How did you arrange that?"

"My part was easy. All I had to do was make a promise

that's out of my hands to keep. They're the ones who had a bit of pain and some shuffling. Their station is a lot smaller than the ISS and only holds three people. With you in the mix, their one replacement became your escort, so instead of a one-for-one, it's a twofer, which means someone's coming home prematurely so you can go up. Learn from old Kip would you? No matter what you face, just remember all the trouble you caused and try to keep harmony down here as well in the heavens."

"Learn from old Kip," Hayden repeated, pursing his lips. "You see, I already know the whole harmony here and heaven means *Tianhe*, the name of their station."

"Very good," Kip said. "Wisdom like that will establish good relations with the *sensei*, whose coattails you'll be riding."

"It's not exactly an ancient Chinese secret."

"I'm glad you can see the humor in this."

"Ora has orders from NASA, so how do you guys work? Do I get orders?"

"Ours are so simple they're verbal. One, don't cause any trouble. Two, stay out of the way. Three, don't touch anything."

"I thought you were going to say something about staying alive."

"You do those three things you will remain alive," Kip said.

"So, I just live up there?" Hayden asked. "What am I supposed to do?"

"*Live* for starters. Why do American's want to take out being alive from living? Knowing the Chinese, all two of them aboard, they'll put you to work so you can earn your keep."

"That's all?"

"No, not exactly," Kip said and blatantly stared at Ora.

At first, she didn't notice, concentrating on her own thoughts, then when she did and saw how brazenly rude his look was, she asked, "Oh, am I supposed to leave?"

"Good thing she's not going with the Chinese," Kip said.

"Fine," she said, as she stormed for the door, then stopped, and turned around. "I assume I'll see you before you leave?" she asked Hayden.

"Certainly…" Hayden started.

Kip interrupted, "He'll try."

Ora turned and stormed out the door.

"Why did you have to do that?" Hayden asked.

"Because, the less she knows, the better for her," Kip said. "Now, listen up and listen up good. The Chinese allow four pounds carry-on on their transport ship. *Four pounds!* That's almost a pound more than the Russians allow. Probably something you hadn't thought about, but your new forearms and hands are actually lighter than the ones your mother gave you."

"Is that why you did both arms?"

"In part, yes. So, guess how much of that four-plus-pounds you get? Two and a half. *Two and a half, Hayden,* that's it! Because you're going to earn your keep from us up there. How you ask? By being our eyes and ears. This is a big deal being on the Tianhe. Even seeing the inside of their transport ship. I want you to remember all that you can. What you don't remember will be video recorded and automatically transmitted back to us. Look around. Move your arms. Be nosy. Wander around the ship. You get caught where you shouldn't be, play the dumb American."

"You want me to spy for you?" Hayden asked.

"Yes!" Kip said. "Let's call it what it is. You'll be doing your country a great service. Back to the weight. You get to pack two and a half pounds. Be stingy. They said they would supply simple toiletries, basic clothes, and etcetera. Your bag needs to be clean. Meaning, nothing goofy in there. The goofy stuff will be throughout your suit. They won't know it and you won't know. It'll be like them trying to find Waldo because the stuff fits right in and looks like part of the suit. We'll communicate by your forearms. One bums out, you have a backup."

"Another reason for two?"

"Yep. Now, we're going to arrive late to avoid any kind of physical examination. I hope to hell it works, but if it does, you're going to have to be stealthy using those screens up there."

"And if being late doesn't work?"

"You're staying on the ground until we can make arrangements with another space station. There's no way we want that technology known."

"Well, just send me to the ISS."

"You know we can't do that. One astronaut will be coming down and Ora will be going up. *Tit-for-tat.* You know how everything is specifically calculated out. Besides, you would be taken into custody."

"Right. The murders I didn't commit. So, you're saying all this stuff will be on my suit, but how will I know what's what?"

"To keep you from getting bored, we'll teach you when we communicate. You'll be surprised how many gadgets are on there."

"Hopefully, they work better than that plastic navigation card."

"They will. At least they should. We're always tinkering with them to make them better."

"Any weapons?" Hayden asked.

"*Hayden Bakley!* I'm shocked," Kip said. "Of course there are weapons."

"Of course," Hayden said smartly. "Not that killing everyone on board would help."

"Good man. Good man. Just the ambassador we need."

"Speaking of which. How in the world are they allowing me on when they aren't allowed on the International Space Station?"

"In trying to keep harmony down here as well in the heavens, we promised them an astronaut spot on the ISS in the future."

"*Holy schmoly!* Isn't that breaking our own law written by

Congress?"

"You're not with OSTP and you're not coordinating anything with the Chinese, who, by the way, wants to work with us and improve relations, so they're willing to take the chance first. They just don't know you're not from NASA, which is what really puts us in the clear."

Hayden stood out of his chair. "What do you mean, I'm not from NASA?"

Kip looked down at the floor, then back up at Hayden. "Yeah, about that. I've been meaning to tell you you've been canned. Eventually, you'll be boxed." Kip's thumb and middle finger touched his temples. "I guess I should explain."

"You think!" Hayden yelled. "A day and a half from leaving Earth, you want to drop this on me. How long have you known?"

"Almost a week … well, four days to be exact."

"Four days!" Hayden couldn't believe it. "Thanks. You're a real pal."

"Okay, so, this is how it is," Kip began. "You've been canned, but not fired. What that means is everything is still intact. Your pension, standing, everything as if you're still on their payroll. A contact at NASA administration is going to try to keep that façade for as long as possible. So, to the Chinese, it'll appear as if they're taking a NASA astronaut into the belly of the CSS in a good-faith gesture. Eventually, admin is going to have to process what they need to process so you're out, but they agreed, for your safety, that you will be deceased."

"What about my pension,?" Hayden asked.

"You are going to take it in a lump sum. It's all been agreed to."

"Without me there? How could that happen?"

"It'll be a great thing. You'll have your money and be off the grid. The only problem will be getting you back into space without any affiliation."

"I thought staying in space was the plan," Hayden said.

"It was," Kip said. "But remember, as time passes and you're off the radar, maybe you won't have to keep going up to space."

"What about them having my DNA? You said they'll find me anywhere."

"Probably true, but if they lose interest …"

Overcome, Hayden plopped into the chair and it wiggled on the post underneath him. He's been jerked around worse—like by Kip.

Seeing the emotion on Hayden's shocked face, Kip said, "Did I you tell you it's been arranged for Ora to receive your death benefit? You two get married and you'll walk away with your pension and the insurance money."

Words didn't seem to exist for Hayden. All his brain envisioned were letters but it lost the ability to arrange them to make a word and even words consisting of a single letter weren't recognized as a word, only a useless letter. Unable to communicate, he just sat there.

Kip stared at Hayden as if this would be the last time his eyes would behold his friend. It's not the image he wanted to capture or the how he wanted to remember him, so he looked away to break the recording memory and said, "I guess that's it then."

Rotating black letters flew across a blanked-white mind's eye inside Hayden's head.

Kip slapped Hayden's leg as he stood and said, "Let me know if you need help packing. We'll be in touch."

With that, Kip left.

A few hours ticked by without Hayden noticing. Coming to, as he had done after the surgery, he wasn't seated in the light-gray leather chair, but inside his room, standing beside his bed with a pair of underwear crumpled in his hand. Not just any pair, but one of his favorites, that is, since his all-time favorite pair with the waistband slightly stretched yet elastic enough to keep them up had been shredded when his house blew up. How he wished he had them on that day.

Underwear broken in like that were barely noticeable when they were on and perfect for a sedentary man, but only lasted so long in that sweet spot before the waistband loosened so much that any kind of movement, even with pants on, they started to slide off.

Just beyond his hand holding the underwear, a bag laid on the bed. Somehow, in that haze, he had started packing. Not trusting what he might have put in the bag, he dumped it out and started again by inserting the underwear. Making the decision process easier, he went over to the already-opened drawer he had pulled the underwear from, reached in, grabbed a pile of them with one hand, and stuffed them inside the bag.

There, he thought, an inactive man in space needs to be comfortable.

The Chinese expected him, but also didn't. His guess was they weren't given much time to plan for his arrival and he wondered what provisions they had made for him. Underwear was a go, but what about the rest? Maybe it was best that he threw some things together more than underwear. *Two and a half pounds,'* Kip had said. *'Be stingy.'*

Under the hurried circumstances, generic Chinese toiletries and clothes awaited him. At least he hoped they awaited him. Whatever toiletries they supplied would be fine, he wasn't terribly picky. However, comfortable clothes should be afforded to the risk-taker and size mattered in comfortableness. He wondered what sizes awaited him, not only from a Chinese to American comparison but also if Kip had intervened. Besides size, style couldn't be discounted when it came to comfort. Leave it to Kip to request underwear unfit for space: bikini, G-string, or even pouchless. A proud American swinging-dick among a people whose philosophy in yin and yang would say size doesn't matter.

Edible was always a possibility and he could hear Kip's explanation they were just in case the Chinese didn't pack enough food for him. Of course, they couldn't be worn and then eaten.

It was decided. Underwear, socks, and t-shirts were going in the bag.

As Hayden packed, his door opened and Ora walked in. Just inside the door, she stopped, either unsure or unbelieving their bad karma in being separated.

Hayden's eyes gobbled her up, but, honestly, he didn't want to deal with her now. He threw the bag and clothes in his hands on the bed.

"Come in," he offered.

Grace refined her strides as she walked over to him, slow and reverent. A framed picture in her hands, held like a bouquet, reminded him of a bride processional. When she came close, he grabbed her and kissed her. Her mouth twisted into a smile against his as he laid it on passionately. After a time, they separated and it became apparent Ora had entered into her own sort of funk.

She tasted her own lips and asked, "What was that for?"

"So there was no doubt about how much I *lo-lo-lo…*" He pretended he couldn't say *love*.

The picture frame slapped onto the bed when it hit flatly and her open hand slapped his chest and she said, "*See!* You can't even say it."

"You didn't feel it? Taste it?"

Her tongue licked her lips again. "Maybe. But sometimes a girl likes to hear it."

"And so does a guy. How about you? Let's hear you say it."

"Fine. I love you!"

Hayden looked around as if she had said it to someone else. "Who do you love? I didn't hear a name."

"Hayden Bakley's the man I love," she said and this time she initiated the kiss.

Pulling his lips away, Hayden said, "I should have said it first. I'll never hear the end of it that you said it first."

Her open hand slapped his chest again. "What do you mean said it first? You're yet to say it."

His hands reached around her to the small of her back and pulled her close to him so the front of their bodies collided. Her body jerked, as did her head, and she said, "Gentle with those things."

He kissed her, looked into her eyes, and told her, "I love you, Ora Frush. For the time I have you, a decade to your senior, I'll love you. And when I die, you'll have another decade or more to love another."

The expression on her face turned serious and she said, "Who says I could love another?"

"Do my hands feel different?"

"No. They're yours. But you start watching T.V. during you know what, I'll rip those forearms off your body."

"Can I pipe in music?"

"As long as it fits the mood."

"Fine, but just remember, my mood might not be the same as yours."

She kissed him again and said, "I don't think you should go up with the Chinese."

"You don't."

"No. I don't think you should go into space at all."

"Why is that?"

"I don't think you're fit for it."

"My age?"

"No."

"John Glenn went up at seventy-seven."

"Prove it then."

Forcefully, she kissed him as if sucking the breath right out of him. Her teeth bit his bottom lip and pulled him onto the bed. When they collapsed, the picture frame was underneath her, so he slid it out and tossed it on the floor. The glass broke.

Between kisses, he said, "I couldn't take the frame anyway. I can only take two and a half pounds."

"Hayden."

"Yeah."

"I don't care."

CHAPTER **SIXTEEN**

Time ticked slow and meaningful for Hayden and Ora. They felt like there was no other place in the universe they would rather be and no one else in the cosmos they would rather be with. Acquaintances in life are just that and don't mean much. Friends, as rare as they are, come and go and lasting friends are almost unheard of. Here, two people, that's it, found life, contentment, and all a human should feel and experience. They would be lasting friends and, perhaps, if Hayden gets the balls to ask, maybe helpmates to each other, officially, in marriage.

They said their goodbyes, for now, and Hayden figured someone would call him soon to tell him it's time to go. It surprised him they hadn't been interrupted by someone already. Kip had mentioned a thousand miles, which would be about a two-hour commercial flight. But those fat-bellied planes had the capability of flying much faster and would probably reduce the flight time quite a bit. Besides, Kip had said he wanted to be late. Someone was keeping tabs on the Chinese and their launch time to ensure nothing changed.

Hayden got himself dressed and packed his estimated two and a half pound bag. Purposefully, he didn't shower as to keep Ora's smell on him as long as he could. However long it lasted, it could be perceived as self-harm and for sure it would hurt, but it could be a catalyst in remembering why he's on the Chinese Space Station (CSS) and motivation for getting off. Not all negative emotions and feelings should be discarded right away, because, if used properly, they could drive someone to turn things around for the better.

Picking the picture frame off the floor, he turned it over and there, through the broken glass, was a picture of Ora and him, heads touching, from one of their missions together. Long forgotten memories of that mission resurfaced and all he had felt so long ago he experienced again.

Over a trash can, he carefully removed the photograph out of the frame. Ora was aging beautifully, but seeing how young she was in the picture made him realize how much of a knockout she was and still is. His own youth in the picture made him think of his life, all he had done, how it's led to now, the things he hasn't gotten to yet, and the ultimate question—will he?

Carrying the photo over to his bag to pack it, he flipped it over. Written on the back, in red nail polish, was, "Marry me, Hayden … before I change my mind! Ora."

Damn her, he thought. She must have been reading his mind. Funny how they knew what each needed and confirmed when they needed confirming.

As he slid the picture into the bag, eyeing the words written on the back until they were hidden, it occurred to him, besides the photograph, there wasn't anything else of a sentimental nature he was taking up. Not that he owned many sentimental things since his house blew up.

Hayden's door opened and one of Kip's men, entirely dressed in black, stepped into the room and said firmly, "Time to go."

The man escorted Hayden to his flight. As they entered a large area acting as a hangar, a penguin-looking plane awaited them, as was Kip. When Hayden reached him, Kip handed him a tray covered with foil.

"Sorry we couldn't have done something with a little more class," Kip said.

They boarded the unorthodox plane and took their seats. As the plane took off, the windows tinted over. In the air, Kip shared how he thought this might go down once they arrived. It would take some acting on both of their parts, mostly playing dumb and blaming the communication barrier, for being late. An innocent misunderstanding needed to be sold for this to work.

As Kip talked, Hayden lifted the foil off the tray and, to his surprise, saw a spread of fruit, sliced meat, and cubed cheese. Not shy, he started eating and, after eating half of it, finally asked Kip if he would like some. A grotesque expression on Kips' face answered he didn't, but, for clarification, he said, "You're dripping fruit juice all over the meat and cheese."

Shrugging it off, Hayden devoured the rest of the tray.

Between Kip talking and Hayden eating, the flight only took an hour and fifteen minutes. They didn't have time to land at Jiayuguan Airport and drive two hours to the Jiuquan Satellite Launch Center, nor did Kip have any plans to do so. The special abilities of the craft allowed it to do extraordinary things. One of them happened to be not needing a landing strip to land. No, this plane could do things a helicopter could without the rotors; its capability like nothing ever seen before in the sky. Perhaps, the closest would be witnesses capturing video and reporting strange and unusual flight patterns, speeds, and maneuvers of unidentified flying objects.

One hundred and thirty miles northeast of the million-person populated city of Jiuquan lies the Jiuquan Spaceport, buffeted in all directions in the Gobi Desert in the autonomous region of Inner Mongolia, a stretch of desert land between Mongolia and China, consisting of five hundred thousand square miles with a meager population of fifty-seven thousand. Conversely, within Manhattan's twenty-three square miles of land live over one and half million people. The fat-bellied, stunted-winged craft touched down on a macadam pad just behind the Launch Center.

The meeting of the United States and the Chinese went about as Kip had expected. The scatterbrained Americans played their part, creating chaos and confusion, while the Chinese, focused on the promise of working with NASA in the future, went along with the American excuses and foolishness, and prepped Hayden for the launch.

Through it all, the physical had been avoided, as did any detection of Hayden's enh*um*anced forearms and hands. Outside embarrassing America and their space agency, the only sign of trouble was when Hayden's bag was weighed and it came in a good one and a half pounds light. The Chinese weigher shot him a look of disbelief, because, typically, astronauts try to bring as much as they can and push the limit.

"I travel light," Hayden said, unsure if his words were comprehended.

During inspection, a pair of bikini underwear was removed from Hayden's bag and held in the air, pinched between the inspector's two fingers like tweezers. Embarrassed, the Chinaman stared at them with disbelief, as did everyone else in the room. Hayden snatched them out of the air, startling the inspector, and threw them at Kip, knowing he had them inserted in his bag on the flight. As the bikini underwear hit Kip's chest and fell to the floor, Kip tried but failed to hold in a laugh, thinking to himself, *The Chinese must be having second thoughts about our little arrangement.*

Stuffed inside the capsule of a *Shenzhou* spacecraft with one Chinese taikonaut and his own personal bag, Hayden and his bag of underclothes awaited launch from the South Launch Site (SLS-1).

All systems a go, the rocket launched and the familiar vibration shook in Hayden a preference toward space that had become dormant during his time on the ground. The awakening felt different and he knew it wasn't the time away, but rather he had someone on the ground that he really cared about. As the rocket ascended, he wondered if Ora was watching.

Upon reaching a certain distance, the Shenzhou spacecraft was shut down and entered an insertion orbit around the Earth. Established, its engines powered again and thrust the craft into an elliptical orbit to establish a higher and more circular orbit. That orbit was established so the Shenzhou craft could phase with the Chinese Space Station (CSS).

After some time, the Shenzhou tracked the CSS and then came the all-important maneuver of situating the vessel for docking. The transport vehicle maneuvered around the CSS and passed it, burned its thrusters to ensure it was well ahead of the CSS, braked, and flipped end-over-end along the CSS orbiting track so its nose now faced the oncoming space station and its thrusters away from it.

At first, Hayden and the Chinese taikonaut didn't see anything. Then, a dot appeared, which enlarged in their vision as the CSS came toward them. The oncoming station wasn't huge, but big enough, not quite half a football field in size. Automated computers on the Shenzhou went to work on docking as the taikonaut monitored the instruments. With the Shenzhou docked to the service module of the CSS, patience needed to be a virtue for both Hayden and the taikonaut, because they knew it would be hours before the hatches opened and they could enter the space station.

Capture and seal completed and verified, the hatches opened and Hayden and the Chinese taikonaut, holding their personal bags, floated into the service module. From launch until this moment, the venture had taken a little under six hours.

Smiles on the faces of the three taikonauts, two male, and one female, expressed how happy they were to see relief arrive. For the two men, their joy was for the obvious reason they were going home to be with their families. New faces, different voices, varying thoughts and ideas, and working with the American had to be on the mind of the female to make her as joyous as she appeared. Perhaps, she had aspirations of one day boarding the ISS.

Since she would be on board with them, she gave Hayden and the taikonaut the grand tour, saving the core module for last. Since meeting her, her short hair fanned out from her head continuously as if zapped with static.

Fitting for the meaning of its core module, the Tiahne, meaning harmony of the heavens, the Chinese Space Station was shaped like a cross, consisting of three core modules and two adjoining sections. Stemming from the docking port just after the service module where they had entered, the space station laid out as such: the horizontal line consisted of a research module docked to the left of the vertical line and another to the right, while the vertical line, top to bottom, consisted of another Shenzhou transport craft, a tiny tubular connector, the core module named Tiahne, and at last a robotic cargo ship named the Tianzhou. In all, five out of six docks on the docking port were occupied; only the top dock remained open for docking.

Also part of the space station, a separate telescope called the *Xuntian* orbited near the CSS.

The rest of the station consisted of solar panels. Three solar arrays extended out from the core module, while the other five sections each had two, making a total of thirteen under the current figuration of the space station.

Not claustrophobic by any stretch of the imagination, Hayden found the Chinese Space Station to be not much different than the International Space Station, only much smaller. Over the years, when asked to describe the ISS, the best answer he could come up with was *'organized chaos.'*

On the last leg of the tour, she led Hayden and the relief taikonaut into the core module with the others. As Hayden floated in, a Chinese taikonaut tossed him an orange, of all things, in a gesture of kindness. All three Chinese taikonauts laughed and tried talking to him. They seemed jovial in doing so, but the conversations ended short, knowing they couldn't understand one another. With all the attention on the American, the Chinese astronaut that came with Hayden kept to himself.

The recycled air inside the core module had a distinct oriental odor. Since exercises took place in the core module, Hayden suspected the astronauts were only partly to blame. The unique bouquet most likely stemmed from meals. In Hayden's experience, the crew gets used to such things and, to him, it didn't smell as bad as other fumes that had tickled his olfactory on the International Space Station.

A live communication with mission control at the Beijing Aerospace Command and Control Center reignited the crew, who situated themselves shoulder-to-shoulder to fit into the camera's view. On mission control's end, only half of the American, Hayden, made it into the picture, floating behind the others and peeling his orange.

The taikonaut, who had piloted Hayden from Earth, didn't want any part of it. Not only did he remain in the back, he held himself down behind those in front, hiding, while holding onto his personal bag as if it contained priceless jewels.

As if in slow motion, Hayden placed a wedge of orange into his mouth and bit half of it off, as he stared at the Chinaman. After looking down at his bag and around, finally, the taikonaut noticed Hayden staring at him. Darkness in his eyes made Hayden nervous. The only other time he had seen eyes like that was on a fellow astronaut, who had gone mad during a space mission and almost killed everyone by attempting to open a hatch, because, he had said later, *'I wanted to go outside for some fresh air.'*

Out of pride, Hayden continued to stare at the man, then, casually, turned away and ate the other half of the orange wedge.

Before Hayden knew it, the rest of the astronauts motioned for him to move front and center, as they made room. Floating there like a doofus, he didn't know what they wanted until they all pointed at the camera and waved. It became apparent to him that those on the ground wanted to see the American aboard the Chinese Space Station and figured NASA had to be piped into the broadcast, too, wanting to see the same thing. Like a chimp, he waved and put on a smile, chewing the orange.

When the communication ended, everyone aboard, except Hayden's journeyman, clapped and patted Hayden on the back. The tour guide motioned for him to move forward and waved the Chinaman, laying low, to follow. She showed them where they were to sleep, said a few things in Chinese, then left.

As Hayden moved past his pilot to go to the bathroom, the taikonaut's eyes followed him coming and going, his hands and arms firmly around the bag. When Hayden returned, the man's bag was nowhere in sight and a thick paranoia between them escalated ever since boarding.

CHAPTER SEVENTEEN

Shift changes occurred rapidly, but thoroughly, on the Chinese Space Station. With limited space, they had to. The size of the CSS was only about a sixth of the International Space Station and with five astronauts aboard, two had to leave. They did, leaving only the female, Hayden, and the Chinaman who came with him in the Shenzhou.

A few hours had passed since the Shenzhou had undocked and headed back toward Earth when the woman taikonaut noticed something of size in the space station's orbit. The way the object moved, it didn't take long for her to figure out it was a craft of some kind and initially thought that something went wrong with the Shenzhou and it had returned to the station. Unable to communicate with the Shenzhou, she contacted the Command and Control Center in Beijing about the ship and they confirmed it was not the Shenzhou and recommended evasive maneuvers.

Before she could make such maneuvers, the craft up ahead had already positioned itself for docking. Much faster than a typical docking, the probe on the unknown craft made contact with the cone on the docking hatch and with a push forward, capture occurred.

She went to the docking port. To her surprise, the new

taikonaut was already at work, ensuring a tight seal by vacuuming and depressurizing.

"I take it you were expecting them," she said in Chinese.

Continuing his work, the man didn't say anything.

When she pushed a second time, he simply nodded and said, *"Shi`."*

"Well, why didn't I know ... *Hey! Hey!* What are you doing?" she said in Chinese.

Much faster than the norm, the male taikonaut began opening the hatch. The other hatch on the craft remained closed. For a procedure that normally took nearly an hour, the hatch had been opened in under ten minutes.

"You could have killed everyone!" she screamed at him in Chinese. "And with an American aboard."

The Chinaman turned and looked at her and she, too, saw the same darkness in his eyes that Hayden had seen.

The hatch to the other spacecraft opened and a brown-skinned man floated aggressively out, holding a handheld weapon. Behind him, came another brown-skinned man, holding a weapon, and, seconds later, a third appeared with a weapon.

At first, the weapons appeared to be bullet-type pistols, but closer now, she wasn't sure, because of the cone-shaped tip. Appearance wise, brown skin, dark hair, and black eyes reminded the female Chinese taikonaut of someone from the Middle East or India. As the male taikonaut closed the hatches behind the three men, she floated off toward the core module and the men yelled something in a language she didn't understand. No sign of her stopping, one of the men handed his laser to another and took off after her.

Using his arms to reach, grab, and pull on what he could to make up the distance, it didn't take long before he grabbed her ankle and pulled her back to him. Kicking and screaming didn't help her, especially in stocking feet. Once he had her, one of the other men had caught up and stuck a laser near her face and she stopped squirming.

The two men escorted her to the core module, where the

third vyomanaut from India and the Chinaman, who had opened the hatch for them, waited. Not wasting any time, the Indian asked the female taikonaut if there was anyone else on board. Asked in Hindu, she couldn't answer, until the Indian pulled from his pocket what looked like a remote control and spoke into it, asking the same question. He floated over to her and stuck it in front of her face and she heard the question in Chinese. The device was a translator.

His eyebrows went up, waiting, and she answered there wasn't. His arm and head dropped at the same time and he peeked at the male taikonaut, who told him there was another on board—an American.

The Indian vyomanaut slapped her face about as firm as anyone could in the microgravity environment. In Hindu, he spoke into the translator and played it back to her in her own language, which said, "Don't lie again. Why do you think we're here? For you?"

He looked at his third Indian brother and said in Hindu, "Take the Chinaman and find him."

The two men floated through the core module to find Hayden.

While one Indian restrained the female taikonaut, the other vyomanaut touched her nose with the coned-tip of his laser and smiled.

Inside the cargo ship, the Tianzhou, Hayden was busy trying to find larger t-shirts, work shirts, and cotton pants. He was tired of being laughed at for their tight fit, mainly his nipples producing tiny bumps in his shirts and bare ankles showing between his pant cuffs and socks. Not finding what he needed, he left the cargo ship emptyhanded and proceeded into the core module, where he ran into trouble.

Seeing Hayden about fifty feet away, the Indian vyomanaut used the female taikonaut to turn himself around and pointed the laser at him. Not holding onto anything, he floated toward the ceiling of the module. The tip of the laser remained pointed at Hayden although the angle of the man's body gradually tilted in such a way it wouldn't be pointed at him long. A mere thirteen feet up and no fear of falling, the Indian pushed off the module above him, and when his feet approached the wall below, he slid them under bars attached there to anchor himself.

At the sight of Hayden, the female taikonaut chanced squirming out of the Indian's grip. Breaking free, she floated toward Hayden. When she reached him, he stopped her movement and held her by her arms. Tears floated around her face like suspended raindrops. There was nowhere to retreat, except the cargo ship. What good would that do? There might be oxygen in there, but the vessel itself wouldn't be oxygenized for a crew flight.

"You're not really going to shoot that in here, are you?" Hayden asked.

The Indian waved the laser for them to come closer and held out the translator.

The tips of her pale fingers touched one another, touched her lips, and as she moved them from her lips, her fingers spread out as if blowing a kiss.

Believing she meant speaking, because, contextually, what would kissing have to do with a time like this, Hayden floated forward with the woman and said again, "You wouldn't shoot that in here, would you?"

A couple of thumb presses on the translator and Hayden's words played in Hindu. The Indian responded in Hindu and played the translator so it came out in English.

"Yes," he had said. "It's very precise."

A nod in the direction of the vyomanaut indicated Hayden understood. Not only the man's candor but also that the two men together were two testicular nut jobs of the same scrotum. The weapons of choice in this game seemed to be lasers and highly explosive bombs, not bullets and grenades. Lasers can be very accurate and he recalled the apparent settings on the orange blasters used by the orange-cloaked bandits. His eyes studied the handheld in the brown-skinned hand and, immediately, noticed it was silver instead of orange. As was the one in the other's hand.

What seemed like eons ago, inside the parallelogram room tucked in the canyon, Kip had presented two main parties in pursuit of the briefcase, now briefcases: us, Kip's group, unofficially associated with NASA, and them, which Hayden had always associated as the orange people. His focus had always been on himself, stuck in the middle of all of this, when *them* could be anybody and certainly more than one.

The third Indian and the Chinaman floated into the core module, where they joined the other Indians. They pointed their lasers down the hull at Hayden and the female taikonaut near the other end. Emphatic as, *game, set, match*, there was no way for Hayden and the female to win the numbers game and three silver lasers set their odds of getting out of this at one. There's always a chance, but with all three lasers pointing in their direction, the match wouldn't be much of a contest.

The vyomanaut handed his laser to the Chinaman and tinkered with his translator. The Chinaman and another Indian floated toward Hayden and the woman, then stopped. The third Indian positioned himself behind the leader from India. When the vyomanaut got the translator to where he wanted it, he floated behind his partners, extended a hand between them, and held out the translator. A pre-recording, which had been previously translated into English, played.

"Hayden Bakley, United States Astronaut, you are our prisoner. Come with us and don't be foolish."

For emphasis, the Indian held the translator still and contorted his face in an expression, which assumed Hayden understood the message and if he tried anything foolish, the Indian would surely kill him.

The translator retreated behind the men and the Indian messed with it some more. Retrieving what he was looking for, he tapped the Chinaman on the shoulder to get his attention and played another message translated into

Chinese.

"You have them?" the translator spoke and the vyomanaut paused the message and waited.

The male taikonaut pointed to the translator. It was easy to see he wished to use it.

When it was all set, he spoke Chinese into it and, when it played, it came out in Hindu.

"My family is safe?" was what the Chinaman had asked, but only the Indians could understand.

The Indian nodded they were.

The male taikonaut turned his eyes down, emotion getting the better of him, and once collected, he looked up and nodded he had them.

The message resumed. "One will remain on board with you. Except for him, do away with anyone left on board with you. Get your bag and wait in the airlock. When outside and they turn gold, you know what to do. If you fail, don't bother coming back down to Earth."

An excited trembling, under the Chinese taikonaut's skin, vibrated fear throughout his body. Not showing it, he merely nodded he understood.

The Indian stowed the translator away and floated toward Hayden and the female. Pushing her aside, he locked eyes with Hayden and waited, lulling him into a deadpan stare. Another Indian and the Chinaman crept closer—something that didn't go unnoticed by Hayden. Neither did the halitosis of the one in front of him. It always amazed him how wonderful-smelling spices, such as curry and others found in Indian dishes, resulted in infernal bad breath.

Surrounded, now, on three sides, Hayden thought of *game, set, match*. Suddenly, the Indian in front of him began to make weird faces and blow on him. Before Hayden knew it, he felt a prick in his shoulder. When his natural reaction turned his head to see what had happened, another pinch struck his other shoulder. His eyes went there and the knee-jerk reactions caused his feet to slip out from under the bar and he began to elevate toward the top of the module. Panic adrenalized him and his eyes bulged with fear when he went to use his arms to stop himself and he couldn't move them.

The sight of the helpless American made the Indians laugh. To say they enjoyed it would be an understatement.

Barbarically, one of the Indians grabbed Hayden's collar and yanked. Before Hayden knew it, he was being dragged through the air like a kite before ascension.

Numbness disseminated through both of Hayden's arms and when he tried to use them, he couldn't. His arms flailed loosely in front of him like barbels on a catfish. The drugging technique of arrest had proven better than handcuffs.

The Indian escorted Hayden through the Chinese Space Station toward the ship the vyomanauts had come on. Relishing in watching the Indian manhandle the American, the leader from India snatched the laser out of the Chinaman's hand and followed. As did the woman's screams, carrying from the core module, the Tiahne.

The only trace the Indians had left behind that they were there was a man from India, remaining on board with the Chinaman. Something big must be at stake by leaving him aboard and leaving nothing to chance, ensuring that their objective gets accomplished. The honor system, in relying on the blackmailed Chinaman to handle it, wasn't enough. The situation required greater assurances that only a native could pledge.

The Indians worked on dressing Hayden in his own spacesuit, identified by the American flag and NASA patch, before stuffing him inside their craft named *Taare ko Nadee*, meaning *River to the Stars* in Hindi. India's crew transport ship resembled the Chinese Shenzhou and the Russian Soyuz in a line of near-copycats, except for the gold color.

Russia had pioneered the crew transport ship and through constant improvements, dominated the market, at times having the only reliable ships to take man into space and bring them home again. Russia partners with the United

States on International Space Station missions, but also works with the China National Space Administration (CNSA), who is banned from the ISS, as well as the Indian Space Research Organization (ISRO). Therefore, both the Indian Taare ko Nadee and the Chinese Shenzhou both utilize Russian Soyuz technology.

With Hayden now in a space suit, a vyomanaut began to place a helmet over Hayden's head, when the female Chinese taikonaut's screaming stopped. A turn of the helmet and it locked onto the suit.

The blackmailed male Chinese taikonaut, still inside the CSS, had already changed the station's orientation so India's craft, docked underneath, could undock and easily separate. This occurred over thirty minutes ago, during which time he used to prepare himself to take a life.

Everyone dressed for space, the hatches were opened, and the vyomanauts seated Hayden first, then, after securing the CSS and their ship, sat. All set, the Taare ko Nadee undocked from the Chinese Space Station and drifted away.

Strain in Hayden's trapezii started to bother him. He wondered what this paralysis would feel like under Earth's gravity. Extremely painful, he guessed. His mind focused on the woman. Not that he tried or even wanted to think of her, it's just where his mind went. Perhaps, the thought of pain triggered an association. A far-reaching one, because, as far as he knew, she no longer felt anything, let alone pain.

Or, maybe, it was the thought of a different time and place, say the International Space Station, and that could have been Ora. His mind's eye imagined the female taikonaut's body floating in the Tiahne with her spiked hair as if a search and rescue diver had found her floating in the East River of Manhattan.

A punishing mind trick jumbled the image around. Now, Ora floated lifelessly in the Tiahne, then, she disintegrated.

Hayden wanted to use his arms to beat his pitiless mind into pulp. Instead, he blared out a hellacious scream, his mouth as large as the visor of his helmet. The vyomanauts thought he had gone mad and disconnected his communication.

Maybe he was. In his estimation, something was wrong. As in, right now, inside the ship. Achieving separation from the CSS, the Taare ko Nadee never entered a deorbit burn. In fact, it appeared to Hayden the Indians had no intention of returning to Earth.

Could a crew transport ship do such a thing? Hayden thought.

He never knew of one. If such sustainability could be achieved, where a vessel could remain in space for a time, not even indefinitely, just dock to a space station, undock, maneuver to another station, dock, and undock before having to return to Earth would give the holder of such technology a nearly insurmountable advantage.

And, if they could accomplish that, increasing sustainability to travel between more stations or the same ones over and over again, man's existence in space would start to take on more of a neighborly structure. With space stations acting as homes, a flying spacecraft with such capability would be the car and black space would be the macadam streets. Space stations would take on new roles, supermarkets, gas stations, banks, and the consumer could get in their flying car, go to those places, and back home again. If only the human body were so sustainable.

A jerk of propulsion knocked Hayden out of starry, and possibly mad, reverie. It may have been a complete overthink unless the future was now and he was riding in it.

The Taare ko Nadee had fulfilled its name by taking India upriver to the stars. Well, three Indians anyway, and now, it appeared to be traveling through space like an alien spaceship or a plane through the sky. Its destination was limited unless India had its own space station under the radar in orbit. The only stations Hayden knew of in orbit, besides the Chinese Space Station, was China's smaller one the Tiangong-2, Space Complex 1, the world's first commercial space station, and the International Space

Station.

The Taare ko Nadee might be on its way to any of them, possibly so the Indians could do what they had done on the CSS. Outside of murder and a kidnapping, Hayden wasn't quite sure what the Indians had accomplished. Yet, there was one thing he knew for sure.

There wasn't harmony in the heavens.

CHAPTER **EIGHTEEN**

The Indian crew ship, River to the Stars, had shut down and established an orbit to phase with the International Space Station. The translator device floated freely inside the transport ship and a pre-recorded message began to play in English for Hayden. The words were direct and to the point. It ended by asking Hayden if he understood.

Gloved fingers manipulated switches, buttons, dials, and levers on the control panel. Once done, one Indian pointed to Hayden he was on.

Knowing what he was to do from the recording, Hayden cleared his throat and spoke, "This is NASA astronaut Hayden Bakley on co-assignment with ISRO, the India Space Research Organization, seeking emergency docking to the ISS. Do you read?"

A woman's voice, thickly accented with German, said, "I read you. Docking granted."

The immediate approval caused one of the Indians to wave his arm not to say anymore.

Clueless as to why the ISS agreed so quickly, Hayden said, "Thank you." With that, the unconventional transmission ended.

It bothered Hayden as to why the German of the

European Space Agency (ESA) wasn't more untrusting. How did she know the craft from India could even dock to the station?

As it had done with the Chinese Space Station, India's craft maneuvered flawlessly, getting into position to dock with the ISS. No one aboard the space station expected a docking, but the River to the Stars docked anyway.

When an astronaut from the Japan Aerospace Exploration Agency (JAXA) had floated his way to the docking station, he found the female German astronaut already there, working on opening the hatch in an expedited fashion. He asked her what she was doing, but she ignored him and kept working. Her actions were putting herself and five other astronauts on board the ISS in grave danger. Sensing she may have gone space-silly in being hell-bent on opening the hatch, he restrained her.

It was too late. Only pulling open the hatch had remained. Everything else had been done. Getting there late, the Japanese astronaut didn't know how far she had gotten. How could he? To his surprise, the hatch began to open.

As he let go of the German woman and tried to get around her in the narrow module, she used her body to block his way, trying to stay between him and the hatch. It was so narrow that the width of one person could block the way and the only way for two to squeeze past each other was if both turned sideways. When he finally got by her and flew toward the hatch, it had already been pushed open all the way inside the ISS and the hatch to India's vessel had been raised inside the transporter craft.

Out of the blackness came one of the Indian vyomanauts like a banded sea krait water snake coming through a hole in white coral; a reflective silver of a pointing laser led the way until the man appeared. His progress pushed back the Japanese astronaut, who raised his hands in the air in surrender. Nearly pushed out of the docking module, the German woman floated just outside a pressurized mating adapter behind the Jap.

A silver laser in hand, the second Indian vyomanaut appeared out of the craft and into the ISS. He handed his laser to his partner, reached back inside the Taare ko Nadee, and pulled, while his partner pointed both lasers at the Jap. Out of the docking ship came another body.

The Japanese astronaut didn't know who Hayden was, but when the German saw him, she pushed past the Jap and the two Indians to reach him. Not to embrace him, but, upon arrival, she hit and kicked him the best she could in the microgravity environment. An opportunity presented itself when the Indian holding both lasers handed one of them to his partner and she almost grabbed it during the exchange, wanting to use it on Hayden.

Defenseless with paralyzed arms, Hayden didn't know why she was attacking him until he saw the black, red, and yellow stripes of the German flag sewn on her shoulder and figured she must have gotten word about the assassination of the German President.

After allowing the German to land a few blows and cut off his breathing by choking him with her hands, an Indian finally waved her away with a laser. A parting blow to the forehead above Hayden's eye and she floated past the Indian vyomanauts and the Japanese astronaut into the mating adapter. Red splotches appeared on her forehead, nose, and cheeks from the exertion.

One of the Indians tilted Hayden so he floated upright. Her attack had been so personal and emotion-filled that Hayden began to wonder what other countries with assassination connections might be on board.

Oxygen in his reopened airway revitalized his brain and an important question resulted from it. *How does she know about my unwarranted connection?* he wondered about the German. *Had something happened he didn't know about?*

A conversation between the Indians and the Japanese astronaut lasted longer than it should have, having to use the translator to communicate. The Jap pointed and directed as he talked. Finally, one vyomanaut motioned his laser for the

Jap to pull Hayden by the collar of his spacesuit. With one arm, the JAXA astronaut pulled himself through the ship, while dragging Hayden through the air with the other, followed by an Indian. One by one, they exited the docking module into the mating adapter, where the German waited, and then floated into node 1 named *Unity*. Floating into the United States Lab named the *Destiny*, Hayden thought he saw Ora but didn't trust his eyes.

Sure now, he said. *"Ora? Ora!* What are you doing here?"

"Hayden? Hayden!" Seeing a Jap and an Indian, Ora's eyes went to the dragged body and floated toward it.

"I thought you weren't launching for another month or so," Hayden said, watching her come toward him. Oh, how he wished he could touch her.

"It got moved up," Ora said. "What's going on? Why are you here?"

The Indian showed the laser for her to back away.

Resolute, she placed her hands over Hayden's ears to hold his head and kissed him.

Seeing this, the JAXA astronaut stopped pulling.

"Hey, watch it!" Hayden said.

Her thumb lightly touched above his eye. "What happened?"

"You're German friend…"

Hard metal of the laser point jabbed into Hayden's side for him to keep moving.

"Chaal!" the Indian said and nodded to the Jap.

Seeing this, the JAXA astronaut pulled Hayden by the collar.

"Wait! What?" Ora said, moving toward Hayden to follow. "Hayden, what's happening?"

The female German astronaut floated behind Ora and wrapped her arms around her while stretching a leg and getting a foot under a bar. Her arms pinned against her body, Ora yelled to Hayden.

"Cooperate with what they want," Hayden instructed, as he was being pulled away. "Don't be difficult."

Silver, an inch away from Ora's eyes, obstructed her vision. It backed away and there was another Indian, smiling, and pointing the metallic silver laser at her for her to stop squirming.

The other vyomanaut waved the laser at the Japanese astronaut, who pulled Hayden through the ship as if driving cattle. They left Destiny and entered another section of the station named Harmony. The JAXA astronaut stopped and pointed down.

The Indian spoke Hindi into the translator and out came Japanese. The Jap worked hard to get Hayden out of his spacesuit. Without the extra padding of the suit, the tip of the metal laser poked into Hayden's body a little harder, a little farther, telling him without speaking to move down into the compartment.

Being on the ISS before, Hayden knew exactly where he was and where the Jap pointed—the Permanent Multipurpose Module (PMM). It was supposed to be moved a couple of years ago to node 3, but there it was, right where Hayden remembered from his last flight.

"You want me down there?" Hayden asked.

Gestures and weapon-pointing answered he was to enter the storage module. As the Jap pushed Hayden into the basement room of the ISS, there wasn't much room for a man Hayden's size inside the cramped space. A supply ship must have visited recently because it was fairly full. The JAXA astronaut held onto a bar and pushed down on Hayden's head and shoulders with his feet for him to descend farther. Once the American's head cleared the doorway, the Jap secured the hatch and left Hayden in the dark.

"Fuck me!" Hayden yelled at the top of his lungs.

Time passed. How much, Hayden didn't know. Paralysis rendered the functionality in the screens lodged in his forearms virtually useless. However, with a spoken word, the screen illuminated and he had light. All the functions enabled by voice command worked, but without the use of his arms, he couldn't see them. Unsure how long he would be caged, he purposely only kept one screen on. It was bright enough to see and that provided some comfort.

Frustration and anger churned his insides. A crook in his neck tightened the muscles there and soreness set in. The entire time, the back of his head pushed against the metal hatch. There was nothing he could do to situate his body differently.

After some time, Hayden tried to give into his current situation by relaxing and closing his eyes. If he could fall asleep, he would have. A voice sounded. At first, he thought it might have come from the other side of the hatch above him. As the voice kept speaking, it occurred to him the voice was in the module with him, specifically, in his forearm.

"Volume up," Hayden commanded and the voice grew louder.

"*Hayden! Hayden Bakley!* You alive? All I see are strange shapes."

"*Kip? Kip!* Is that you?" Hayden asked, his mouth dry.

"*Yeah.* Where are you?" Kip asked. "What am I looking at?"

"Cargo. Plain old cargo. In the PMM."

"PMM? The Permanent Multipurpose Module? Well, I suppose it's an improvement, but I would rather be talking to your face."

"Believe me, seeing another face is preferable for me, too. Even if it's yours."

"Just hold your arm up," Kip said. "The cargo can wait."

"I've been jailed in here and I can't use my arms," Hayden said.

"*Holy crapoli!* What happened?"

"I've been drugged and the CSS has been taken over. It's a Chinaman, but don't be fooled. The Indians must have gotten to him."

"*Indians?* Like cowboys and Indians?"

"No, like India Indians."

"Hai-hai-hai-hai!" Kip said, imitating an Indian war cry. "So they are on board."

"How about that?" Hayden said. "I know something before you."

"Hayden, you've been ahead of me the whole time. You've experienced things firsthand."

"Floating here like a dead man in water doesn't feel like it."

"Baldy," Kip said, not talking to Hayden. "Where's Hayden Bakley?"

The module became brighter when the screen in Hayden's other forearm illuminated and, now, both were on.

"The bald man made it, *huh?*" Hayden asked Kip.

"Oh, yeah," Kip said. "The assailants never made it down that far."

"Mr. Bakley is in the PMM on the ISS, Mr. Stanton," the bald-headed hybrid reported.

"The ISS?" Kip said. "What are doing you there? I thought you meant in a PMM on the CSS."

"The Indians brought me here," Hayden answered.

"Brought you there? How? Didn't they dock to the CSS?"

"They did. And without reentry, their vessel located and docked with the ISS."

"How the hell did it do that?"

"Damned if I know. My guess is that the U.S. will drop the Soyuz for this one."

"And there goes the budget."

"Hey, Kip," Hayden said in a lower voice. "Without my arms, what can I do to get out of here?"

"You're in a tough spot, my friend," Kip said. "The ISS was the last place we wanted to send you, so we didn't. It's bad news. Real bad news. First off, four of the six ISS astronauts are female. That hasn't happened since almost a decade ago. Ora's one. There's a German…"

"Met her," Hayden interjected. "She kicked my ass. I'm

guessing she knows about the assassination of the German President, but how does she know I'm a suspect?"

"*Oh, man. Oh, man.* Bad to worse. That's a good question," Kip said and then said to the bald man-machine, "Baldy. Find out when these women boarded, will you?"

"Yes, Mr. Stanton."

"You know what, still do that, but, first, see if there's any news on Hayden Bakley."

"Right away, Mr. Stanton."

To Hayden, Kip said, "I wonder if the Anthrax is out of the envelope. Anyway, while we're waiting, there's a U.S. astronaut that has a father-in-law from the Czech Republic. Anything happen with her?"

"No. Probably didn't see me being drug through the station by a Jap."

"Fair enough. Last, but not least, there's another U.S. astronaut with Slovenian descent. Three out of four have Presidential assassination ties. I would argue you're in a very precarious position. I guess the Lord's good in not having an astronaut from Niger on board. Of course, he's had some help in that there's never been anyone from Niger in space."

"Lucky me," Hayden said sarcastically.

"If you say so," Kip said. "Three astronaut-skilled women are bad enough, let alone three pissed-off women who happened to be astronauts. Worst of all, you've got nowhere to go. They've got your balls viced so tight the only thing left to happen now is for them to be clipped off."

"I can't even get comforting words from a friend."

"Hey, I'm not a pair of underwear here," Kip said.

"Just make sure Ora gets through this okay," Hayden said. "Promise me, Kip."

"Mr. Stanton," the bald head said. "Mr. Bakley is all over the news for assassinating four presidents and an attempted assassination of a prime minister."

"Well, as a suspect, right?" Kip asked.

"No, Mr. Stanton," the balded man said. "It appears everyone's jumped the gun, asking citizens with any information to contact respective investigative agencies and have placed Bakley on respective most wanted lists."

"No shit," Kip said. "What number is he?"

"Fuck, Kip!" Hayden yelled. "You got me into this black hole, now get me out!"

"Nothing comes back out of those. Ever. Not even light. I'm not a miracle worker you know. Besides, how do the Indians get absolved of this?"

"Just … get off the line if you're not going to help. And you never promised about Ora."

"I know. I'm sorry. You know I'll do everything I can. I'm working on it. *We're* working on it."

Pain in Hayden's neck felt like it carried the weight of the universe; weight in a microgravity environment.

"I know," Hayden said softly.

Dead air occupied time. Baldy unoccupied the other screen in Hayden's forearm, but its light remained on.

Finally, Kip asked Hayden, "Any feeling in those arms yet?"

"No … I don't know. Maybe some. They're deader than the air."

"Well, my mind's not dead. I think some more downtime is needed to see if your arms return to normal. If not, I don't think you'll be much use to this mission. Either way, we need to get Ora over to you to open that hatch."

"Not Ora. That'll put her in more danger than she's already in."

"And who do you suppose we get? One of the other ladies, who wants to munch your balls off and spit them down your throat so you choke on them and die? Here you thought they were kissing you. You're naïve, Hayden. Maybe the Jap, but the Indians sure aren't going to help you. They have their own agenda."

"The Jap, then," Hayden said.

"I know you don't want to hear it," Kip said, "but we can get in touch with her directly and more easily. You weren't the only one sent up with gadgets on your suit."

"So, that's the plan to wait and see if I get my arms back and Ora will be by to get me out?"

"Sorry, buddy, but it's the best I got right now."

They said their goodbyes and the screen on Hayden's forearm where Kip had appeared shut off, rendering the module darker.

It remained like that for a while and then Hayden verbally commanded the other screen off.

There, he floated at an angle, resembling a dead man trapped inside a compromised submarine that had sunk to the ocean floor.

CHAPTER **NINETEEN**

Five hours had passed since Hayden's incarceration. In that time, another crew transport ship already in transit, the Taare ko Nadeem, had carried another trifecta of Indian vyomanauts upriver to the stars and had landed on the first and only commercial space station, Space Complex 1 (SC1), where they had successfully taken over the station. No one knew why the Indians, so far, had ignored China's smaller space station, the Tiangong-2.

Additionally, preparations for coordinated spacewalks had been either completed or currently underway at the other three space stations. On the Chinese Space Station, the Indian vyomanaut dressed the Chinaman into a spacesuit and has him waiting in the equipment lock. On the International Space Station, an Indian dressed the female German astronaut, who was finishing a pre-breathe in the equipment lock. Precursors on Space Complex 1 had fallen behind schedule, where the final dressing of an American astronaut neared completion and then the Indian vyomanaut would conduct a pre-breathe for the American, which would last another two hours.

Wakened by the sound of the hatch opening above him,

Hayden pushed on the hatch above his head to move away from it. With bent forefingers, he rubbed his eyes. As the hatch opened, artificial light shined down and blinded him like the sun blinding a prisoner who had been shut away in darkened solitary confinement for days. His hands moved slowly away from his face and his squinting eyes absorbed the wonderful sight. Light enveloped his hands and arms like a spiritual aura—a modern-day miracle.

A hand reached down through the light and Hayden reached up and grabbed it as desperate as grabbing for a life preserver in water. A crude connection occurred when their hands locked and, despite Hayden experiencing a lost sense of touch, the contact with another human still satisfied him all the same.

The helping hand wasn't needed, because his body floated out of the Permanent Multipurpose Module as if resurrected out of a tomb. His eyes beheld his helper. The savior was the Jap. The only one aboard the ISS. The same one, who had used his feet to stuff him down into the hole. A confused, half-hearted smile formed mechanically on Hayden's face as he looked up at the JAXA astronaut, because, immediately, he thought, *Where's Ora?*

"Where's Ora?" Hayden asked.

"Come on," the Jap said.

"Where?"

"Kibo."

"The Japanese Lab. Figures."

"It means *hope*."

"I know. Let's just hope we find some there."

The Japanese Experimental Module (JEM) named the *Kibo* was located on the same end of the ISS as the PMM. A short trip, they ventured out of the PMM, across Harmony, and into the Kibo module. Once inside, the Jap secured the hatch. The brevity of the journey and the movement it required was enough to aggravate the tingling soreness in Hayden's arms.

The Jap opened a compartment, pulled out some

pouches, and took them over to Hayden.

"My name is Fahim," the JAXA astronaut introduced himself.

"Hayden," Hayden said. "Thanks for getting me out of there."

Fahim released the pouches in his arms to let them float and said, "After I put you in." His own words made him smile.

Hayden's eyebrows raised. "*Yeah*, bust a gut funny."

"Sorry. I brought you some drinking water, coffee with cream and sugar, cashews. And best of all," Fahim floated over to the compartment and tossed to Hayden, of all things, another orange, "fresh fruit."

"Any brandy stashed in there?" Hayden asked, smiling, as he caught the orange. "Just kidding. I'm famished."

"I thought you might be."

Fahim let Hayden eat and drink.

After Hayden's confinement, more silence was the last thing he needed. There's sound, silence, and beyond the absence of sound, sound again. Hayden knew it to be true, because it rasped in his brain like a cheese grater, shredding his soft tissue. One of the most annoying sounds he'd ever experienced.

"What are you trying to do, torture me?" Hayden asked. "Make some noise. Talk. Do something."

"I can't make too much noise," Fahim said and gestured about the others outside.

Hayden waved it off. "Fine. Then talk quietly."

"About what?"

"I don't care. Anything. *Fahim*. Does that mean something?"

"Yes. *Learned man*."

"And that knowledge brought you all the way up here to space."

"JAXA started when I was a teenager and I knew then I wanted to be an astronaut."

Hayden washed down some cashews with some cream

and sugared coffee out of a pouch and then pointed at Fahim. "That's good. Talk about that."

As the Jap told his story, his soft voice soothed Hayden like a healing ointment massaged into his arms. Having something in his stomach produced the same sensation inside his body and, together, they made a complete contentment. For a moment, the predicament he, Fahim, and the other astronauts aboard the ISS were in had been forgotten.

Then, like an alarm clock waking him out of a pleasant dream, Hayden's screen implanted in his right forearm illuminated.

Seeing light come through Hayden's shirt, Fahim floated back.

"You have a light in your arm," Fahim said as he pointed toward it.

"See. You are a learned man," Hayden said.

An image of Kip clearly appeared within the light as if Hayden's skin or shirt weren't there. Fahim moved in for a closer look, looking down at the screen.

"You're not Hayden," Kip said out of the screen. "Where's Hayden? What have you done with him?"

Nervously, Fahim answered, "I brought him out of the darkness and gave him food and drink."

"*Oh*. Okay. Well, that's good, then," Kip said flatly. "I take it you're an ally."

"Yes."

"It's true he did all that, but don't mind him," Hayden said as he raised his arm and looked into the screen at Kip.

"*Wow!* I can't believe you finally made a friend during this whole mess. You're so unlikable."

"You should talk."

"I'm about to. Hayden, listen. Did your friend tell you anything useful?"

"No, not yet."

"What do you mean not yet? What has he told you?"

"How he came to wanting to be an astronaut."

"That's fucking dandy at a time like this," Kip said. "He wined you, dined you, told you his life story. What were you guys on—a date? Never mind that. My group's just as progressive as any other. I can't wine and dine you from down here, but you'll be interested in what I have to say."

"We're all ears," Hayden said.

"*We? Ugh, jeez.* Can't he go somewhere?"

"No. Fahim saved me and we're in the JEM."

"Okay, fine," Kip agreed. "Remember all of those presidents you killed?"

Fahim turned to Hayden wide-eyed and Hayden shook his head side-to-side it wasn't true.

"Well, add the President of Hungary," Kip continued.

"I was in space, so … How are they going to get around that?"

"Someone will think of something crazier than the one who thought it."

"Life doesn't make sense," Hayden said. "So, your people's theory that this dealt with the Outer Space Treaty was correct?"

"It appears so," Kip said. "Out of the one hundred and twenty-eight countries listed, only a quarter of them never signed, ratified, or accessioned, which doesn't matter, because none of them will ever get into space. Their worries on the ground are too great. But out of the one hundred or so countries that ratified or came in on it late and accessioned, only eight came in after India. Not exactly staunch is it?

"See, India's always had a lot of people, but not a lot of wealth," Kip continued. "I think, once they started getting some moola, they're like, what, in the top ten or something, and space became a possibility, and the treaty became more applicable to them, things changed. I don't think today's India ratifies or accessions, let alone signs."

"What's the Outer Space Treaty?" Fahim asked.

"Don't worry about it," Kip said. "You guys signed and ratified right away so you guys are all-in. That's why you two are sitting in the largest module on the ISS."

"Okay, so what's the big deal about the treaty?" Hayden asked. "How does it fit in with what's happening?"

"When I say we're working on something, take it to heart we really are," Kip started. "Our take on it is India's beliefs concerning the treaty changed as they changed. If they don't believe the articles in the treaty are worth abiding by anymore, then their actions will mirror those new beliefs. Meaning, take Article 1 for example. If India doesn't believe that the exploration of space should benefit all of mankind, but only India, or that space shouldn't be free to all who venture there, because the Indians want to control it, then India's newfound problem with the treaty and its governing principles becomes everyone's problem. And I haven't even told you the problem and how big it truly is."

With Hayden's mouth opened to say something, the Japanese astronaut spoke to Kip as if he were having the conversation.

"What is it and how big?" Fahim asked.

"A billion more people than the United States big," Kip answered, referring to India's population.

Hayden shot Fahim an annoyed look, then asked Kip his question. "What's India's plan? They hijacked the CSS and the ISS, but for what purpose? To just occupy them up here?"

"In a way, you could say that, yes," Kip answered. "Occupancy has always been a vital element in war."

"Mr. Stanton," the bald-headed half-man, half-machine said, as his face appeared on the second screen infixed in Hayden's other forearm. "We just got word that the vyomanauts from India now have control of Space Complex 1."

At the sight of the screen lodged in Hayden's other forearm, Fahim's eyes inflated from pointed American footballs into round basketballs.

"Unbelievable, Baldy!" Kip said. "I mean, who do you work for? How about informing *me*, in private, before you go blabbing it."

"Sorry, Mr. Stanton," the bald-headed man said. "I figured everyone on the comm was in the know. Mr. Bakley could dispose of the Jap and that would limit the intel."

The suggestion opened and rounded the mouth on the JAXA astronaut's round head, which shook side-to-side and he waved his hands out in front of him that disposing of him wasn't necessary.

"Could you do it? Kip asked Hayden.

The question itself, but also the calm everyday tone Kip used made the pupils in the Jap's uncharacteristically round eyes enlarge as if dilated.

"He did stuff me into that hole," Hayden said, having a little fun with the Jap, but then said, "No. Not after he helped me out. Besides, there's already been enough killing. I think they murdered a female taikonaut on the CSS."

"Baldy, any casualties or injuries aboard SC1?" Kip asked. "Check all of the space stations, would you?"

"On it, Mr. Stanton," the man-machine said.

"Yes, Mr. Stanton," Hayden said sarcastically. "How about it? The Indians are occupying space stations. Other than the hijackings, what's the point? It's not like they can just stay in them?"

"I guess I owe you one," Kip said. "Especially, after I took the liberty of switching out both of your forearms."

When no laughter or any indication Hayden had found that funny silenced the airwaves, Kip continued.

"Fine. You deserve it and more. Here's the deal. My team and I have had bad dreams about those golf ball-sized soccer balls inside that briefcase, Hayden, since we first learned of something like that coming down the pike. You have no idea. Conceptually, anyway. We didn't know exactly the form they would use, but from the last intel, I can't say we were entirely surprised. What is surprising is, here, we thought the orange people were coming up with these. Not India. Hell, the oranges probably think we're making them."

"So, the first guy I saw, carrying the briefcase in

Manhattan, wasn't from India," Hayden said. "So, he got the briefcase from someone else? Had to, right?"

"The orange folks had to have gotten it from the Indians and then our man got it before it landed in your car. Either way, the oranges knew about India before we did, because they sent an agent there to retrieve the case. We only had an agent there, because we knew the orange was there."

"How did they know about India and you didn't?"

"Foresight. Poor ass job, I guess. We never expected them. India's space program used to be about sharing technology for everyone's benefit, not trying to control the spheres for themselves." Frustration and embarrassment contorted Kip's face. "It's so clear now, isn't it? I went through their progressions moments ago."

"That was hindsight. As you said, the oranges might have had the foresight. My guess is India didn't have the foresight either until the technology presented itself while trying to produce something else."

"That's how it normally works, doesn't it? Accidental creation. Potential power in an unformed lump held in one's hands is a dangerous thing. Then, when it takes form and real power lies in it, watch out!"

"So, what are they?" Hayden asked. "What's the power?"

Kip sighed and then said, "They're communication devices. Miniature satellites. After hijacking the stations, we believe these one-inch satellites are relays."

"Relays?" Hayden questioned. "From what to what…"

"Mr. Stanton," the hybrid interrupted. "Here are the updates on the space stations and their crews. China's Tiangong-2 and its crew are intact and unvisited by the Indians. The commercial Space Complex 1 and its crew are intact, as is the International Space Station and its crew. China's space station is intact, but one of the crew is dead."

"The female taikonaut Hayden pointed out," Kip stated. "What about the others?"

"Well, Mr. Bakley is now aboard the ISS and the other Chinese taikonaut is still aboard the CSS."

"So, why kill one and not the other?" Kip asked.

"To help," Fahim answered.

"Help?" Kip questioned.

"Yes. Help," Fahim said. "There is a German astronaut aboard, female, who opened the hatch for the Indians when they docked."

"Ah, shit," Kip said. "That kind of help. Where's the flag-waving these days?"

"But, maybe not *willing* help," Hayden suggested. "The male taikonaut on the CSS didn't seem right. Like, maybe, he was coerced."

"How about the German, Fahim?" Kip asked.

"No," Fahim answered. "But, German faces are carved in stone."

"Fair enough," Kip said. "You never quite know what's swimming inside a German's head. You need to cast zombies, hire the Germans. No other race resembles the living dead more."

"Speaking of dead, Mr. Stanton," The hybrid said. "I got a flatline reading on one of the astronauts on the ISS. It appears to be … *uh* … one of the Russians."

"Maybe he or she took off their biomonitoring shirt," Kip suggested, unworried.

"No! Oh, shit!" Baldy blurted. "It appears to be legit. *Holy fuck!* Another one flatlined! And another! *Oh* … and another!"

CHAPTER **TWENTY**

"**F**our out of six isn't good, Baldy!" Kip said. "Who are they? Talk to me!"

"Any of them Ora?" Hayden yelled.

"Sh!" Fahim said with an index finger over his mouth. "You have to stay quiet. Let's hope it's the German."

"We have to get out there," Hayden demanded of Fahim.

"No," Fahim said. "Let me think."

"No matter what, Hayden," Kip said. "The Jap is right. You can't give up the ship."

"What is this, the Navy?" Hayden asked. "Staying in the module isn't going to help Ora or anybody else."

A snap from the Jap's fingers and he said, "That's it. Yes, we stay in here and ..." he was busy opening compartments, looking for something, "we ... use ..." When he turned around, he held out a ball in his hand and said, "This."

"What's that?" Hayden asked.

"A drone," the JAXA astronaut said.

"A drone. On the ISS?" Hayden said.

"Yes. We send this out and we can track it on the computer," Fahim said.

"These weren't around when I was on board last," Hayden explained. "Won't they see it?"

"Probably, yes," Fahim answered. "It just hovers, but it's better than us going out there."

"It's smart, Hayden," Kip offered. "See how far it gets without the danger."

"Any word on Ora, Baldy?" Hayden asked.

"The biomonitoring is going bananas," the half man, half machine reported. "It's a jumbled mess."

A long sigh expelled out of Hayden. The man in the hat with a tan, *Manhattan*, had methodically ventured from taking things from Hayden that were replaceable, like his home and most of what was in it, now into the arena of the unreplaceable, such as some of the items he had in his house, the secure feeling of sanctuary he had felt there, his freedom, his innocence, and now maybe Ora.

Hayden headed for the hatch. "I have to know."

The JAXA astronaut grabbed him and said, "You will," and then showed him the drone-ball in his hand, "with this."

"He's dropping all kinds of wisdom on you, Hayden. I would take it," Kip persuaded.

"You're foggy now and not seeing clearly," Fahim said. "Nor, thinking clearly. You go out there, you'll get yourself killed. I go out after you and you'll get me killed. The drone will show us clearly. However long it lasts."

"Well put, Fahim," Kip said out of the screen.

Glossed-over eyes in Hayden's sockets looked at the Jap. The calm confidence in his eyes and on his face of the plan convinced Hayden it was the right thing to do.

All Hayden could muster was a nod to proceed.

A reassuring smile fought to form on Fahim's face. "Okay. I got it," the JAXA astronaut said and went to work.

Suited up and entirely prepped for a spacewalk, the Chinaman was alone inside the sealed airlock on the Chinese Space Station. Similarly, the female German was alone in the airlock on the International Space Station and the American was alone inside the airlock on Space Complex 1. Synchronization of all three astronauts depended on the

Indians who had helped them up to this point. Now, the threat held over each spacewalking astronaut would have to be enough for them to execute the plan on their own, a plan, which rested solely upon the cause of the bulge in their utility pockets, sewn to one of the thighs in their respective spacesuits.

Inside the Japanese Experimental Module (JEM) named the Kibo, Fahim got the ball-shaped drone ready, while Kip relayed more information Baldy had just reported from agents in the field on Earth.

"Well, well," Kip started. "Remember when I said that those golf balls were relays, mini-satellites for communication purposes? We knew of two briefcases, Manhattan and Sydney, but Hayden, there are four of those suckers out there. Maybe more, but we believe four."

"Four!" Hayden acknowledged. "For what? Do we know their purpose?"

"Not exactly, but one of my agents, abreast of everything, has a theory. Four briefcases. Four operational space stations in orbit. She believes there was one briefcase assigned per station. Supposed to be, anyway. The one we have here botched up the Tiangong-2 hijacking, so they skipped it. Apparently, someone on India's end had decided that the sixty satellites in the three briefcases and the three larger space stations were enough to pull off whatever it is they're trying to do."

Exhausted, hurt, and confused impatience came out of Hayden when he asked, "Which is?"

"They're setting up for some kind of relay."

"So, are those ball satellites up here on the ISS?"

"We're not sure. We haven't figured out a way of using the ones we have to track the others. We're not even sure we can."

"Well, let Fahim and I go see if we can find them."

"No, Hayden, really. You're not fooling anybody. You just want to check on Ora. If that ball-drone the Japanese have can look for her, it can look for the small satellites."

A defeated sigh leaked out of Hayden in his helplessness.

"Remember, Hayden, you saw them," Kip continued. "Each of these tiny satellites has twelve panels, like a soccer ball. Our researchers determined that each panel could relay information. My agent with the theory had calculated that twelve relay panels on a ball times twenty balls in a briefcase mean a potential of two hundred and forty relays per briefcase. Multiply that by three and it means seven hundred and twenty transmissions could take place. Simultaneously, I might add. If they had that fourth briefcase, we're talking almost a thousand transmissions."

"So what?" Hayden asked. "I follow your math, but satellites handle way more than that."

"True, but they're parked over a footprint of Earth and handle transmissions for that area. Not these balls. Their panels in a circle go out in every direction."

Overhearing as he worked, Fahim chimed in, "They're so small, I doubt they're powerful enough to reach Earth."

"Not reliably, anyway," Kip agreed. "Which my agent feels she has an answer for that. What if the signal just needs received from Earth and is transmitted a shorter distance?"

"I think that would work fine," Fahim said.

"If it's a danger," Hayden said, "then let's find them. There's no one left aboard the CSS to help us, but what about SC1? You contact them? If we can get ours and they can get theirs and you have one, what good would the one do on the CSS?"

"I hear you loud and clear," Kip said. "The problem is we don't know. Without knowing what their goal is, it's impossible to know. Maybe all it takes is one and the rest are contingent."

"Okay," the JAXA astronaut said. "We're ready. You open the hatch and, once I drive it out, secure it."

Hayden cracked the hatch and peeked out into the Harmony module. No one around, he opened it wider. The thought of venturing out on his own crossed his mind, but perhaps he wasn't thinking clearly. After another check outside, his eyes wondered at the white, baseball-sized drone floating toward him. One lone dark-glassed dot at its center had to be the camera. As it passed him, it appeared there were more cameras, one in each direction, north, south, east, and west. Outside of the camera dots, the white drone camouflaged with the white and off-white enclosure inside the Japanese module. Stealthily, it cruised out the hatch as if a line drive hit baseball captured in slow motion.

"Okay, close the hatch," Fahim said.

The opened hatch tempted Hayden.

"Close it!" Fahim said.

As Hayden secured the hatch, Kip's voice spoke out of Hayden's forearm.

"I wish I could have seen that," Kip said.

"Scary, if you ask me," Hayden said.

"Sci-fi has come to life," Kip agreed. "The military uses them all the time on bombing strikes. How weird is that to see men running and hiding from a flying machine?"

"Or helpful," Fahim reasoned. "It's going into danger out there, while we get to stay in here."

"Wisdom, Hayden," Kip said. "Keep that man alive. He just might save your life."

Hayden smiled at the Japanese astronaut and said, "Maybe."

"Well, I'm going bolt and leave you two to your work," Kip said. "Keep me posted, *hey.*"

"We will," Fahim said for Hayden.

Hayden's mouth closed and left it at that. It was all he was going to say himself.

Being the only Japanese aboard, Fahim must have felt like part of a team, which he was on the ISS, an important one, but perhaps more essential on this smaller team.

"Come," Fahim invited.

Hayden floated over to the computer. Its screen was split into four quarters, where a visual of Harmony, the node 2 module, could be seen in each direction through the cameras on the ball-drone as it slowly floated forward.

"We'll both watch so we don't miss anything," Fahim said. "You watch those two and I'll watch these two."

"Fine," Hayden agreed. "Does this thing have sound?"

"Yes. The closer the better, so I don't know how helpful it will be."

"Anything's good at this point."

Visually seeing the progress across node 2 with his own eyes tricked Hayden into sensations he was out there himself on a casual float as if having an out-of-body experience. Only charged with monitoring two quadrants, he found his eyes wandering to the other two, the experience exhilarating.

Creeping along, the ball-drone would not draw attention to itself, but would also be an easy target. A space-aged piñata, hanging to be struck, or a plump peach, hanging on a limb to be plucked.

Undetected, the ball-drone crossed node 2 and into the *Columbus* science laboratory. It was empty. The floating sphere didn't turn around, it backed up, where the camera on the backside became the forward camera and the views in each of the quadrants on the computer screen changed so now that camera became Camera 1 and appeared in the top left box.

Back in node 2, the floating sphere went a little farther and entered the Permanent Multipurpose Module. It, too, was void of life.

"That looks familiar," Hayden said.

"Sorry," Fahim said and shrugged his shoulders.

Back inside node 2, the module was still empty. Through one of the cameras, Hayden saw a patch with ORA FRUSH stitched into it above her crew quarters where she sleeps.

"Go in there," Hayden said.

"I don't think we should waste time…" Fahim began.

"I think you owe me one," Hayden interrupted. "Don't you?"

"Fine. Quick."

"Of course it will be quick. It's a broom closet."

Slowly, the floating drone went into Ora's sleep quarters. The only picture attached to one of her walls near her hanging sleep pod, or sleeping bag, was the same one she had framed and given to Hayden on the ground.

Seeing it now through the computer screen made him think of her in more detail. This time, there were no thoughts of himself as he had thought on the ground. His life, all he had accomplished, the things he hadn't done, would he get the chance to do them, all paled in comparison to the task now, this moment. Everything before and whatever awaited him after was in black and white, while right now came through in color.

"Okay, thanks," Hayden said. "You're right. Let's go."

The drone exited node 2 and entered Destiny, the U.S. laboratory.

"The place is a ghost town," Hayden said.

"Where is everybody?" Fahim asked.

Out of Destiny and into node 1, named the Unity, the drone didn't detect any human life in its cameras or sound.

"Eerie isn't it," Hayden said.

"Maybe we're alone," Fahim said.

"*Oh*, don't say that. Where would everyone else be?"

"Maybe the Indians took them or made them leave the ship in the Soyuz."

"Maybe they're on their way to Earth right now."

Just then, a body floated into the module.

"*Holy fuck!*" Hayden reacted and, simultaneously, the Jap made an unintelligible sound.

Another body floated into the module and crashed into the first, causing the newcomer to turn in midair.

"*Whoa!*" Hayden yelled.

A different inarticulate sound expelled out of Fahim as if this body deserved its own or the first sound simply couldn't be reproduced.

The bodies were both female and neither wore anything on their clothing to signify what country they were from. The hair on the one, floating on her stomach, covered her face and the color and length looked like it might be Ora.

"I'm not staying in here," Hayden said. "Come on!"

"No!" Fahim replied. "I feel the same way, but we must know what we're dealing with."

"Two Indians! *Two!* You and I can take them."

"They have lasers. And who knows, maybe more of them came aboard."

The lasers Hayden knew of, but the idea that more Indian vyomanauts may have boarded just might be a possibility. So far, they haven't seen them, but there was still half of the ISS left.

Fahim's good thinking had Hayden pondering and he said, "Why haven't they come looking for us?"

The JAXA astronaut took his eyes off the computer monitor, looked at Hayden, and said, "Easy. We're not important."

Fahim's eyes remained fixed on Hayden's a moment, then returned to the screen.

"Can you get over there?" Hayden asked.

"I'll try," Fahim said. "I'll hide within the bodies."

The ball-drone moved forward toward the floating bodies.

"They're pretty limp," Hayden said.

The JAXA astronaut didn't say anything, concentrating on maneuvering the drone.

As it floated among the bodies, its speakers picked up the sound of voices.

"Can we turn that up?" Hayden asked.

The volume was turned up and Hayden recognized the language.

"It's the Indians," Hayden said.

Concentrating on his work, Fahim said, "Let's see what's happening in there."

The drone floated in view of the open hatch of the *Quest* airlock. One of the woman's floating legs blocked the drone's camera until the sphere lowered to where it could see.

This time, neither man said anything. Floating limp among the two Indians inside the equipment lock was Ora's body.

CHAPTER **TWENTY-ONE**

The ball-drone caught a glimpse of a man coming into node 1. By process of elimination, the only other male crewmember aboard the ISS was the Russian. As he moved closer, the white, blue, and red striped flag on his shirt verified his Russian nationality. The women's floating bodies in node 1 stopped him cold. His head snapped toward the equipment lock and when he began to move that way, pushing the women's bodies out of the way, a flash of golden light tinted the camera's view.

Seeing it on the computer screen, Hayden asked, "What was that?"

"Not good," Fahim said.

When the Russian had pushed the women's bodies, they had floated into the drone and sent it into a spin. Fahim and Hayden knew they had lost their drone, because, in space, what started in motion, remained in motion.

Psychedelic whirls of color in each quadrant on the computer screen became difficult to look at and it didn't take long for Hayden to give up on it.

"Whew!" Hayden said, rubbing his eyes. "You should record that so we can use it as a form of torture on the Indians."

The spinning view didn't seem to bother Fahim as much, so he continued to watch. Hope, most likely, motivated the Jap to stay with it so he and Hayden wouldn't have to venture outside the JEM.

Darkness filled the main camera on the drone and the floating sphere appeared to stop spinning. From Fahim's view on the computer, the darkness rested and then light appeared with the camera stable. Seeing the Russian cosmonaut's body afloat, he realized the Russian's body had shadowed and collided with the drone, wedged it to a stop against the floating women, and then floated away.

"He's dead," Fahim said.

"He's what?" Hayden asked surprised.

"Now we know what the gold flash was."

"A laser?"

"Had to be," Fahim answered and turned toward Hayden. "They're not messing around. We can't go out there."

"Let me see," Hayden said and made his way to view the computer screen. "Those assholes are dragging him into the equipment lock. Follow them."

"They'll see us."

"They're going to see us anyway. Let's see what they're doing."

Nestled against the dragged Russian body, the drone-ball entered the equipment lock. The danger intensified for Fahim and Hayden as if they had floated in themselves. An Indian vyomanaut opened the hatch to the crew lock and he and his partner stuffed the Russian's body inside.

Seeing Ora's body, floating in the equipment lock, Hayden said, "They're casting them into space and Ora's next."

"The German must be outside to pull them out," Fahim said.

"We need to stop this!"

"*Wait!* Look at the screen."

Hayden did and his anger amplified by what he saw.

A close-up of an Indian's face filled a quadrant on the computer screen. For a moment, he just looked and then a smile elongated his mouth. He said something in Hindi and then in accented English said, "Watch."

The vyomanaut floated over to the hatch and pushed the drone-ball inside the crew lock.

The camera views on the computer screen exhibited that the drone had entered a slow turn, but not enough to where they couldn't see anything as before. In panoramic view, they could see the inside of the crew lock and the hatch closed.

Moments passed and the outside hatch opened, exposing space and the female German astronaut. She reached in and grabbed the drone-ball, looked at it through the visor in her helmet, and tossed it into space. The toss resulted in a controlled tumble, similar to a knuckleball pitch in baseball.

As the drone moved away from the airlock, the cameras on each of its sides captured bizarre happenings like a third-party witness to a murder who may never report it. *'Watch,'* the Indian had said, wanting those operating the drone to see the bodies discarded.

Hayden and Fahim watched the German pull the Russian body out of the crew lock and let it float off into space.

"Are we recording this?" Hayden asked, without taking his eyes off the computer screen.

"Yes," Fahim said, "but because of the earlier time constraints, the drone doesn't have much power left."

The German closed the outside hatch.

As Hayden floated toward the hatch inside the JEM, he said, "Close the hatch behind me and stay here to record what you can for evidence. They're not going to do that to Ora. She suffers from Astrophobia."

The words caused a sweeping rupture of splintering emotion inside him, burning his brain and stomach, and colliding at his throat. Caught there and unable to breathe, it choked him until a spitting ejection came out of his mouth and tears and heavy breathing followed. He wasn't okay and he swore he heard a snap like a ruptured tendon. The only problem was it came from inside his head.

He knew she was dead and they were disposing the body.

Despite their fracture, his heart and mind wandered a bit into the future now, which they had failed to do earlier, remembering what she had written in red nail polish on the back of the picture she had given him, *'Marry me, Hayden … before I change my mind! Ora.'*

"What are you going to use?" Fahim asked.

"What do you mean?" Hayden said.

"They have lasers. What do you have?"

Only a moment ago, Hayden's hands had felt invincible, like shields of the strongest, thickest steel, destructive weapons that could kill anything. Now, Fahim's sobering question left him hungover; his face dazed and confused.

"Check the logistics module up there," Fahim offered. "There might be something."

Hayden floated into the logistics module attached to the JEM. An overwhelming number of compartments covered the entire wall space of the module. Luckily, for Hayden, like most things on the ISS, they were all labeled. Floating and scanning, he searched for a weapon that would kill or at least stun until he got his hands on them.

He wished he knew where his spacesuit was. When the drone had scanned half of the station and he didn't see it, including in the equipment lock, where suits are typically kept, he wondered if it had been discarded into space the same as the Russian body.

Knowing he was running out of time, Hayden had to grab something and make it work. As many times he had been on board the ISS, it always amazed him how every crew docking station was located only on one side of the ship, opposite where he was now. A pistol out of a Soyuz would almost equal the playing field against the Indian's lasers.

Almost. Maybe a pistol wouldn't be enough. There were two of them with two lasers and one of him without a weapon to match. The thought of puncturing something long and sharp through a space station wall had crossed his mind. So did opening a hatch or detaching a section of the ship. But outside of killing the Indians, everyone else inside, and the female German astronaut outside, once her air ran out, then what? Such an act would thwart the vyomanaut's plan, but at the expense of destroying himself, Fahim, along with hundreds of billions of dollars invested in the ISS.

Time again tugged on Hayden like a person inhaling their last breaths. Opening a drawer, he settled on a long-handled dead-blow hammer and a crowbar and returned to the JEM.

"Anything new?" Hayden asked.

"Not yet," Fahim said, "The German's waiting," and when he saw the weapons Hayden had chosen, he added, "Good choices and good luck."

"Don't say that. The way my luck's been running, I'm a dead man."

"But you're angry. Anger can bring a lot of power and hide a lot of pain."

"Lock the hatch behind me, would you?"

Hayden opened the hatch to the JEM, peeked out, turned back to the JAXA astronaut, and said, "Nice knowing you, Fahim. And thanks."

"Go," Fahim said. "This isn't goodbye."

A half-hearted smile dimpled one of the corners of Hayden's mouth as he turned and floated through the hatch into node 2. With the weapons he had, he knew he had to get close to use them. Aggressive momentum propelled him through modules node 2, the U.S. lab, node 1, and with one last pull to thrust himself forward, he entered the equipment lock, swinging the long-handled hammer in his left hand and the crowbar in his right.

As if Japanese himself, yielding swords, Hayden had gained the element of surprise. The crowbar hit an Indian vyomanaut along the side of his head at the ear and down onto the trapezius. Anger had added power to his swing. Hard steel walloped flesh and bone, effective in dazing the

Indian, who's floating body moved down to the floor, then buoyed up again into a limp hover.

That was the extent of Hayden's attack because the other floating Indian pointed a laser at him. Unable to communicate and the vyomanaut unwilling to use the translator, they remained in a passive confrontation for a time. From Hayden's perspective, as long as they remained like that, Ora remained inside and the German outside was consuming the air in her tanks.

Wanting to keep the hatch to his back, Hayden floated forward a little, grabbed Ora, and pulled her close to him near the hatch. For the time being, the vyomanaut didn't mind Hayden's actions.

The lack of vital signs verified she was gone. Undeniably gone. He stroked her hair as if she lied on the couch tucked into him asleep, while his eyes bashed the vyomanaut's head in until all the pulp had leaked and splattered out of it, rendering it flat at the back of his skull. Killing these bastards became his life mission. After that, he didn't know.

The Indian, Hayden had struck with the crowbar, wasn't right. His eyelids slowly closed as if falling asleep and then startled open. Each time, the Indian's brown eyelids remained closed for longer stretches, until the last time, they remained closed and his body appeared to relax, even noticeable in near-zero gravity.

Upon Hayden's attack, the Indian must have half-pulled the laser out of his holster, because it clung there like a leaf stuck in the grass and flapping in the wind. It broke loose and floated in the air; the Indian's body blocking the free weapon from his partner.

The Indian checked on his partner, shaking him to wake up. Hayden bent down and kissed Ora's dead lips. Carefully, keeping an eye on the floating laser, without making it obvious, he moved Ora's hovering body to the side, pushed off the wall with his feet, and grabbed the laser. Knowing the vyomanaut from India had the bead on him before he could point and fire the laser, he turned and pushed off another wall as if doing laps in the pool, grabbed Ora, and floated out of the equipment lock into node 1. Without stopping, he kept going into node 3, named *Tranquility*.

Upon entering, a floating space suit startled him because, at first glance, its posture could have passed as a person. Even the helmet was attached to the suit. Despite the suit being deflated in spots, he checked it to make sure someone wasn't in it. It was empty and he realized it was his suit. Kip had told him there were weapons and other gadgets on it, but never shown, as Kip had promised, there wasn't time to find them now. Besides, he couldn't imagine there being anything more deadly than the laser in his hand.

As if he waded in water and Ora floated on her back, Hayden held onto her with one hand and pointed the laser toward the hatch with the other. A view of Earth, blue and white, behind them through the cupola windows their water.

Something was wrong. Either Hayden's luck was changing or there was another reason why the Indian had let him go so easily. All it would have taken was one blast from the laser and that would be it. So why the hesitation?

Hayden wouldn't make the same mistake. Reluctantly, his hand let go of Ora and her body floated beside him as he waited.

Sure enough, the vyomanaut darkened the opening to the hatch and entered node 3, controlled and confident.

Resolute, Hayden fired the laser. A solid gold beam, surrounded by a yellowish-gold glow, extended out of the tip of the laser and across node 3. Its power penetrated the Indian, whose wide eyes and opened mouth expressed his surprise that Hayden had a laser. Within a few seconds, his eyes stilled, as did his body. His hand relaxed and the laser floated out of it.

The laser beam extinguished when Hayden stopped firing. Now, the vyomanaut resembled Ora and the others on board. His body hovered in node 3 like a drowned man upheld by the water that killed him, forever silenced.

Leaving Ora's body floating there in front of the cupola,

Hayden returned to the equipment lock, where the other Indian floated. A hint of ethical judgment questioned him. Only a whisper, and to avoid later problems, he lasered the unconscious Indian, making sure he was dead.

The Indians had used him to gain access to the ISS and, now, Ora, and nearly everyone else was dead. Hayden had a lot to live with, but killing the vyomanauts from India wouldn't be part of the nagging in his conscious. Ensuring their deaths by his hand had become his life mission and now that it was accomplished, he didn't know.

Before leaving the equipment lock, he secured the hatch so it couldn't be opened from the outside, ensuring the female German, who had helped the Indians, would run out of air and die. This, too, wasn't something that would bother him later. A black and white thinker in a gray world, he easily validated an accomplice to multiple murders and hijackings had an equal right to die as the assailants themselves. An enemy was an enemy. Kill or be killed.

While retrieving Ora in node 3, the sight of Earth, through the cupola windows, spurred in Hayden a new mission: get Ora back to Earth for a proper burial. Looking at her, he vowed to do it or die trying. As he moved her body from node 3 into node 1, where two female bodies floated, the mission expanded to include them, if he was able. Without question, Ora was his priority.

Outside the hatch of the JEM, he realized he and the Japanese astronaut never arranged for opening the hatch if he were to return. Maybe the Jap never expected that. All he knew to do was yell through the hatch.

"Fahim! Fahim! It's Hayden and Ora!"

Time passed and he tried again.

"Fahim! Fah…"

"How do I know?" Fahim's voice muffled through the hatch.

"Ask me something from our conversation earlier."

"Fine. What does my name mean?"

"Learned man," Hayden answered.

The hatch to the JEM opened. Hayden entered first and the smiling Jap awaited with opened arms. But when Hayden dragged in Ora's body behind him, the Jap's face elongated as if gravity had pulled on his round chin.

"I thought you said she was with you," Fahim said.

"She is," Hayden answered, but knew what he had meant.

A home within the ISS, the Japanese hope module, strangely, provided Hayden some relief.

"The Indians?" Fahim wondered.

"Dead," Hayden answered. "Both of them."

"I should have gone with you."

"Na," Hayden said. "You were our last line of defense. It was best you remained here. Speaking of which, anything new?"

"No. The Russian cosmonaut's body started to balloon and is out of sight now and the German's thoroughly frustrated outside."

"Probably wondering why the hatch hasn't opened. She should have tried before because it's not going to open now. I secured it."

"She seemed preoccupied with whatever's in her utility pocket."

"How so?"

"She kept checking it all the time. As much as she checked the hatch."

The female German astronaut didn't know what had transpired inside the ISS. It didn't seem conceivable to her that anyone could have detained the vyomanauts, let alone kill them. Believing she was still under the threat of the Indians, the only thing she could do was carry out what they had asked so she could get back to her husband and son.

She opened the outermost hatch to the airlock so no one inside could open the one inside and come out without endangering everyone inside the ISS. Her oxygen gauge said she had a few hours of air left, but she sure hoped the signal would come soon.

Not long after that wish, it came.

CHAPTER **TWENTY-TWO**

Inside the JEM, Fahim monitored the computer to check what he could still see from the drone floating in space, while Hayden remained with Ora's body, dealing with the loss and everything that came with it.

"Hey, Hayden," Fahim said. "You may want to see this."

Without thinking about it, Hayden kissed Ora's dead lips and floated over to the computer.

On the screen, the German outside the ISS, held her utility pocket open. There's no mobility in the helmet when it's attached to the bodysuit, but based on her posture, they assumed she was looking down the best she could. If they were her, they would be looking down, too, because a golden hue of light leaked out of the utility pouch as if it were a miner's pack containing the shiniest gold nuggets ever found.

The light was the same gold color that had shot out of the Indian lasers and the color of their crew transport ship, the River to the Stars. Pre-planned, the Indians use of the color gold came from the colors in India's flag: saffron, white, and India green. When these colors are mixed, ignoring the navy blue Ashoka Chakra on the twenty-four-spoked wheel, they produce a golden color.

"Can you zoom on that?" Hayden asked.

The view in the top-left quadrant zoomed in a little more on the computer screen.

"That's it," Fahim said. "The ISS is moving away from the drone for it to zoom any closer."

"No, no, that's fine," Hayden said then pointed at the screen. "She's getting something."

Tethered to the International Space Station, the female German astronaut pinched two thick-gloved fingers into her utility pocket and pulled out a golden-lit tiny ball. Holding it between her fingers, she eyed it and then separated her fingers and let it go. As hurriedly as she could in dealing with padded gloves, utility pouch, and an uncooperative helmet, one-by-one she let them go into space—twenty in all. Scattered, they resembled lightning bugs, emitting the brightest bioluminescence in the blackness of space.

Inconceivably, every one of them brightened simultaneously. Golden round orbs of light expanded their glow, looking like floodlights used in search of something in the darkest night. Tiny thrusters propelled the miniature satellites higher into space, creating a golden smear and leaving a white tail, dangling underneath them like launched fireworks.

The sight of the German in her spacesuit, tethered to the space station, with golden-glowing, golf-ball sized satellites, hovering in dark space, was otherworldly.

"Okay," Hayden said. "Kip said they were satellites, relays, so what are they for?"

"Look," Fahim said, pointing at the computer screen.

A crew transport ship, similar to the Russian Soyuz and the Chinese Shenzhou, approached the open docking station.

"Fuck, who's that?" Hayden blurted out.

At first, the ship appeared tan, shielded slightly by the solar arrays on the ISS. But as it entered a clearing, it became quite apparent its color was orange.

"Shit," Hayden leaked as he thought. "Let's split up and

make sure all of the hatches are secure so no one can get in. You take the closer ones and I'll take the farthest."

"Okay," Fahim agreed.

"*Oh*, and here. I got you something." Hayden handed the Jap an Indian laser.

A loud gulp moved the JAXA astronaut's throat, apparently knowing where and how Hayden had gotten it.

"Take it, man!" Hayden said. "We don't have time to waste."

"You have one?" Fahim checked.

Hayden waved it as he floated for the hatch to the JEM.

Hayden secured his hatches and, as long as the Jap sealed his, the ISS should be locked down. On his way back to the JEM, the screen nested in his forearm illuminated and Kip's voice sounded out of the speakers.

"Got an update for you, partner," Kip said. "And it isn't good. We have satellite images of someone on the China Space Station and another on Space Complex 1, disbursing those balls. They're for something, Hayden. Something big!"

"The German did the same here," Hayden said. "They must have been timed up. Could you tell if the balls looked golden?"

"They were. That was their trigger, then?"

"Must be, because Fahim watched the German the entire time and she didn't launch them until they were lit."

"This is some scheme."

"*Yeah,* well, what's ours?"

"I'm working on it," Kip said, then asked, "The ISS secure?"

"I believe so," Hayden answered.

"Well, make sure."

While Kip worked on it, Hayden met Fahim back at the JEM.

"All locked up?" Hayden asked.

"Yeah," Fahim answered. "Now what?"

"Kip contacted me and is working on it. You have any ideas?"

"No. We can't continuously thrust the ISS so the ship doesn't dock and about those balls …"

"I don't have anything either."

"I do." Out of the screen embedded in Hayden's left forearm, Kip's voice interrupted their conversation.

"That didn't take long," Hayden said.

"I have a feeling we're running out of time," Kip said. "Now, look. We can't launch anything from the ground. Those tiny satellites are too small. However, there are a couple of satellites up there that are weaponized."

"Whoa! Weaponized?" Hayden said. "I thought that couldn't be done because of the treaties."

"For the sake of time, let's just say some countries with the experience and means thought it might be a good idea to have something up there in case of an asteroid or something was on a collision course with Earth. I don't know about you, but I'm okay with it. One of them is ours, meaning the United States. If you can get to it, we can use it."

"For what? To shoot them down? There's no way at these orbital speeds I could hit a one-inch target."

"Understood. We know that. Ours has a magnet."

"A magnet?"

"To collect space junk without destroying it in orbit and keeping orbital lanes clear. Some designs are using nets for the bigger stuff. They collect the stuff and, once full, escort it into the atmosphere to burn. A little expensive for my taste, but …"

"Do we know if these things are magnetic?" Hayden asked.

"Through our testing performed on them, they are," Kip answered.

"Well, why not just steer it from the ground?"

"We need those twenty satellites for phase two."

"Phase two! What's phase two?"

"Let's just get by phase one first, shall we?"

"Which is I find my way to the magnetized satellite and then what? Can I operate it?"

"It can be manned. One man. And it can be controlled. Once you're in it, we'll talk you through it."

"Why doesn't this sound easy?"

"It's not and you might die. Speaking of which, if you do make it inside, you're going to want to get out of there just in case someone down here accidentally commands it into the Earth's atmosphere for destruction."

"Well, you're going to let them know I'm going in it, right?" Hayden asked, leery.

"We're having a hard time getting ahold of them," Kip said flatly. "But don't worry, we will. You'll be fine. You still have your spacesuit?"

"I'll have to look it over, but yeah."

"Then get dressed."

"You're going to owe me big time for this," Hayden said.

"Maybe the world will owe you," Kip said. "Checkbook's out with pen in hand as we speak. Don't go too crazy, *huh*. We have a budget to think about."

After Hayden checked his spacesuit, Fahim helped him put it on, shortening the process where they could, including an abbreviated pre-breath. During that time, Kip introduced a specialist on the magnetized satellite, who talked Hayden through what they were doing on the ground and what he would attempt to do in space.

The plan was to have the much smaller magnetic satellite thrust to slow down, allowing the ISS to catch up. Once they achieved near-parallel orbital vicinity with the ISS higher than the magnetic satellite, the idea was for Hayden to exit the ISS as if performing a spacewalk, untether himself, and use the latest maneuvering technology built into his spacesuit to fly over to the target satellite. It was a little like two same-speed airplanes, traveling with one slightly higher than the other, and a person jumping off the higher plane into a freefall and using a jetpack to fly over to the lower plane. His window of start had to be to the second and his power usage, speed, and charted course all had to be near perfect to intercept the satellite.

Another challenge, the technology Hayden was about to use had never been tested in space. On the ground and in a similar environment, yes. Used to perform such a complicated maneuver, no. Although, untethered space exploration was why this space suit had been created in a long line of prior attempts.

The days of strapping on a pack to maneuver around were over. This maneuverability came straight from a cartoon superhero, only its energy source was different and much simpler. Built into the gloves and boots of Hayden's space suit were thrusters that used his exhaled carbon dioxide as fuel for propulsion, which escaped evenly out from the palm of the gloves and the bottom of the boots. One-hundred percent pure oxygen was stored in a bladder sewn into the back of Hayden's space suit instead of tanks strapped to his back and the suit contained carbon dioxide filters. Instead of removing the carbon dioxide, it was used as a propellant and its warm denseness pushed against the less dense air of space.

This same idea was what would slow Hayden down once he reached the magnetized satellite. All he'd have to do is position his hands and feet out in front of him to resist his forward progress.

After all the Godspeeds and good lucks by Kip and the others, who had helped derive the plan, Fahim helped Hayden into the crew lock with his head outward.

"I normally don't believe in killing," Fahim said. "But kill that German bitch." It was his Godspeed.

"I got it," Hayden said and he crawled forward in the crew lock, holding the laser above his head.

Once the airlock depressurized, Hayden started opening the outside hatch. Holding the laser, it was difficult, but then, a pleasant surprise occurred. Maybe things were going to turn his way because the female German astronaut outside began to assist in opening the hatch. Perhaps, she thought the Indians had loaded another dead body to dispose of in space, as was done with the Russian. More important than that, with her air running out, she probably wanted back inside.

Immediately, Hayden stopped helping. The German unsecured the hatch and swung the door open. She didn't know why the body had been positioned headfirst or why it was in a spacesuit. To the dead, it didn't matter. The only thing that mattered to her was it needed out, so she could get in. She reached in, grabbed the helmet, and pulled.

Helmets were usually sturdy and fastened to the suit tightly, but Hayden began to worry she might separate the helmet from the suit and that would squash the best-laid plan. His body remained as limp as it could under the circumstances. Near-zero gravity certainly helped in selling it. The laser had been stowed away before she opened the hatch.

With his body entirely out of the airlock, she shoved him off in a direction away from the solar arrays and hoped that he would clear the station without incident.

The way she had discarded his body, as if flicking a cigarette butt onto the street, rekindled an anger brewing inside him. Tension tightened his body, which, being away from her, was okay. He needed to get jacked up to do what he was about to do.

As the German bent down to enter the crew lock, Hayden reached for his laser and fired it at her. The gold beam tracked to the Primary Life Support System (PLSS), covering her entire back. The laser caused an ignition of the oxygen tank where it hit and burned right through it to the German. Her slightly hunched body straightened and there she remained for a time with a smoldering blue fire, not having much of a flame, consuming the PLSS, suit, and flesh. Attempted reaches for her back slowed and eventually ceased. Thickly-gloved hands came off the hatch and booted feet separated from the station. Her rigid body drifted away until the tether yanked like a leash on a dog and there she floated.

Hayden puffed some carbon dioxide through the boosters in his suit to get back to the station, where he tethered himself and secured the outside hatch. After one more look at the German, he unhooked her tether and she floated away from the ISS like a stringed balloon.

From here on out, he thought he was on his own, until both screens, inlaid in his forearms, illuminated, showing through his skin, clothing layers, and spacesuit as if they weren't there.

"We're with you, buddy," Kip said through the headset inside Hayden's helmet, as his face donned one screen and the face of the scientist, who had thoroughly explained every detail of the plan to Hayden, on the other, who only said, "Hello, again."

"What are you guys doing?" Hayden asked.

"We have a lot riding on this," Kip said. "Besides, we'll live vicariously through you."

"I assume the danger by going through everything, while you get to watch from comfortable safety."

"Of course. Why change that now."

"You should see the target satellite now," the scientist said.

At first, Hayden couldn't see it, then, from behind the solar arrays of the International Space Station, the magnetized satellite came into view.

"I see it," Hayden said.

"Good," the scientist said. "You have two minutes to get into position and untether yourself."

"Copy."

Hayden accomplished what needed done and held onto the station, waiting.

"Twenty seconds to shove off," the scientist said.

"Copy."

"On my mark."

Starting from twenty seconds, the scientist counted down.

"Five. Four. Three. Two. One. Mark."

Hayden pushed off the ISS with his hands and feet. Backing away from the space station reminded him of his dream, where he was tumbling in space away from a spaceship. Thank the cosmos he wasn't tumbling, and before something happened to cause him to tumble, he positioned and firmed his body into an erect, headfirst projectile, heading right for the target satellite. His arms straight down his sides, wrist bent so his palms faced straight back, his legs straight and together, and his boots flat, he began to wonder if the carbon dioxide boosters would be needed at the speed he gained in the significantly lighter and mobile space suit.

"Boosters on my mark," the scientist said. "And … Five. Four. Three. Two. One. Mark."

The space suit had processed Hayden's carbon dioxide since he first put on the helmet, through pre-breathe up to now, discharging out of the boosters in the palms of his gloves and the bottoms of his boots like rocket exhaust. The speed at which he traveled increased and Hayden found it both exhilarating and terrifying.

"Three hundred feet," the scientist said. "Initiate counter booster position in one hundred and fifty feet. Two twenty-five. One ninety-five. One fifty-nine. One fifty-six. One fifty-three. One fifty. Mark."

Hayden brought his hands over his head so the carbon dioxide shot out in front of him and swung his legs in front of him like a gymnast swinging on the parallel bars. His body assumed a seated position and he moved his hands out in front of him as if doing a pushup. All four boosters pushed against his momentum and he felt himself begin to slow down.

"Approaching the target satellite," the scientist said. "In seventy-five feet. Forty-five. Thirty. Fifteen. Extinguish boosters. Coasting now. Nine feet. Six. Three … and capture."

Hayden lowered his legs; his panicked eyes searching for something to grab on the satellite.

"Capture what?" Hayden yelled. "It's smooth on this side."

"Find what you can, daredevil," Kip said in support.

Hayden's hands collided into the cylinder of the satellite harder than he expected, relaxed them, and moved them out from in front of him altogether to avoid breaking his arms. The visor of his helmet banged against the cylinder and then his chest hit, almost knocking the wind out of him. His body slid against the side of the satellite as it continued to move and he was running out of satellite. As soon as his hand clamped onto a bar supporting solar arrays, something rammed into his back and the momentum squashed him against the spacecraft.

"What the fuck!" Hayden said, surprised.

Orange-gloved hands and arms were wrapped around his chest when he glanced down. An effort to swing his other hand up to grab onto the bar failed and there he was, holding himself and an orange assailant with one arm. It was a good thing they were in near-zero gravity.

"Hayden, what's happening?" Kip asked. "I'm seeing orange."

A second attempt proved true and, with both hands on the bar, Hayden pulled his body toward it, hoping the orange bastard hanging on him would drop off and float away into space.

Whoever held onto him was strong. So strong the person in orange used Hayden by climbing up his back and grabbing the support bar to the solar arrays themselves. Both holding on, they fought to gain an advantage, knowing whoever gained the higher ground first could use their feet and kick the other off.

Busy trying to stay alive, Hayden caught a glimpse into the tinted visor of the enemy's helmet and swore the face was a woman's. There are some very strong women out there, but her strength didn't match the sex.

For a moment, the orange warrior halted the fight and looked at Hayden. Kip's elevated voice sounded in Hayden's helmet as Hayden continued to struggle for another moment, then, instead of taking advantage of the cease, he ended up ceasing himself.

Hayden's foe was too beautiful to be a man. A stealing glance of the body next to him with breasts and a woman's shape, experience told him this was no man.

Squinting into the opposing visor facing him, he saw the most beautiful of the beautiful. Green eyes on clean whites. Dark eyebrows curved above them. Crisp facial features contrasted against light fair skin. A thin nose went to thick rosy lips. He knew if he could remove her helmet, he would find dark auburn hair. Her beauty apprehended him. Spellbound, he let his guard down in the surprise of it all.

Her lips moved inside her helmet as if talking, but Hayden couldn't hear her, only Kip. A loud screeching rasp of interference intruded inside his own helmet, drowning out Kip's voice, followed by settling cracking, and then he heard her; Kip no longer had sound or visual.

"I'm pretty sure this is my seat," she said.

It was her.

CHAPTER **TWENTY-THREE**

Only four space stations occupied space. Without question, mankind's quest for the stars resided in a minority few. Therefore, with today's current technology and self-imposed cost restrictions for space exploration, the maximum number of people who could occupy space could be counted on three hands, maybe four, but no more. The lack of humans physically in space meant something else would do the warfare for us, albeit, an extension of man, through his knowledge and craftsmanship, that would reach the stars on our behalf. The war for the spheres would be won or lost through the satellites.

And it was so. Despite two humans, Hayden and the beautiful female orange assailant from Manhattan and Sydney, risking their lives by literally fighting over the control of the satellite in their grasp, it was the one-inch satellites, hovering in space, that would win or lose the day.

Through their small thrusters, the tiny satellites, a set of twenty set free from the ISS, CSS, and SC1, sixty in all, had moved higher and scattered in the atmosphere. Farther away from the sun, they orbited a tad slower than the space stations, which averaged sixteen complete orbits around the Earth a day, while other artificial bodies orbited at their own pace. Two keys for the miniature satellite's success were many of the artificial bodies, orbiting beneath the miniature satellites, would pass by at least once and some moving faster multiple times. But despite, their orbital pace, everything rotating between the one-inch satellites and the Earth was in range.

The Indian Space Research Organization (ISRO) had gotten off easy in both duty and costs. Sure, the vyomanauts risked the voyage up to the space stations and such an endeavor is never automatic or safe, but they were spared the task of bringing the one-inch round satellites and the spacewalk to disburse them. Trained as they were, they could have accomplished both. But if the transporter had been caught carrying the tiny satellites, the bringer and their country would have born the blame. Not to mention, the mini-satellites were transported on proven crew vessels, the Russian Soyuz and the Chinese Shenzhou, instead of India's unproven Taare ko Nadee. Based on the superior mobility, demonstrated by India's crew transport ship, unproven didn't mean inferior.

There was another benefit to India's plan. Instead of having to launch their own space station and build it out module by module, they could take over existing orbital assets, namely space stations and satellites, via technology.

Understanding this and having the sixty golf ball-sized satellites spread out above the space stations and most satellite's orbital tracks, the ISRO on the ground went to work. Here was the moment of truth. Years of planning cumulated in the next few moments.

Most of those years had been spent collecting the unique identification codes specific to over a thousand operating satellites, including the space stations, all necessary security codes and passwords to gain access as a believed authorized user, as well as understanding frequencies, encryptions, and modulating schemes. Having this information, the ISRO initiated the takeover by transmitting an uplink from the largest dish antenna of India's Deep Space Network (IDSN), located in the village of Byalalu, India, up to the twenty satellite balls that had been released from the Space Complex 1 space station. Three hundred miles above the Earth, the golden lights on the tiny satellites brightened in dark space when the uplink reached them. The steady-state lights began to flicker as power lights do on computers when processing.

The process inside the twenty, one-inch balls bolstered the uplink's power. With each miniature satellite configured like a twelve-paneled soccer ball with twelve pentagon patches sewn together, twelve uplink signals went out from each of the panels in all directions across space and didn't stop until they located the other forty satellite balls.

In a game of connect the dots, one-by-one their golden lights radiated when the uplinks reached them, then blinked as the processing inside strengthened the already bolstered uplink signal.

A web of unseen communication became more complex as out of every panel of every satellite ball, seven hundred and twenty enhanced uplink signals in total reached out and connected to every Tracking and Data Relay Satellite (TDRS) in space. The initial uplink signal transmitted from India had spread and strengthened across space like some kind of cosmic cancer.

The transmission of terror rained down on the four space stations and more than a thousand operational satellites orbiting below. This was where all the research had to be right for the communication to be recognized and accepted as an authorized user. Once into the computers, the attack of orbital jamming and interference began.

A webbed network, intertwined within the spheres around Earth, had been achieved by India, capable of handling enough power to override any intruding power source or attempted reclamation of the satellites or space stations. The uplink spread and strengthened around all operating orbiters in space like one continuous choking weed. Some seizures were quick, while the size and scope of the space stations were a little more involved and the takeover more gradual.

Now it was time to gain complete control of the satellites and stations by turning their efforts to the ground. Complicating matters, another uplink was sent from India's Deep Space Network to the satellite balls and relayed through to every Tracking and Data Relay Satellite in space. From all these relays, an equally lethal downlink returned to Earth and breached every tracking, telemetry, and control center (TT&C), Deep Space Network (DSN), and every other antenna and communication device capable of reaching space like an undiscriminating disease. Except for India, of course, who had already swallowed the antidote and was spared.

The ground attack had been achieved without the use of military intrusion and bypassing all physical security that typically guarded such assets.

Controlling all Tracking and Data Relay Satellites and Deep Space Networks were just as important as gaining control of the space stations and satellites themselves because they provided India continuous orbital tracking capability of every operational orbiter in space. Just as the acquisitions of the space stations were more complex than satellites, the TT&Cs and DSNs would be gradual. The Indians involved at the ISRO would have to be diligent in heading off countermeasures and be patient as the planned uplinks and downlinks did their damage.

On Earth, at the Indian Space Research Organization's headquarters in Bengaluru, India and all other ISRO centers across India, nervousness moistened every witnessing body and thickened the air inside all facilities. The anticipation of taking over the world, a new empire, was in India's sweaty palms.

But that was all and way too early for celebration. Many things could go wrong and it all could slip right through their fingers. Not to mention, after such a drastic, bold attempt to rule the spheres and therefore Earth, if they failed, the wrath of every country in the world with military power would rain down on them and any partnerships in dealing with space or even imports and exports of trade would isolate them from the rest of the world.

When the first downlink of a specific identification code returned to Earth and appeared on the monitoring screens that India had successfully assumed control of that particular satellite, a unified cheer among ISRO participants expressed relief and excitement. As a results-oriented people, the celebration didn't last long and an even heavier nervousness lathered them and the air.

In a slow build-up, more identification codes of operational orbiters appeared on the screens until the codes started coming in so fast that they scrolled on the monitors. Hundreds of orbiters had been taken over by the Indians.

Then, a sizable jackpot. A main identification code and all of its subsequent codes appeared on the monitoring screens, indicating that they had now assumed control of the commercial space station, Space Complex 1. At first, there was silence at the victory. Then, an eruption of joy, louder than the first satellite code, sounded in all ISRO facilities.

More satellites came under their control followed by all the codes identifying China's smaller space station, the Tiangong-2. Still more codes of satellites poured in and shortly after identification codes for the Chinese Space Station showed on the screen. A major victory. At this point, near disbelief of their success wowed the Indians.

In chunks, more satellite codes came in, scrolling the screens. A recognizable code appeared on the monitors, followed by all of its subsequent codes, silencing nearly every witness in every ISRO location across India—codes for the International Space Station.

Literally, their ship had come in. Exuberance was tempered with having more work to do to ensure their success.

Within an hour of the codes appearing for the ISS, codes for tracking, telemetry, and control centers began appearing on the screens across all ISRO locations.

It would be hours before any of the Deep Space Networks came in, but, eventually, they did. What started as a dream began to materialize in their palm, soaking up the blood, sweat, and tears in a desperate fight for life to become a reality.

Having control of each of the four space stations and nearly every other artificial orbiter, it was now the Indians wished they had gotten those other twenty satellites in the fourth briefcase, in Kip's possession, into space. They would have provided an additional two hundred and forty relay signals, which certainly would have captured the last remaining satellites in orbit, instead of having to resend codes once they passed by the one-inch satellites a second time over the next few hours.

However, not having the satellites from the fourth briefcase in space didn't warrant panic. They had achieved what they had set out to achieve. Years of detailed planning, research, organizing, and implementing had been worth the effort. From the forefathers of scientists, who had started the initial work on India's space program inside the Saint Mary Magdalene Church in the village of Thumb, where science and spirituality had met in harmony, leading up to this moment, India had entered glory unto glory on an atmospheric river to the stars and achieved space glory by winning the war for the spheres.

With complete control of the four space stations, nearly every operational satellite in orbit, and a growing number of TT&Cs and DSNs as tenacious uplinks and downlinks took hold, India controlled the spheres, and the ISRO had the capability to configure the satellites however they wished. They could disable them, destroy them by ramming them into each other or even into the space stations, or use any weaponized satellites to do the damage. Unlimited access to mission packages and other information was at their fingertips. Communication. Reconnaissance. Navigation. Remote Sensing. Space Exploration. Everything a satellite could do and relay was in their control, eliminating, more than anything, military reliance on such equipment, which had become so important in increasing their power, and debilitating them, sending not only militaries, but every country, other than India, back a hundred years to relying on ground communication.

Hayden heard her breathing inside his helmet, not knowing how she had gained communications access, but she had. As he reconciled the beautiful woman wearing an orange spacesuit, her hand had slithered over his chest in search of something to pull or pinch to cause his demise. His spacesuit had been specifically designed to keep most workings of the suit insulated inside. A realization that she would kill him woke him out of his funk and his hand grabbed her hand and bent it back to get it off his chest.

Accepting defeat, she pulled her hand away and decided that the importance of killing him with her own hands, which had been shredded by holding onto the shattered window of Hayden's rental car in Manhattan, wasn't as important as removing him from the game forever. This American astronaut had ruined many of the orange assailants' plans by keeping a briefcase and its satellites from them and when they did get another briefcase on the harbor boat in Sydney, he had let Kip and his group know about it and, in turn, the Indians caught wind, and ended up with all briefcases but the one in Kip's possession. It could have been the orange assailants who had controlled the spheres instead of India. The American had to die.

While holding onto the bar with one hand, she went for her orange laser. Seeing it, Hayden chose to reach for her's, instead of playing the draw game and going for the Indian laser he had brought with him. The mind tends to think strange things, even during times when one's life was on the line. It happened to Hayden here, thinking, unlike taking care of business on the ISS, where he hadn't hesitated in killing the two Indians, his delay now, because of who she was and her beauty might get him killed.

Again, her strength surprised him. Over the years, he had easier bouts with men. Ticks of time were running out if they hadn't already and he had to kill her. The choice hung in space as they did, but, really, after everything, if he wanted things to end right, there wasn't a choice.

Each fought for the laser with one hand. They resembled two monkeys hanging from the same branch, fighting over a banana.

In the midst of the struggle, the laser fired.

When India had devised their plan, they accounted for a counter-control attempt by another nation or nations, so control wasn't taken from them. Once they had gained control of as many operational satellites as they could, the plan was to move the space stations and satellites into higher orbits to avoid anti-satellite weapon attacks from Earth and the sky as well as to uplink cyber protection to all orbiters, even to the oldest technology, making them virtually unhackable. If such an intrusion should occur, self-destruction of information and even the satellite or space station itself would occur.

The third stage of their plan was forced warfare on the ground at TT&C and DSN locations. Through recruitment and training, the number of India's military and scientists of all branches, in particular space and aeronautics, had increased dramatically and India intended on using as many willing participants as they could of their one point three billion population.

The fourth stage of their plan entailed using the space stations and satellites under their control for their intended use laid out in their plan as well as gather as much intelligence and information as they could.

Returning functionality to the nearly three thousand non-operational satellites, as to not waste the hardware in an equivalency of adding more troops to the front lines, was the fifth step. Once operational, these, too, would be used to strengthen their dominance of the spheres and Earth.

The finality of their plan culminated in taking control of the space probes orbiting other bodies, starting with the closest—the Moon—and branching out from there to Mercury, Venus, Mars, Jupiter, and Saturn, including artificial bodies in orbit around asteroids and the Sun.

First things first. Captures of satellites, passing in orbit under the golf ball-sized relays a second time, TT&Cs, and DSNs on Earth continued to trickle in on the screens at ISRO locations all over India.

An orange beam, from the fired laser, just missed Hayden's helmet and passed by the solar arrays of the magnetic satellite.

Hayden let go of the bar and initiated his carbon dioxide thrusters so he could use both hands. His heavy breathing had released much of it to convert. The woman's intelligence displayed when she, too, let go of the bar to fight Hayden with both hands for the laser, but holding onto the laser and Hayden's hands, never burned her thrusters, saving the fuel.

Her only miscalculation, his thrusters had provided him leverage and, with it, he gained control of the laser and pulled it out of her hands.

Her body followed, colliding into Hayden and bouncing off. Each of her reaches toward him was deflected by Hayden's swinging hand. With Hayden out of reach, she stretched and got her fingers around the bar supporting the solar arrays. It occurred to Hayden that she didn't activate her boosters earlier, not to save power, but because they didn't have power.

Heavy breathing and grunts of the woman, working to get a firm grip around the bar, buzzed into Hayden's helmet. Another missed opportunity to kill her, Hayden questioned why he let it pass by. As she held onto the bar, sporadic, winded words among her heavy breathing sounded through the speakers in his helmet, pleading him to spare her life.

Without any more dramatized wastefulness, Hayden pointed the orange laser at her and, in the middle of her supplication, fired. Its force on her body pushed her away from him. Her thick-gloved hand released the bar. A loud screech screamed inside his helmet and he could see her wide eyes and gaped mouth through her visor. The lack of movement on her part told him she didn't have another weapon on her to use. If she had, he was sure she would have attempted to use it in a final act of life.

He could see black space through the hole in her torso. Black death crept into it and filled the void. Moment by moment, space claimed more and more of her as its own, in the same way the sea had insisted on many by filling their bodies with itself. As the orange spacesuit floated away, the mauling of her body continued inside.

CHAPTER **TWENTY-FOUR**

Watching the orange assailant float away and die, it dawned on Hayden that her laser had been set to kill instead of disintegrate. It gave him an idea. Kip had told him that the golf ball-sized satellites were needed for phase two, but never explained what phase two was.

When he entered the magnetized satellite and pressurized the cabin, it must have alerted Kip to his successful arrival, because the screen in Hayden's right forearm illuminated with Kip's face up close and personal.

"*Hayden!* Can you hear me?" Kip asked.

"A little grainy, but yeah," Hayden answered.

"We got blocked out down here."

"Nothing you could have done, anyway."

"Well, glad you made it. What the hell happened up there, anyway?"

"I got mugged by that woman I met in Sydney. She had to be the same one from Manhattan."

"Makes sense," Kip said. "The oranges are pissing orange juice the same as we are that the Indians have everything and we have nothing. They outsmarted both of us."

"Why?" Hayden asked. "What do you know?"

"That we're too late. India controls nearly everything in orbit and on the ground."

Failure silenced Hayden. Replays of what had happened flashed across his mind as he wondered if he could have done anything differently.

"Is it a continuous signal?" Hayden asked.

"We believe so," Kip said. "Why?"

"Because I have an orange laser with a disintegration setting on it that maybe we could use to destroy those relays. I'm just not sure yet how I can reach all of them or if the laser reaches that…"

"Don't worry about it," Kip interrupted. "Sorry for the change of plans, but we need them spread out and working."

"For what?"

"But we need you to disburse those other twenty satellites," Kip said.

"I don't have them," Hayden said.

"They're packed in the right utility pocket of your suit."

"From the briefcase? They're on me now?" Hayden couldn't believe it.

"Yeah," Kip acknowledged. "Packed in there like a quart of plump strawberries."

"But the vyomanauts have control of them, too, right?"

"Probably. They have damn near everything else."

"I'm not doing anything until you answer the question," Hayden insisted. "You need those additional relays spread out for what? And while you're at it, what's phase two?"

"Not bad, Hayden. I knew you were cut out for this shit. Regaining control. That's what phase two is."

"I figured, but how?"

"Well, it's going to be tricky and we need a lot of things to go right," Kip said. "The main problem is, they took over all TDRSs up there and nearly every TDRSS satellite ground terminal, TT&C, and DSN down here."

"Now, why did they do that?" Hayden asked. "I thought India had their own dish tracking?"

"They do. In India. They can't track an entire orbit

around the globe from there. Now listen. We have people ready to help defend Goldstone as we speak, but one complex isn't going to cut it. They'd just take back control as everything up there orbits past Australia and Spain. Teams are assembling there, but aren't ready yet. Our greatest fear is that the Indians already deployed some kind of cyber protection. If they did, we may never crack it and never get control."

"Get control how?" Hayden asked. "That's the sticking point for me. Don't you have to see their uplink to get an idea..."

"We have our own uplink," Kip interrupted.

The words slapped Hayden's mind silly, refusing to sink in. Thirsty for knowledge, his mind grabbed the words and they registered understanding, but it wasn't complete, because he wondered why Kip would have his own uplink?

There could be umpteen reasons why. Kip and his group had thought the orange assailants were working on the miniature satellites, not knowing about India, and maybe had derived their own uplink to counter for a situation just as this.

"I just hope it's powerful enough," Kip continued.

"Okay," Hayden said. "So I disburse the twenty in my pocket for more satellite relays and someone on the ground will use Goldstone in California to send the initial uplink."

"And from every other means necessary of countries willing to work with us."

"I see. Now, will that give you control of everything or return things to how they were?"

"Come now, Hayden," Kip said. "You know I couldn't send an uplink to return things how they were. It would take China, Japan, Russia, Europe, India, and any other country with tracking dishes to send their own signals. Besides, would you rather have India control everything or the United States?"

Hayden didn't want to see control lie with any one country, but of all of them, of course, he preferred the

United States.

"You know the answer to that," Hayden answered.

"Alright then," Kip said. "Let's get those balls disbursed and get your butt back to the ISS."

"Speaking of which, do I have enough power to get back?"

"You've been breathing heavy?"

"Alright. Got it. What about that scientist to help make sure I have a good track? Is he around?"

"I'll look for him, but first, let's get control before India cock blocks us out."

"Before you go, can you or someone patch me into Fahim on the ISS?" Hayden asked.

"The Jap," Kip said. "I'll have someone get on it. Dispatch those balls."

And with that, the screen in Hayden's forearm went black.

After depressurizing the magnetic satellite and opening the hatch, Hayden opened the utility pocket sewn into the thigh of his spacesuit. A bright golden hue emitted out because every one-inch ball was lit. Two thick-gloved fingers pinched one and brought it out. In front of his face, its light permeated his visor, casting a golden hue on his face. Sitting in nothing more than an amusement car with the hatch opened above him to exposed space, he stared at it. The tiny satellite in his fingers had caused all of this. If it didn't exist, none of it would have happened. Amazing how something so small can change everything. Within hours, the balance of power on Earth had changed and the world wasn't the same.

With his fingers, he flung the tiny satellite into space. Another, he tossed in a different direction. Another, and, working faster now, he tossed another. Each one launched in differing directions so they were as spread out as possible.

As he tossed the thirteenth ball into space, something reflective moved in his direction like an approaching shark in dark water. Closer now, it appeared to be glass; half of a glass bubble like the windows found on submarines and aquariums. Behind the domed glass was a solid box, as tall as it was wide, maybe four or five feet, with its length elongated, perhaps ten feet. The oblong box, connected to the semicircle of glass, reminded him of a coffin.

More than anything, Hayden hoped it wasn't an omen and would miss him and the satellite in passing. Based on its orbital path, it would be close. If it did happen, it would be his own fault, guessing his struggle with the orange warrior and the fired laser must have moved the magnetic satellite in the path of the oncoming object.

In a hurried fashion, nearly all the one-inch sized satellites were disbursed into space. If this was his final act in life, there were worse acts than stopping a foreign country from single-handedly controlling the spheres.

The artificial object moved within mere feet of Hayden and the magnetic satellite. He started to duck inside the ship, intent on preparing himself for impact but found he couldn't. Because, as the domed glass neared overhead, eyes of a human face, a man's face, looked out of the glass and down at him. Looking was accurate because the eyes in the sockets moved.

As it passed overhead, just missing Hayden and the magnetic satellite, it became apparent a human head occupied the glass dome: hairless, skinless, with the brain exposed as if the parietal bone of the skull had been removed. Many arched wires extended from the brain to inside the box. Without question, the head was alive, the tissue living. It was natural for Hayden to wonder if the orbiting casket behind the glassed dome contained the body—man's next evolution in space.

The images of the head lingered with Hayden, as he watched the oddity float away. He hoped the man had only agreed to such an arrangement as a last-ditch, life-saving experiment and hadn't been forced into it by an oppressive government.

One-by-one, exhaust spewed out of the satellite balls he

had freed into space, pushing against the thermosphere, taking them higher. He closed the hatch and pressurized the magnetic satellite, where he waited for the scientist to appear on the screen to help him get back to the ISS.

Too much time had passed. Thank goodness, he had an unlimited air supply as long as he breathed. Impatience and all of its associations filled Hayden until they overflowed out of his mouth in cusses and complaints. The wait had outlasted him.

Just about to take matters into his own hands, he positioned the screen implanted in his forearm to use it for navigational purposes, when it illuminated before he started.

"*Hayden. Hayden.* This is Fahim. Do you read?"

"I read you," Hayden acknowledged. "I take it there'll be no call from the scientist?"

"No call," Fahim said. "But you want back to the ISS, correct?"

"That's the plan. I just don't have one."

"I have one, but I'm afraid to do it. There's someone in an orange spacesuit on board."

"They still got in. I'm not surprised. You still in the JEM?"

"Yeah."

"You think only one of them is aboard?"

"From what I can tell. Without the drone, I've been relying on what NASA and JAXA could tell me, until that stopped, too."

"Yes, about that, Fahim. You should know that India apparently controls nearly everything in orbit and on Earth. You experience any changes with the ISS?"

"No. The flight feels the same."

"Okay, what's your plan," Hayden inquired.

"A cosmic catch," the Japanese astronaut said. "Or, at least, a cosmic stop. You thrust your craft toward the ISS and I'll use the Canadarm2 to stabilize it. Once you're settled, you can use those thrusters in your suit and I'll meet you at the Quest airlock."

"Thanks, Fahim," Hayden said, meaningfully. "You put some thought into this."

"I had time to kill."

"Speaking of kill, you'll have to leave the Hope module, get to the cupola to control the arm, and then get to an airlock to open it so I can get in. You might find resistance."

"I know. That's why I'm afraid."

"I don't blame you. *Can't* rather. It's a tough decision."

"I want to help you, but…"

"You want to stay alive and get back to your family. Whatever you choose, I'm fine with it, and you should be, too."

It was hard for Hayden to see the contemplation on Fahim's face because of his nationality, but it was there. Mute space pressed against Hayden as he waited. His life was in the hands of the Japanese astronaut. In fairness, not entirely. There was an orange assailant on board, who also had a lot to say whether Hayden lived or died. The Jap for that matter. Because if they killed the Jap, they would also kill Hayden in the process.

Fahim's head turned on the screen. In Hayden's limited view, he didn't know the Jap looked at Ora, still floating inside the JEM. Fahim turned his head and looked straight into the screen.

"I'll do it," Fahim said.

"Oh, boy!" Hayden said, relieved. "You had me going there. Are you sure? It might get nasty."

"I'm sure."

"So, let's talk navigation. How do I find the ISS?"

"I thought Kip sent you something."

"If he did, I haven't seen it."

"Check your screens."

Hayden brought up the screen nested in his other forearm. Sure enough, Kip had sent navigation capability to track the ISS and a note that the magnetized satellite had a bit of fuel left for maneuvers because it hadn't been launched all that long ago.

"I got it," Hayden said to Fahim. "And I see you coming. I'm going to fire this thing up and booster closer as you had said in your plan."

"Okay," the JAXA astronaut said. "I'll be ready."

Based on the navigation on the screen embedded in Hayden's forearm, the ISS should be in front of him. Looking through a narrow, rectangle-shaped window in the magnetized satellite, he didn't see anything. After rechecking the navigation, he looked out the window and, this time, caught a visual of the space station. There was plenty of room between them for him to use the thrusters to puff the magnetic satellite closer. A jettison of propulsion and the one-man satellite floated toward the ISS.

The space station exponentially grew in the satellite's narrow window frame. Its sheer size and the speed at which it approached worried Hayden that the gap between them had lessened so much that there might not be enough space or time to avoid hitting its far-reaching solar panels. Consecutive, corrective puffs, in an attempt to slow and steer the orbiter clear, expelled out of the craft.

The ISS no longer fit within the satellite's window frame and Hayden doubted he was going to clear its path. It was up to Fahim and his operation of the long, mechanical arm on the ISS, which, so far, hadn't moved.

Stacking worry for himself, Fahim, and whether he could get Ora and the others home safely for proper burials, overwhelmed him. As Kip had said, the satellite he sat in wasn't made for reentry, but to burn in the atmosphere, incinerating it and all the space junk it had collected. Nor was it made for docking. Staying in the small satellite wasn't an option.

"Come on, Fahim," Hayden whispered, watching.

Thoughts of Fahim genuinely occupied Hayden's mind, feeling unworthy of the man's willingness to risk and, apparently, lose his life to save his.

Through the narrow window, a flash of light in the

distance caught Hayden's attention. Debris, burning within it, spewed out like a spitting sparkler. Something had exploded.

His eyes checked the arm on the ISS again and it hadn't moved.

Another combustion of light flared its brilliance in black space, closer than the last.

Frantically, Hayden stretched to see what he could out the near-worthless window of the craft, then checked the navigation screen, lodged in his forearm, to see if there was a weaponized satellite or something nearby causing the explosions. From what he could tell, there wasn't.

He couldn't remember if Kip had said this satellite was weaponized or not, so his eyes scanned the minimal controls in front of him. If it was weaponized, he didn't see how.

His eyes looked out the window in time to witness another blast, this one even closer. When it dissipated, the arm on the ISS remained unmoved and the outer stretches of the space station's solar panels drew dangerously close.

CHAPTER **TWENTY-FIVE**

Hayden was going to fail, and somehow, someway die. It might be fast, exploding upon impact with the International Space Station or ricocheting off, plunging into the Earth's atmosphere, and incinerating. Or, it might be slow, ricocheting off the ISS and spinning uncontrollably in that tin can into deep space where dehydration and hunger would do him in.

Minutes, days, or weeks, it didn't matter. Death was a way of stopping more death. Ora's dead. Their unborn children never had a chance to live. The female Chinese taikonaut is dead. The crew of the ISS is no more. Fahim must be dead in trying to save him. Somewhere along the line, he went from being an astronaut to a killer, taking the lives of two Indian vyomanauts and the orange assailant. Why shouldn't he die, too?

Reserved to his fate, he closed his eyes and waited for death to claim him.

Too much time had passed. He should have hit the space station by now. When he looked out the narrow window, the fifty-eight foot Canadarm2 on the ISS slowly extended toward him like a giant reaching down to save him.

A jerky collision rocked the magnetic satellite to a stop. In a cosmic catch, the *hand* had caught him before the satellite crashed into the space station.

The plan to reclaim Hayden on the ISS had worked. Waiting inside the crew lock for it to pressurize, Hayden couldn't wait to get inside. Flying through space, relying only on his spacesuit, had been exhilarating, but stressful. He had enough for a while and placing his faith in something bigger, like the space station, would relieve some of that stress.

The hatch opened and a bloodied, round face looked in at him. Without needing to see or know more, Hayden knew he owed his life to the JAXA astronaut and vowed to get him home safely with the others.

Hayden floated into the ship, while Fahim secured the hatch. When the Japanese's eyes met Hayden's, Hayden knew he had been through hell and the murder he committed of another soul would most likely keep him there for a while.

Fahim helped Hayden out of his helmet.

"Thanks, buddy," Hayden said and hugged him. "Anything happened to you, I was a goner, too."

"I know, my friend," Fahim said and continued to help Hayden out of his spacesuit.

"You won't believe what I just saw."

"And you won't believe all I heard."

"*Heard? How?* Aren't all of the satellites and communications under India's control?"

"Let's get you undressed and I'll show you."

Under the circumstances, undressing and re-acclimating Hayden to space station conditions was rushed and crude. Occasionally, Fahim would ask Hayden if he was doing okay, and every time Hayden answered he was, despite some irregular breathing.

They floated out of the equipment lock and into node 1, where the dead bodies of two female American astronauts still floated. Through the U.S. lab and through node 2, they entered the Japanese Experiment Module.

Seeing Ora's body dead float sent Hayden over the edge. Wishful thinking had him hoping that she might have woken up and would be there to greet him as he entered. There's nothing more unsettling about death than being in the presence of an unanimated body. While some cultures live with them for a time, most dispose of them by burial or cremation to get it out of sight. Composure gave way to pain and anger and Hayden couldn't look at her. Conflict between him wanting to eject her into space and getting her home safely split his allegiances.

Sensitive to how this was tearing Hayden apart, Fahim placed his hand on Hayden's shoulder and squeezed.

The touch of life welled up to the surface every emotion associated with all that had happened that Hayden had buried and tried to avoid. It spewed out of him uncontrollably; he didn't have a say in the matter. There was no way for him to stop it, even if he wanted to. All of it was coming out in its own way.

Pouring out, the gushed release reduced to a trickle of sniffles and the occasional cough. Vacated graves left voids, leaving Hayden feeling empty.

"Would you like to hear what I know?" Fahim asked. "Take your mind off things."

Hayden remembered how the Jap's smooth voice had helped him recover after being locked inside the Permanent Multipurpose Module (PMM) for hours.

"What did I miss?" Hayden asked in a near whisper. "What were those explosions nearby?"

"It seems the Russians fired anti-satellite weapons from the ground to destroy India satellites in orbit," Fahim explained.

"That's good. Any more countries doing the same?"

"Not that I last heard."

"Once again, the Russians stand alone," Hayden said. "Speaking of standing alone, can I show you something?"

Fahim nodded.

Hayden opened his hand and one of the golf ball-sized satellites floated out of it.

"Do you have any expertise with electronics?" Hayden asked.

"I'm not bad. Why?"

"Can we identify India's uplink and downlink and alter them somehow?"

"Alter?"

"Yeah. Maybe some of the identification codes that relayed through it could be manipulated to control those particular satellites. Maybe even get lucky and find the ISS on it."

"It's a long shot. I don't know if I have what I need, but there is something I can try."

"I hate to ask you for another favor, but would you?"

Fahim snatched the ball out of the air and went to work. It didn't take long before he turned to Hayden and said, "It's wiped clean."

"What do you mean?" Hayden asked.

"There's nothing on it. No information whatsoever."

More devastating for Hayden than Fahim's findings was the possibility the whole thing had been more complicated than what he realized, which meant it was unlikely that Kip's group had altered India's uplink since their takeover and had created their own uplink some time ago, prior to all that had happened.

"What's your take on this?" Hayden asked, very interested in Fahim's viewpoint.

"Well, I think it's been done," Fahim said.

"We know it's been done," Hayden said, disappointed. "The Indians have control."

"No, I mean I think Kip uplinked, downlinked, sidelinked, whatever, and everything is back to normal."

"Do you know that for sure? Is there a way to check the ISS?"

"Already did. Everything was fine, then kablooey, now, everything seems okay again."

"So you received all of this information *after* everything was okay again?" Hayden asked.

"Oh, no," Fahim said. *"Before."*

"Kip's been in touch with you the whole time and left me out there?"

"No, not Kip. The bald guy."

"That's not a guy," Hayden said. "Not entirely, anyway."

"Come. I'll show you."

Fahim floated toward Ora, stopped, and said, "Even in death, she saved us."

"Why?" Hayden asked through a sudden, bumbling burst of emotion. "What do you mean?"

"This," Fahim said and rolled up her sleeve.

At first, there wasn't much of a reaction by Hayden, seeing her arm. Then, his eyes widened when he got it.

"She has a screen implanted in her forearm?" Hayden asked, pointing at it.

"Like yours," Fahim answered, pointing at his.

"So, this is how Baldy contacted you?"

"Yes. Had to. Remember, everything was kablooey."

"Come to think of it, mine worked, too."

"The bald guy said something about them not having a kind of code for the Indians to latch onto."

"And you saw that, too. Just a few minutes ago. The relay was wiped clean."

"It seemed that way, yes."

"Give me a minute."

Hayden thought everything through. Despite all the branches hanging near the ground, only one was still attached to the trunk.

Snapping his fingers, Hayden said, "That's how Kip's going to do it. Or, you think maybe he's already done it. He used his uplink to gain control and then wiped them clean, relays, satellites, space stations, everything, so once he had control, nobody could hack them."

"That's a good idea."

"But is that what you think may have happened?"

"Sure. I guess so. Maybe there's code there. I just couldn't see it."

"Invisible?"

"Or in a state of constant scrambling to make it appear nothing's there," Fahim said. "Right now, when there's nothing to find or latch onto, it can't be manipulated."

"So the U.S. link can find India's and take control?"

"Maybe," the Japanese astronaut said and turned his thoughts elsewhere, obviously disturbed by them based on the expression on his face. "Let me ask you a question. You said the United States taking control. If Kip already did it, then is the United States in complete control as India was?"

"If Kip already did it, then yes," Hayden answered. "Kip said so himself that was the only way of doing it. I'm sorry. I thought that's how you understood it."

"No. I thought everything might be back to normal."

"It's bothersome, I know. I'm American and I don't like it."

"If that's true and I believe it is, then you're not going to like this. The Usuda Deep Space Network in my country had been disabled and is no longer tracking orbiters."

"Well, of course not. Not now. None of them are tracking, because there's nothing for them to track."

"This was *before*, Hayden—not after. I don't think we really know what's happening down on the ground."

"Before India's control or before U.S. control?"

"Both."

CHAPTER **TWENTY-SIX**

Inside the new secret location of the unknown agency Kip belonged to, Hayden waited inside the same trapezoid-shaped room, where some time ago Kip had informed him he was going to the Chinese Space Station and Ora to the International Space Station. Since that meeting, the construction of the room had been completed. The same gray-colored industrialized rug covered the floor. A darker shade of gray had been painted on the walls. All twelve light-gray leather chairs had been installed evenly apart, surrounding a large, round conference table.

Decorative green vegetation covered the tabletop with pockets of meat, exotic cheeses, caviar, dessert, and other food. Fruit sprinkled the unoccupied areas as did glass bottles nested within the leaves, filled with brandy, cognac, and wine.

Above the table, all the light-gray metal grids had been filled in with animated tiles, which, congruently together, played a video of the whitest clouds slowly moving over the clearest blue sky.

When Hayden sat down, the chair felt solid underneath him. There wasn't a helmet on the hooks by the door, because he didn't wear one when he was escorted to the room by one of Kip's men dressed in black. At the pace the facility was coming along, there were probably things that no outsider should see, but after everything Hayden had seen and been through, he doubted Kip considered him an outsider any longer.

A sound of a plane flying took Hayden by surprise and he doubted they were that close to the Earth's surface to hear anything outside. When he looked up, an old-time double-winged plane flew across the ceiling panels with a banner attached to its tail, fluttering in the wind, that read, "Thanks a million, Hayden! So here's two!"

On cue, Kip entered the room with his arms spread like a true showman.

"Huh! Huh!" Kip exclaimed. "What do you think of the spread? Welcome home partner."

Hayden remained seated.

Pointing to the animated tiles, Kip said, "And we mean that, too. Two million greenbacks have already been deposited into a retirement account for you."

Hayden's thumb rhythmically tapped the leather armrest of his chair.

"On top of that," Kip continued, "we're going to make your choice of living quarters as nice and automated as any in the world. Within reason, of course. We have a budget we're trying to maintain."

Hayden's thumb tapped the armrest one last time and stopped.

As Kip walked toward the table, he asked, "How about a drink? The finest brandy? Cognac? … *Geez*, you haven't touched a thing."

Hayden sat still.

"Well, I'm having some," Kip said. "Cognac sounds good." While Kip surveyed the bottle, he continued, "You know, Hayden. You're not the only one who lost things in the name of space."

The sound of the double-winged airplane annoyed Kip as it flew across the ceiling tiles a second time, so he commanded the animation of the plane to stop. It never finished its flight and disappeared from the tiles as if swallowed by the Bermuda Triangle.

"Take Baldy, for example." Kip opened the bottle and poured himself a drink. "Whose thirst for space counted himself worthy as one of the first full-blown attempts at hybridizing man to be better equipped for the harshness of space. Particularly, and I know you can sympathize with this, the lack of gravity on the legs over extended periods of time. Countless others had followed in his footsteps. Now, I'm not a religious man, but I've been to enough hero funerals. Didn't Jesus say something about there's no greater love than a man laying down his life for another?"

Kip walked the cognac he just poured around the table over to Hayden and offered it to him.

"Aren't you going to say anything? … *Hero*," Kip said.

"Don't call me that again!" Hayden said. "And stop treating me like one. What did I do, exactly?"

"You know what you did," Kip said. "You lived it."

"No, I don't know," Hayden said, shaking his head. "You explain it to me. Explain everything to me."

"For starters, you allowed us to get complete control of the spheres and ground before the Indians could cock block us out."

"*Oh, no!*" Hayden said, shaking his head. "I didn't do that. You already had an uplink ready to go *way* before I even got involved in all of this."

"Not entirely true, but …" Kip took a distinguished sip of the cognac he had offered Hayden.

"So what is the truth?" Hayden asked.

"You want to play twenty-one questions?" Kip took another sip. "Go ahead—shoot."

"You were going for the spheres all along, weren't you? Sole control for the United States?"

"Double-barreling me out of the gate. Well, of course, Hayden. This is a war and most don't end in a tie. Somebody wins and somebody loses."

The expression on Hayden's face told Kip that he needed more.

"Okay, look," Kip continued. "India was a complete surprise, but after some analysis, we should have seen it. Once they got this ball rolling, we figured they wouldn't waste any time and go for the juggler right away, so we began piggybacking their processes. Thank goodness there's nothing expedient about the process or else we'd be all working on our Hindi right now."

"And Usuda was part of that?" Hayden asked.

"*Usuda!* The Jap again. All ground communications were part of it. To control the spheres we had to control the ground." Kip shook his head in disgust. "Just so you know, I'm well aware of that little stunt you and the Jap tried to pull on the ISS."

"His name is Fahim," Hayden said. "I would try it again if I knew it would have worked."

"Whose side are you on?"

"What about you? Whose side are you on?"

A sigh released out of Kip and he consumed a larger swallow of the cognac, then said, "I'm many things, Hayden, but I'm no traitor."

"It's not just countries that can be betrayed," Hayden said. "You said you had my back. More like shred my back with a chainsaw. And Ora's."

Pointing a finger at Hayden, while holding the glass, the cognac swirling inside, Kip said, "*You leave Ora out of this!* I loved her, too, damn it!"

"Why was she up there earlier, then?"

"Her orders got moved up! That wasn't me! What was I supposed to do?"

"Help her. Help me."

"Well, it's too late for one of you," Kip said and gulped the rest of the cognac in his glass. "I can't help her now."

"Or the man's head inside the glass dome on that satellite," Hayden said. "Tell me, is the rest of his body inside that floating coffin?"

Kip shook his head and answered, "I heard about him when I first started. Honestly, I don't know."

"It must be easy not to care enough to know."

"This business…"

"*Blah! Blah! Blah! Blah! Blah!*" Hayden interrupted. "This business kills and hurts a lot of people."

"And avoids pain and saves many times more," Kip rebutted. "You're no Mother Theresa. You're a dangerous man with a growing number of kills notched in your belt."

"Why do I have a feeling not as many as you."

"I've been at it longer than you is all. But you're off to a fast start."

"You know I didn't kill those country leaders."

"I know."

"Was it you?"

"In a matter of speaking."

"Then take the credit."

"I can't afford the responsibility."

"Why? Why put the blame on me?"

"I believe the Outer Space Treaty is outdated. The damned thing is over half a century old."

"*You* think it's outdated or *your agency*?" Hayden asked.

"Both," Kip answered. "When in war, no one pays attention to the law of war."

Frustrated with the discussion, Kip surveyed the table, pinched two fingers on a toothpick stabbed in a piece of cheese, and ate the cheese cube.

"They honestly were your bullets out of the East River," Kip continued. "I gave the orders, but I didn't pull the trigger. You may think there's not a difference, but there is. *A big one.* It's my job to divert attention away from me and the group. I needed a scapegoat. Quite frankly, I didn't think you would survive this. Believe me, if I had, I never would have pinned it on you."

Standing before Hayden was the man in the hat with a tan, *Manhattan*, who had turned Hayden from a man into a scapegoat, taking his innocence and, with it, his freedom.

Maybe he hadn't directly influenced what had happened in Manhattan, or could be blamed for the orange assailants following him to his house and blowing it up, or claim sole responsibility for Ora's death, but he sure invested the last so many years of his life to the war for the spheres, that he never had a problem investing other's lives. The man in the hat with a tan had a name—and it was Kip Stanton.

CHAPTER **TWENTY-SEVEN**

"Fuck!" Hayden yelled. "Where do I begin?"

"I hope a truce," Kip said.

"A truce?"

"Yeah! You know, forgive, and forget."

"I've seen how far you will go, but how far can you take it?"

"The plan is to control every planet, dwarf planet, small bodies, and get the hell out of this solar system and eventually into interstellar space. As much as I can and as far as I can while I'm alive."

"Whatever happened to good-old-fashioned world domination?"

"It's outdated. Just like the treaties."

"World domination outdated? *Really?* How can something never achieved be outdated?"

"Beating around the bush is outdated. Skipping the beat-down, hoping they get the message, and going straight for the kill is where the world is today."

Kip set his glass within some leaves on the table and tossed his toothpick into it. He sat down beside Hayden, swiveled his chair to face him, and looked him in the eyes.

"Join us," Kip said with a straight face.

"What?" Disbelief of the request twisted Hayden's face as if he had tasted something sour. "After everything? How you treated me? Treated Ora? You got major cojones."

"In this job, you need them," Kip said. "How about it? Sure, you could live the rest of your days comfortably under our witness protection program. Everything will be taken care of and provided for. Even your taxes. It's a tall order, though, with half of the world looking for you. Your name still isn't cleared for those murders. With your face all over the news and everyone convinced you did it, I just don't see how you can survive on your own as a civilian. And don't say you have, because I've helped you. You must have a horseshoe wrapped around your dingy in a dead ringer to be so lucky. You're done flying missions for NASA. There's no way they can have a murderer on staff. So, instead of being forced out, stay on indirectly and become one of us. I can't offer job safety, but I can offer job security, because there'll always be some *yo-yo* out there, scheming to take what rightfully belongs to the United States."

"Belong?" Hayden asked. "The universe? To the United States? How?"

"Haven't we protected those who couldn't protect themselves? Stuck our nose in affairs we had no right getting involved in, but we did to even the odds or play peacekeeper? How about all of the good we've done and for so long? Every great empire ends, but it looks like this empire's not ending anytime soon. The universe belongs in our hands. Can you think of another country who should own it?"

"I can think of *countries*, working together to accomplish the same thing on behalf of all mankind and Earth."

"And if everyone thought like you, we would be okay. *Hell*, I would be okay. But I guess you forget about India's attempt. It won't be their last. They're going to want revenge. Or the tangerines, who want the same thing. Trust me, more will raise their ugly mugs."

"And have you let me die like your agent on the ferry?

Or Ora. I don't think so."

"Ouch."

"You say believe you, trust you—I can't. I don't."

"I wasn't going to go there, but since you did, then, how about revenge for Ora?"

"Maybe," Hayden said, as he shrugged his shoulders. "You have that retirement information?"

"Now you're talking," Kip said, reaching inside his suit jacket and handing Hayden a card with information on it. "Right here."

Hayden's eyes studied it and then he asked, "This is the account number?"

"Yep. Deposited offshore in your name. Ready for you to use when you're ready."

"And you said something about housing?"

"Witness protection will take care of that."

"What if I wanted to choose my own place? You know, with their recommendation of course."

"It's your funeral, but if that's how you want to play it."

"How do I get the money?"

"It can be arranged."

Hayden's lips pursed and he shook his head once and said, "No rush."

"Well, let's celebrate," Kip said. "What'll it be?"

"Brandy. Neat."

"I knew that," Kip said, reaching for the bottle.

Hayden started to stand.

"Oh, no you don't," Kip said. "I'll get it. You take it easy."

As Kip poured, he said, "So, that time up there jacked up your legs, *huh*? What was it—the uniqueness of the assignment or just you getting old?"

"Probably both," Hayden said. "Hey, would you mind grabbing that box over there?"

"Sure," Kip said, handing Hayden his brandy. "What is it? There's not a head or other body part in there is there?"

"No. It's a gift."

"No shit! For me?" Surprise raised Kip's voice a little.

Kip picked up the box, brought it over to the table, sat down, and asked, "What is it?"

"You're worse than a child," Hayden said. "Just open it."

The flaps of the box spread and Kip's hands disappeared inside. When they came out, a ball of material was in their grasp. Kip stood up and the material unrolled.

"Are you kidding me?" Kip said. "A new overcoat."

"I hope you didn't buy one already."

Kip slipped it on. "Not bad. Fits pretty good. Thanks."

"Looks a little snug. I can return it," Hayden joked and then said, "Here, hand me that box and I'll flatten it."

"I have something better," Kip said, reaching into the left coat pocket. "What? No gloves? Never mind," he said and pulled out something small, wrapped in newspaper comics, and handed it to Hayden.

Hayden took it but didn't want to open it. When he had said he didn't believe or trust Kip, he meant it. When he unwrapped it, it was a souvenir of a miniature Statue of Liberty.

Hayden's eyes shot up at Kip. "Is this from my house?"

"Is it," Kip answered. "If I were you, I would hold onto that. Who knows how much longer those things will be around."

"But how did you get it into the coat?"

With a somber face, Kip asked, "Why did you want the box, Hayden?"

"Your gift …" Hayden said.

"So your hands would appear busy and reach for this?"

Kip's right hand flipped back the overcoat and reached into the right pocket of his suit jacket. Out came the silver laser Hayden had acquired after killing one of the Indians on the ISS. At first, Kip just held it in his hand and then he pointed it at Hayden.

"This was the real gift, wasn't it?" Kip asked. "I know you tucked it in the chair beside you. Everyone believes you're a murderer. Now, there'll be no question."

Hayden's face contorted. This hadn't gone as he had planned. Kip had picked up the laser when he had sat in the chair next to Hayden and asked him to join them.

The screen in Kip's forearm illuminated. It was Baldy.

"Yeah, Baldy," Kip said, irritated. "What is it?"

"Mr. Stanton, you know who wants to see you in his office right away. It's urgent."

"All I need is a second. Can't it wait?"

"I wouldn't with the mood he's in, Mr. Stanton."

"Tell him I'll be there in a few minutes."

"It's your funeral."

"*Dammit!* All right, fine. I'll be down."

Kip waved the laser in front of Hayden's face and said, "This will give you time to make your peace with death."

Under the circumstances, Hayden reasoned he might have to.

As Kip headed for the door, he commanded into the air, "Secure the room once I'm out."

"Right away, Mr. Stanton," the same smooth female voice from the canyon replied into the room.

The door opened on its own as Kip approached. Before it opened all the way, something happened and Kip froze in place. Hayden stood faster than he wanted to out of the chair to see what had happened. Kip's body dematerialized near the door as Baldy rolled in on what looked like the bottom wheeled-legs of an office chair; the top-half of his body where the seat would be. In the robot's hand was an orange laser.

The door closed behind him and Baldy said aloud, "Door secure?"

"Door secure, Baldy," the near-perfect female voice said into the room.

"We better file an internal missing report on Mr. Stanton," Baldy said. "He's been missing for a few hours now."

"I'll get on that right away," the silky sleek voice said.

"Why?" Hayden asked.

"All you have to do is look at me and when the canyon was attacked, he left a vast majority like me there. He uses people. And I'm still a person. So are they."

What could Hayden say, other than, "Thank you."

CHAPTER **TWENTY-EIGHT**

After meeting Ora's family, paying for Ora's burial, and attending the services, Hayden went to the place where he was going to propose to her and, in her absence, made the proposal.

After much protesting by the neighbors, Hayden had taken some of the retirement money, purchased a new floating home, and docked it to one of the newly built docks on Friday Harbor in Washington State. Winter had rolled in once again and had sprinkled snow on the deep green treetops, buried rocky shorelines, and banks.

The longest hair he ever had in his life, covered his head and shoulders as a shawl, and his beard warmed his neck like a turtleneck. On the coffee table in the living room sat a dirty plate beside a half-drank glass of brandy and the bottle nearby. A fire crackled in the fireplace as Hayden sat on a chair, cleaning the silver laser he had given to Fahim on the International Space Station, but who had since returned it as a Christmas gift. The Jap would never use it, so instead of wasting it, he thought Hayden might find a use for it.

Unlike last year, Hayden planned to stay home this holiday season, in an attempt of recapturing a sense of sanctuary in his new home.

If the orange assailants, Indians, Kip's group, or any of the countries who had lost their world leader ever wanted to pay him a visit, let them come—he'll be ready.

ABOUT **THE AUTHOR**

W. G. TUTTLE is an American writer of riveting science fiction, thriller, and suspense novels and short stories. He is the author of the novels Try To Sleep, Those Who Long, October Midnight, and War For The Spheres. He has also written numerous short stories, including Scranton October 1894, Vacation's End, Where Did THEY Come From?, and Standard Issue Spirits.

He also writes screenplays and intelligent non-fiction about stocks, investing, and trading.

Born: January 27, 1972, Binghamton, New York

Full name: Walter George Tuttle, Jr.

Spouse: Shawn M. Tuttle (m.1997)

Children: 1 son & 1 daughter

Alma mater: The Pennsylvania State University

Influenced by: Frank Herbert, H. G. Wells, Ramsey Campbell (Carl Dreadstone), Arthur C. Clarke, Isaac Asimov, Stanislaw Lem, William Peter Blatty, Ira Levin, Robert Bloch, Ian Fleming, Alistair MacLean

wgtuttle.com

Made in the USA
Middletown, DE
08 May 2023